THE
LONG WAY
TO A SMALL,
ANGRY PLANET

THE
LONG WAY
TO A SMALL,
ANGRY PLANET

BECKY CHAMBERS

HARPER Voyager
An Imprint of HarperCollins*Publishers*

THE LONG WAY TO A SMALL, ANGRY PLANET. Copyright © 2014 by Becky Chambers. All rights reserved. Printed in the United States of America. No part of this book may be used or reproduced in any manner whatsoever without written permission except in the case of brief quotations embodied in critical articles and reviews. For information address HarperCollins Publishers, 195 Broadway, New York, NY 10007.

HarperCollins books may be purchased for educational, business, or sales promotional use. For information please e-mail the Special Markets Department at SPsales@harpercollins.com.

Originally published in Great Britain in 2015 by Hodder & Stoughton, a Hachette UK company.

FIRST EDITION

Harper Voyager and design is a trademark of HarperCollins Publishers L.L.C.

Designed by Paula Russell Szafranski

Library of Congress Cataloging-in-Publication Data has been applied for.

ISBN 978-0-06-244413-4

23 24 25 26 27 LBC 25 24 23 22 21

For my family, hatch and feather

THE
LONG WAY
TO A SMALL,
ANGRY PLANET

From the ground, we stand;
From our ships, we live;
By the stars, we hope.

—EXODAN PROVERB

TRANSIT

As she woke up in the pod, she remembered three things. First, she was traveling through open space. Second, she was about to start a new job, one she could not screw up. Third, she had bribed a government official into giving her a new identity file. None of this information was new, but it wasn't pleasant to wake up to.

She wasn't supposed to be awake yet, not for another day at least, but that was what you got for booking cheap transport. Cheap transport meant a cheap pod flying on cheap fuel, and cheap drugs to knock you out. She had flickered into consciousness several times since launch—surfacing in confusion, falling back just as she'd gotten a grasp on things. The pod was dark, and there were no navigational screens. There was no way to tell how much time had passed between each waking, or how far she'd traveled, or if she'd even been traveling at all. The thought made her anxious, and sick.

Her vision cleared enough for her to focus on the window. The shutters were down, blocking out any possible light sources. She knew there were none. She was out in the open now. No bustling planets, no travel lanes, no sparkling orbiters. Just emptiness, horrible emptiness, filled with nothing but herself and the occasional rock.

The engine whined as it prepared for another sublayer jump. The drugs reached out, tugging her down into uneasy sleep. As she faded, she thought again of the job, the lies, the smug look on the official's face as she'd poured credits into his account. She wondered if it had been enough. It had to be. It had to. She'd paid too much already for mistakes she'd had no part in.

Her eyes closed. The drugs took her. The pod, presumably, continued on.

||||||||||||||||||||||||||||||||||||||||||||||||||||||||||||||||

A COMPLAINT

Living in space was anything but quiet. Grounders never expected that. For anyone who had grown up planetside, it took sometime to get used to the clicks and hums of a ship, the ever-present ambience that came with living inside a piece of machinery. But to Ashby, those sounds were as ordinary as his own heartbeat. He could tell when it was time to wake by the sigh of the air filter over his bed. When rocks hit the outer hull with their familiar pattering, he knew which were small enough to ignore, and which meant trouble. He could tell by the amount of static crackling over the ansible how far away he was from the person on the other end. These were the sounds of spacer life, an underscore of vulnerability and distance. They were reminders of what a fragile thing it was to be alive. But those sounds also meant safety. An absence of sound meant that air was no longer flowing, engines no longer running, artigrav nets no longer holding your feet to the floor. Silence belonged to the vacuum outside. Silence was death.

There were other sounds, too, sounds made not by the ship itself, but by the people living in it. Even in the endless halls of homestead ships, you could hear the echoes of nearby conversations, footsteps on metal floors, the faint thumping of a tech climbing through the walls, off to repair some unseen circuit.

Ashby's ship, the *Wayfarer*, was spacious enough, but tiny compared to the homesteader he'd grown up on. When he'd first purchased the *Wayfarer* and filled it with crew, even he'd had to get used to the close quarters they kept. But the constant sounds of people working and laughing and fighting all around him had become a comfort. The open was an empty place to be, and there were moments when even the most seasoned spacer might look to the star-flecked void outside with humility and awe.

Ashby welcomed the noise. It was reassuring to know that he was never alone out there, especially given his line of work. Building wormholes was not a glamorous profession. The interspatial passageways that ran throughout the Galactic Commons were so ordinary as to be taken for granted. Ashby doubted the average person gave tunneling much more thought than you might give a pair of trousers or a hot cooked meal. But his job required him to think about tunnels, and to think hard on them, at that. If you sat and thought about them for too long, imagined your ship diving in and out of space like a needle pulling thread . . . well, that was the sort of thinking that made a person glad for some noisy company.

Ashby was in his office, reading a newsfeed over a cup of mek, when one particular sound made him cringe. Footsteps. Corbin's footsteps. Corbin's *angry* footsteps, coming right toward his door. Ashby sighed, swallowed his irritation and became the captain. He kept his face neutral, his ears open. Talking to Corbin always required a moment of preparation, and a good deal of detachment.

Artis Corbin was two things: a talented algaeist and a complete asshole. The former trait was crucial on a long-haul ship like the *Wayfarer*. A batch of fuel going brown could be the difference between arriving at port and going adrift. Half of one of the *Wayfarer*'s lower decks was filled with nothing but algae vats, all of which needed someone to obsessively adjust their nutrient content and salinity. This was one area in which Corbin's lack of social graces was actually a benefit. The man *preferred* to stay cooped up in the algae bay all day, muttering over readouts, working in pursuit of what he called "optimal conditions." Conditions always seemed optimal enough to Ashby, but he wasn't going to get in Corbin's way where algae was concerned. Ashby's fuel costs had dropped by 10 percent since he'd brought Corbin aboard, and there were few algaeists who would accept a position on a tunneling ship in the first place. Algae could be touchy enough on a short trip, but keeping your batches healthy over a long haul required meticulousness, and stamina, too. Corbin hated people, but he loved his work, and he was damn good at it. In Ashby's book, that made him extremely valuable. An extremely valuable headache.

The door spun open and Corbin stormed in. His brow was beaded with sweat, as usual, and the graying hair at his temples looked slick. The *Wayfarer* had to be kept warm for their pilot's sake, but Corbin had voiced his dislike for the ship's standard temperature from day one. Even after years aboard the ship, his body had refused to acclimate, seemingly out of pure spite.

Corbin's cheeks were red as well, though whether that was due to his mood or from coming up the stairs was anyone's guess. Ashby never got used to the sight of cheeks that red. The majority of living Humans were descended from the Exodus Fleet, which had sailed far beyond the reaches of their ancestral sun. Many, like Ashby, had been born within the very same homesteaders that had belonged to the original Earthen refugees. His tight black curls and amber skin were the result of generations of mingling and mixing aboard the giant ships. Most Humans, whether spaceborn or colony kids, shared that nationless Exodan blend.

Corbin, on the other hand, was unmistakably Sol system stock, even though the people of the home planets had come to resemble Exodans in recent generations. With as much of a hodgepodge as Human genetics were, lighter shades were known to pop up here and there, even in the Fleet. But Corbin was practically *pink*. His forerunners had been scientists, early explorers who built the first research orbiters around Enceladus. They'd been there for centuries, keeping vigil over the bacteria flourishing within icy seas. With Sol a dim thumbprint in the skies above Saturn, the researchers lost more and more pigment with every decade. The end result was Corbin, a pink man bred for tedious lab work and a sunless sky.

Corbin tossed his scrib over Ashby's desk. The thin, rectangular pad sailed through the mistlike pixel screen and clattered down in front of Ashby. Ashby gestured to the pixels, instructing them to disperse. The news headlines hovering in the air dissolved into colored wisps. The pixels slunk down like swarms of tiny insects into the projector boxes on either side of the desk. Ashby looked at the scrib, and raised his eyebrows at Corbin.

"*This*," Corbin said, pointing a bony finger at the scrib, "has got to be a joke."

"Let me guess," Ashby said. "Jenks messed with your notes again?" Corbin frowned and shook his head. Ashby focused on the scrib, trying not to laugh at the memory of the last time Jenks had hacked into Corbin's scrib, replacing the algaeist's careful notes with 362 photographic variations of Jenks himself, naked as the day he was born. Ashby had thought the one of Jenks carrying a Galactic Commons banner was particularly good. It had a sort of dramatic dignity to it, all things considered.

Ashby picked up the scrib, flipping it screen-side up.

ATTN.: Captain Ashby Santoso (Wayfarer, GC tunneling license
  no. 387-97456)
RE: Resume for Rosemary Harper (GC administration certificate
  no. 65-78-2)

Ashby recognized the file. It was the resume for their new clerk, who was scheduled to arrive the next day. She was probably strapped into a deepod by now, sedated for the duration of her long, cramped trip. "Why are you showing me this?" Ashby asked.

"Oh, so you *have* actually read it," Corbin said.

"Of course I have. I told you all to read this file ages ago so you could get a feel for her before she arrived." Ashby had no idea what Corbin was getting at, but this was Corbin's standard operating procedure. Complain first, explain later.

Corbin's reply was predictable, even before he opened his mouth: "I didn't have the time." Corbin had a habit of ignoring tasks that didn't originate within his lab. "What the hell are you thinking, bringing aboard a kid like that?"

"I was thinking," Ashby said, "that I need a certified clerk." Even Corbin couldn't argue that point. Ashby's records were a mess, and while a tunneling ship didn't strictly *need* a clerk in order to keep its license, the suits at the GC Transportation Board had made it pretty clear that Ashby's perpetually late reports weren't earning him any favors. Feeding and paying an extra crew member was no small expense, but after careful consideration and some nudging from Sissix, Ashby had asked the Board to send him someone certified. His business was going to start suffering if he didn't stop trying to do two jobs at once.

Corbin folded his arms and sniffed. "Have you talked to her?"

"We had a sib chat last tenday. She seems fine."

"*She seems fine,*" Corbin repeated. "That's encouraging."

Ashby chose his next words more carefully. This was Corbin, after all. The king of semantics. "The Board cleared her. She's fully qualified."

"The Board is smoking smash." He stabbed his finger toward the scrib again. "She's got no long-haul experience. She's never lived off Mars, as far as I can tell. She's fresh out of university—"

Ashby started ticking things off on his fingers. Two could play at this game. "She's certified to handle GC formwork. She's worked an internship at a ground transport company, which required the same basic skills I need her to have. She's fluent in Hanto, gestures and all, which could really open some doors for us. She comes with a letter of recommendation from her interspecies relations professor. And most important, from the little I've spoken to her, she seems like someone I can work with."

"She's never done this before. We're out in the middle of the open, on our way to a blind punch, and you're bringing a *kid* aboard."

"She's not a kid, she's just young. And everybody has a first job, Corbin. Even you must've started somewhere."

"You know what my first job was? Scrubbing out sample dishes in my father's lab. A trained *animal* could have done that job. *That's* what a first job should be, not—" He sputtered. "May I remind you of what we do here? We fly around punching holes—very literal holes—through space. This is not a safe job. Kizzy and Jenks scare the hell out of me with their carelessness as it is, but at least they're experienced. I can't do my job if I'm constantly worried about some incompetent rookie pushing the wrong button."

That was the warning flag, the *I can't work under these conditions* flag that indicated Corbin was about to go nonlinear. It was time to get him back on the rails. "Corbin, she's not going to be pushing any buttons. She's not doing anything more complicated than writing reports and filing formwork."

"*And* liasing with border guards, and planetary patrols, and clients who are late on their payments. The people we have to work with are not all nice people. They are not all *trustworthy* people. We need someone who can hold their own, who can bark down some upstart deputy who thinks he knows regulations better than us. Somebody who knows the difference between a *real* food safety stamp and a smuggler's knockoff. Somebody who actually knows how things *work* out here, not some blank-eyed graduate who will wet herself the first time a Quelin enforcer pulls up alongside."

Ashby set his mug down. "What *I* need," he said, "is someone to keep my records accurate. I need someone to manage our appointments, to make sure we all get the required vaccinations and scans before crossing borders, and to get my financial files sorted out. It's a complicated job, but not a difficult one, not if she's as organized as her letter of recommendation makes her out to be."

"That's a standardized letter if ever I saw one. I bet that professor has sent the exact same letter on behalf of every milquetoast student that came mewling through his door."

Ashby arched an eyebrow. "She studied at Alexandria University, same as you."

Corbin scoffed. "I was in the science department. There's a difference."

Ashby gave a short laugh. "Sissix is right, Corbin, you *are* a snob."

"Sissix can go to hell."

"So I heard you telling her last night. I could hear you down the hall." Corbin and Sissix were going to kill each other one of these days. They had never gotten along, and neither of them had any interest in trying to find common ground. It was an area where Ashby had to tread very lightly. Ashby and Sissix had been friends before the *Wayfarer*, but when he was in captain mode, both she and Corbin had to be treated equally as members of his crew. Moderating their frequent sparring matches required a delicate approach. Most of the time, he tried to stay out of it altogether. "Should I even ask?"

Corbin's mouth twitched. "She used the last of my dentbots."

Ashby blinked. "You do know we've got huge cases of dentbot packs down in the cargo bay."

"Not *my* dentbots. You buy those cheap hackjob bots that leave your gums sore."

"I use those bots every day and my gums feel just fine."

"I have sensitive gums. You can ask Dr. Chef for my dental records if you don't believe me. I have to buy my own bots."

Ashby hoped that his face did not reveal just how low this tale of woe ranked on his list of priorities. "I appreciate that it's annoying, but it's just one pack of dentbots we're talking about here."

Corbin was indignant. "They don't come cheap! She did it just to get at me, I know she did. If that selfish lizard can't—"

"Hey!" Ashby sat up straight. "Not okay. I don't want to hear that word come out of your mouth again." As far as racial insults went, *lizard* was hardly the worst, but it was bad enough.

Corbin pressed his lips together, as if to keep further unpleasantries from escaping. "Sorry."

Ashby's hackles were up, but truthfully, this was an ideal way for a conversation with Corbin to go. Get him away from the crew, let him vent, wait for him to cross a line, then talk him down while he was feeling penitent. "I will talk to Sissix, but you have got to be more civil to people. And I don't care how mad you get, that kind of language does not belong on my ship."

"I just lost my temper, was all." Corbin was obviously still angry, but even he knew better than to bite the hand that feeds. Corbin knew that he was a valuable asset, but at the end of the day, Ashby was the one who sent credits to his account. *Valuable* was not the same as *irreplaceable*.

"Losing your temper is one thing, but you are part of a multispecies crew, and you need to be mindful of that.

Especially with somebody new coming aboard. And on that note, I'm sorry you have concerns about her, but frankly, she's not your problem. Rosemary was the Board's suggestion, but agreeing to take her on was my call. If she's a mistake, we'll get someone new. But until then, we are all going to give her the benefit of the doubt. Regardless of how you feel about her, I expect you to make her feel welcome. In fact . . ." A slow smile spread across Ashby's face.

Corbin looked wary. "What?"

Ashby leaned back in his chair, lacing his fingers together. "Corbin, I seem to recall that our new clerk will be arriving around seventeen-half tomorrow. Now, I have a sib scheduled with Yoshi at seventeen on the nose, and you know how he loves to talk. I doubt I'll be done by the time Rosemary docks, and she's going to need someone to show her around."

"Oh, no." A stricken look crossed Corbin's face. "Have Kizzy do it. She loves that sort of thing."

"Kizzy's got her hands full replacing the air filter by the med bay, and I doubt she'll be done before tomorrow. Jenks will be helping Kizzy, so he's out."

"Sissix, then."

"Mmm, Sissix has a lot of prep work to do before the punch tomorrow. She probably won't have the time." Ashby grinned. "I'm sure you'll give her a great tour."

Corbin looked at his employer with baleful eyes. "Sometimes you're a real pain in the ass, Ashby."

Ashby picked up his mug and finished off the dregs. "I knew I could count on you."

||||||||||||||||||||||||||||||||||||||||||||||||||||||||||||||||

ARRIVAL

Rosemary rubbed the bridge of her nose as she accepted a cup of water from the wall dispenser. The lingering edges of the sedatives made her head feel foggy, and so far, the stims that were supposed to counter those effects had done nothing but make her heart race. Her body longed for a stretch, but she couldn't undo the safety harness while the pod was in motion, and the pod didn't have enough room for anything except standing up and walking out anyway. She leaned her head back with a groan. It had been nearly three days since the deepod launched. Solar days, she reminded herself. Not standard days. She needed to get used to making the distinction. Longer days, longer years. But she had more pressing things to focus on than differences in calendars. She was groggy, hungry, cramped, and in all her twenty-three years—Solar, not standard—she could not remember ever needing to pee quite so badly. The brusque Aeluon attendant at the spaceport had told her the sedatives would suppress that need, but nothing had been said about how she would feel once they wore off.

Rosemary imagined the lengthy letter of complaint her mother might write after such a trip. She tried to imagine the circumstances in which her mother would travel by deepod at all. She couldn't even picture her mother setting foot within a public spaceport.

Rosemary had been surprised to find *herself* in such a place. The dingy waiting area, the twitching pixel posters, the stale smells of algae gunk and cleaning fluid. Despite the exoskeletons and tentacles milling around her, *she* had felt like the alien there.

That was the thing that had hammered home just how far from Sol she was—the menagerie of sapients standing alongside her in the ticket line. Her homeworld was fairly cosmopolitan, but aside from the occasional diplomat or corporate representative, Mars didn't see much in the way of non-Human travelers. A terraformed rock inhabited by one of the GC's least influential species was hardly a destination of choice. Professor Selim had warned her that studying the concepts behind interspecies relations was vastly different from having to go out there and *talk* to other sapients, but she hadn't truly understood that advice until she found herself surrounded by clunky biosuits and feet that didn't need shoes. She'd even been nervous speaking to the Harmagian behind the ticket counter. She knew that her Hanto was excellent (for a Human, anyway), but this was no longer the safe, controlled environment of the university language lab. No one would gently correct her mistakes or forgive her for an unwitting social transgression. She was on her own now, and in order to keep credits in her account and a bed beneath her back, she had to do the job she had assured Captain Santoso she could do.

No pressure, or anything.

Not for the first time, a cold fist appeared deep within her stomach. Never in her life had she worried about credits or having a place to go home to. But with the last of her savings running thin and her bridges burned behind her, there was no margin for error. The price of a fresh start was having no one to fall back on.

Please, she thought. *Please don't screw this up.*

"We are beginning our approach, Rosemary," chirped the

deepod's computer. "Do you require anything else before I begin docking procedures?"

"A bathroom and a sandwich," said Rosemary.

"Sorry, Rosemary, I had difficulty processing that. Could you please repeat your request?"

"I don't require anything."

"Okay, Rosemary. I will now open the outer shutters. You may wish to close your eyes in order to adjust to any external light sources."

Rosemary dutifully shut her eyes as the shutters whirred open, but her eyelids remained dark. She opened her eyes to find that the only significant source of light was coming from within the pod. As she had expected, there was nothing beyond the window but empty space and tiny stars. Out in the open.

She wondered how thick the pod's hull was.

The pod swung up, and Rosemary shielded her eyes from a sudden burst of light, pouring out of the windows of the ugliest ship she'd ever seen. It was blocky and angular, with the exception of a bulging dome that stuck out from the back like a warped spine. This was not a ship designed for fussy commercial passengers. There was nothing sleek or inspiring about it. It was bigger than a transport ship, smaller than a cargo carrier. The lack of wings indicated that this was a ship that had been built out in space, a ship that would never enter an atmosphere. The underside of the vessel held a massive, complex machine—metallic and sharp, with rows of toothlike ridges angled toward a thin, protracted spire. She didn't know much about ships, but from the mismatched colors of the outer hull, it looked as though whole sections had been cobbled together, perhaps originating from other vessels. A patchwork ship. The only reassuring thing about it was that it looked sturdy. This was a ship that could take (and had taken) a few knocks. Though the ships she was used to traveling in were far easier on the eye, knowing that there would be a solid, stocky hull between her and all that empty space was heartening.

"*Wayfarer*, this is Deepod 36-A, requesting permission to dock," said the computer.

"Deepod 36-A, this is the *Wayfarer*," replied a female voice with an Exodan accent. Rosemary noted the softness of the vowels, the pronunciation that was a little *too* polished. An AI. "Please confirm passenger identification."

"Acknowledged, *Wayfarer*. Transmitting passenger details now."

There was a brief pause. "Confirmed, Deepod 36-A. You are cleared to dock."

The deepod moved alongside the *Wayfarer* like some sort of aquatic animal swimming up to suckle at its mother. The hatch at the back of the pod slipped into the *Wayfarer's* sunken docking port. Rosemary could hear the mechanical sound of catches connecting. There was a hiss of air as the seal expanded.

The hatch door slid upward. Rosemary moaned as she stood. Her muscles felt as if they would splinter. She collected her duffel bag and satchel from the luggage rack, and limped forward. There was a slight gravitational discrepancy between the pod and the *Wayfarer,* enough to make her stomach lurch as she crossed the seam between the two. The feeling only lasted a few seconds, but combined with her foggy head, jittery pulse and aching bladder, it was enough to make Rosemary cross the line from *uncomfortable* to *vaguely miserable*. She hoped her new bed was soft.

She stepped into a small decontamination chamber, empty except for a glowing yellow panel affixed to a waist-high stand. The AI spoke through a vox on the wall. "Hello! I'm pretty sure I know who you are, but can you swipe your wristpatch over the panel, so I can be sure?"

Rosemary pulled her sleeve back, exposing her wristwrap—a woven bracelet that protected the small dermal patch embedded within the skin of her inner right wrist. There was a lot of data stored in that thumbnail-size piece of tech—her ID file, her bank account details and a medical interface used to communicate with the half million or so imubots that patrolled her bloodstream. Like all GC citizens, Rosemary got her first patch during childhood (for Humans, the standard age was five), but the patch she had now was only a few tendays old. The seam of skin surrounding it was still shiny and tender. The new patch had cost almost half of her savings, which seemed exorbitant, but she had hardly been in a position to argue.

She held her wrist over the yellow panel. There was a soft pulse of light. A twinge of adrenaline ran alongside the stims. What if something had gone wrong with the patch, and they pulled her old file instead? What if they saw her name, and put two and two together? Would it matter to people out here? Would it matter that she'd done nothing wrong? Would they turn away from her, just as her friends had? Would they put her back on the pod, and send her crawling back to Mars, back to a name she didn't want and a mess she hadn't—

The pad blinked a friendly green. Rosemary exhaled, and scoffed at herself for being nervous at all. The new patch had worked just fine ever since it was installed. She'd had no trouble confirming her identity or making payments at any stops along the way. It was unlikely that the patch scanner on this clunky tunneling ship would have picked up any discrepancies that the high-end scanners at the spaceports hadn't. Even so, this was the last hurdle to clear. Now all she had to worry about was whether or not she'd be good at her job.

"Well, there you are, Rosemary Harper," said the AI. "My name is Lovelace, and I serve as the ship's communication interface. I suppose in that regard we have relatively similar jobs, don't we? You liase on behalf of the crew. I liase on behalf of the ship."

"I guess that's true," Rosemary said, a little unsure of herself. She didn't have much experience with sentient AIs. The ones back home were all bland and utilitarian. The university library had an AI named Oracle, but she had been a more academic sort. Rosemary had never spoken to an AI as personable as Lovelace.

"Should I call you Rosemary?" Lovelace asked. "Or do you have a nickname?"

"Rosemary is fine."

"Okay, Rosemary. You can call me Lovey, if you like. Everyone else does. Feels good to be off that pod, doesn't it?"

"You have no idea."

"True. But then, you don't know how good it feels to have your memory banks recalibrated."

Rosemary considered this. "You're right, I don't."

"Rosemary, I have to be honest with you. The reason I've kept you chatting for this long is so that you don't get bored while I scan you for contaminants. One of our crew members has very specific health needs, and I have to do a more thorough scan than some ships require. It shouldn't be much longer."

Rosemary hadn't felt that she'd been waiting long at all, but she had no idea what qualified as a lengthy amount of time to an AI. "Take all the time you need."

"Is that all the luggage you have?"

"Yes," Rosemary said. In fact, she was carrying everything that she owned (that is, everything she hadn't sold off). She was still marveling at the fact that she could fit it all into two little bags. After a life in her parents' enormous home, full of furniture and knickknacks and rarities, the knowledge that she didn't need anything more than what she could carry gave her a remarkable sense of freedom.

"If you put your bags into that cargo elevator to your right, I can move them to the upper crew deck for you. You can pick them up whenever you head to your room."

"Thanks," Rosemary said. She pulled open the hinged metal door on the wall, set her bags into the corresponding compartment and latched the door shut. There was a rushing sound within the wall.

"Okay, Rosemary, I just finished my scan. Hate to say it, but you do have a few blacklisted bugs in your system."

"What kind of bugs?" Rosemary asked. She thought back with dread to the spaceport's smudged handrails and sticky seats. Three tendays since she'd left Mars, and already she'd picked up some alien plague.

"Oh, nothing that would affect *you*, but they are things our navigator can't handle. You'll need to have our doctor update your imubots accordingly before you leave the ship again. For now, I'm going to have to give you a decontamination flash. Is that okay?" Lovey sounded apologetic, and for good reason. The only good thing about a decontamination flash was that it was over quickly.

"Okay," Rosemary said, gritting her teeth.

"Hang in there," Lovey said. "Flashing in three . . . two . . . one."

Harsh orange light filled the room. Rosemary could feel it move right through her. A cold sting cut through her pores, her teeth, the roots of her eyelashes. For a brief moment, she knew where all her capillaries were.

"Oh, I'm so sorry," Lovey said as the flash ended. "I hate having to do that. You look sick."

Rosemary exhaled, trying to shake off the needlelike twinges. "It's not your fault," she said. "I wasn't feeling very well to start." She paused, realizing that she was trying to make an AI feel better. It was a silly concept, but something about Lovey's demeanor made any other response feel a bit rude. Could AIs even take offense? Rosemary wasn't sure.

"I hope you feel better soon. I know there's dinner planned

for you, but I'm sure you can get some rest right after that. Now, I've kept you long enough. You're free to go on through. And may I be the first to say: welcome aboard."

The vox switched off. Rosemary pressed her hand against the door panel. The inner airlock door spun open to reveal a pale man with a sour face. He changed his expression as Rosemary stepped forward. It was the most insincere smile she had ever seen.

"Welcome to the *Wayfarer*," the man said, extending his hand. "Artis Corbin. Algaeist."

"Nice to meet you, Mr. Corbin. I'm Rosemary Harper." Rosemary shook his hand. His grip was limp, his skin clammy. She was glad to let go.

"Just Corbin is fine." He cleared his throat. "Do you . . . ah . . ." He nodded toward the opposite wall. There was a door painted with the Human symbol for bathroom.

Rosemary ran for it.

She came back out a few minutes later in a more positive mood. Her heart was still fluttering, her head still clearing, the lingering tingle of the flash still making her teeth hurt. But at least *one* of her physical complaints could be checked off the list.

"Deepods are the worst way to travel," Corbin said. "They run on scrub fuel, you know. Bunch of accidents waiting to happen. They really should be better regulated." Rosemary tried to think up a response, but before she could, Corbin said: "This way." She followed him down the corridor.

The *Wayfarer* wasn't any fancier inside than it was outside, but the mismatched corridors had a humble charm. Small windows broke up the walls at regular intervals. The wall panels themselves were held together with bolts and screws of varying shapes. Like the exterior, the walls were different colors—coppery brown to one side, dull brass to the other, the occasional sheet of soft gray thrown in for good measure.

"Interesting design," said Rosemary.

Corbin scoffed. "If by 'interesting,'" you mean it looks like my grandmother's quilt, then yes. The *Wayfarer*'s an old ship. Most tunneling ships are. Incentives are provided to captains who upgrade old vessels instead of purchasing new ones. Ashby took full advantage of that. The original ship is about thirty-five standards old. Built to last, but not built with the comfort of the crew in mind. Ashby added bigger quarters, more storage space, water showers, those kinds of things. All salvaged, of course. Don't have the money to kit it all out from scratch."

Rosemary was relieved at the mention of improved living conditions. She had been bracing herself for the possibility of tiny bunks and sanidust showers. "I assume that Lovey was a later addition as well?"

"Yes. Ashby purchased her, but she's Jenks's pet." Corbin continued on without explanation. He nodded at the wall. "There are voxes in every room and in major junctions. No matter where you are, Lovey can hear your requests and transmit messages on your behalf. They broadcast to the whole ship, so be selective about what you say. Voxes are a tool, not a toy. Fire extinguishers are available throughout the ship as well. Kizzy can send you a map of their locations. Exosuit lockers are in the docking hatch, the crew deck and the cargo bay. Escape pods are available on all decks. We also have a shuttle that is accessible through the cargo bay. If you see those emergency panels on the wall light up, head for a suit, a pod or the shuttle, whichever is closest." The corridor split in two up ahead. He pointed to the left. "Med bay is that way. It's nothing state of the art, but it's enough to keep someone alive until we get to port."

"I see," said Rosemary. She tried not to read too much into the fact that the only things Corbin had mentioned were related to emergencies or injuries.

Loud, jovial voices came from a junction up ahead. There

was a *clang* as something fell to the floor. This was followed by a brief argument, then laughter. Corbin's eyes narrowed as if warding off a headache. "I believe you're about to meet our techs," he said.

They rounded the corner to find a bird's nest of wires and cables strewn about the floor. There was no order or sense to any of it, not that Rosemary could see. Algae tubes poured like innards from an open wall panel. Working within the wall itself were two people, a man and a woman, both Human—or were they? There was no question about the woman, who was somewhere on the cusp between her twenties and thirties. Her black hair was tied back in a lopsided bun, held together with a frayed, faded ribbon. She wore an orange jumpsuit smudged with grease and gunk, patched on the elbows with bright fabric and big stitches. There were hasty notes handwritten on her sleeves, things like "CHECK 32-B—OLD WIRES?" and "DON'T FORGET AIR FILTERS YOU DUMMY" and "EAT." Perched on her flat nose was a set of curious optical lenses. Rather than just one lens per eye, there were no fewer than half a dozen attachments welded onto hinged supports. Some bulged and magnified, others flickered with tiny digital panels. They appeared to be handmade. As for the woman herself, her dark olive skin looked as if it had spent a lot of time bathing in natural sunlight, but her indistinct features were undeniably Exodan. Rosemary thought it likely that she had grown up on an extrasolar colony—"out of the sun," as they would say back on Mars.

The man, on the other hand, was not so easily categorized, though he looked Human in most respects. His blended facial features, his body shape, his limbs and digits, they were all familiar. His copper coloring was even quite similar to Rosemary's, though several shades darker. But while his head was an average size, the rest of him was small, as small as a child. He was stocky, too, as if his limbs had filled out while refusing to lengthen. He was small enough to fit atop the woman's shoulders, which was exactly where he was standing. As if his physique were not noteworthy enough, he had gone to great lengths to decorate himself. The sides of his head were shaved, and a tuft of curls popped up atop his scalp. His ears were adorned with constellations of piercings, his arms sleeved in colorful tattoos. Rosemary did her best not to stare. She concluded that he was indeed Human, but he had to be a genetweak. It was the only explanation she could think of. But then again, why would anyone go to that much trouble to make himself small?

The woman looked up from her work. "Oh, hooray!" she said. "Jenks, get off me, we have to be sociable."

The small man, who had been operating some noisy tool within the wall, turned his head and lifted up his safety goggles. "Aha," he said, climbing down. "The newbie approaches."

Before Rosemary could have any say in the matter, the woman stood up, removed her gloves and wrapped Rosemary in an enormous hug. "Welcome home." She pulled back, wearing an infectious grin. "I'm Kizzy Shao. Mech tech."

"Rosemary Harper." She tried not to appear too startled. "And thank you."

Kizzy's grin grew wider. "Ooh, I love your accent. You Martians always sound so *smooth*."

"I'm the comp tech," the man said, cleaning the gunk from his hands with a rag. "Jenks."

"Is that your given name or your family name?" Rosemary asked.

Jenks shrugged. "Whichever." He reached out to shake her hand. Even with his small hands, he had a better grip than Corbin. "Nice to meet you."

"Nice to meet you, too, Mr. Jenks."

"*Mister* Jenks! I like that." He turned his head. "Hey, Lovey. Patch me through to everybody, please." A nearby vox switched on. "Attention all hands," Jenks said in a pompous voice. "As per our clerk's example, I will now only respond to my full title of 'Mr. Jenks.' That is all."

Corbin leaned toward Rosemary and lowered his voice. "That's *not* what the voxes are for."

"So," said Kizzy. "Was your trip okay?"

"I've had better," said Rosemary. "Though I'm here in one piece, so I guess I can't complain."

"Complain all you want," Jenks said. He pulled a worn metal tin from his pocket. "Deepods are a shit way to get around. And I know they're the only way to get you here fast, but those things are dangerous as hell. Stims make you shaky?" Rosemary nodded. "Ugh, yeah, trust me, you'll feel better after you get some food in you."

"Have you been up to your room yet?" Kizzy asked. "I made the curtains, but if you don't like the fabric, just say so and I'll tear 'em right down."

"I haven't been there yet," Rosemary said. "But I've been admiring the rest of your handiwork so far. Must not be easy adding on to an old model."

Kizzy's face lit up like a globulb. "No, but see, that's why it's so fun! It's like a puzzle, figuring out what kind of circuits the old ones will talk to, adding new bits to make things more homey, staying on top of all the old framework's secrets so we don't blow up." She gave a contented sigh. "It's the best job ever. Have you seen the Fishbowl yet?"

"The what, sorry?"

"The Fishbowl." Kizzy beamed. "Just wait. It's the bestest."

Corbin's peering eyes snapped to the comp tech. "Jenks, you cannot be serious!"

Jenks's metal tin was full of redreed. He had stuffed a hefty pinch of it into a small, curved pipe, and was now lighting it with a welding tool. "What?" he said, his voice muffled through clenched teeth. He sucked air into the pipe, causing the shredded fibers to spark and smoke. The faint scent of burnt cinnamon and ash hit Rosemary's nose. She thought of her father, who was always puffing the stuff as he worked. She pushed the unwanted reminder of family aside.

Corbin placed a hand over his nose and mouth. "If you want to fill your lungs with toxins, fine, but do it in your quarters."

"Calm down," said Jenks. "This is that tweaked strain the Laru cooked up. Bless their eight-valved hearts. All the mellow of fresh redreed, without any of the toxic stuff. One hundred percent good for you. Well, not *bad* for you, anyway. You should try some, it'd do wonders for your mood." He exhaled a stream of smoke in Corbin's direction.

Corbin's face tightened, but he seemed reluctant to press the issue further. Rosemary got the impression that for all his bluster about the rules, Corbin didn't actually have any authority over the techs. "Does Ashby know about this mess?" Corbin said, gesturing at the floor.

"Relax, grumpy," Kizzy said. "It'll all be fixed and put away by dinnertime."

"Dinner is in half an hour," Corbin said.

Kizzy's hands went to the top of her head. She grimaced dramatically. "Oh, no! For serious? I thought dinner was at eighteen?"

"It's seventeen-half now."

"Balls!" Kizzy said, diving back into the wall. "We'll talk later, Rosemary, I've got work to do. Jenks, get on my shoulders, buddy, posthaste!"

"Hup!" Jenks said, placing the pipe between his teeth and climbing up.

Corbin continued down the corridor without another word.

"It was nice meeting you," Rosemary said, hurrying after Corbin.

"Nice meeting you, too!" called Kizzy. "Ah, shit, Jenks! You got ash in my mouth!" There was the sound of spitting, and a twin set of laughter.

"It's a wonder we're not all dead," Corbin said to no one. He said nothing else as they continued down the corridor. Rosemary had deduced that small talk was not his forte. As uncomfortable as the silence was, she felt it best not to break it.

The corridor curved inward, connecting to the other side of the ship. At the apex of the curve was a door. "This is the control room," Corbin said. "Navigation and tunneling controls. You won't have much need for this room."

"Is it all right to see it anyway? Just to get my bearings?"

Corbin hesitated. "Our pilot is probably working in there now. We shouldn't disturb—"

The door opened, and a female Aandrisk stepped out. "I thought I heard a new voice!" she said. Her accent was husky around the edges, but it was the clearest Rosemary had ever heard from her species. Not that Rosemary had much experience with Aandrisks. As one of the Galactic Commons's three founding species, they were a familiar sight throughout the galaxy. Or so Rosemary had been told. The Aandrisk standing before her was the first that she had ever spoken to directly. Her mind raced, scrambling to remember what she could of Aandrisk culture. *Complicated family structures. Virtually no concept of personal space. Physically affectionate. Promiscuous.* She mentally slapped herself for that. It was a stereotype, one that every Human knew whether they wanted to or not, and it smacked of ethnocentrism. *They don't pair up like we do*, she chided herself. *It's not the same thing.* Somewhere in her head, Professor Selim was frowning at her. "*The very fact that we use the term 'cold-blooded' as a synonym for 'heartless' should tell you something about the innate bias we primates hold against reptiles*," she pictured him saying. "*Do not judge other species by your own social norms.*"

Determined to do her professor proud, Rosemary braced herself for some of that Aandrisk cheek nuzzling she'd heard about, or perhaps another unexpected hug. However this person wanted to greet her, she was going to flow with it. She was part of a multispecies crew now, and she was going to be graceful about it, dammit.

But to Rosemary's disappointment, all the Aandrisk woman did was extend one of her clawed hands, initiating a handshake. "You must be Rosemary," she said warmly. "I'm Sissix."

Rosemary wrapped her fingers around Sissix's scaled palm as best she could. Their hands did not fit well together, but they made the best of it. Sissix was too alien for Rosemary to label her as beautiful, but . . . *striking.* Yes, that was a better word. She stood a head taller than Rosemary, and her body was lithe and lean. Moss green scales sheathed her body from the top of her head to the tip of her tail, fading into a paler shade over her belly. She had a smooth face, no nose or lips or ears to speak of, just holes for breathing and holes for hearing and a small slit of a mouth. A multicolored shock of feathers covered her head like a short, festive mane. Her chest was as flat as a Human man's, but the contrast between her thin waist and her muscular, saurian thighs gave the illusion of feminine hips (though Rosemary knew that impression also stemmed from cultural bias; male Aandrisks were built exactly the same as females, only smaller). Her legs were slightly bowed, as if poised to spring, and her fingers and toes were capped with thick, blunt claws. Each claw was painted with lazy swirls of gold, and looked to be filed down. She wore a pair of loose, low-slung trousers, and a vest held together with one button. Rosemary recalled Professor Selim saying that Aandrisks only wore clothes to make other species feel more comfortable. Between the clothes, the accent and the handshake, Rosemary got the impression that Sissix had been around Humans a long time.

Sissix had not been the only thing to exit the control room. A waft of hot, dry air had followed her out the door. Rosemary could feel waves of heat emanating from the room beyond. Even at the doorway, it felt smothering.

Corbin's eyes narrowed. "You do know that interface panels start to warp if they get too hot."

Sissix flicked her yellow eyes toward the pale man. "Thank you, Corbin. I've only been living on ships for my entire adult life, so I have no idea how to safely manage internal temperature settings."

"I think this ship is hot enough as it is."

"If anyone else had been working in there with me, I would've cranked it down. Honestly, what is the problem?"

"The problem, Sissix, is that—"

"Stop." Sissix raised a palm. She looked back and forth between Corbin and Rosemary. "Why are *you* showing her around?"

Corbin clenched his jaw. "Ashby asked me to. It's no trouble." His words were noncommittal, but Rosemary could hear the same insincerity that had masked his face when she stepped through the airlock. The cold fist reappeared in her stomach. Ten minutes on the ship, and already somebody didn't like her. Fantastic.

"Right," Sissix said. She squinted, as if trying to figure something out. "I'd be happy to take over as tour guide if you have other things to do."

Corbin pressed his lips together. "I don't mean to be rude, Rosemary, but I do have some salinity tests that should be started sooner rather than later."

"Great!" said Sissix, putting her hand on Rosemary's shoulder. "Have fun with your algae!"

"Um, it was nice meeting you," Rosemary said as Sissix led her away. Corbin was already disappearing down the corridor. The whole exchange had been bewildering, but Rosemary was glad of what appeared to be more friendly company. She did her best not to stare at the way Sissix's bare feet flexed, the way her feathers bounced as she walked. Everything about the way she moved was fascinating.

"Rosemary, on behalf of the crew of the *Wayfarer*, I would like to apologize," Sissix said. "Coming into a new home deserves a better welcome than anything Artis Corbin can give. I'm sure you know all about the escape pods by now, and nothing about who we are and what we do."

Rosemary laughed despite herself. "How did you know?"

"Because I have to live with that man," Sissix said. "As do you. But fortunately, you get to live with the rest of us, too, and I think we're pretty likable." She stopped beside a metal staircase that stretched both up through the ceiling and down through the floor. "Have you even seen your room yet?"

"No."

Sissix rolled her eyes. "Come on," she said, walking up the stairs, doing her best to keep her tail out of Rosemary's face. "I always feel better on a new ship once I know where my place is."

The Aandrisk woman was right. Rosemary's place, it turned out, was a room tucked into the corner of the topmost deck. The only furniture was a boxy apparatus built right into the far wall, which housed drawers, a tiny closet and a nook just big enough for a bunk. But the sparseness of the room had been softened by a few Human touches (or sapient touches, Rosemary supposed). The bunk was covered with a fuzzy blanket and a heap of colorful pillows, transforming what might have been a spartan shelf into a cozy little nest. The curtains that Kizzy had mentioned were made from a flower-patterned fabric—no, not flowers, jellyfish. The print was a bit too busy for Rosemary's taste, but she was sure it would grow on her. On the adjoining wall, there was a small hydroponic planter trailing tear-shaped leaves. Beside it was a mirror, upon which hung a printed note: "WELCOME HOME!" It was the smallest, simplest, humblest living space Rosemary had ever seen (dingy spaceport hotels notwithstanding). And yet, all things considered, it was perfect. She couldn't think of a better place to start over.

TIP OFF

Ashby forced a smile as Yoshi rambled on over the sib. He had never liked the man much. There was nothing *wrong* with him, exactly, but stars, he could talk for days. Checking in with the Transport Board was an empty formality to begin with, a verbal confirmation that Ashby wouldn't be punching through any space that didn't belong to him. He of all people understood the need to measure twice and cut once, but Yoshi always managed to turn what should've been a simple matter of *Did you get the flight plan? All right then, safe journey* into an hour-long conversation.

The pixels displaying Yoshi flickered slightly, the result of signal decay. He pushed back his long sleeves and stirred his mek—cold, Ashby noted, in the Harmagian style. He refrained from rolling his eyes at the well-crafted charade. The cold mek, the Aeluon-influenced tailoring, the practiced Central accent that still betrayed a Martian cadence if you knew what to listen for. The trappings of a bureaucrat trying to pretend he had the same clout as the powerful species around him. Ashby was not ashamed of his heritage—quite the opposite—but there was something irritating about seeing a Human get too big for his britches.

"But enough about me," Yoshi said with a laugh. "How's life aboard the *Wayfarer*? All well with your crew?"

"Yeah, we're all fine," Ashby said. "And we've got one more, as of today."

"Yes, yes, the new clerk! I was going to ask you about her. Is she settling in all right?"

"I haven't actually met her yet. I heard her pod dock a short while ago."

"Ah, then I won't keep you long." *Ha.* "You know, Ashby, bringing on a clerk puts a few points in your book as far as the Board's concerned. You've always been dependable when it comes to tunneling, but this shows that you're committed to upholding our administrative standards as well. Smart move on your part."

"Just practical, really. I need the extra help."

Yoshi leaned back in his chair, his face blurring as he moved back from the sib camera. "You've been doing level-three work for a long time now. Have you ever considered taking things up a notch?"

Ashby raised his eyebrows. Yoshi was a faker, but he wasn't incompetent. He knew the *Wayfarer* wasn't equipped for high-level jobs. "Sure, but we're not kitted out for it," Ashby said. He couldn't afford to be, either. His ship was geared for single-ship transport lanes—colony hops, mostly. There was a lot of money to be made in cargo convoy tunnels, but you needed some serious equipment to make a stable passage that big. Ashby didn't know of any Human-owned ships doing that kind of work.

"True, but that doesn't mean you should limit yourself, either," Yoshi said. He glanced over his shoulder with sly importance. Again, Ashby stopped himself from rolling his eyes. As far as he could tell, Yoshi was alone in a closed room. "Just watch out for some *interesting* work coming down the line. In your usual bracket, but—ah, a little different."

Ashby leaned forward a bit. It was hard to trust much coming from a Human who forced his *R*s into a Harmagian burr, but even so, he wasn't going to ignore advice given from someone sitting in a Parliament office. "What kind of work?"

"I'm not in a position to say *what*, exactly," Yoshi said. "Let's just say it'd be a nice change of pace from what you're used to." He looked Ashby in the eye. The pixels twitched. "The kind of thing that might give you a leg up."

Ashby gave what he hoped was a congenial smile. "That's a little vague."

Yoshi smirked. "You follow the news?"

"Every day."

"Make sure that you do over, say, oh, the next five days or so. Don't worry about it now. Take care of your clerk, get through the punch tomorrow, and then . . . then you'll see." He took a smug, knowing sip from his chilled cup. "Trust me. You'll know it when you see it."

THE TUNNELERS

☆

After tucking away her two pieces of luggage (which Sissix had approved of—"packing light saves fuel"), Rosemary followed her guide back down the stairs. Something caught her eye, something she hadn't noticed on the way up. Each grated metal step was carefully covered with a thick strip of carpet.

"What's this for?" Rosemary asked.

"Hmm? Oh, that's for me. So my claws don't catch in the grating."

Rosemary cringed. "Ugh."

"You have no idea. I snapped one clean off a few years back, before Kizzy put the runners down. Shrieked like a hatchling." She stepped off onto the next deck, nodding toward doors. "Rec room's over there. Exercise machines, gaming hub, comfy couches, all that stuff. The hub's got a few good outdoor sims you can patch into. Everybody's supposed to use it for at least a half hour every day. In theory. It's an easy thing to forget, but it *is* good for you. On a long haul, *this*"—she tapped the top of Rosemary's head—"needs to be the most important thing you take care of."

Rosemary paused as they walked down the corridor. "Is it just me, or is it getting darker in here?"

Sissix chuckled. "You really haven't lived out in the open,

have you?" she said, though not unkindly. "The lighting in the corridors and communal areas gets lighter and darker as the day goes on. What you're seeing now is sunset, or an approximation of it. You can turn on the work lamps in individual rooms whenever you need more light, but having ambient lighting throughout the ship helps us keep a rhythm."

"You follow standard days here, right?"

Sissix nodded. "Standard days, standard calendar. Are you still on Solar time?"

"Yeah."

"Go easy your first tenday. Adopting a new body clock can really take it out of you. Honestly, though, as long as you get your work done and know what day it is, it doesn't matter what sort of schedule you keep. None of us get up at the same time, and we all work weird hours. Especially Ohan. They're nocturnal."

Rosemary wasn't sure who Ohan was or what Sissix had meant by the plural pronoun, but before she could ask, Sissix directed a grin toward the door ahead. "I'm going to let you go through first."

There was a hand-painted sign affixed to the wall beside the door. "THE FISHBOWL," it read. The bright letters were surrounded by smiling planets and cheerful flowers. New as Rosemary was to the ship, she had an inkling that the sign was Kizzy's doing.

She opened the door, and gasped. Before her was a wide, domed room, constructed from interlocking sheets of plex. It was a window, a giant, bubblelike window, with the entire galaxy spilling out beyond. And on their side, everything—*everything*—was green. Large hydroponic planters were arranged in spiraling rows, bursting with broad leaves, perky sprouts and dark, fat vegetables. Handwritten labels were affixed to skewers at regular intervals (the alphabet used was not one that Rosemary recognized). Some of the plants were flowering, and delicate trellises encouraged the climbers to grow tall. A branching path stretched out from the doorway, lined with repurposed cargo crates and food cans filled with bushy tufts of grass. Bits of tech junk painted with bright shapes peeked out here and there, adding dabs of color. At the end of the path were three steps, which led into a sunken garden. A ramshackle fountain chattered quietly there, with a few benches and chairs nearby. Behind the benches, small decorative trees stretched up toward the sunlamps that hung overhead. But once Rosemary noticed the lamps, her attention was drawn back to the bubbled window, to the stars and planets and nebulae waiting just outside.

After a few seconds of gaping, Rosemary had the presence of mind to note the smaller details. The window frame looked worn, and of a completely different make from the rest of the room. The hydroponic planters were of all shapes and sizes, and were banged up enough to suggest that they'd been purchased secondhand. But the room was one of those strange, wonderful places that benefited from a lack of uniformity. The plants were healthy and well-tended, but somehow, the scuffs and dents and painted scraps were what made them truly come alive.

"This . . ." Rosemary blinked. "This is incredible."

"And necessary, believe it or not," said Sissix. "It may seem like an extravagance, but it's got three useful purposes. One, living plants ease the strain on our air filters. Two, we can grow some of our own food, which saves us money on market trips, and is healthier than eating stuff kept in stasis all the time. Three, most important, it keeps us from going crazy after being cooped up in here for a few tendays. The rec room's good for a moment of quiet, but this is where we all come to really slow down. A lot of long-haul ships have places like this. Ours is the best, though, if you'd like my entirely unbiased opinion."

"It's beautiful," said Rosemary, tearing her eyes away from the window. She thought for a moment, remembering the opaque dome she'd seen from the deepod. "Why couldn't I see this coming in?"

"Neat trick, isn't it?" said Sissix. "It's made out of switch plex, so it's only transparent when we want it to be. Gives us some privacy, and keeps things cool if we're near a sun. It used to be part of some Harmagian's yacht. Kizzy and Jenks have a whole network of scavenger buddies who give us a call whenever they find some scrap we might put to good use. The dome has been the jackpot so far." She gestured for Rosemary to follow her. "Come on, I'll introduce you to the guy who grows all this stuff."

They followed the right side of the path to an oval-shaped dining table, set for dinner. The chairs surrounding the table were mismatched, and about a third of them designed to fit non-Human posteriors. Soft lights hung from long wires over the table, capped with shades of different colors. It was far from the fanciest table Rosemary had ever seen—the napkins were faded, a few plates had dents, the condiments were all cheap brands—but it felt inviting nonetheless.

Near the table was a counter, with three stools on one side and a big kitchen on the other. The smell of baking bread and sizzling herbs flooded Rosemary's nostrils, and her body reminded her of how long it had been since she last ate. Her entire torso felt hollow.

"Hey!" Sissix called over the counter. "Come meet our new crewmate!"

Rosemary hadn't seen the curtain covering the doorway in the back until a member of the strangest species she'd ever seen threw it aside and lumbered forward. The sapient—*guy*, Sissix had said—was at least twice Rosemary's size. He was rotund and fleshy, with dappled gray skin. She would have pegged him as some sort of amphibian if it weren't for the tufts of long whiskers that stood out from his balloonlike cheeks. The major-ity of his face was dominated by a broad, split upper lip, which

Rosemary found endearing, though she couldn't say why. She thought back to the picture programs of ancient Earth animals she'd pored over as a kid. If you crossed an otter with a gecko, then made it walk like a six-legged caterpillar, you'd be getting somewhere.

The sapient's legs were especially difficult to categorize, because they could have just as easily been arms. He had six of them, whatever they were, all identical. When he came through the door, he'd been walking on one pair, and holding two tubs of food with the others. But once he set the tubs down, he folded his body down onto two pairs and walked to the counter.

"Well, well, well," the sapient rumbled. There was a weird harmony to his voice, as if five people were talking at once. As she continued to process his appearance, Rosemary noticed that he was wearing Human-style clothing. His upper torso—if you could call it that—was covered by a huge short-sleeved shirt printed with a logo of a green Human thumb zooming through space. The surrounding text was printed not in Klip, but in Ensk: "Littlejohn's Plant Emporium—Your One-Stop Shop for Transgalactic Hydroponics." Extra armholes had been cut into the sides to allow for his middle pair of limbs. His lower section was covered by an enormous pair of drawstring trousers. Or not trousers. More like a pouch with room for legs.

The sapient's whole face curved upward in a surreal approxima- tion of a smile. "I bet you've never seen one of me before," he said.

Rosemary smiled, relieved that he'd broken the ice. "Can't say that I have," she said.

The sapient bustled about behind the counter as he spoke. "Interspecies sensitivity training always falls a bit short when you see something new, doesn't it? The first time I saw one of you lanky brown things, I fell dead quiet."

"And for his species," Sissix said, "that's really saying something."

"That it is!" said the sapient. "Silence doesn't suit us." A sound exploded from his mouth—a warbling, rumbling coo.

Rosemary glanced at Sissix as discordant bursts continued to flow from the sapient's strange mouth. "He's laughing," Sissix whispered.

The noise cut off, and the sapient tapped his chest. "I'm Dr. Chef."

"I'm Rosemary," she said. "You have an interesting name."

"Well, it's not my *actual* name, but I cook the food and I work in the med bay when the need arises. I am what I do."

"What species are you?"

"I am a Grum, and I'm currently male."

Rosemary had never heard of a Grum. Had to be a non-GC species. "Currently?" she asked.

"Biological sex is a transitional state of being for my species. We begin life as female, become male once our egg-laying years are over, then end our lives as something neither here nor there." Dr. Chef reached over the counter and placed a cup of juice and a small plate of thick, grainy crackers in front of Rosemary. "Here you go. Sugar, salt, vitamins, calories. Dinner will be soon, but you look ready to faint." He shook his head at Sissix. "I hate deepods."

"Oh, stars, thank you." Rosemary fell upon the crackers. In some distant part of her head, she knew that they were nothing special, but in that moment, they were the best thing that she had ever eaten. "May I ask your given name?" she said, once her mouth was less full.

"You won't be able to say it."

"Can I try?"

Again, the warbling laugh. "Okay, get ready." Dr. Chef's mouth opened, and a cacophony fell out, layers upon layers of baffling sounds. It lasted a full minute. His cheeks puffed three times once it ended. "That's me," he said. He pointed at his throat. "Branching windpipes, six sets of vocal cords. There's not one word in my language that doesn't have several sounds blended together."

Rosemary felt a little stunned. "Learning Klip cannot have been easy for you."

"Oh, it wasn't," said Dr. Chef. "And I won't lie, it's still tiring at times. Synchronizing my vocal cords takes a lot of effort."

"Why not just use a talkbox?"

Dr. Chef shook his head, the skin on his cheeks shivering. "I don't like implants that aren't medically necessary. Besides, what's the point of talking to different species if you don't take the time to learn their words? Seems like cheating to simply *think* things and let a little box do the talking for you."

Rosemary took another sip of juice. Her head was already feeling better. "Does your name mean something in your language?"

"It does. I am 'A Grove of Trees Where Friends Meet to Watch the Moons Align During a Sunset in Mid' . . . I'd guess you'd say 'autumn.' Mind you, that's just the first bit. It also includes my mother's name and the town in which I was born, but I think I'll leave it there, or else you'll be listening to me translate all night." He laughed again. "And you? I know most Humans don't put much stock in names, but does yours have any meaning?"

"Er, well, I don't think my parents meant anything by it, but rosemary is a kind of plant."

Dr. Chef leaned forward, resting his weight against his upper arms. "A plant? What kind of plant?"

"Nothing special. Just an herb."

"Just an herb!" said Dr. Chef, his whiskers trembling. "Just an herb, she says!"

"Uh-oh," said Sissix. "You said the magic word."

"Rosemary, Rosemary," said Dr. Chef, taking her hand. "Herbs are my very favorite thing. They combine both the medicinal and the gastronomical, which, as you may have guessed, are my two best subjects. I am an avid collector of herbs. I pick up new specimens wherever I go." He paused, grumbling and whistling to himself. "I don't think I've heard of your namesake herb. Is it for eating or healing?"

"Eating," said Rosemary. "I think it goes in soups. Breads, too, I guess."

"Soups! Oh, I like soups," said Dr. Chef. His solid black eyes shifted to Sissix. "We're making a stop at Port Coriol soon, right?"

"Yep," said Sissix.

"Someone there will have it for sure. I'll send a message to my old friend Drave, he'll know where to look. He's good at finding food-related things." His mouth curved up as he looked back to Rosemary. "See? You've got a proper name after all. Now, you finish those crackers, I'm going to check on the bugs." He bustled back into the kitchen, growling and sighing as he bent over the grill. Rosemary wondered if he might be humming.

Sissix leaned close to Rosemary and whispered, her voice shielded by Dr. Chef's vocalizations and the general sounds of cooking. "Don't ask about his homeworld."

"Oh," Rosemary said. "Okay."

"Trust me on this. And don't ask about his family, either. It's . . . not good dinner talk. I'll explain later."

Dr. Chef proudly lifted a large arthropod from the grill with a pair of tongs. Its shell was blackened, and its legs curled under in even rows. It was about the size of Rosemary's hand, wrist to fingertip. "I hope you like red coast bugs. Fresh, too, not from the stasie. I have a few breeding tanks in the back."

Sissix gave Rosemary a friendly nudge. "We only get fresh ones for special occasions."

"I've never had them, but they smell wonderful," Rosemary said.

"Wait," Sissix said. "You've never had red coast bugs? I've never met a Human who's never had red coast bugs."

"I've always lived planetside," Rosemary said. "We don't eat many bugs on Mars." She felt guilty just saying it. Insects were cheap, rich in protein and easy to cultivate in cramped rooms, which made them an ideal food for spacers. Bugs had been part of the Exodus Fleet's diet for so long that even extrasolar colonies still used them as a main staple. Rosemary had, of course, at least *heard* of red coast bugs. The old story went that a short while after the Exodus Fleet had been granted refugee status within the Galactic Commons, a few Human representatives had been brought to some Aeluon colony to discuss their needs. One of the more entrepreneurial Humans had noticed clusters of large insects skittering over the red sand dunes near the coastline. The insects were a mild nuisance to the Aeluons, but the Humans saw food, and lots of it. Red coast bugs were swiftly adopted into the Exodans' diet, and nowadays you could find plenty of Aeluons and extrasolar Humans who had become wealthy from their trade. Rosemary's admission that she'd never eaten red coast bugs meant that she was not only poorly traveled, but that she belonged to a separate chapter of Human history. She was a descendant of the wealthy meat eaters who had first settled Mars, the cowards who had shipped livestock through space while nations starved back on Earth. Even though Exodans and Solans had long ago put their old grudges behind them (mostly), her privileged ancestry was something she had become ashamed of. It reminded her all too well of why she had left home.

Sissix eyed her with suspicion. "Have you eaten mammals? I mean the real thing, not vat grown."

"Sure. There are a few cattle ranches on Mars."

Sissix recoiled, making sounds of amusement and disgust. "Oh, no, *yuck*." She looked apologetic. "Sorry, Rosemary, that's just so . . . *blech*."

"*Psh*. They're just big sandwiches on hooves," said Jenks, walking in with a grin. "I've had planetside beef, too, y'know. It's *awesome*."

"Oh, gross. You're all gross," Sissix said, laughing.

"I'll stick with bugs, thanks," said a male Human voice. Rosemary turned, and stood up. "Welcome aboard," Captain Santoso said, shaking her hand. "It's good to finally meet you."

"You as well, Captain," Rosemary said. "I'm very happy to be here."

"Please, just call me Ashby," he said with a smile. He glanced around, looking for someone. "Did Corbin give you the grand tour?"

"He started it off," Sissix said, taking one of Rosemary's crackers. "I took over so he could run some tests."

"Well. That was . . . nice of you," Ashby said. He stared at Sissix for a moment, asking a question that Rosemary couldn't discern. He turned his attention back to her. "I'm afraid I won't have much time to show you the ropes over the next couple of days. We're tunneling tomorrow, and there're always some odds and ends to take care of afterward. But I'm sure you need some time to settle in anyway. Once we've put this job behind us, you and I can sit down and start going through my reports."

"You have my sympathies," Sissix said, patting Rosemary's shoulder.

"They're not *that* bad," Ashby said. Dr. Chef cleared his throats pointedly. "Okay, they're pretty bad." Ashby shrugged and smiled. "But hey! That means you have a job!"

Rosemary laughed. "Don't worry. I'm one of those weirdos who likes formwork."

"Thank the stars for that," Ashby said. "We're a good crew, but formwork is not one of our strengths."

"Sissix!" Kizzy cried, entering the room. "I need to talk to you about this super-scandalous sexy vid I saw today."

Ashby's eyes fell shut. "Neither is tact."

Sissix looked bemused. "Kizzy, I told you, I am done watching your vids. I swear, Humans are the only species who can make coupling *tacky*."

"No, listen, it's important." Kizzy strolled behind the counter, inspecting Dr. Chef's cooking. She had shed the grubby jumpsuit in exchange for a smart yellow jacket, a skirt that could only be described as a short petticoat, bright orange polka dot tights, a massive pair of boots trussed up in all manner of buckles and straps and a scattering of cloth flowers woven through her hair. The ensemble would've been clownish on anyone else, but somehow, Kizzy made it work. "It was a multispecies vid, and I now have a bucketful of questions about Aandrisk anatomy."

"You've seen me naked before," Sissix said. "You've probably seen a lot of Aandrisks naked before."

"Yes, but . . . Sissix, the flexibility on this guy, holy *shit*—" She stuck her hand toward a bowl of vegetables. Dr. Chef smacked her wrist with a spatula without even glancing her way.

Sissix sighed. "What's the name of this vid?"

"Prison Planet 6: The Zero-G Spot."

"Aaand, we're done," Ashby said. "Honestly, would *one day* of being polite have killed you?"

"Hey, I'm polite," Jenks said. "I didn't even *mention* Prison Planet 7."

Ashby sighed and turned to Rosemary. "There's probably still time for you to call the deepod back, if you've changed your mind."

Rosemary shook her head. "I haven't had dinner yet."

Dr. Chef let out a hearty, squawking laugh. "At last, someone with the same priorities as me."

Sissix leaned across the counter. "Kizzy, your shoes are amazing. I wish I could wear shoes."

"I know, right?!" Kizzy exclaimed, lifting her right foot as if she had never seen it before. "Behold, my wonderboots! All the kick-ass of an Aeluon assault squad, combined with total ergonomic perfection! It's podiatric madness! What are they? Are they big tough stompers? Are they comfy kick-arounds? No one knows! There are feats of science happening right over my socks as we speak!" She turned to Dr. Chef, who was pulling a pan of rolls out of the oven. She plucked one up and tossed it between her fingers. "Stars, these smell good. Come to my face, love bun!"

Ashby turned to Rosemary. "You're good at languages, right?"

Rosemary dragged her attention away from the mech tech, who was doing a little dance of pain after searing her tongue on the hot bun. "I do all right," she said. Truthfully, she was *very* good with languages, but that wasn't the sort of thing one said to new colleagues over dinner.

"Well, if you're going to live on this ship, you're going to have to learn to speak Kizzy."

"It's one of those you sort of pick up as you go along," said Sissix, who had begun shuttling heaping bowls of food to the table. Rosemary picked up a bowl filled with some mashed purple root vegetable and followed suit. As she set the bowl down beside the place settings, she was struck with an odd realization: this was the first time she'd ever set a table.

"Oh, oh, by the way," Kizzy said, hopping over to Ashby. "Air filter's fixed, but I was so scared I was gonna be late for dinner, and I had to change, too, so I just bundled up all the wires into the wall good enough so they wouldn't catch fire or anything, and I promise I'll finish it up right after we eat, I promise promise—"

"If you want, Kiz, I can take care of cleaning up the cables on my own," Jenks said. "I know you've got a hell of a to-do list before tomorrow."

"This is why you're the best," Kizzy said. She met Rosemary's eyes and pointed at Jenks. "Isn't he the best?"

"Okay," Dr. Chef said, lifting a platter stacked with steaming bugs. "Grub's up."

Sissix, Kizzy and Jenks all sat down on the same side of the table. As if on cue, Corbin entered the room. He sat on the opposite side. He said nothing. Neither did anyone else. Ashby, at least, gave him a polite nod.

The captain sat at the head of the table; Dr. Chef took the chair opposite him. Ashby gestured for Rosemary to take the empty seat to his right. He smiled at everyone and raised his glass of water. "To our new crew member," he said. "And to a problem-free day of work tomorrow."

They all clinked glasses. "I should've gotten something fancier to drink," Dr. Chef muttered.

"We all need water, Doc," Ashby said. "And besides, you've rather outdone yourself." He nodded at the heaping bowls of food. Rosemary clapped a hand over her stomach to muffle the growling.

Filling one's plate was a free-for-all affair. Bowls and trays were traded back and forth without following any clear pattern. By the time the serving bowls had all been set back down, Rosemary's plate was stacked with salad, a heap of the mashed purple stuff (tuskem roots, Dr. Chef had called them), two grainy rolls and one of the red coast bugs. Melted butter flecked with shredded herbs oozed out from the gaps in the bug's spindly joints. Rosemary noticed that there was a tiny hatch cut into the shell, where Dr. Chef had administered seasonings before grilling them. The bug was nightmarish to look at, but it smelled incredible, and Rosemary was hungry enough to try anything. There was just one problem. She didn't know how to eat it.

Sissix must've seen her hesitancy, for the Aandrisk woman

caught her eyes across the table. Sissix slowly, deliberately raised her knife and fork with her four-fingered hands, and began removing the shell in a practiced manner, popping off the legs first, then working open the underbelly at the seams. Rosemary mirrored her actions, trying not to appear too obvious in her lack of expertise. She appreciated Sissix's subtlety, but she could not ignore the irony of an Aandrisk teaching her how to eat a Human dish.

If Rosemary had committed any transgressions in the act of dismantling the bug, none of the other crew members mentioned it. They were too busy shoveling down food, heaping praise on Dr. Chef for his cooking and laughing at jokes that Rosemary couldn't follow. Her embarrassment at being unfamiliar with the food disappeared the moment she placed the first bite of bug in her mouth—tender, savory, comforting. A bit like crab, only denser. The rolls were hearty and hot, the mash salty sweet, the salad (picked from the garden that day, she was told) crisp and refreshing. All her fears about spacer food were eradicated. She could get used to bugs and hydroponic vegetables. Easily.

Once her hunger had been quelled enough for her to eat at a less desperate pace, Rosemary noticed the empty chair and unused place setting that separated her from Corbin. "Who sits here?" she asked.

"Ah," said Dr. Chef. "A tricky question. No one, technically, but it's meant for Ohan."

Rosemary registered the name. "Right, Sissix said xe's nocturnal," she said, choosing a neutral pronoun. It was the only polite thing to do when no gender signifiers had been given.

Ashby smiled and shook his head. "*They*. Ohan's a Sianat Pair. Male, but we still say 'they.'"

Rosemary thought back to the airlock. Lovey hadn't been talking about a navigator, but a *Navigator*. Her mind raced with excitement. Sianats were the stuff of urban legends back home—a reclusive race who could conceptualize multidimensional space as easily as a Human could do algebra. Their mental aptitude was not innate, however. Sianat culture was structured around a neurovirus they called the Whisperer. The effects of the Whisperer were largely unknown to the rest of the GC (Sianats barred other species from researching it), but what *was* known was that it altered the brain functions of the host. As far as Rosemary knew, all Sianats were infected with the virus during childhood, at which point they ceased thinking of themselves as individuals, but rather as plural entities—a Pair. They were then encouraged to go out into the galaxy in order to share the Whisperer's gifts with species that could never know them first-hand (the virus had yet to jump to other species). Sianat Pairs' ability to think in ways other species couldn't made them invaluable members of research projects, science labs . . . and tunneling ships. In all the hullabaloo of getting herself out to the *Wayfarer*, the likelihood of meeting a Sianat Pair hadn't occurred to her.

"Do they not eat dinner with us?" she asked, trying to hide just how badly she wanted to meet this—person? People? The plural thing was going to take some practice.

Ashby shook his head. "Pairs are paranoid about their health. They're wary of anything that might inadvertently affect the Whisperer. Ohan never leaves the ship, and they don't eat the same food that we do."

"Though it's perfectly sanitary, I assure you," Dr. Chef said.

"That's why I had to get flashed when I docked," Rosemary said. "Lovey said I had a few contaminants one of the crew couldn't handle."

"Ah, yes," Dr. Chef said. "We'll need to update your imubots' databases. We can take care of that tomorrow."

"It's not just a health thing," Sissix said. "Pairs don't socialize well, even with other Pairs. Ohan doesn't leave their room much. They're . . . you'll see when you meet them. They're on their own little plane."

"You would be, too, if you could map out tunnels in your head," Jenks said.

"But Dr. Chef always sets a place for them anyway," Kizzy said, tucking a bite of food into her cheek. "Because he's a sweetie."

"I want them to know that they're always welcome," Dr. Chef said. "Even if they can't eat with us."

"Aww," said Kizzy and Jenks in unison.

"Technically, I don't eat dinner, either," Sissix explained. Rosemary had already noticed that while Sissix had taken some of everything, her portions were tiny. "I just eat little bits of stuff throughout the day. One of the benefits of not being able to keep myself warm is not needing as much food." She smiled. "But I like sitting down with everybody in the evening. It's one of my favorite Human customs."

"I heartily agree," said Dr. Chef, taking another red coast bug. "Especially since I only eat once a day." He balanced the bug atop a tall stack of empty shells. Rosemary counted six.

"So what do Sianat Pairs eat?" Rosemary asked.

A violent ripple passed through Dr. Chef's cheeks. Even with his unfamiliar anatomy, Rosemary got the feeling that it was an expression of disgust. "This horrible nutrient paste. That's all, just tubes and tubes of it, shipped from the Sianat homeworld."

"Hey, you never know," Jenks said. "It could be pretty good."

"Nope," Kizzy said. "Definitely not. I snuck a tube of it once, for research."

"*Kizzy*," Ashby said.

Kizzy ignored him. "Imagine something with the consistency of dry, cold nut butter, but with no flavor at all. No salt or anything. I tried putting it on toast, but it was just a waste of good toast."

Ashby sighed. "And this from the woman who throws a fit if anybody even so much as *glances* at a bag of her fire shrimp."

"Hey," Kizzy said, pointing her fork at him. "Fire shrimp are a rare delicacy, okay."

"They're a cheap snack," Sissix said.

"A cheap snack you can only get from my colony, which makes them a rare delicacy. There are *crates* of Ohan's paste tubes in the cargo bay. I knew they wouldn't even notice if I sampled one. Supply and demand."

"That's not what supply and demand means," Jenks said.

"Sure it does."

"'Supply and demand' does not mean 'please wantonly steal shit because there's more than enough to go around.'"

"You mean like this?" She darted a hand forward and stole a bun off his plate. She crammed the whole thing in her mouth, forcing it in with her fingers, and began grabbing more from the bread basket.

Ashby turned toward Rosemary, ignoring the war of the baked goods. "So. Rosemary. Let's hear about you. Any family back on Mars?"

Rosemary took a calm sip of water. The question made her heart hammer a bit, but it would all be okay. She'd practiced this. "Yeah. My dad works in off-world imports, my mom owns an art gallery." It was a true statement, just missing a few key details. "I have an older sister, too, but she lives on Hagarem." True. "She works for the GC. Resource allocation bureau. Nothing fancy, just pushing formwork." True. "We're not very close, though." Definitely true.

"Where'd you grow up?"

"Florence." True.

Jenks pulled his attention away from wrestling with Kizzy over buns. He whistled. "That's some prime real estate," he said. "You must come from money."

"Not really." Lie. "It's just close to my dad's business." True. Sort of.

"I was in Florence once," Kizzy said. "When I was twelve. My dads saved and saved and saved so we could go there for the Remembrance Day thing. Stars, I'll never forget when everybody let those floating lanterns go out in that big open place." Rosemary knew where she meant. New World Square, the capital's central gathering space. A wide stone plaza watched over by a statue of the city's eponym, Marcella Florence, the first Human to set foot on Mars. "All those little lights, going up and up like tiny ships. I thought it was the prettiest thing I'd ever seen."

"I was there for that," Rosemary said.

"No way!"

She laughed. "I don't think anybody missed the All Stories Festival." In fact, her father had been a major sponsor of the event, but she felt it best to leave that out. Remembrance Day was a Human holiday commemorating the day that the last homesteader set off from Earth—the day the last Humans left their inhospitable homeworld. The holiday had originated as an Exodan custom, but Remembrance Day had quickly gained popularity in both the Solar Republic and the extrasolar colonies. The All Stories Festival had marked the bicentennial Remembrance Day, and the surrounding event had been organized as a joint effort between Solan and Exodan officials. Practically the entire Diaspora had turned up, down to every last handler and bureaucrat. The festival was meant as a gesture of friendship and unity among a fractured species, an acknowledgment that despite their difficult pasts, they could work together toward a bright galactic future. Not that anything had really come of it. The Diaspora was still ineffectual in the GC Parliament. Harmagians had money. Aeluons had firepower. Aandrisks had diplomacy. Humans had arguments. No festival, no matter how lavish, was going to change that. But it had been a fine party, at least.

Kizzy grinned at Rosemary. "Maybe we saw each other's lanterns. Oh! Did you get one of those ice creams there? The real milk ones, in one of those waffley bowl things, all covered with berry sauce and little chocolate bits?"

"Ugh, that sounds sweet," Dr. Chef said.

"If memory serves, I had two of those," said Rosemary. She smiled, hoping that it masked the tangle of homesickness filling her chest. She had worked so hard to get away, jumped through so many hoops, spent so many sleepless nights being afraid of getting caught, and yet . . . yet there were bugs on her plate, and artigrav nets beneath her feet, and a table full of strangers who could never know what she'd left behind. She was out in the open now, far from everything and anything that was familiar.

"Speaking of sweet things," Dr. Chef said, setting his fork down with finality. "Who wants dessert?"

Even though her stomach was now full to bursting, Rosemary found it easy to make room for three of what Dr. Chef called "spring cakes"—delicate, chewy, reminiscent of almonds, dusted with some zingy spice she couldn't identify. Not quite Remembrance Day ice cream with berry sauce, but then, nothing ever would be.

After he'd helped clear the table, Ashby settled into one of the benches tucked away in the garden. He pulled out his scrib, and took a bite out of the last spring cake. Captain's prerogative.

He gestured at his scrib, directing it toward one of the Transport Board's job feeds. "Establishing connection," the screen read. "Verifying access." As the progress icon pulsed in thought, he glanced back to the kitchen. Dr. Chef was behind the counter, showing Rosemary how to stack dirty dishes in the cleanser. She looked attentive, but a little lost. Ashby smiled to himself. First days were always hard.

Sissix approached, a mug of tea in hand. "So?" she asked quietly, making a small gesture with her head back toward the kitchen.

Ashby nodded and made room for her on the bench. "So far, so good," he said under his breath. "She seems friendly enough."

"I have a good feeling about her," Sissix said, sitting down.

"Yeah?"

"Yeah. I mean, she's a bit . . . oh, stars, there isn't a good word for it in Klip. *Issik*. You know that one?"

Ashby shook his head. He could muddle through Reskitkish, if spoken slowly, but his vocabulary wasn't extensive.

"Literally means 'egg soft.' Like a hatchling's skin, when it first comes out of the shell."

"Ah, okay. So . . . inexperienced?"

She rocked her head in thought. "Yes, but not quite. It implies that you'll toughen up in time."

He nodded, glancing at her thick scales. "I'm sure she will."

"Well, that's the thing about being *issik*. If your skin doesn't harden . . ." She let her tongue fall out of her mouth and made a choking sound. She laughed.

Ashby gave her a wry look. "You are talking about *babies* here."

She sighed. "Mammals," she said, with fond exasperation. She rested her head on his shoulder and put her hand on his knee. Coming from a Human, the gesture would've been intimate, but he was used to it with Sissix. This was her version of casual. "Still trying to find us a follow-up?" she asked, nodding toward the scrib. The feed had connected, displaying a neat table of contract offers.

"Just seeing what's out there."

"You won't get far with this feed."

"Why?"

"Because these are upper-level gigs." There was amusement in her voice. "You're tired."

"No," he said. "I'm just . . . looking." He would've left the explanation there, but he could feel her looking at him, waiting for more. He exhaled. "Just one of these pays more than our last three jobs combined."

"Big ships get big money," she said. "That's always been the way of things."

"You don't need a *big* ship. Just a well-equipped ship." He looked around the garden. Recycled crates, a scavenged window, hand-me-down planters. "With the right upgrades, we could start applying for these jobs."

Sissix started to chuckle, but stopped when she saw his face. "Are you being serious?"

"I don't know," Ashby said. "I wonder if I've gotten so comfortable in this kind of work that I never stopped to consider doing more. And we could, in theory. We're capable enough. We're good enough."

"We are," Sissix said slowly. "But we're not talking new circuit boards here. We'd need a new bore, and that'd cost you a standard's worth of profits right there. I'd want a new nav panel, because the one we've got is sticky enough as it is sometimes. We'd need a bigger ambi stock, more stabilizers, more buoys—I'm sorry. I don't mean to stomp all over your daydream here." She gave his knee a friendly scratch with her claws. "Okay, let's say you saved up enough, and we got all kitted out, and we could start taking high-level jobs. What would you do with that?"

"What do you mean?"

"I mean why do you *want* that, other than whatever Yoshi said that got under your skin."

He raised his eyebrows and smirked. "How did you know?"

She laughed. "Just a guess."

Ashby scratched his beard and thought. What *did* he want it for? After he'd first left home, all those years ago, he'd sometimes wondered if he'd go back to the Fleet to raise kids, or if he'd settle down on a colony somewhere. But he was a spacer through and through, and he had the itch for drifting. As the years went on, the thought of making a family had dwindled. The point of a family, he'd always thought, was to enjoy the experience of bringing something new into the universe, passing on your knowledge and seeing part of yourself live on. He had come to realize that his life in the sky filled that need. He had a crew that relied on him, and a ship that continued to grow, and tunnels that would last for generations. To him, that was enough.

But was it enough as it was now? He was content, sure, but he *could* do more. He could build grander things meant for greater numbers of people. He could give his crew a bigger cut, which he'd long wanted to do, and they certainly deserved. He didn't share Yoshi's hubris, but he couldn't deny that the idea of a Human captain doing work traditionally left to the founding species gave him a spark of pride. He could—

"Oh, not to change the subject, but I meant to tell you," he said. "I got a vid pack from Tessa today. Ky started walking."

"Aw, that's great," Sissix said. "Tell her I say congratulations." She paused. "Okay, I have to be honest, I always forget learning to walk takes so long for you guys. Whenever I pictured your nephew, I pictured him running around."

Ashby laughed. "He will be soon enough." He would be, chasing after his big sister, banging knees, breaking bones, burning an ever-increasing amount of calories. Tessa always protested whenever Ashby sent her credits, but she never outright said no, either. Neither did his father, who was having trouble with his eyesight despite repeated surgeries. What he needed was an optical implant, just as Tessa needed healthier food for her kids than a Fleet job in a cargo bay could provide.

He could do more.

TECHNICAL DETAILS

☆

The sound of stimthump met Jenks as he walked through the corridors of the engine room. Pounding notes echoed off the fluid-filled pipes that stretched along the ceiling. He followed the sounds of drums, pipeflutes, grating strings, the wails of several Harmagians—and one unabashedly off-key Human woman who was not part of the recording.

He entered a roomy access area. This was Kizzy's lair, a well-lit space full of workbenches heaped with spare parts, hand-labeled containers and forgotten amusements. A tool cage stood sentry by one of the entrances, laden with every sort of implement imaginable. Two green armchairs, their balding fabric covered with patches, rested strategically near the warm tubes that pumped spent fuel down to the processing tanks. Between the chairs was a mek brewer, jerry-rigged into one of the engine's powerlines. It was in need of cleaning.

The mech tech herself was perched on a work ladder, her head and hands up inside an open ceiling panel. Her hips rocked in time with the drumbeats. She belted along to the throbbing music as she worked. "Punch 'em in the face! Monkeys like it, too!"

"Hey. Kizzy," Jenks said.

"I ate a har—monica! These socks—match—my hat!"

"Kizzy."

A tool clattered to the ground. Kizzy's hands clenched into fists as the music swelled to a stormy crescendo. She danced atop the shuddering ladder, her head still in the ceiling. "Socks! Match—my hat! Socks! Match—my hat! Step on—some—sweet—toast! Socks! Match—my hat!"

"*Kizzy!*"

Kizzy ducked her head down. She pressed the clicker strapped to her wrist, turning down the volume of the nearby thump box. "'Sup?"

Jenks quirked an eyebrow. "Do you have *any* idea what this song is?"

Kizzy blinked. "Socks Match My Hat," she said. She went back up into the ceiling, tightening something with her gloved hands.

"*Soskh Matsh Mae'ha.* It's banned in the Harmagian Protectorate."

"We're not in the Harmagian Protectorate."

"Do you know what this song's about?"

"You know I don't speak Hanto."

"Banging the Harmagian royal family. In glorious detail."

"Ha! Oh, I like this song so much more now."

"It's credited with setting off the riots on Sosh'ka last year."

"Huh. Well, if this band hates the establishment *that* much, then I doubt they'll care about me making up my own words. They can't oppress me with their 'correct lyrics.' Fuck the system." She grunted, fighting with a stuck valve. "So what's up?"

"I need the axial circuit coupler and I have no idea where you put it."

"Left-side toolbench."

Jenks looked from side to side. "My left or your left?"

"My left. No. Wait. Your left."

Jenks walked to the bench, dragged over an empty crate and

climbed up to have a look. The piles of junk that covered the bench had merged, creating one nebulous omnipile. He sifted through the contents. A bundle of three-gauge fuel tubing. A half-eaten bag of fire shrimp ("Devastatingly Hot!" the label boasted). An assortment of dirty mugs. Several sets of schematics with added notes and doodles. An unopened box of—Jenks paused and craned his head toward Kizzy.

"Out of curiosity," he said. "What are you doing?"

Kizzy showed him her palms. Her work gloves were caked with dense green slime. "Gunk trap's clogged."

He looked back to the box on the bench. "You could have that done in three seconds if you used fixbots."

"I don't have any bots."

"Um, so, this box of bots I'm looking at is *what*, then?"

Kizzy's head reappeared. She squinted at the bench. "Oh, those bots." She disappeared into the ceiling again.

He ran a finger over the box. It came back dusty. "You've never even opened these." The company logo caught his eye. "Holy shit, Kiz, these are Tarcska bots. Do you have any idea how top of the line these are?"

"Bots are boring," she said.

"Boring."

"Mmm-hmm."

Jenks shook his head. "Once upon a time, the Human race would've killed for the computing power stored in these little guys—*literally killed*—and you've got them buried under old snacks. Why do you even have these?"

A glob of green gunk ran over the edge of the ceiling panel, spattering the floor. "If ever we find ourselves in a situation so mind-fuckingly dire that you can't lend me a hand and Lovey can't shut things down, then I'll need them. Thankfully, that's never happened." She took a tool from her belt and stretched up onto the tips of her toes. Something metallic groaned in protest. "Oh, *ass*, just *work*, you stupid bastard thing—"

Jenks brushed aside an empty glue packet and found the coupler. He clipped it to his toolbelt. "Air filter's done, by the by. I'm gonna go check on Lovey. You wanna smash before bed?"

There was a reply, but it was muffled beneath clanging and swearing and dripping gunk. Jenks chuckled and walked out of the room. Kizzy remained in the ceiling, filthy and profane. He knew she was having a wonderful time.

There were other Lovelaces out there, of course. Her core software platform could be purchased through any AI dealer. There were probably dozens of versions of her traveling through the galaxy—maybe hundreds, who knew. But they weren't *her*. The Lovey that Jenks knew was uniquely molded by the *Wayfarer*. Her personality had been shaped by every experience she and the crew had together, every place they'd been, every conversation they'd shared. And honestly, Jenks thought, couldn't the same be said for organic people? Weren't they all born running the Basic Human Starter Platform, which was shaped and changed as they went along? In Jenks's eyes, the only real difference in cognitive development between Humans and AIs was that of speed. He'd had to learn to walk and talk and eat and all the other essentials before he'd begun to have a sense of identity. Lovey didn't have to worry about those things. There hadn't been a need for her to spend years learning how to monitor systems or switch off circuits. She had started life out with all the maturity and knowledge she needed to do her job competently. But in the three standards since she'd been installed, she'd become much more than just a ship's AI. She'd become someone wonderful.

"Hey, you," Lovey said as Jenks stepped into the AI chamber.

"Hey, yourself," he said, bending down to untie his boots. He slipped them off and stepped into a pair of sandals that never left the room. He found the idea of walking around in there with grubby, gunky shoes quite rude. The walls were covered with circuit panels, each a vital component of Lovey's framework—effectively, her brain. In the middle of the room was her central core, resting on a pedestal within a temperature-controlled pit. Jenks spent a lot of time in the pit, even though his job didn't require it, and going in there with boots on felt like kissing somebody in the morning without brushing your teeth.

"Good day?" she asked.

He smirked. "You know how my day was." Lovey had cameras and sensors throughout the ship. She kept a protective eye on them at all times. It was a comfort, knowing that an accident or injury wouldn't go unnoticed, even in the most out-of-the-way corners. Lovey was always there to call for help. But it was the sort of thing that made a man pause before scratching his balls or picking his nose. Having an AI around forced good manners.

"I still like to hear you tell it."

"Fair enough. It was a good day. I think we're ready for the punch tomorrow. Everything's working fine, far as I can tell."

"What do you think of Rosemary?"

"She seems nice. Hard to say. She's a little quiet, and was pretty lagged to boot. We'll all need sometime to get to know her."

"I felt so bad about having to flash her when she came aboard. She looked rough afterward. Not a very nice thing to do when meeting someone for the first time."

"I'm sure she understood you were only doing your job." Jenks walked along the wall panels, looking them over for the little red lights that meant trouble. Lovey hadn't alerted him to any problems, but if something went *really* wrong, she might not be able to let him know. He did the rounds twice a day, just in case.

"Do you think she's pretty?"

Jenks raised an eyebrow toward the nearest camera, then glanced back at one of her analytical pathways. The filament was old; it would need replacing in a tenday or two. "Sure, I guess. Not, like, falling-out-of-my-seat pretty, but if I were a lady, I'd be content looking the way she does." He stepped up onto a workstool and examined the upper circuit row. "Why do you ask?"

"She seemed like the sort you'd find pretty."

"How so?"

"Do you remember that adventure sim you played two years ago? *Black Sun Falling*?"

"Of course I do. Great sim. There were archeologists who said they couldn't tell the difference between the Arkanic ruins in the sim and the real deal."

"Do you remember the love interest you chose?"

"What was her name . . . Mia. Yeah, well-written character. I liked her storyline a lot."

"Mmm-hmm. And it occurred to me when Rosemary boarded the ship that she's got a nice smile and a short crop of curls, just like Mia did. So, I thought she might be your cup of tea."

Jenks chuckled. "That's a fair line of reasoning. I didn't know you kept track of these things."

"I like to know what you like."

"I like you." Jenks got off the stool, set down the coupler and walked to the pit. The inspection could wait. He put on the heavy sweater that lay folded by the edge of the pit, just where he'd left it the day before. He climbed down into the temperature-controlled air, a cool contrast to the warm yellow light that pulsed from Lovey's core. "If I *had* found her pretty, would that bother you?"

Lovey laughed. "No. Jealousy's stupid."

"Just because it's stupid doesn't mean you can't feel it."

"True, but what would be the point of me getting jealous over someone who actually has a face? Or breasts, or hips, or however it works. You're designed to find bodies attractive, Jenks. Enjoy them." She paused. "If it were legal for me to have a body, what kind would you want me to have?"

"Well, there's a question," said Jenks. "I hadn't really thought about it."

"Liar."

Jenks sat down and leaned back against the wall. He could feel the light vibration of her cooling system buzz against his scalp. He had, of course, thought about Lovey in a body. Many, many times.

"What kind of body would you *want* to have?" Jenks countered. "That's way more important."

"I'm not sure. That's why I've been paying attention to what *you* pay attention to. I don't know what it's like to be in any form other than what I am, so it's hard to voice my desires on that front. It's not as if I'm in here pining away for legs all day long."

"Tell that to the FDS." The Friends of Digital Sapients were one of those organizations that had their hearts in the right place but their heads firmly up their asses. On paper, Jenks believed a lot of the same things they did, namely that AIs were sapient individuals worthy of the same legal rights that everyone else had. But the FDS went about it all wrong. For starters, they didn't have a lot of techs in their ranks. They ignored the actual science behind artificial cognition in favor of a bunch of fluffy nonsense, making AIs out to be organic souls imprisoned within metal boxes. AIs weren't like that. Comparing an AI to an organic sapient was like comparing a Human to a Harmagian. You could find similarities, and they deserved equal respect, but under the hood, they operated in fundamentally different ways. Jenks was all for proper recognition of AI rights, but the FDS's inability to speak about digital minds with any sort of accuracy was more of a hindrance than a help. Acting all sanctimonious while spouting bad info was a terrible way to win a debate, but a great way to piss people off.

"That's exactly what I mean," Lovey said. "They act like all AIs want a body. Granted, I think *I* do, but that doesn't mean all of us do. That's such an incredibly organic bias, the idea that your squishy physical existence is some sort of pinnacle that all programs aspire to. No offense."

"None taken." He thought for a moment. "That's kind of hypocritical, isn't it? We assume organic bodies are so awesome, everybody else must want them, then we go off to get genetweaks to look younger or slimmer or whatever."

"You've got a few modifications yourself. No tweaks, but still. Do you think that's different from someone wanting to look a few years younger? Aren't all bodily changes about vanity?"

"Hmm," said Jenks. He felt the weight of the spacers in his ears. He recalled the thin sunburn sting of a needle driving ink down into his skin. "That's a good question." He tapped his mouth with his fingers. "I don't know. You know I get pretty squicked over tweaks, so I guess my opinion there isn't exactly objective. But I do think something like an antiaging tweak is done out of a lack of self-esteem, because you feel like you're not good enough as you are. All the things I've done to my body, I've done out of love. Seriously. I've gotten ink to remind me of all sorts of places and memories, but at the core, everything I've had done has been my way of saying that this is *my* body. That I don't want the body everybody else told me I should have. Dr. Chef's the only doctor I've ever had who's never *once* told me that my life would be easier if I got a few tweaks. You know, so I could be a *normal* height. Fuck that. If I'm going to make changes to my body, they're going to be changes that were my idea."

"I think I feel the same way," Lovey said. "Even though it's a moot point for me. Any body talk is entirely hypothetical for me unless some laws change."

"Do you really *want* to have a body?" He hesitated, feeling awkward about what he wanted to ask next. "It's not just because of me, is it?"

"No. I go back and forth on it, but I think the pros outweigh the cons."

"Okay," Jenks said, folding his hands across his stomach. "Cons first."

"Cons. Can only be in one room at a time. Unable to simultaneously look inside the ship and outside it. Needing to physically jack my head into the Linkings anytime I want to look something up. Or, well, I could use a scrib, I guess, but that seems so *slow*."

"I have always been jealous of that," Jenks said. For Lovey, checking a reference or reading a feed was as simple as activating the part of her cognitive processor that had Linking access. He'd always imagined it to be like having a download library inside your head, full of books you could read through in a matter of seconds.

"Honestly, I think most of my cons stem from concerns about perception and spatial awareness. That's why I think the pros carry more weight. They're more varied. I could get used to having only one set of eyes, I think. It could be restful. Or boring, I'm not sure."

"Maybe a little of both. Let's have your pros."

"Leaving the ship. That's a big one. I don't feel like I'm missing out as I am now, but you all seem to have so much fun when you hop over to orbiters or down planetside."

"What else?"

"Having dinner with the crew. Face-to-face conversations.

Seeing the sky from the ground." She paused. "Having the ability to be a real companion for you. You know, with all the trimmings."

Even sitting down, Jenks felt his knees go weak.

Lovey sighed. "It's a frivolous line of thinking, with things as they are. But even so, you haven't answered my question."

"What question?"

"What kind of body would you want me to have? Or perhaps a better question is, what do you find pretty?"

"That's . . . I'm not sure I can sum that up easily. It really depends on the person."

"Hmm. Okay, what did the women you've coupled with before look like?"

Jenks let out a hearty laugh. "Are you making a database?"

She paused. "Maybe."

Jenks gave a fond smirk. "Lovey, if you were able to have a body, it should look how *you* want it to look." He relaxed back into the wall and trailed his fingers down a bundle of cables. "I'd find you pretty in any package."

"Stars, you're so full of it," Lovey laughed. "But that's why I love you."

☆

FEED SOURCE: The Thread—The Official News Source of the Exodan Fleet (Public/Klip)
ITEM NAME/DATE: Evening News Summary—Galactic—130/306
ENCRYPTION: 0
TRANSLATION PATH: 0
TRANSCRIPTION: [vid:text]
NODE IDENTIFIER: 7182-312-95, Ashby Santoso

Hello, and welcome to our evening update. I'm Quinn Stephens. We begin tonight's headline summary with news from the Fleet.

Yesterday marked the fourth anniversary of the Oxomoco disaster. Memorial events were held throughout the Fleet in commemoration of the deaths of the 43,756 Exodans who lost their lives after a transport crash, compounded by fatigued bulkheads on the Oxomoco, led to rapid decompression of several lodging decks. Yesterday, all major Fleet vessels turned off their lights for two minutes at fourteen-sixteen, the time of the accident. The disaster was also commemorated on Mars this year, with the unveiling of a memorial statue in the Samurakami Botanical Gardens. Martian President Kevin Liu was present at the ceremony, and dedicated the memorial to "the families aboard the Oxomoco, and to all our courageous brothers and sisters in the Fleet." Fleet Admiral Ranya May thanked the Martian government for the gesture, stating, "Our two societies no longer turn a blind eye to the tragedies that befall the other. This is a testament to how far we have come in our efforts to close the gap between us."

In other Fleet news, the Marabunta scare aboard the Newet is finally over. The last remaining patient has been released from quarantine and granted a clean bill of health. The Fleet health office is confident that no traces of the virus remain aboard Fleet vessels. A statement released this morning reminds all Fleet denizens and boarders to schedule regular imubot upgrades with their health care providers, and to not take chances with unlicensed tech implant clinics. It is believed that the Marabunta virus was brought aboard the Newet by an individual who recently patronized a fringe colony implant clinic. In response to the outbreak, the health office is working to upgrade docking bay scanners throughout the Fleet, in order to better detect individuals carrying hijacked bots.

Next tenday is the thirty-first annual Bug Fry Festival aboard the Dou Mu. The transportation office anticipates high amounts of shuttle traffic and docking bay delays throughout the duration of the festival. All persons traveling between ships are advised to plan accordingly, even if you do not intend attending the festival.

In the news from the Solar Republic, former Phobos Fuel CEO Quentin Harris the third was officially indicted on charges of weapons smuggling, conspiracy and crimes against sapient kind. Harris is alleged to have been instrumental in a smuggling ring that delivered illegal weapons, including gene-targeters, to several Toremi clans, who are currently engaged in a civil war. Harris was arrested earlier this standard after a data cache of evidence documenting his involvement with the smuggling ring was uploaded to several Linking feeds. Harris claims that the evidence has been falsified by business rivals, and has pled not guilty.

In the news from the independent Human colonies, the construction of a new water reclamation plant on Seed was halted last tenday after the discovery of ancient Arkanic artifacts. A satellite scan has confirmed the presence of expansive Arkanic ruins throughout the Refuge Foothills region. Though the GC academic community is hailing the find for its historical significance, the discovery has caused problems for the Seed municipality, who have been suffering chronic water shortages. Alexandria University and the Hashkath Institute of Interstellar Migration have assembled a joint archelogical survey team to study the site. The Seed municipal government has filed an official aid request to the Diaspora, in hopes of receiving funding to purchase portable water reclamators as a stopgap measure.

In galactic news, the Hok Pres border war continues to intensify as Aeluon troops enter their third standard year of armed conflict with the Rosk Synergy. The deaths of twenty-six GC civilians on Kaelo were reported this morning, following a Rosk bombing run. Though the Aeluon government has released few details concerning their military efforts, reports from the area indicate that there has been an increase in Aeluon troop deployment throughout the Kaelo region.

This concludes the evening update. Our morning update will be ready to access at tenth hour tomorrow. For more in-depth coverage on these stories and more, provided in both vid and text, connect to the Thread feed via scrib or neural patch. Thank you, and fly safely.

BLIND PUNCH

☆

Breakfast was laid out on the kitchen counter when Rosemary returned to the Fishbowl in the morning. Two big bowls of fruit (stored in the stasie, by the look of the pale skin), a basket of unfamiliar pastries and a large hotpot full of some sort of dark brown porridge. Dr. Chef stood behind the counter, chopping vegetables with two handfeet, drying cutlery with another pair. His cheeks puffed out as she approached.

"Good morning!" he said. "How'd you sleep?"

"Not bad," she said, climbing onto a stool. "Woke up a little confused a few times."

Dr. Chef nodded. "It's never easy sleeping in a new place. You're lucky we had a Human-style bed already installed in that cabin. When I first joined the crew, I had to wait a few days before we got furniture I could fit myself into." He gestured to the food on the counter. "Breakfast here is a help-yourself affair, as is lunch. Snacks are available throughout the day, so stop by whenever you're hungry. Oh, and there's always tea. You can get yourself a cup anytime you like." He pointed toward two large decanters, perched on the far end of the counter. A rack of mugs rested alongside. There were two hand-drawn labels affixed to the decanters. "Happy Tea!" read one, above a drawing of a wide-eyed, grinning Human with frizzy hair standing

68

on end. "Boring Tea," read the other. The Human drawn there looked content, but indifferent. The handwriting was the same as the sign on the Fishbowl door. Kizzy's.

"Boring tea?" Rosemary asked.

"No caffeine. Just a lovely, normal herbal tea," said Dr. Chef. "I'll never understand why you Humans like the jittery stuff so much. As a doctor, I hate starting off your mornings with stimulants, but as a cook, I understand how important breakfast habits are." He wagged one of his pudgy fingers at her. "But no more than three cups a day, and definitely not on an empty stomach."

"Don't worry," Rosemary said, reaching for a mug. "I'm more of a boring tea person myself." Dr. Chef looked pleased. She pointed at the rolls. "These smell wonderful. What are they?"

The answer came from behind. "Smoky buns!" Kizzy cheered. She jumped onto a stool and grabbed one of the yellowish pastries. She began to eat with one hand and dished out some porridge with the other.

"Smoky buns?"

"Yet another thing from my home that doesn't have an easily translatable name," said Dr. Chef.

"He makes 'em every time we tunnel," Kizzy said, loading up a plate with an additional bun and a pile of fruit.

"They're good, solid fuel for a hard day of work." He squinted at Kizzy as she filled a mug with happy tea. "Unlike *that*."

"I know, I know, three-cup limit, I promise," she said. She turned to Rosemary, cupping her mug between her palms. "What's the verdict on the curtains?"

"They're great," Rosemary said. "They make things feel homey." It was true. She'd almost forgotten that she was no longer living planetside until she'd drawn the curtains back that morning and found a stellar system floating majestically right outside. Even though she had traveled between planets before, the notion that she was now *living* out in the open still hadn't sunk in.

She bit down into a smoky bun. The bread was airy soft, the unidentified filling rich and savory, somewhat reminiscent of roasted mushrooms. Smoky, yes, but also lightly spiced, with just the right amount of salt. She looked up to Dr. Chef, who was watching her eagerly. "These are amazing."

Dr. Chef beamed. "The filling's made from *jeskoo*. I think you Solans call it white tree fungus. Rather different from the ingredients I grew up with, but it's a good approximation. And the buns are high in protein, too. I supplement the grain with mealworm flour."

"He won't tell us his recipe," Kizzy said. "Bastard's going to take it to his grave."

"Grum don't have graves."

"To the bottom of the ocean, then. That's even *worse* than a grave. Graves you can at least dig up." She shook a bun at him. "Some dumb fish is going to eat whatever part of your brain stores this recipe, and we'll all be lost without it."

"Better eat them while you can, then," Dr. Chef said. His cheeks gave a fluttering puff. Rosemary had deduced that the faster the puffs, the bigger the "smile."

"So," Kizzy said, turning her attention to Rosemary. "This is your first time tagging along for a punch, right?"

"Sorry, a what?" Rosemary said.

Kizzy chuckled. "That answers my question. A *punch* is the act of making a tunnel."

"Oh, right." Rosemary sipped her tea. Slightly sweet, nothing special. Okay, so it *was* a little boring, but comforting nonetheless. "I was actually wondering . . ." She paused, not wanting to sound stupid. "I know I'll never have to help out with the tunneling stuff, but I'd like to have a better understanding of how it works."

Kizzy pressed her lips together with excitement. "You want me to give you a crash course?"

"If it's no trouble, that is."

"Oh, stars and buckets, of course it's no trouble. I am flattered and you are adorable. Um, right, okay. Have you taken any courses in interspatial manipulation? Probably not, huh?"

"Can't say that I have."

"Space-time topology?"

"Nope."

"Transdimensional theory?"

Rosemary made an apologetic face.

"Aww!" said Kizzy, clasping her hands over her heart. "You're a physics virgin! Okay, okay, we'll keep this simple." She looked around the counter for props. "Okay, cool, here. The area above my bowl of porridge"—she gestured importantly—"is the fabric of space. The porridge itself is the sublayer—basically the space in between space. And this groob"—she picked up a small black fruit from her plate—"is the *Wayfarer*."

"Oh, I can't wait to see this," Dr. Chef said, resting his top arms on the opposite side of the counter.

Kizzy cleared her throat and straightened up. "So, here's us." She swooped the berry over the bowl. "We've got two ends of space to connect, right? *Here* and *here*." She pressed her finger down into the porridge, making indentations on opposite ends of the bowl. "So we travel to one end—*whoosh*—and all the people seeing us fly by are like, oh my stars, look at that totally amazing ship, what genius tech patched together such a thing, and I'm like, oh, that's me, Kizzy Shao, you can all name your babies after me—*whooosh*—and then we get to our start point." She hovered the berry above the disappearing dent in the porridge. "Once we're in position, I turn on the interspatial bore. Did you see it when you flew in? Big ol' monstro machine strapped to our belly? It's a *beast*. Runs on ambi cells. Our entire ship couldn't hold the amount of algae you'd need to power it. Oh, and fair warning, it's noisy as hell, so don't freak out while it's doing its thing. We're not blowing up or anything. So, yes. Bore warms up. Then we punch." She slammed the berry down into the porridge. "And then it gets weird."

"Weird how?" Rosemary said.

"Well, we're just squishy little three-dimensional creatures. Our brains can't process what goes on in the sublayer. Technically, the sublayer is outside what we consider *normal time*. Understanding what's going on in there is like . . . it's like telling someone—a Human, I mean—to see in infrared. We just can't do it. So, in the sublayer, you feel that something is wrong with the world, but you can't put your finger on what it is. It's very, very weird. Have you ever done daffy?"

Rosemary blinked. Where she was from, people didn't casually ask about illegal hallucinogens over breakfast. "Ah, no, I haven't."

"Hmm. Well, it's kind of like that. Your visual perception and sense of time get all fucked up, but the difference is that you're fully in control of your actions. When you're studying for your tunneling license—that's separate from basic tech studies, so believe me when I say I'm super glad I'll never have to set foot in a school again—you have to practice stuff like fixing the engines or entering in commands after taking a dose of sophro, which is basically a dumbed-down, government-issued version of daffy. Worst homework ever, I assure you. But you get used to it." She stuck her fingers into the porridge, getting a grip on the hidden berry. "Okay, so while we're all tripping balls, the ship's pushing through the sublayer, dropping buoys to force the tunnel open. The buoys are there for two reasons. One, they keep the tunnel from collapsing, and two, they generate this field made up of all the same strings and particles and stuff that normal space is made out of."

Rosemary nodded. "Artificial space." Finally, a concept she somewhat understood. "But why do that?"

"So that it's an easy ride for anybody traveling through. That's why you don't notice a difference when you tunnel-hop."

"And none of this messes up the space outside? I mean, here in our space?"

"Nope, not if you do it right. That's why we're pros."

Rosemary nodded toward the porridge. "So how do we get out of the sublayer?"

"Okay," Kizzy said. She started pushing the groob through the porridge. "Once we get to our exit point, we bust back through." She shoved a spoon under the groob, catapult style, and raised her fist.

"Kizzy," said Dr. Chef, his voice even. "If you launch porridge all over my nice clean countertop—"

"I won't. I just realized this won't work. My genius demonstration is flawed." She frowned. "I can't fold porridge."

"Here," said Dr. Chef. He handed her two cloth napkins. "One for your hands, one for educational purposes."

"Ah!" said Kizzy, cleaning the porridge from her fingers. "Perfecto." She held up the clean napkin, gripping two opposite corners. "Okay. You know the big gridlike spheres surrounding tunnel openings, with all the blinky warning lights and crackly lightning stuff coming off the joints? Those are containment cages. They keep space from ripping open any farther than we want it to. You have to have one cage on each end of the tunnel." She gestured with the corners of the napkin. "So if we've got one cage at *this* end, and another cage at *this* end, we've got to construct a tunnel that effectively makes it so that *this*"—she stretched the corners far apart from each other—"is the same thing as *this*"—she brought the corners together.

Rosemary frowned. She had a rough idea of how tunnels worked, but she'd never been able to make the idea stick. "Okay, so, the cages are light-years apart. They're not in the same place. But . . . they behave as if they were in the same space?"

"Pretty much. It's like a doorway connecting two rooms, only the rooms are on opposite sides of town."

"So, the only place the distance between those two points has been changed is . . . within the tunnel?"

Kizzy grinned. "Physics is a bitch, right?"

Rosemary stared at the napkin, struggling to make her three-dimensional brain work with these concepts. "How do you get the cages in place? Wouldn't it take forever to travel from one end to the other?"

"Gold star for the lady in the pretty yellow top!" Kizzy said. "You are totally correct. That's why there are two different ways of building a tunnel. The easy way is what we call an *anchored punch*. These take place in systems that already have existing tunnels connecting them to other places. So, say you want to connect Stellar System A to Stellar System B. Both System A and System B already connect to System C. You drop a cage in System A. You hop through the existing tunnel from System A to System C. Then you hop from System C to System B. You drop the second cage, then you punch back to System A."

Rosemary nodded. "That makes sense. Sounds like a round-about way to get there, though."

"Oh, definitely, and it's rarely a two-hop trip like that. Especially if the tunnels connect to different planets within the system. Usually takes us a few tendays to get between jobs, sometimes more if we've got a lot of space to cover. That's part of what Sissix does, charting the fastest ways to get between existing tunnels."

Rosemary took a second bun and cracked it open. A puff of steam rose from the fragrant pocket within. "What if the system you're tunneling to isn't connected to anywhere?"

"Aha. Then you do a blind punch."

"What's that?"

"Drop a cage at one end, punch through and find your way to the other side—which is crazy hard to do without the second cage to guide you. Once you get back out, you're working against the clock to get the cage up. Cages are self-constructing, so all you can really do is deploy the pieces and wait a day. But still, you have to deploy it as soon as you get out. Having a cage on one end of the tunnel and none on the other makes things inside unstable. At first, it's no problem, but the longer you wait, the faster it starts to tear. If that happens, it all goes to shit. And when the fabric of space goes to shit, you've got a really big problem."

"Like the Kaj'met Expanse." Learning about the Kaj'met Expanse was something of a rite of passage for youngsters, the moment when you realized that space, for all its silent calm, was a dangerous place. The Kaj'met Expanse was a Harmagian territory, half the size of the Sol system, in which space had been completely rent asunder. The pictures from there were terrifying—asteroids drifting into invisible holes, planets snapped in half, a dying star leaking into a debris-crusted tear.

"Yeah, that's a leftover from way back when the Harmagians started building tunnels. All the first ones were blind punches. Had to be. No other way to get from system to system except for going FTL."

"Right," said Rosemary, nodding. The ban against FTL was one of the oldest laws on the books, predating the founding of the GC. While traveling faster than light was technologically possible, the logistical and social problems caused by what basically amounted to time travel far outweighed the gains. And aside from the administrative nightmare, few people were keen on a method of transportation that guaranteed everyone you knew back home would be long dead by the time you reached your destination. "But why not get between systems with a . . . oh,

I don't know what it's called. The things deepods use."

"A pinhole drive. Right, so, a pinhole drive dips you in and out of the sublayer really fast, like a needle and thread. They basically make a bunch of tiny, temporary tunnels to get between places super fast."

"That much I knew."

"Okay. Pinhole jumps are fine with a little bitty single-person craft like a deepod, because the holes it makes are too small to do any real damage. Without a cage, the hole closes right up. Think of it like a baby blind punch, only the trajectory is mapped out with a series of marker buoys ahead of time, so the deepod is always following the exact same sublayer path. That's also why deepods have designated travel lanes in populated areas, and why they're equipped with multidimensional warning beacons. You don't want a deepod jumping out of the sublayer into your hull."

"You can't use pinhole drives with big ships?"

"You *can*, but it's not a good idea. Holes that big really wear on space, and if you have a lot of them relatively close together, like you would in a deepod lane, they could potentially tear into each other. As a once-in-a-while thing, doing pinhole jumps with a big ship is okay. But if you were sending something the size of our ship in and out of the sublayer as often as a deepod—yeah, that wouldn't be good. Also, pinhole drives are expensive as hell to install, so pretty much no big ships bother with them. Now, if you *really* need to get somewhere fast—and I mean *need*, like serious business need—you can put in a request for a pinhole tug. A tug can drag a big ship to wherever it needs to be. Same risks apply, but tugs are super regulated, and they're careful with how they use them. You have to get approval from the Transport Board to use a tug. You see tugs for things like, I dunno, if you need to get a med ship to a bunch of refugees fast, or if the government's sending someone outside GC space, where we don't have tunnels. So, for ordinary stuff like tunneling, using a pinhole drive isn't worth the cost, or the risk."

Rosemary took a long sip from her mug. The boring tea was growing on her. Something sweet and unassuming was the perfect complement for the smoky buns. Dr. Chef sure knew what he was doing. "Blind punches sound pretty risky on their own, though."

"They are. There aren't many tunnelers licensed to do them. That's why we get paid well. Well enough, anyway."

"This ship does blind punches?" Rosemary didn't like that idea. Burrowing through the space in between space without a clear idea of where you'd be coming back out did not sound like something she wanted to tag along for.

"Yup. We'll be doing one today." She patted Rosemary's shoulder. "Don't worry. I know it sounds scary, but we do this all the time. Trust me, we're super safe."

Trust me. This coming from the tech in a grubby jumpsuit with to-do lists written on her sleeve. Rosemary needed a little more reassurance than that. "How do you know where the ship should come back out?"

"Well, *we* don't. The best any computer program can do with a blind punch is an educated guess, and that's not good enough. That's why you need a Sianat Pair."

"You can't do blind punches without a Navigator, not legally or practically," said Dr. Chef. "You need someone who can comprehend what's going on in the sublayer. Someone who can *visualize* what's going on."

"An AI can't do it?" Rosemary said. She knew that there were still things that technology couldn't do, but being reminded of it always surprised her.

"Nope. Think about it," Kizzy said. "AIs can't be any smarter than the people who create them. We can code in all the crazy maths and theories we want, but we can't make an AI do things that we don't understand ourselves. And not to freak you out, but we definitely don't understand the sublayer. We've got ideas about it, sure, but the only species who really *gets it* are the Sianat. Which means the only people who could make an AI on a par with a Sianat Pair are the Sianat themselves. And they sure as hell aren't going to do that."

"Why not?"

"Because it's heresy," Dr. Chef said. "The Sianat believe that the abilities the Whisperer gives them are sacred gifts. They believe that since the virus doesn't affect other species, other species aren't meant to possess those abilities. They're happy to do the work for us, but they're not going to share their understanding, not even with software."

"Interesting," Rosemary said. *Weird*, she thought. "Okay, so, regardless of what kind of a punch you're doing, isn't it possible that you can come out not just in another place, but in another time?"

"Absolutely," Kizzy said. "That's why we do our very, very best not to fuck things up. Oh, that reminds me!" She hopped off the stool and ran over to the vox in the kitchen. "Lovey, can you get me Jenks, please?"

There was a pause. The vox snapped to life. "Mmmwha?" said Jenks on the other end.

"Come get your smoky buns, sleepy, before I eat them all," Kizzy said.

"What time is it?"

"Ninth hour, ish. You're late."

"What? Are we at the punch site yet?"

"About an hour out."

"Shit. Kizzy. Kizzy, I am so hungover."

"I know."

"This is entirely your fault."

"I know, sweetie. Come get smoky buns."

"Don't 'sweetie' me. We're not friends anymore. Are you in the kitchen?"

"Yes."

"Dr. Chef, please tell me you have some SoberUps on hand."

"There's an unopened box in the med bay," said Dr. Chef, puffing his cheeks.

"Okay," sighed Jenks. "Okay." The vox clicked off.

Dr. Chef gave Kizzy a look. "Just what did you two get up to last night?"

Kizzy took a bite of porridge. "Waterball semifinals. I thought it would be more fun as a drinking game."

"Who was playing?"

"Skydivers versus Fast Hands. Jenks and I each picked a team, and we had to drink when the other scored."

"Who did you pick?"

"Fast Hands."

"I take it they won?"

Kizzy grinned. "By twelve."

Dr. Chef exhaled a disparaging rumble and fixed his beady eyes on Rosemary. "Some advice? If Kizzy ever says the words 'you know what would be a great idea?,' ignore whatever comes after."

"Don't listen to him," Kizzy said. "All my ideas are great."

Dr. Chef studied Rosemary, considering something. "You know, I always sedate myself before a punch. I've never gotten used to the sublayer, so I find it easier to sleep through it. No one will fault you if you care to join me."

"Thanks," Rosemary said, "but I think I'd like to see how it's done."

"Attagirl," said Kizzy, clapping Rosemary on the back. "Don't you worry. It's a kick in the head, but it's a *fun* kick in the head."

An hour later, in the control room, Rosemary was buckling the safety harness on her chair when the Sianat Pair entered the room. Rosemary could not help but stare. She had seen pictures of Pairs before, but seeing one in the flesh was different. Ohan had a lanky, four-limbed body, with broad feet and unsettlingly long fingers. He—*they* walked on all fours, back bowed, rather like the archival vids Rosemary had seen of Earthen primates. Ohan was covered from scalp to toenails with dense, ice blue fur, trimmed short and decorated with shaved fractal patterns that revealed coal gray skin beneath. Their eyes were enormous, long-lashed and visibly wet (Rosemary had read the night before that overactive tear ducts were one of the Sianat virus's many quirks). Their furry face looked relaxed, almost drugged—a look that was corroborated by their loosely held shoulders, the slowness of their motions. They wore robes, of a sort, a snug garment so simple in design that it seemed like an afterthought. Rosemary knew it was unfair to judge other sapients by Human social norms, but Ohan gave her the impression of a stoned college student, showing up late to class in nothing but a bathrobe. She reminded herself that this stoned college student could outmatch an AI when it came to interdimensional physics.

"There's the other half of my team," Sissix said with a friendly smile. "This should be a fun one, hmm?"

Ohan nodded once toward her, moving with polite formality. "We always enjoy our work with you," they said.

"Hey, Ohan," Ashby said, looking up from his control panel as the Sianat Pair took their seat. "How are you today?"

Ohan sat hunched on their back haunches. Their joints folded up tightly, making the Pair appear much shorter than when they walked in. "Very well, thank you, Ashby," they said. They curved their head toward Corbin, before turning their attention back to their workstation. They flicked their long fingers over the controls, bringing the visual readouts to life. Several seconds went by before they raised their head again, noticing that something in the room was different. Their head turned toward Rosemary, owl-like. "Welcome," they said with a single nod. As they spoke, Rosemary could see a row of flat teeth. She had read that Pairs filed down their carnivorous points. The thought made her shiver.

Rosemary returned the nod, making sure not to break their gaze. Chin down, eyes up. That was how the Linking reference said Sianats greeted others. "It's nice to meet you," she said. "I'm looking forward to seeing you work."

Ohan gave another small nod—pleased, perhaps?—and turned back to their workstation. They pulled out a scrib and a thick pixel pen. Rosemary's eyes widened when she saw that the scrib was running a basic sketch program. They weren't honestly going to puzzle out the inner workings of a wormhole by *hand*, were they?

"Okay," Ashby said, buckling his safety harness. "Let's do this thing. Lovey, patch me through to the techs."

"You're on," Lovey said.

"Roll call," Ashby said.

"Flight controls, go," said Sissix.

"Fuel check, go," said Corbin.

"The interspatial bore is go," said Kizzy over the vox. "But I can't find my crackers and you know I don't like to do this without snacking—"

"Think of it next time, Kiz," said Ashby. "Jenks?"

Jenks's voice chimed in. "Buoys are go."

"Lovey, ship status," said Ashby.

"All ship systems performing normally," said Lovey. "No technical or structural malfunctions."

"Ohan, are you ready?"

"We are eager to begin."

"Fantastic," said Ashby. He glanced back to Rosemary. "You strapped in?"

Rosemary nodded. She had checked the buckle three times.

"Right then. Kizzy, start it up."

Deep down in the bowels of the ship, the bore awoke with a baritone howl. Rosemary was glad that Kizzy had warned her about the bore beforehand. It was the sort of sound that felt capable of ripping bulkheads apart.

Ashby tapped the arm of his chair ten times, evenly spaced. As he tapped, a trembling grew within the hull. The thing on the underside of the ship pulsed and bellowed. The floor panels shuddered.

With a terrible silence, the sky ripped open.

It swallowed them.

Rosemary looked out the window, and realized that she'd never really seen the color black before.

"Give me a heading, Ohan," said Sissix.

Ohan stared at the readouts on their screen. Their hand was already darting over the scrib, writing equations in a text that Rosemary did not recognize. "Ahead sixteen-point-six ibens. Full speed, please."

"That's what I like to hear," said Sissix. She threw back her feathered head with a cheer as she sent the *Wayfarer* hurtling through nothing.

There was no real way to say how much time it took to build the wormhole, because, as Kizzy had said would happen, time ceased to have any meaning. There was a clock silently counting minutes and hours above the window, but within the sublayer, they were mere numbers to Rosemary. She kept feeling as if they had just arrived, only to then feel that they had been in there forever. She felt drunk, or worse, like trying to wake from a fever dream. Her vision swam and shifted. There was nothing beyond the screen, though that same nothingness sometimes seemed to shimmer with color and gauzy light. The buoys they launched blinked and drifted, like plankton caught in waves.

Voices blurred all around her, calling out complex terms that would have meant nothing to her even if she could have processed the words at normal speed. Ohan's voice was the only thing that remained steady, the eye of the storm, directing course changes to Sissix as their hand tirelessly scrawled numbers across the scrib.

"All buoys deployed," Jenks said over the vox. "We're ready to set up the lattice." The words seemed to hang, as if the air carrying them had thickened, even though the world itself was playing back in double-time.

"Initiate coupling," said Ashby.

"Ashby, I think we've hit a pocket," said Sissix.

"Get us out before we get stuck," said Ashby.

"Ashby, I think we've hit a pocket."

"Get us out before we get stuck."

"Ashby, I think we've hit a pocket."

"Get us out before we get stuck."

"Ashby, I think we've—"

"Thirty ibens to port, now!" cried Ohan.

The ship lurched and groaned as Sissix jolted them aside. Somehow, despite the artigrav nets, it felt as if they had flipped upside down. Or maybe that they had been upside down to begin with.

"The hell was that?" said Ashby.

"Temporal pocket," said Ohan.

"Where?"

Ohan gave their readout screen a glance. "Twenty ibens starboard. Five and a half ibens wide. Give it a wide berth."

"Am doing," Sissix said. "Good thing we didn't get stuck."

Corbin scowled at his screen. "Looks like we *did* get stuck. Fuel levels are down point-oh-oh-six percent from where they should be."

"Buoys holding?" Ashby asked.

"Holding," Jenks and Kizzy said in tandem.

"Ohan, where's our exit?"

"Three-point-six ibens, ahead," Ohan said. "Two-point-nine ibens, up. One . . . no, no, zero-point-seven-three ibens starboard."

Sissix's claws flew over the controls. "Ready?"

Ashby nodded. "Punch it."

The bellowing below returned. Everyone slammed back into their seats, eyes snapping shut. Time returned with a thud. Rosemary caught her breath, and pulled her fingernails out from the arms of her chair. She looked to the window. The view had changed. A red dwarf lay in the distance, surrounded by several planets. One was partially terraformed, with a small fleet of GC cargo carriers and transport ships clustered nearby. A new colony was being built. A sphere of blinking safety buoys hung in the space around the ship, their yellow lights directing others away from the *Wayfarer*'s work area.

"And that is what we call perfect," said Ashby. He flicked through the readouts on the panel before him. "No spatial degradation. No temporal tears. We're exactly where and when we should be." Sissix whooped. A double cheer came up over the vox, muffled behind Lovey's congratulations. Ashby nodded, satisfied. "Kizzy, Jenks, I'll leave you two to deploy the cage. The rest of you, call it a day. Great work, everybody. Well done."

"You know, Ashby," said Sissix. "If memory serves, big transport ships like that one there have some nice recreational facilities for weary travelers."

"You don't say," said Ashby with a smirk. "Well, we've just earned ourselves a nice paycheck. I'd say that calls for a few hours off ship. That is, if Ohan and Lovey don't mind keeping an eye on the cage for us." The Sianat Pair and the AI both voiced their agreement.

Sissix cupped her hands toward the vox. "Party on the carrier in two hours," she announced. Kizzy's jubilant cry nearly drowned out Jenks, who was moaning something about SoberUps. Sissix turned back toward Rosemary. "So, newbie. What'd you think?"

Rosemary forced a wan smile. "It was great," she said. She managed to turn away from the console before throwing up.

THE JOB

"I hate this game," Sissix said, frowning over the checkered pixel board.

Ashby took a bite of spice bread. "You're the one who wanted to play."

"Yeah, well, I'm going to win one of these days, and then I can be done with it forever." She rested her chin on her fists, sighed and gestured toward her bishop. The game piece moved itself forward, leaving a faint trail of pixels in its wake. "The fact that you people have been playing this for centuries says a lot about your species."

"Oh? What's it say?"

"That Humans make everything needlessly difficult."

Ashby laughed. "I could just let you win."

Sissix's eyes narrowed. "Don't you dare." She glanced out the Fishbowl's bubbled window, watching the joints of the new containment cage fasten themselves together. A few more hours, and they could be out of here. Not that they had another job lined up yet, but there wasn't any reason to linger. They were due for a market stop, and Sissix was looking forward to having her feet on the ground for a while.

"You know, Aya laughed at me for still playing pixel games. She said they're not cool."

Sissix blinked. "Tell me she doesn't have a brain jack."

"Oh, no, no, she just uses slappers."

"Okay, then. Whew." Slap patches weren't anything to worry about. They had a box of them in the rec room, little sticky sheets applied below the brain stem, a necessary accessory if you wanted to create a neural link between yourself and a sim, a vid or the Linkings. Slappers had come around after Sissix had reached adulthood, so while she used them on occasion, she still preferred the more tangible comforts of a pixel board and a scrib. Brain jacks, on the other hand, made her skin crawl. She couldn't imagine loving any hobby so much that it warranted putting a techport in her head.

Ashby gestured at a pawn. "Besides, I can't believe there's a doctor out there who'd put a jack in an eight-year-old. Not to mention a parent who'd let it happen."

"Have you *met* any of Kizzy and Jenks's friends?"

"Fair point."

Sissix took a sip of mek. She didn't usually start her mornings with the sleepy brew, but she had nothing to do until the cage was finished. She could justify being lazy. She tugged at the heat blanket wrapped around her shoulders, trying to coax away the lingering torpidity. "Little brains have enough going on without getting all wired up. So do big brains, for that matter."

"That's what I told Aya."

"And what'd she say?"

"She called me old." He rubbed his stubbled chin as he studied the board. "I am officially the old, boring uncle."

Sissix laughed. "I highly doubt that. You let her fly our shuttle last time we visited the Fleet."

Ashby chuckled. "I thought my sister was going to kill me."

"Exactly. And that makes you cool. Your move, by the way."

Dr. Chef lumbered down into the garden, walking on two handfeet, carrying gardening supplies in the other four. "How's the spice bread?" he asked Ashby.

"The crust's a little crisper than last time," Ashby said. "I like it."

"Glad to hear it. I thought you could all do with some complex carbohydrates after last night."

Ashby smirked. "Hey, *I* left the carrier bar at a reasonable time, with my reputation intact. I am the very picture of restraint."

"*Ha*," Sissix said.

A guilty grin spread across Ashby's face. "Okay, maybe I got a *little* happy."

A chorus of laughter erupted from Dr. Chef's throat. "At least you were quiet about it. Unlike a particular trio of inebriated Humans I found raiding the med bay at sixth hour."

"Oh no," said Sissix with a smile. "What did they do?"

"Nothing scandalous. Kizzy and Jenks were in search of some SoberUps, and Rosemary had fallen over onto one of the examination tables. Dead asleep. I think she actually tried to match drinks with those two."

Sissix laughed. "Oh, I bet she did, and I'm sure they talked her into it. By the time I left, they were six rounds of kick deep, and had just ordered sugarsnaps. Poor thing, she'll be miserable today. Did you get her to her room?"

"Kizzy did. I think she put her in the freight elevator. Her feet and her brain were operating on completely different frequencies."

Ashby shook his head with amusement as he moved his rook. "Well, hopefully she understands that the techs just wanted to give her a welcome. And that she never has to go through it again." He leaned back in his chair. "Also, checkmate."

"What?" Sissix cried, leaning forward. "No, that's . . . wait . . . shit." Her shoulders sagged. "But I had a strategy and everything."

"Sorry to mess it up."

She studied the board, trying to figure out where she'd gone wrong. Nearby, Dr. Chef was tending to one of his planters, breathing out a low, droning whisper, as always. His version of silence. Sissix watched his pudgy fingers weave bracing knots of twine around the wandering shoots. Sissix never failed to be surprised by how agile Dr. Chef's movements were. The man looked like a pudding with legs, yet his handfeet let him move as nimbly as a dancer.

"How's your ginger?" Sissix said.

"Fat and happy," he said, tying back the tall stalks. Dr. Chef puffed his cheeks with pride. The ginger had been Jenks's idea, and few things made Dr. Chef happier than meeting the crew's culinary requests. "Although, I have to admit, I like eating the flowers much more than the root. Far too potent for my taste. Nice and crunchy, though."

Ashby turned his head. "You know ginger's an accent, right? Like a spice?"

"What? No. Really?"

"Did you try to eat it whole?"

"Oh, dear. Yes." Dr. Chef rumbled a laugh. "I thought it was some sort of spicy potato."

"I have never understood potatoes," Sissix said. "The whole point of a potato is to cover it with salt so you don't notice how bland it is. Why not just get a salt lick and skip the potato?"

"Don't ask me," Ashby said, standing up. "Potatoes are a grounder thing."

"You done playing?" asked Sissix.

"Yeah, it's a little after tenth hour. The newsfeeds will be updated." His tone was easy, but there was a serious look in his eye as he said it.

"Okay," she said. She knew what feeds he'd be checking, and it made her want to hug him. Not a quick, stiff Human hug—a long hug, the kind you give to friends when you know something's bothering them. But she'd learned long ago that those kinds of embraces just didn't happen platonically among Humans. It was one of the many social instincts she'd learned to temper.

Dr. Chef tied one more knot, grumbled with satisfaction and took Ashby's empty seat. In his top handfeet, he held a mug printed with an Ensk expression: "KISS THE COOK." A past birthday gift from Kizzy, who always ignored the fact that none of the non-Human crew members traditionally celebrated birthdays.

Sissix lifted the pitcher of mek sitting beside the pixel board. "More?"

Dr. Chef considered. "Just a half cup," he said, extending the mug. "I suppose we're all entitled to a lazy day once in a while."

"That we are." Sissix filled Dr. Chef's mug halfway, then filled her own to the brim. She could feel the muscles in her cheeks and throat relax as the warm, bittersweet brew washed over them. The feeling bloomed throughout her shoulders, her neck, her arms, washing away all the remaining scraps of tension that the previous cup had softened. Stars, she loved mek.

Dr. Chef cradled his mug in his handfeet. He nodded toward the pixel board. "A very typical Human game."

"How so?"

"All Human games are based around conquest."

"Not true," she said. "They've got lots of cooperative games. What about Battle Wizards?" Scarcely a tenday went by in which Kizzy and Jenks didn't plug into that game—with slappers; even those two weren't dumb enough to jack—exploring magical worlds and sharing merry adventures inside their heads.

Dr. Chef waved a free handfoot dismissively. "I don't mean brain games. I mean stuff like this," he said, gesturing to the pixel board. "The classics. Things Humans have been playing since before they even knew there were other planets out there. All conquest, all competition. Come to think of it, even Battle Wizards is like that. The players work together, but they're still working to defeat a common enemy—the game itself."

Sissix mulled this over. The idea of Humans as conquerers had always been a laughable one. Not just because they had meager resources or because the Diaspora could never get anything done, but because the Humans she knew personally were so unassuming. Ashby was one of the kindest individuals she'd ever met, of any species. Jenks didn't have any ambitions beyond living comfortably alongside people he liked. Kizzy had managed to drop a sandwich into an air duct last tenday, so they hardly needed to worry about her launching a coup. Corbin was a hateful pain in the ass, but harmless, and a coward, too. And yet, Human history—pre-Exodus, at least—was rife with cruelty and endless war. Sissix had never been able to make sense of that.

Dr. Chef pushed the chess pieces around the board. "Grum games are rather similar, thematically. I think our species are rather alike, in some ways. Humans would've died out, too, if the Aeluons hadn't chanced upon the Fleet. Luck's what saved them. Luck, and discovering humility. That's really all that makes Humans different from Grum. Well, aside from the obvious." He chuckled, gesturing to his body.

Sissix laid her hand across Dr. Chef's closest foreleg. There would be no more Grum in a century or so, and there was nothing to be done about it. She knew that Dr. Chef had long ago made peace with his species' impending extinction. Even as he referred to it now, there was no sadness in his voice, no bitterness. But that didn't mean that she couldn't feel it on his behalf.

Dr. Chef patted her hand, more for her sake than his. He glanced over his shoulder toward Ashby, who was leaning against the kitchen counter, reading feeds on his scrib. Dr. Chef spoke in a low whisper, quieting all the voices that came from his mouth. "Am I wrong, or has Ashby been checking the news a lot these days?"

Sissix nodded, knowing what he was asking. "The Rosk have been hitting the colonies at Kaelo hard."

"And that's where . . . ?"

"She was headed last, yeah. Not that the feeds give many details."

Understanding passed between them. They both knew that Ashby wasn't worried about a war that would never come to his doorstep. His concern revolved around one of the Aeluons stuck on the fringes of that war. Her name was Pei, and she and Ashby had been coupling as often as they could for years now. She was a civilian cargo runner, hired to haul medical supplies, ammo, tech, food, whatever the Aeluon forces needed. Given the nature of her work, she couldn't always send text or jump on the ansible when she was heading into contested territory, for fear of giving away troop locations or becoming an easy target. Ashby often went tendays without hearing from her, and during such times, it was not unusual to find him checking newsfeeds. When he *did* hear from her, and had a rough idea of her location, the checking became all the more targeted. It didn't help Ashby's well-being at all, not that Sissix could see, but Humans always got a little dumb when sexual partners were involved.

Close as Sissix was to Ashby, she'd never met Pei, or even *seen* her. The woman was an enigma. But Ashby's lack of forthcoming had nothing to do with Sissix, and everything to do with Aeluon prudishness. An Aeluon—especially one working alongside respectable soldiers—could get in a hell of a lot of trouble for pairing up with someone from another species. Everybody aboard the *Wayfarer* knew about Pei, of course, but they understood why Ashby needed to keep it quiet. Everyone had stopped asking questions about her—at least, while Ashby was in the room—and even Kizzy was smart enough to keep her mouth shut about it when they were around other people.

"It's not good for him to check the news all the time," Dr. Chef said. "It's not as if they'd print her name if anything happened."

"You tell him that," Sissix said.

"I can't," Dr. Chef sighed. "I did the same thing when my daughters were off at war. That's why I don't like that he's doing it. I know how all that wondering can eat away at a person." He shook out his cheeks, as if brushing himself off. "This conversation has become entirely too heavy. Would you like to play a game with me? Or have you had enough for one morning?"

"I'm down for another. You want to play chess?"

"Stars, no. Let's play something Aandrisk. One of your lovely 'let's team up and solve a puzzle' games."

"Tikkit?"

"Oh, I like tikkit. I haven't played it in years, though, not since I lived in Port Coriol."

"Well, I'm not very good at it, so we'll be a balanced team." She voiced the change in game to the board. The pixels reassembled themselves accordingly. "So, what about Aandrisk games?"

"Hmm?"

"What do Aandrisk games tell you about us?"

"That you're clever, fond of sharing and just as dysfunctional as everybody else."

Sissix laughed. "I can't argue that."

They began the game, and the conversation segued into tikkit strategy. Sissix was just starting to think that they might actually win when Ashby broke his silence. "Whoa," he said to himself. Then again, more publicly, as he hurried back toward them. "*Whoa.*"

"Everything okay?" Sissix said. All spacers knew that a lot

of bad things could happen to a ship in a short amount of time, especially when sitting in the mouth of a brand-new tunnel. Seeing a crewmate in a hurry always made her adrenaline kick.

"We're fine," he said. He laid his scrib down beside the pixel board and gestured over the screen. The vid feed playing on the screen leaped into the air and hovered above the scrib. It was a Human news program—Fleet based, from the sound of the reporter's accent. Sissix and Dr. Chef leaned forward to listen.

"—yet to confirm how long membership talks have been in place, but sources indicate that a small team of GC ambassadors have been secretly in communication with the Toremi Ka for at least two standard years."

"The Toremi?" Dr. Chef said, his whiskers rustling in surprise. Sissix could not mimic his physical response, but she shared the feeling. The Toremi were not a species that was mentioned often in the news. They were not a species that was mentioned often *at all*. Sissix knew little of them, other than that they controlled a tight ring of territory surrounding the galactic core, and that they had been industriously killing each other for decades.

Ashby shook his head, a gesture of both confirmation and disbelief. "One of their clans has just been granted GC membership."

Sissix set down her mug. "What?" Her brain reeled. "Wait, *what*?" If that was true, the Commons Parliament had gone insane. The Toremi clans, from what few accounts of them there were, came across as both vicious and incomprehensible. Never a good mix. The clans had been discovered by the Harmagians nearly five hundred standards prior, when a probe found Toremi ships skip-driving (which was dangerous as hell) around and around the galactic core, like fish following a current. No one knew why, and the Toremi themselves showed no interest in talking to their galactic neighbors. They kept up their nomadic loop until about forty standards back, when they stopped in their tracks and started slaughtering each other over claims to stationary territories. And again, no one knew why. No one could get close enough to ask. The Toremi blocked all access to the core. Ships that got close were pushed back. Ships that slipped through came back in pieces, or not at all. But aside from butchering trespassers, the Toremi had kept to themselves, of no concern to anyone except the scientists and entrepreneurs frustrated by a walled-off core.

Ashby put his finger to his lips, and pointed to the scrib. "—official statement from the GC ambassadorial committee explains that the Toremi Ka are the only Toremi clan currently taking part in this membership agreement," the reporter explained. "Other clans have remained neutral in this agreement, and reportedly have displayed no hostility toward the GC. The GC has vouched for the Toremi Ka, stating—quote—'we stand by the good intentions of our new allies, who are committed to enjoying the benefits of a more unified galaxy.' As part of the new membership agreement, the GC will *not* aid the Toremi Ka in offensive attacks against other Toremi clans. However, use of military force *will* be authorized to defend territories shared by the Toremi Ka and the GC."

Dr. Chef scoffed. "In other words, the Toremi Ka get big GC battleships sitting on their borders, and the GC gets easy access to all the ambi sitting on the other side." He shook his head. "No good can come from a species at war with itself. Never has, never will." His eyes grew small, and he *hrummed* deeply. Sissix knew his thoughts had gone to his own people, his own war. She reached out and squeezed his topmost shoulder. His eyes grew large again, focusing on her. He came back. He puffed his cheeks and laid one of his handfeet atop her claws.

"Wait," Ashby said. "Huh."

"What?" Sissix said.

He blinked. "This is what Yoshi was talking about." He looked at Sissix. She understood.

"We could do this," she said, and nodded. "Yeah, we could handle this."

"Handle what?" Dr. Chef said.

"If they're going to be mining and pulling ambi, they need a way to get their hauls back home."

"And they're going to need single-ship hops in place before they can start thinking about convoy tunnels," Ashby said. He straightened up, deep in thought. "This is exactly the kind of work that could get us ahead. A job like this, they're not going to pay small."

"Work," repeated Dr. Chef. "You want to work out there? With those people?"

"Every tunneler's going to jump on this once they hear the news," Sissix said.

"Then we better beat them to it," said Ashby. "Let's go draft a letter of intent. We need to call Yoshi, too."

"You think he's big enough to lead a project like that?"

"Oh, no chance. But he'll know who to contact. I'll have Lovey send him a sib invite, I have no idea what time it is there. And you'll need to help me figure out roughly how long it would take us to get to Central space from our current location. I'm assuming that's where they'll want us to punch from. Is Rosemary up yet?"

Sissix remembered the last time she'd seen Rosemary the night before: head propped against her palm, smiling from ear to ear, words slurring thickly. "I'm going to guess she's still asleep."

Ashby rolled his eyes. "Get her some SoberUps. This is exactly the sort of thing I hired a clerk for."

"I'll fix her a plate of breakfast," Dr. Chef said. He wagged a finger at Sissix. "You tell the techs they picked a terrible night to break her in."

"To be fair," Sissix said, getting to her feet, "I don't think they were planning on the GC losing its mind."

☆

RECEIVED MESSAGE
ENCRYPTION: 1
FROM: Vlae Mok Han'sib'in (path: 4589-556-17)
TO: Ashby Santoso (path: 7182-312-95)
SUBJECT: Tokath/Hedra Ka project

Kind greetings, Captain Santoso. My name is Vlae Mok Han'sib'in, and I am writing to you on behalf of the GC Transportation Board. We have received your letter of intent regarding tunnel construction into Toremi Ka space. Connecting our allies to existing GC territories is a high priority for the Commons Parliament, and we have great need for skilled contractors such as yourself to help us enter into this new chapter of interspecies cooperation.

After reviewing your work record and assessing our needs, we agree that the *Wayfarer* would be an excellent choice to assist in our endeavors with the Toremi Ka. This assessment is reflective not only of your professional expertise, but also of your recent decision to employ a certified clerk. We see the latter as a sign of your dedication to upholding the standards of the GC Transportation Board.

We are pleased to offer you the following project. The GC is in need of a new single-ship tunnel connecting Central space (Tokath Gateway) to Hedra Ka, the capital planet in Toremi Ka territory. This would eliminate our current reliance on pinhole tugs in that sector, and would be our first step toward establishing cargo convoy tunnels. Before you accept, we ask you to carefully consider the conditions of this project.

Normally, a blind punch would be the most expedient means

of connecting to an unanchored territory. However, Hedra Ka is located in a soft zone. As I am sure you are aware, the environmental risk factors in such an area make a blind punch from Tokath nearly impossible. In the interest of protecting both spatial stability and sapient life, this project would require an anchored punch between Hedra Ka and the Tokath Gateway. As there are currently no tunnels that connect GC and Toremi space, this poses a challenge. We propose that the *Wayfarer* travel to the Del'lek Lookout Station, at the GC border. This is the closest anchored point between GC space and Hedra Ka. A pinhole tug would rendezvous with you there, in order to bring your ship through to Hedra Ka. Given your current position, we estimate that a journey to Del'lek would take between 0.8 and 0.9 standards, depending on your choice of route. The pinhole jump would take an additional four days. To help cut down your travel time, the GC would hire another contractor to place the exit cage at Tokath in advance.

We understand that this is an unusual proposal, but given the circumstances, we do not have (nor require) a more expedient plan for completing this project. We also understand that the required travel time represents a significant commitment from yourself and your crew. The GC is willing to cover your basic living and operational expenses for the duration of your travels, in addition to your payment for the project. We also understand that space travel can impose unexpected delays, and that the mental health of your crew will require occasional rest stops along the way. In light of these needs, we do not demand a specific arrival date, but instead require that you arrive at anytime before 165/307. You will also have the freedom to chart your own flight path and make stops as you see fit, though an efficient route is obviously a priority. If you are not confident that your crew or your ship can withstand this journey, it is best that you do not accept this project.

The offered payment for the Hedra Ka project is 36M credits (expenses not included; nonnegotiable). We will expect a reply from you by 155/306. This project will not be offered to any other contractors during that time, so please do not make a hasty decision. If you have any questions regarding this project, feel free to contact my office. If I am not available, my AI, Tugu, will be able to assist you.

With gracious regards,

Vlae Mok Han'sib'in

☆

ASHBY (00:10): sissix, are you there?

(00:11): pick up your scrib

(00:14): hello?

SISSIX (00:15): text

(00:15): realy

(00:16): how fuckng quaint

ASHBY (00:16): did i wake you up?

SISSIX (00:17): yes

(00:17): im goin to complain my boss bout this n th mornin

ASHBY (00:17): sorry. it's important

(00:17): i just forwarded you a letter

SISSIX (00:18): why cnt yo come to my room i hat typng

ASHBY (00:18): because i don't want anyone to hear what we're saying

SISSIX (00:18): ship ok?

ASHBY (00:18): yes, just read the damn letter

SISSIX (00:19): give me minut

(00:19): need to heat bed i can barly mov

ASHBY (00:19): get a heat blanket and let's go

SISSIX (00:24): ok better
(00:24): can actually use my hands now, hooray

ASHBY (00:24): READ IT

SISSIX (00:24): ok ok
(00:27): HOLY SHIT

ASHBY (00:27): shh, i could hear you yell through the wall

SISSIX (00:27): ashby
(00:27): this
(00:28): holy shit
(00:28): we just won the jackpot

ASHBY (00:28): sis, if you don't stop making noise in there, i'm going to
   space you

SISSIX (00:28): how are you NOT making noise
(00:28): are you seeing how much money this is
(00:29): PLUS EXPENSES
(00:29): ashby this is more than we brought in all of last
   standard
(00:29): and this would be just profit
(00:30): pure profit, no expenses

ASHBY (00:30): i know
(00:30): i still can't wrap my head around it

SISSIX (00:30): we could get a new bore for this, easy
(00:31): and all sorts of new tech
(00:31): just like we talked about
(00:31): stars, ashby
(00:32): and not to be pushy, but your crew could get a bonus
(00:32): for example

ASHBY (00:32): yes
(00:33): it's incredible, i know
(00:33): but we need to be smart about this
(00:33): this is one hell of a haul

SISSIX (00:34): we're used to long hauls between jobs
(00:34): we'll be okay

ASHBY (00:34): this is the better part of a standard we're talking about
(00:35): that means no vacations, no visiting family unless they're in our flight path and a lot of stasie food

SISSIX (00:35): it's not like we won't dock when we can. i can plot us a nice smart course that gives us plenty of market stops and places to put our feet on the ground

ASHBY (00:36): i know

SISSIX (00:36): but?

ASHBY (00:36): it's toremi space
(00:36): those people have been at war forever
(00:37): and i don't know anything about them

SISSIX (00:37): ashby, the GC wouldn't send us in if it wasn't safe
(00:38): we're an unarmed tunneling ship, no one will be concerned with us
(00:38): if anything, that long haul gives them plenty of time to get their diplomatic shit sorted out before we arrive
(00:39): and i am sure that place will be swarming with bureaucrats and GC troops
(00:39): all we have to do is get there, punch a hole and jump back home

ASHBY (00:40): so long as they don't start murdering each other again once we're there
(00:40): i don't even know what language they speak

(00:41): oh
(00:41): wait

SISSIX (00:41): what

ASHBY (00:42): rosemary
(00:42): i hadn't even thought of her
(00:43): do you think she's up for this?

SISSIX (00:43): in terms of job or psyche?

ASHBY (00:43): both
(00:44): a standard's a lot to ask even for spacers like us
(00:44): this is all new to her

SISSIX (00:45): well, as far as the job goes, she's got plenty of time to get her claws sharp
(00:45): so to speak
(00:46): as for her personal life, she's dodged every question i've asked about family, and she's single, too
(00:46): i don't get the impression that she's in any rush to visit home
(00:47): besides, you read the letter
(00:47): hiring her essentially got you this job
(00:47): so even if she's useless the rest of the way, at least she did that much

ASHBY (00:48): ouch

SISSIX (00:48): i'm kidding
(00:48): kind of

ASHBY (00:49): it's so much money
(00:49): we could do so much with this
(00:50): and what a project

SISSIX (00:50): like i said
(00:50): jackpot

(00:51): you've earned this

(00:51): i've known you a long time, ashby

(00:51): trust me

(00:51): you've earned this

ASHBY (00:52): thank you, sis

(00:52): sorry for waking you, i just needed to pick your brain

(00:52): i'll need to discuss it with the crew before i decide anything

SISSIX (00:53): so let's discuss it with them

ASHBY (00:53): no sis wait

Throughout the ship, the voxes snapped to life. "EVERYBODY, WAKE UP! BIG NEWS! CREW MEETING! REC ROOM IN FIVE!"

ASHBY (00:54): i'm going to space you, sissix

SISSIX (00:55): you love me

☆

FEED SOURCE: Galactic Commons Reference Files (Public/Klip)

ITEM NAME: Astronomy > Home Galaxy > Regions > Galactic Center (Core) > Natural Resources

ENCRYPTION: 0

TRANSLATION PATH: 0

TRANSCRIPTION: 0

NODE IDENTIFIER: 9874-457-28, Rosemary Harper

The Galactic Center, colloquially called the Core, is home to several unusual astronomical phenomena, including a supermassive black hole and a high concentration of stellar clusters. These unique conditions indicate that the Galactic Center is the Home Galaxy's largest source of raw fuel materials, such as ambi, as well as metals and minerals used in spacecraft construction and terraforming. Estimates of the available resource yield are speculative at best, but the scientific community widely accepts that the amount of harvestable ambi sources in the Galactic Center contain a supply more than four times the amount present in all combined GC territories. Though the presence of such materials has been confirmed by Harmagian long-range survey probes, the Galactic Center remains largely unexplored by GC member species, due to Toremi territorial claims.

Related topics:

Black holes
Accretion disks
Stellar clusters
Ambient energy theory
Commercial fuel sources
Ambi harvesting
Toremi
Interstellar exploration (Harmagian)
Spacecraft construction
Terraforming
Galactic regions and territories (Home Galaxy)
Traditional names for the Home Galaxy (by species)

PORT CORIOL

☆

Ashby wasn't a judgmental man, but anyone who didn't like Port Coriol lost a few points in his book. GC space had plenty of neutral markets that welcomed spacers of all species, but the Port was something special. Even if you didn't need to stock up, the spectacle of it was well worth the trip. Sprawling streets stuffed with open-air shopfronts, overflowing with clothes and kitsch and sundries. Grounded ships, gutted and transformed into warehouses and eateries. Towering junk heaps lorded over by odd tinkerers who could always find exactly the part you were looking for, so long as you had the patience to listen to them talk about their latest engine mod. Cold underground bunkers full of bots and chips, swarming at all hours with giddy techs and modders sporting every implant imaginable. Food stalls offering everything from greasy street snacks to curious delicacies, some with rambling menus of daily specials, others with offerings so specific that the only acceptable thing to say at the counter was "One, please." A menagerie of sapients speaking in a dizzying array of languages, shaking hands and clasping paws and brushing tendrils.

How could you *not* love a place like that?

On some level, Ashby could understand how Port Coriol might be a little jarring to someone accustomed to the glossy prefab trade centers you could find throughout the GC, each as sterile and uniform as the other. The markets of the Port were anything but corporate, and the colony's independent, anything-goes attitude was exactly what made it so beloved—or, to some, rather unsavory. Ashby conceded that the Port was a little dirty, a little scuffed around the edges. But dangerous? Hardly. Crime, for the most part, was limited to low-stakes scams aimed at tunnel-hopping students or gullible tourists. So long as you had two brain cells to rub together, Port Coriol was as safe as anywhere else. Trade was well regulated, too—that is, as regulated as you wanted it to be. Merchants who risked the ire of the port authority didn't last long, and even those dealing in shadier merchandise had plenty of honest permits and legitimate goods on hand to keep watchful eyes happy. Port Coriol's black market was no secret, but it was carefully managed. Not that Ashby ever tried his luck with such things. Losing his license would ruin him, and possibly his crew as well. Despite Kizzy's regular pleas to let her buy something that would give the engines "a li'l more kick," it was smarter to keep things aboveboard.

The Port's soft orange sun warmed Ashby's skin as he led his crew through the crowded shuttle dock. Accustomed as he was to living behind sealed walls and thick plex, being outside was refreshing. As usual, though, he had forgotten about the smell—a heady mix of fuel, dust, spices, fire, perfume, kitchen grease, solder and the natural odors of a dozen or more sapient species. Behind it all was the constant mossy funk emanating from the surrounding shores. The moon of Coriol was tidally locked, which allowed an uninterrupted source of sunlight to fall upon the skins of matted scum that capped its quiet seas. The merchants and traders who kept permanent residence on the moon often made their homes on the dark side, away from the sun and the stink.

For many sapients—Sissix and Dr. Chef included—the smell

was too much to handle unfiltered. Respirators and breathing masks were a common sight, even among the people who lived there. The shuttle docks were lined with booths selling masks to newcomers who had not been forewarned of the Port's signature scent. But Humans, with their relatively poor sense of smell, could wander the streets with nostrils fully exposed. Most Humans, anyway. Corbin had opted to wear a full breathing helmet—the Exolung Deluxe, a weighty contraption that boasted the best airborne allergen and pathogen filtration system available. Ashby thought it looked like a jellyfish tank fitted with limp balloons.

"Destination, please," droned the AI at the quick-travel desk. It wasn't a free-thinking program like Lovey, but a limited model, unable to do anything beyond scripted tasks. Its casing was meant to resemble a Harmagian head, complete with chin tendrils for making facial gestures. The long, doughy face was coated in a skinlike polymer, and it was not *entirely* unlike the species it mimicked. But its digital voice cracked around the edges, and the tendrils twitched with palsied age. Nothing about it could be confused with something alive.

"Two to the bug farms," said Ashby, indicating himself and Dr. Chef. The AI chirped in acknowledgment. Ashby pointed to Corbin. "One to the algae depot." Chirp. Ashby pointed to Jenks. "One to the tech district." Chirp. Ashby turned to Sissix. "And you guys can walk, right?"

"Yeah," said Sissix. "Our sundry run starts right through the gate here."

"That's all," Ashby said. He waved his wristwrap over the scanner on the counter. A short beep indicated that payment had gone through.

"Very good," said the AI. "Your quick-travel pods will be dispatched momentarily. Should you need additional transport or directions, look for the quick-travel symbol, as displayed atop this kiosk. If you lack a sense of sight, you may request a complimentary location indicator from this or any—"

"Thank you," Ashby said, though the AI was still speaking. He led the crew away from the booth. Jenks remained behind.

The AI continued on, unfazed by the departure of its audience. "Location indicators come in models fit for all species, and can provide alerts in a variety of sensory inputs, such as smell, taste, sound, dermal stimulation, neural stimulation—"

"Is Jenks coming?" Rosemary asked.

"Jenks always waits until the end of the speech," Kizzy said with a fond smile. "Just to be polite."

Rosemary looked back to the jittery AI. "That's not a sentient model, is it?"

"I don't think so," said Ashby. "But try telling Jenks that. He always gives AIs the benefit of the doubt."

"Which is absurd," Corbin said. His voice was muffled by the breathing mask.

"So is that thing on your head," muttered Sissix.

Ashby jumped in, addressing the group before Corbin could fire back. "Okay, folks. You know how this works." He saw Jenks give the AI a courteous nod before walking over to join them. "Same drill as always, but this time, we've got GC expense chips to buy stuff with. *Necessary purchases only.* Everything else goes on your wristpatch. The GC's not going to like it if they get a bill for four-course meals and body massages."

"Well, there goes my afternoon," Jenks said.

"Rosemary, everybody's got their chips, right?"

"Right," Rosemary said. "And everyone should have a list of approved expenses on their scribs, just for reference."

"Good. Once you've knocked everything off your list, you're free to do whatever you like until morning. Let's try to be on our way by tenth hour." His scrib pinged, indicating he had a new message. "Sorry, just a sec." He pulled his scrib out from his satchel and gestured at the screen. The message appeared.

RECEIVED MESSAGE
ENCRYPTION: 3
TRANSLATION: 0
FROM: Unknown sender (encrypted)

Ashby's heart skipped.

I couldn't help but notice a hideous tunneling rig that just
docked in orbit. I'm back from the border, but heading out soon.
In three hours, I'll officially be on two days of shore leave. I've
already made it clear that I'm taking some alone time. Are you
free to share it with me?

No signature, but Ashby didn't need one. The message was from
Pei. She was here. And most important, she was okay. She was
alive.

Even though he could feel tendays of tension leaking away,
Ashby managed to remain nonchalant. He placed his scrib back
in his satchel and rubbed his hand over his chin. Shit. He hadn't
shaved. Ah, well. Pei was a cargo runner. Even though her species lacked hair, she of all people could understand a lapse in
personal grooming.

Sissix was eying him as he turned back to the group. He
raised his eyebrows at her, then put his captain face on. "Well,
what are you all waiting for? Go buy stuff."

Rosemary hurried after her crewmates, anxious to not get lost.
The shuttle dock had been crowded enough, but now that they
were weaving their way through the market gates, the likelihood
of her getting swept away in a sea of traders had increased. *Getting
lost* wasn't what scared her, exactly. It was more the prospect of

getting mugged. Or harassed. Or stabbed. She'd seen a few people that definitely looked stabby. And weren't wristpatch thieves a thing in places like this? Hadn't she heard a story about someone who had visited Port Coriol, wandered their way into the wrong shop and woken up in an alley with their patch arm amputated? Okay, maybe that was a little far-fetched, but given that she'd just walked past an Aeluon whose entire face was a mosaic of implants, she wasn't ready to rule out the possibility of arm-stealing patch thieves just yet. She was grateful to be with Sissix, whose presence was reassuring, and Kizzy, who was probably loud enough—in both volume and clothing—to deter stealthier criminals. They both looked like people who knew what they were doing. She hoped some of that might rub off on her.

"You sure you don't want to go to the tech caves, Kiz?" Sissix asked.

"Nah," said Kizzy. "Jenks has my list. I'll pop in later to say some hellos and ogle the gizmos. But I'm all space twitchy. I need open sky and fresh air." She threw her arms wide and inhaled dramatically. "*Ahhhhhh.*"

"Mmm. Yeah. Fresh air," Sissix said, huffing through her breathing mask.

"You know the feeling, right, Rosemary?" Kizzy bounced over to her. "You grew up planetside."

"It's nice having real gravity," Rosemary said.

"Aww, have you been spacesick?"

"Just a little around the edges. But it's no trouble, I'm getting used to it."

"We'll look around for balance bracelets. I'm sure somebody's selling them."

Sissix scoffed with amusement. "Those things are such a scam."

"Are not," Kizzy said. "My grandma, she wears 'em every time she goes up and she says they work like awesome."

"Your grandma also thinks she can talk to her imubots."

"Okay, yeah, but she never gets spacesi— Oh, shit." Kizzy looked down at her boots. "Don't make eye contact. Don't make eye contact."

Rosemary averted her eyes once she saw the source of Kizzy's panic: a simple, friendly table, covered with sealed terrariums and clay (clay!) bowls filled with info chips. Such tables were a common sight in the public squares of Florence, and the outfits of the table's keepers were instantly recognizable. They wore heavy biosuits, like ancient Lunar explorers, sealed and padded to a degree that made Corbin's helmet look almost sensible. Rosemary had heard that their used suits were placed into sealed containers and shot into space. Standard decontamination processes weren't enough for them. There could be no risk of corrupting their immune systems—or worse, the natural flow of Human evolution.

Gaiists. They certainly were their own brand of crazy.

"*Shit*," Kizzy said. "I made eye contact."

"Nice job, Kiz," Sissix said.

"I didn't mean to!"

A Gaiist man beelined for them, cupping a round terrarium in his gloved hands. "Hello, sisters," he said. A small vox below the suit's faceplate transmitted his voice. His Klip was good but heavily accented, full of imprecise consonants that hinted at a lack of regular use. "Would you like to see one of the small wonders of your mother planet?" He held the terrarium out to Kizzy and Rosemary, ignoring Sissix altogether.

Rosemary mumbled a "No, thanks." Kizzy babbled about being "Late for a thing."

"I'd like to see it," Sissix said.

The Gaiist man's face went stony within his helmet. With a strained smile, he held up the terrarium. Behind the plex, a complicated yellow flower sprang up from a cradle of moss. "This is an *orchid*," he said, the foreign word jutting oddly into the surrounding Klip. "A delicate plant that once grew in Earthen swamps and rainforests. Like much of Earth's diverse flora, these beautiful flowers went extinct in the wild during the Collapse." His eyes kept darting between Kizzy and Rosemary, anxious to see them take interest. "Thanks to the efforts of our hardworking folks back home, orchids have successfully taken root in a few restored rainforests."

"It's beautiful," Sissix said. She sounded like she meant it. She pointed at the flower and turned her head to her companions. "Your genitals look kind of like this, right?"

Kizzy burst out laughing. Rosemary felt her cheeks flush.

"Hey, I have a question," Sissix said, addressing the now-stammering Gaiist. She reached out to touch the terrarium. Within his suit, the Gaiist recoiled at the sight of alien claws hovering over Earthen moss. "The scientists in the Samsara Project, do they work with *orr-kids*, too?"

The Gaiist frowned. "They may," he said thinly. "But one cannot have much success with dirt if one lives with his feet in the sky." A hint of piousness crept into his friendly tone.

Rosemary almost felt sorry for the Gaiist. Sissix was baiting him, trying to make him drop the nature lesson pretense and come out swinging with the tenets of Gaian Purism. On the surface, the Gaiist goal of healing their species' barely habitable homeworld was a noble one. But this was the same goal shared by the scientists of the Samsara Project, who lived in the silvery orbital ring that encircled Earth—a ring built not by Humans, but by philanthropic Aeluons and Aandrisks. And though restoration efforts on the ring were headed by Humans, many scientists working alongside them were from other worlds. Diehard Gaiists—especially the kind who braved shuttle docks in search of lost souls—hated that.

The Gaiist turned to Rosemary and Kizzy, the edge leaving his voice, a bit of desperation creeping in. "If you should have some time to yourselves during your stay here"—in other words, *away from the alien*—"please come see us again. We have many more Earthen wonders to share, and even more in the habitat tanks aboard our ship." He switched the terrarium into his left hand and reached into his satchel. "Here," he said, handing them each an info chip. "Take these as a gift. They contain videos of some of the magical places that await you on our homeworld. Just stick them in your scrib and enjoy." He smiled, as if the mere mention of Earth brought him peace. "Do come see us again, sisters. You are always welcome among us."

The Gaiist man retreated to his table, leaving the three crew-mates to make a hasty departure.

"And that," said Kizzy, tossing the chip into the first trash box she saw, "is why you never make eye contact. *Way to go, self.*"

"You know, there are crazy speciest Aandrisks, too," Sissix said. "But they don't go bugging other people about it."

"What do your crazy speciests do?" Kizzy asked.

Sissix shrugged. "Live on gated farms and have private orgies."

"How is that any different from what the rest of you do?"

"We don't have gates and anybody can come to our orgies. Except the Laru. They're allergic to us."

"Stars," Kizzy said, leading the way into the marketplace proper. She pulled a bag of algae puffs from her satchel and began crunching away. "I can't believe Mala used to go for that stuff."

"I can't believe she used to be a *Survivalist*," said Sissix. "She seems so grounded. No pun intended."

"Sorry, who?" asked Rosemary.

"Mala. Jenks's mom," said Kizzy. "She's in the Samsara Project. Works with mammals. You should ask Jenks to show you some pictures of her little fuzzballs. Oh my stars, the *wombats—*"

Rosemary paused. She must've heard something wrong. "Wait, she was a Survivalist?" That couldn't be right, not if this woman lived on the ring. Survivalists were as extreme as Gaiists could go. They weren't just xenophobic, but technophobic to boot. They believed that technology was what doomed their planet from the beginning, and the only way to achieve redemption was to live like the animals they were. Survivalists were strict hunter-gatherers and genetic purists, abstaining not just from routine gene therapies, but from vaccinations, too. Weakness, they believed, had to be bred out. They seemed to ignore the fact that the only reason Earth had land capable of supporting them at all was because the Solar Republic had given them a large territory of restored grassland, filled with edible plants and herds of prey all brought back to life by scientists using frozen DNA and gestation chambers. Rosemary didn't know Jenks well at all yet, but how could that level-headed, laid-back *comp tech* come from a Survivalist mother?

"Yeah, she fell into it during her teens," said Kizzy. "Ran away from home, hitched a ride to Earth, joined a clan, ate honest-to-God *wild meat*, the whole thing. Can you imagine?" She fell into a theatrical stalking crouch. "You're like, all sneaking through the grass"—she skipped from side to side—"dodging snakes or rats or whatever, and you've just got this big pointy stick, and you have to run up to this fucking buffle—"

"Buffle?" said Sissix.

"It's like a big cow or something. And then you stab it and stab it and stab it, and it's all throwing you around like *oh, shit*—" Kizzy flailed in nonspecific pantomime, unaware or uncaring of the other marketgoers eying her cautiously. A few stray algae puffs flew from the bag. "And there's hooves in your face and blood everywhere, *everywhere*, and then it's dead, and then you have to take it apart with your hands. *And eat it*." She raised her hands to her mouth, making messy chewing sounds.

"Ugh, the end, please," Sissix said, grimacing.

"Did Jenks grow up down on Earth? In a clan?" Rosemary asked.

"No, but he was born into one. That's why he's small," said Sissix. "No prenatal therapy."

"Oh," Rosemary said. "I thought he was a genetweak, but I wasn't sure how to ask."

"Yeah, no, it *is* a genetic thing, but he was born with it," Kizzy said. "And by the way, I'm sure you scored some points with him by not pointing it out right off the bat. He doesn't mind questions, but he does get tired of it."

Sissix continued. "See, Mala didn't get any routine screenings after she got pregnant. She—"

"She almost *died* during childbirth," Kizzy said. "Seriously almost *died*. Can you believe that? Who dies in childbirth? Fucking archaic. And Jenks'd totally be dead, too, if Mala hadn't decided to be awesome. Her buying into the crazy Survivalist stuff stopped the moment there was talk of killing her kid."

Rosemary's mouth dropped. "They were going to kill Jenks?"

Kizzy nodded, stuffing a handful of puffs into her mouth. "Srvsts mmdn mmf—hrm." She swallowed. "Survivalists abandon babies if they're sick or different or whatever. Just like, oh, hey, this one's kind of weird, better leave it behind so we can weed out the weak genes." Kizzy clenched her fists, crushing the puffs within the bag. "Gah! It's so *stupid*!" She looked down at the bag as if seeing it for the first time. "Aww."

"So what happened?" Rosemary asked.

"I made crumbs."

"No, I mean to Mala."

"She ran away again," Sissix said. "She got away from the clan, found a group of scientists working planetside. See, they—"

"No, you're missing the badass part," Kizzy said. "She had to *walk*, okay, like a crazy long way, just hoping she'd find someone past the Survivalist border. No skiffs, no skimmers, no shuttles. Just *walking*. Bare-bloody-foot. With, like, lions everywhere. *Lions*."

"Not *everywhere*," Sissix said.

"Listen, when you're talking about lions, it doesn't matter if they're *literally* everywhere," Kizzy said. "Knowing there are a few lions that *might* be around is bad enough."

"Well, anyway, the scientists on the Ring gave Mala and Jenks safe haven, and she came around to the fact that they weren't so bad. She took a shine to biology, and that's where she's been ever since."

"No university or anything," Kizzy said. "Just started shoveling shit in the breeding pens and learned the ropes from there. She's still a Gaiist, though, just in a mellow way. A lot of the Human scientists on the Ring are, actually. They believe in all the souls-tied-to-the-planet stuff, and they don't like being far from Earth, but they scrap all the speciest whatever for the fuckery that it is. And apparently she was only *mildly* freaked out when teenage Jenks decided to go see the rest of the galaxy. She's totally fine with it now. A lot of Gaiists are cool people. Unlike *those* assholes." She jerked her head back toward the missionaries.

"Could Jenks not get gene therapy when they went to the Ring?" Rosemary asked. "I mean, even the Gaiist scientists must be okay with standard medicine."

"Yeah, they are. They've got imubots like the rest of us, and they vaccinate, thank goodness. Gene therapy's kind of iffy. They're usually cool with tweaking for quality-of-life reasons, but not cosmetic ones."

"Then, why—"

"Why didn't Jenks get tweaked? Like I said, only for quality of life. Just look at that happy bastard. His life would be total quality at any size."

"But they couldn't know that when he was a baby."

"Mala wouldn't let them do it. Jenks says once she got the doctors to admit that him being small didn't mean he wasn't healthy, it wasn't even a question for her. Didn't have anything to do with the Gaiist stuff at that point. He says she was just sick of people telling her that there was something wrong with her kid." She stopped and looked around. "And I've totally been walking the wrong way."

"What's first on our list?" asked Sissix.

Kizzy pulled out her scrib. "Plex cleaner," she said. "Followed by scrub bot dispensers."

"Can we get unscented ones this time?" Sissix begged. "Ashby always gets the lemon ones, and I hate coming into the bathroom after cleaning day and smelling *citrus*."

"You've got something against being lemony fresh?"

"You know iski?"

"No."

"Yes, you do. Little green fruit, grows in clusters of three?"

"Oh, yeah."

"Smells like lemons, right?"

"Kind of."

"Yeah, we anoint our dead with iski juice."

Kizzy laughed. "Oh, no, eww. Okay, unscented scrub bots it is." She took another look at her list, and tapped it emphatically, like a politician making a speech. "Listen, we are going to be a rock-solid shopping team today. We're sticking to the list, and that's it. I always spend way too much here on shit I don't need." Something over Rosemary's shoulder caught her attention. "Like *those*." Without another word, Kizzy ran off toward a stall full of juggling supplies.

Sissix sighed. "And so it begins," she said, watching Kizzy dig through a box of shimmering batons. "If you thought today was about getting supplies, you're wrong. Today is about Kizzy wrangling."

As they walked after the mech tech, Sissix put her arm around Rosemary's shoulder. The easy familiarity made Rosemary blink, but she also felt a spark of pride. Even if she got mugged before the day was out, at least she was in good company.

Jenks walked down the ramp to the underground tech district— or, as it was better known, the caves. At the entrance, an Aandrisk man with a stun gun sat on a stool near a multilingual sign. The text read:

THE FOLLOWING ITEMS CAN CAUSE HARM TO TECH, BOTS, AIs, MODDED SAPIENTS AND SAPIENTS USING PERSONAL LIFE SUPPORT SYSTEMS. DO NOT BRING ANY OF THESE ITEMS INTO THE CAVES. IF ONE OR MORE OF THESE ITEMS IS IMPLANTED ONTO OR WITHIN YOUR BODY, DEACTIVATE IT BEFORE ENTERING.

- ☆ Ghost patches (surface-penetrating ocular implants)
- ☆ Hijacker or assassin bots
- ☆ Hack dust (airborne code injectors)
- ☆ Improperly sealed radioactive materials (if you're not sure, don't chance it)
- ☆ Anything running on scrub fuel
- ☆ Magnets

At the bottom of the sign was a handwritten addendum, only in Klip:

seriously, we are not fucking around.

As Jenks passed by, the Aandrisk nodded congenially, his twin ocular implants glinting in the busy artificial light. Every shop and stall in the caves had different lighting mechanisms to help distinguish themselves from the others. The caves were a cyclone of ambient blues, shifting rainbows, simulated sunrises, projected starfields. Within each shop, the lighting could be appreciated, but in the corridors in between, the overlapping effects created an odd mishmash of color and shadow. It was like walking through a drunk kaleidescope.

Jenks felt at home in the caves, and not just for the endless rows of neatly packaged, hand-hacked goodies. Many of the folks there were hardcore modders, people prone to removing their own limbs in favor of synthetic replacements. Walking through the caves, you might see metallic exoskeletons, or swirling nanobot tattoos, or unsettlingly perfect faces that betrayed a weakness for genetweaks. Facial patches, dermal ports, home-brewed implants. Alongside such oddities, his small stature was nothing special. It was hard to feel weird in a place where *everybody* was weird. He took comfort in that.

He walked through the pathways, making mental notes of places he'd have to check out later. Jenks was a veteran of the Port, and he knew that there was only one acceptable place to begin before he started throwing credits around.

The shopfront he arrived at wasn't as fancy as some. A sign made from a broken circuit board hung overhead. Old bits of junk had been stuck to it in the shape of letters. "The Rust Bucket," the sign read, and in smaller letters, "Tech Swap and Fix-It Shop," and in smaller letters still, "Pepper and Blue, Proprietors."

Jenks stood on tiptoe to look over the top of the counter. Pepper was hunched over a workbench, her back to him, muttering to herself. She reached up to scratch the back of her hairless Human head, leaving behind a smudge of machine grease. If she noticed, she did not seem to care.

"Hey, lady!" Jenks barked. "You know where I can score some stim bots?"

Pepper turned around, not bothering to mask her irritation at being asked such a stupid question. Her face brightened once she realized who was doing the asking. "Jenks!" she said, wiping her hands on her apron and coming around the counter. "What the hell are you doing here!" She knelt down to give him a friendly hug. The hug was warm, but her arms were thin. Too thin. For as long as Jenks had known Pepper, her hugs always prompted a burst of sympathy within him.

Pepper and her companion Blue were escapees from a fringe planet called Aganon, one of the last bastions of the Enhanced Humanity movement. Unequivocally cut off from the Diaspora and the Galactic Commons, Enhancement colonies bred their people in gestation chambers, basing their genetic makeup on calculations of what their society would be in need of once they reached maturity. Their genes were tweaked beyond recognition, improving health, intelligence, social skills—whatever was needed for the jobs they were destined to fill. Menial labor was performed by people bred without any genetic alterations at all, save two: infertility and a lack of hair (to make them easy to spot). The Enhanced were so convinced of their superiority over the laboring class that they had been utterly unprepared for Pepper's improbable exodus, which began with a lucky late-childhood escape from a tech manufacturing plant, and culminated within a massive junkyard that became her temporary home. There, among countless other cast-off things, Pepper found hidden treasure: a derelict interstellar shuttle. Using only what scraps she could find, Pepper patched and hacked and coaxed the shuttle back to life. It took her over six standards to get the thing flying, and nearly a standard more to steal enough fuel. The cost of her freedom was severe malnutrition, which had almost killed her by the time her shuttle was picked up by a GC patrol ship. She'd been on Port Coriol for eight standards, long enough to become a staple of the local modder community, and her health had been well looked after during that time. But though she loved to eat (she had taken her name after discovering the joys of seasoning), her metabolism just couldn't catch up. Her waifish body was never going to fill out.

The fact that Jenks and Pepper could be standing in the same place—she from a world where genetweaks were a mandate, he from a mother who had shunned traditional health care altogether—was a real testament to the openness of the Port, as well as the weirdness of Humanity. It was also probably why he and Pepper had always gotten along so well, be it out of compassion or sheer amusement. Well, that, and their deep, undying love for all things digital. That undoubtedly helped.

"How's the *Wayfarer*?" Pepper asked. This was always her first question, and it was not small talk. Her interest in his ship—in all ships, for that matter—was genuine.

"Flying smooth as ever," Jenks said. "Just did a blind punch to Boras Welim."

"That's the new Aeluon colony, right?" Pepper asked.

"Yup."

"How'd it go?"

"Textbook. Except our new clerk didn't take to the sublayer well. *Blehhh*." He pantomimed an explosion from his mouth.

Pepper laughed. "Oh, I want to hear all the gossip. You got time for a cup of mek after we get our business sorted? I've built a brewer that'll change your life."

"Well, I can't say no to that."

"Good. So what's next? You got something else lined up?"

"Yeah, actually," Jenks said with pride. "You hear about the Toremi alliance?"

Pepper rolled her eyes. "Honestly, what the fuck are they thinking?"

Jenks laughed. "I dunno, but we're getting some awfully good work out of it. Tokath to Hedra Ka. That's us."

"No way," Pepper said, her mouth falling open. "You're going to the *Core*?"

"Yup. And an anchored punch, to boot."

"Shit. Really? Wow, that's a serious haul. How long?"

"About a standard. GC's got our tab, though. All we got to do is get there and punch back."

Pepper gave her head a quick shake. "Good for you guys, but I'm glad it's not me." She laughed. "Oh, man, I'd get so twitchy on a ship that long. Still, though. The Core. How many people can say they've been there?"

"I know, right?"

"Wow. Well, that explains why you're here. I take it you have a shopping list for me?"

"Most of it's from Kiz. She's off getting sundries." Jenks handed her his scrib.

"You tell her she better poke her head in here before you guys leave orbit. I won't let her leave without a hello."

"Like she'd let that happen. We could meet up with you and Blue on the dark side later, if you guys don't have plans. Do dinner or something. I did just get paid."

"I like that idea a lot. Especially the part where you're buying." She scrolled through his list, slowly. Reading wasn't her strongest suit. "Okay, current modulators. Go to Pok, the Quelin down by the bot alley. You know him?"

"I know *of* him. He's creepy as hell."

"I can't argue there, but he's not a bad guy, and he doesn't package his stuff in grax like the others do. Trust me, his modulators are top notch."

"What's wrong with grax?"

"It's good, cheap protection for your tech, but it'll dull your receiver nodes if you leave them wrapped up too long."

"No kidding?"

"Well, folks who sell grax disagree, but I swear my tech's been pluckier since I stopped buying anything packaged in it."

"I'll take your word for it."

Pepper continued with the list. "Switch couplers, go to Hish."

"Hish?"

"Open Circuit. Hish is the owner."

"Ah, okay. I've never been to Open Circuit. I've always gone to White Star."

"She charges more than White Star, but I think she's got way better stuff. Tell her I said so, she might knock a few credits off." She read on. "Six-top circuits I can do you for, as long as you don't mind getting them used." She reached up to a shelf, grabbed a hand-wrapped circuit pack and set it on the counter.

"Your version of used is usually better than new," Jenks said. He meant it. Pepper was a wizard when it came to bringing tech back from the dead.

Pepper smirked. "You charmer, you." Her eyes flicked over the scrib. "Coil wraps," she said. "Hmm. I think I've got some tucked away somewhere . . ." She pawed around, then tossed a bag of tiny metallic bundles onto the counter. "There ya go. Coil wraps."

"How much?" Jenks asked, pushing back his wristwrap.

She waved her hand. "You're buying me and my man a meal. We're square."

"You sure?"

"Positively."

"Fair enough," he said. He cleared his throat and lowered his voice. "Pepper, there's something I'm looking for that's not on the list."

"Go for it," Pepper said.

"Just out of curiosity. Nothing serious." It was, of course, a very serious request, but even with a friend like Pepper, it required a bit of caution.

Pepper gave a slow, understanding nod. She leaned forward on the counter, speaking in a hush. "Purely hypothetical. I gotcha."

"Right." He paused. "How much do you know about body kits?"

Pepper raised her eyebrows—or rather, the spot where her eyebrows would be if she had any hair. "Damn, you don't start small, do you? Oh. Uh, no offense."

"None taken. Look, I know kits are tricky to find . . ."

"Tricky to find? Jenks, that kind of tech is so banned it practically doesn't exist."

"There's got to be somebody, though. Some modder with a bunker somewhere—"

"Oh, I'm sure there is. But nobody I know offhand." She searched his face. "What do you want a body kit for anyway?"

Jenks tugged at the spacer in his left ear. "If I said it was personal, could we leave it at that?"

Pepper said nothing, but he could see in her eyes that she was putting pieces together. She knew what his job was. She'd heard him talk about Lovey, however casually. Jenks could feel himself begin to sweat. *Stars, I must look pathetic*, he thought. But Pepper just gave a lazy smile and shrugged. "Suit yourself." She thought for a moment, her face growing serious. "But may I say, as a friend, that if a body kit comes your way—and yes, if by some astronomical stroke of luck I find a supplier, I'll contact you—I really, really hope you know what you're doing."

"I'll be careful."

"No, Jenks," Pepper said. All room for discussion was gone from her voice. "I'm not talking about you getting arrested. I'm talking about you doing something dangerous. I hate to pull the my-past-is-a-sad-story card, but listen: I am the end product of a few very stupid, well-intentioned people who thought it would be a great idea to redefine Humanity. It didn't start with much. A tweak here, a splice there. But things escalated, as they always do, until it became something completely beyond reason. That's exactly why body kits are banned. Some people who know a hell of a lot more about ethics than you or me decided that they didn't think the GC was ready or equipped to support a new kind of life. And yeah, as things are now, AIs are treated like shit. You know I'm all for giving them full rights. But this is murky territory, Jenks, and much as I hate to say it, I'm not sure body kits are the solution. So however innocent your intentions, think about what you're doing first. Ask yourself if you're ready for that kind of responsibility." She held up her thin hands. Her palms were thick with old scars, left over from a decade of digging through sharp junkyard scraps. Memories of hunger and fear and a world gone wrong. "Ask yourself what the consequences might be."

Jenks thought hard. "If you feel that strongly about it," he said at last, "then why would you tell me if you found a supplier?"

"Because you're a friend," she said, the edge leaving her voice. "And because making connections is what I do. And if you're serious about this, I'd rather you go through me than some back-alley hack. Though, truth be told, I'm also hoping that by the time I find someone, you'll have decided I was right about it being a bad idea." Pepper put a little sign on the counter: "In The Back, Yell For Service." "Come on, we need some mek. And I want to hear about this spacesick newbie of yours."

Ashby sat in the hotel room he'd paid for an hour earlier. He was thinking about waterball. Not that he particularly cared about waterball, but it was easier to handle than the alternative. When he'd woken up that morning, he'd been ready for a day of haggling and spending credits, the high point of which might've been drinks and a good meal in a sleepy bar. Now, he was on the dark side of Coriol, surrounded by thick pillows and ugly wall hangings while he waited for Pei, who was not only alive and well, but close by and intent on having sex with him. Waterball was easier to process.

Okay. Titan Cup finalists, year 303. Let's see. The Whitecaps had to have been playing, because Kizzy freaked out when Kimi St. Clair tore a ligament. The Starbursts were there, right? Yeah, you bought Aya a Starbursts jersey for her birthday that year. She said they were her favorite.

Left unchecked, his thoughts jumped like a deepod, ducking in and out before he could lay any of them to rest. He had too many feelings lobbying for attention. Relief over Pei's safety. Joy over seeing her at any moment. Baseless worry that her feelings had ebbed. Determination to follow her lead (stars only knew how she was feeling after tens of tendays spent skirting war zones). And fear. Fear, which he felt every time they met. Fear that in the tendays ahead, after she'd returned to more dangerous space, this hello might end up being a good-bye.

No, no, the Starbursts had to have been 302, not 303. That was the same birthday Aya got her first starter scrib, which means she was starting school. Which means 302.

There was a vague anxiety, too, the concern that they'd get caught this time. He couldn't think of anything he'd left unchecked. Their system for avoiding notice was old hat by now. He always found the hotel—nothing flashy, something off the beaten path and preferably somewhere they hadn't been before. He'd make it clear to the desk staff that he needed some rest and didn't want to be disturbed for any reason. Once in his room, he'd send Pei a message with nothing but the hotel name and the room number, which she'd delete after reading. Two hours later, long enough to prevent anyone from suspecting anything, she'd arrive at the hotel, and request whatever room number was adjacent to his. This was easily done, as complex numerology was a well-known component of traditional Aeluon culture. There were so many conflicting systems for finding meanings within numerical sequences that no matter what room number Ashby got, Pei could find a way to put a positive spin on the number she requested. A non-Aeluon desk worker would assume that Pei wanted a room with a number that symbolised peace or good health, whereas an Aeluon would just see her as unusually old-fashioned for her age (and perhaps a little silly). After settling into her room, Pei would knock on the adjoining wall. Ashby would make sure the hallway was empty, then leave his room. After that, they were good to go.

A lengthy song and dance to go through just to see each other, but a necessary one. As open and generous as Aeluons generally were to their galactic neighbors, interspecies coupling remained a mainstream taboo. Ashby didn't understand the logic behind that—it was a nonissue for most Humans, at least where bipedal species were concerned—but he understood the danger for Pei. An Aeluon could lose her family and friends over an alien relationship. She could lose her job, especially when on a government contract. And for someone like Pei, who took pride in being a hard worker with a honed skill set, that kind of shame would cut deep.

Ashby, focus. The Whitecaps. The Hammers. The . . . the Falcons? No, they haven't made it to a semifinal match since you were crewing aboard the Calling Dawn. *What about the—oh, stars, Ashby. Come on. Waterball.*

Alongside all the emotional distractions he was trying to subdue, Ashby was engaged in a battle of wills, a fight between brains and biology. He knew it was pretty much a given that he'd be getting laid any moment, but he didn't want to be presumptuous. He had no idea what she'd been through prior to this meeting, and until he had a clear sense of where she was at, he was going to let her make the first move. And even if she *was* on the same page as him . . . well, he still had good manners. Even if his body was getting ahead of itself.

Ashby. Waterball semifinals. Year 303. The Skydivers won. Who else was—

A knock came through the wall, quiet but clear.

He left the Titan Cup behind.

"Soap!" Kizzy cried, pointing to a stall full of bathing goods. "Look at 'em! They're like cakes!" She ran off, her hefty bag of purchases bouncing against her back.

"I guess I could use some scale scrub," Sissix said. She and Rosemary followed after the mech tech, who was already poking through display baskets.

The shop was run by a Harmagian merchant, whose offerings catered to the needs of many species. Coarse brushes and bundles of herbs for Aandrisk steam baths, fizzing tablets and warming salves for the icy plunges preferred by Aeluons, skin scrapers and cleansing tonics for Harmagians, a modest yet cheerful selection of Human soaps and shampoos and dozens more jars, bottles and cans that Rosemary could not identify. The galaxy's sapient species could find many cultural commonalities, but few topics were quite as contentious as the proper way to get clean.

The Harmagian—a male, as Rosemary could tell by the color of the spots across his back—whirred over on his treaded cart as they approached. "A pleasant day to you, dear guests," he said, his chin tendrils curling happily. "Have you come to browse, or do you have something special in mind?" The dactyli on the ends of his three front tentacles spread open in a helpful gesture. He was elderly, and the pale yellow skin covering his amorphous body lacked the moistness of youth.

Rosemary had known Harmagians before—her Hanto professor, for one, and several of her father's regular dinner guests—but she always had trouble reconciling their appearance with their history. The person before her was, like all his species, a mollusc-like blob who couldn't move around quickly without the help of his cart. He didn't have teeth or claws. He didn't have *bones*. Yet somehow, there had been a time when this squishy species had controlled a significant portion of the galaxy (and they still did, if you watched where the credits flowed, but they weren't in the habit of subjugating indigenous sapients anymore). She had once read a paper by an Aeluon historian who suggested that the Harmagians' physical frailty was exactly what had helped them develop a technological edge over other species. "Want and intelligence," the historian had written, "is a dangerous combination."

When she considered the historical context, Rosemary thought their presence in the shop made for a rather odd tableau: a Harmagian (an aging son of a former empire), an Aandrisk (whose people had moderated the talks that granted independence to Harmagian colonies and ultimately founded the GC) and two Humans (a meager species that would've been ripe for the picking if they had been discovered during the days of Harmagian conquest). All standing together, amicably discussing the sale of soap. Time was a curious equalizer.

Kizzy poked around the Harmagian's offerings. "Have you got any—Ooh! Can I ask you in Hanto? I've been taking a course on the Linkings and I want to practice."

Sissix eyed Kizzy with skepticism. "Since when?"

"Dunno, five days ago?"

The slits on the ends of the Harmagian's eyestalks crinkled with amusement. "Please, let me hear."

Kizzy cleared her throat and coughed out a few wobbly syllables. Rosemary cringed. Not only had Kizzy spoken nonsense, but without the accompanying gestures, the attempt had come across as a bit rude.

But the Harmagian ululated in laughter. "Oh, my dear guest," he said, tendrils quivering. "Forgive me, but that was the worst pronunciation I have ever heard."

Kizzy gave a sheepish grin. "Oh, no," she said, and laughed.

"It is not your fault," said the Harmagian. "Humans have much difficulty in mimicking our tonal shifts."

Rosemary put a hand near her collarbone and waggled her fingers, as she had done many times. It was a crude imitation of tendril gestures, but it was the best a Human could do. *"Pala, ram talen, rakae'ma huk aesket'alo'n, hama t'hul basrakt'hon kib,"* she said. *Perhaps, dear host, but with some extended effort, we can share your fine words.*

Kizzy and Sissix turned their heads toward Rosemary in unison, as if seeing her for the first time. The Harmagian flexed his tendrils with respect. *"Well and successfully done, dear guest!"* he said, speaking in his own tongue. *"Are you a spacer merchant?"*

Rosemary stretched her fingers. *"Not a merchant, and only recently a spacer,"* she said. *"We three crew are aboard a tunneling ship."* The words were true, but they still sounded strange, as if they belonged to someone else's life. *"My friends and I have come to the Port to acquire supplies."*

"Ah, tunneling! A well-traveled life. You will need plenty of things to keep you clean along the way." The Harmagian straightened his tendrils cheekily. His eyeslits dilated as he shifted his gaze to Kizzy. "Have you found something to your liking?" he asked in Klip.

Kizzy held a brick of blood-red soap. "I need this," she said, pressing her nose against it and inhaling deeply. "Oh my stars, what *is* this?"

"That's made with boiled eevberry," the Harmagian said. "A very popular scent on my homeworld. Though, of course, we don't mix it into soap. What you hold there is a fine blending of our two cultures."

"I'll take it." Kizzy handed the Harmagian the soap. He took hold of it with two of his smaller tentacles, each covered in a sheathlike glove to protect his delicate skin. He zipped behind the counter and busied himself with foil and ribbon.

"There you go, dear guest," said the Harmagian, handing her the attractively wrapped bundle. "Just chip off a little piece of it at a time; it'll last longer that way."

Kizzy stuck her nose to the wrapper again. "Mmph, that smells good. Check it out, Rosemary."

Rosemary couldn't help but inhale as Kizzy shoved the block of soap into her face. The scent was thickly sweet and sugary, like a cake. She imagined using it would be like bathing in a meringue.

"That's eight hundred sixty credits, if you please, thank you," the Harmagian said.

Kizzy stuck out her hand to Rosemary. "Can I have the chip?"

Rosemary blinked, not sure if she had understood. "You want the company chip?"

"Yeah, it's soap," Kizzy said. "Soap is cool, right?"

Rosemary cleared her throat and looked down at her scrib. No, soap *wasn't* cool, not fancy soap, but how could she tell Kizzy that? She had come onto Kizzy's ship, been welcomed by Kizzy with open arms, let Kizzy buy her too many drinks, had vastly less experience than Kizzy in things like tunneling and shopping in neutral ports. But even so—"I'm sorry, Kizzy, but, um, we can only use the chip for common-use soap. If you want special soap, you have to get it yourself." She felt the words come out of her mouth, and she hated them. She sounded like a killjoy.

"But—" Kizzy started.

Without a word, Sissix grabbed Kizzy's wrist and pressed it to the merchant's scanner. There was a corresponding chirp, indicating her account had been accepted.

"Hey!" Kizzy said.

"You can afford it," Sissix said.

"A pleasure doing business with you," said the merchant. "Do come back when you are next in port." His voice was friendly, but Rosemary could tell by his twisting tendrils that the exchange over payment had made him awkward. She gestured a quick, silent apology. He gave her a respectful flex, and scooted off to help other customers.

Sissix frowned at Kizzy as they exited the shop. "Kiz, if we're flying through a rough patch, and I tell everybody to drop what they're doing and strap down, what do you do?"

Kizzy looked confused. "What?"

"Just answer the question."

"I . . . stop what I'm doing and strap down," Kizzy said.

"Even if it's inconvenient?"

"Yeah."

"And if *you* need everybody to not use water taps for a while because you need to fix the lines, which is *hugely* inconvenient, what do we do?"

Kizzy scratched the tip of her nose. "You stop using taps," she said.

Sissix pointed at Rosemary. "This woman here has the worst job of all of us. She has to live on our ship, with all us gloriously stubborn dustheads, and tell us which of our well-worn habits are against the rules. That sounds scary as hell to me, but she's done it without coming across like a hatch parent. So even though it's not always convenient, we're going to listen to her when she needs to do her job, because we expect her to do the same in return." She looked to Rosemary, who was busy hoping the ground might swallow her up. "And you, Rosemary, have the right to kick our asses over stuff like this, because not passing inspections or getting grounded over unpaid invoices is every bit as much trouble for this crew as anything else."

"Unpaid invoices won't suck you into space," mumbled Kizzy.

"You know what I mean," said Sissix.

Kizzy sighed. "Rosemary, I am sorry for being a jerk," she

said, looking at her toes. She lifted up her block of soap as if she were paying homage to royalty. "Please accept my soap as an apology."

Rosemary gave a little laugh. "It's no problem," she said, relieved that *she* hadn't been perceived as the jerk. "Keep your soap."

Kizzy considered this. "Can I buy you lunch at least?"

"Really, it's okay."

"Let her buy you food," said Sissix. "Otherwise she's going to come up with some other ridiculous gift out of penance."

"Hey, you liked the Twelve Days of Jam Cakes," Kizzy said.

"That I did," said Sissix. "I almost wish you'd break my scrib more often."

"Knocked it into a pot of soup," Kizzy confessed to Rosemary.

"And stuck her arm in after it," said Sissix.

"Out of reflex!"

"And spent the next hour in the med bay getting her burns treated."

"Whatever. You got jam cakes, stop being mean."

Sissix pointed at Rosemary's scrib. "We need anything else in this district before we eat?"

Rosemary scrolled through the list. "I don't think so. Didn't you say you wanted some scale scrub?"

"Yeah, I didn't like what he had, though," Sissix said. "Mind if we keep looking?"

The three crewmates drifted from stall to stall, inquiring after scale scrub. After several apologetic noes, one puzzled look and one long-necked Laru who swore that his holistic desert salts would work just as well, Kizzy tugged on Sissix's vest. "I bet that lady's got some," she said, pointing.

"Where?" said Sissix, turning around. Her face softened when she saw the merchant, an old Aandrisk woman seated beneath a small woven canopy, surrounded on three sides by tables full of handmade goods. The woman's feathers were faded, their frills worn and sparse. Her skin was cracking, like old leather, and though the single garment she wore—a soft pair of trousers—was bright and clean, something solemn hung around her scaled shoulders.

Sissix said something to herself in Reskitkish. The sibilant words were lost on Rosemary, but she saw Kizzy's eyebrows knit together. Sissix pressed a palm toward her companions. "Sorry, ladies, wait here. I'll try not to be long." She headed for the merchant, who was too busy stirring a cup of something hot to see Sissix approach.

Rosemary and Kizzy looked at each other. "Do you know what she said?" Rosemary asked.

"My Reskitkish sucks," Kizzy said. "But she sounded upset. Dunno what she's up to." She nodded at a nearby bench. "Guess we'll chill for a bit."

They took a seat. Across from them, the merchant looked up at Sissix. The old Aandrisk smiled, but she looked hesitant, as if she were embarrassed about something. Rosemary could see Sissix's mouth moving, but the words were lost to distance (not that Rosemary could understand the language anyway). As Sissix spoke, her hands weaved in subtle patterns, shifting and darting like small flocks of birds. The old woman's hands moved in response. At first, their respective motions were discordant, but as their conversation continued, they began to mirror each other.

"Do you know Aandrisk hand speak?" Rosemary asked.

Kizzy glanced up from the lock of hair she was braiding. "Not really. Sis taught me a couple of 'em. Just basic stuff. 'Hello.' 'Thanks.' 'I enjoy your company but I don't want to have sex.'" She watched Sissix and the merchant for a moment. She shook her head. "I have no idea. They're way too fast. But Sissix is speaking out loud, too, which is interesting."

"Why would she speak if she's using sign language?"

"No, no, it's not like a sign language. Hand speak doesn't match up with Reskitkish."

Rosemary was puzzled. "This is a stupid question, but then what is it? Is it like facial expressions? Or Hanto gestures?"

"No." Kizzy pulled a ribbon from her pocket and tied off the braid. "Hand speak expresses things that are either too basic to waste words on or too personal."

"Too personal?"

"Yeah, stuff that's really important or hard to say. Like about love or hate or stuff you're scared about. You know how when you have something big to tell someone, you stammer through it or sit in front of your mirror practicing what to say? Aandrisks don't bother with that. They let the gestures take care of all the awkwards. They figure that big, deep feelings are universal enough to be defined with just a flick of the hand or whatever, even though the events that cause those feelings are unique."

"That must save them a lot of time," said Rosemary, wondering how much of her life had been spent trying to find the right words in difficult conversations.

"Seriously. But back in the day, you could *also* use hand speak while you spoke. It was used to add emphasis to stuff you said out loud, so that folks knew you *really* meant it. Sissix says you can still use it like that, but it's old-fashioned, and you only do it in special circumstances." She nodded toward the stall, where the two Aandrisks were now moving in sync. "What we're seeing here is Sissix being *super* respectful. And honest."

"But she doesn't know that merchant, right?"

"Dunno. Don't think so. But that lady's old, so maybe she's just being old-fashioned for her sake."

Rosemary watched the Aandrisks. Their hands moved in a graceful, hurried dance. "How are they matching each other?" she asked.

Kizzy shrugged. "I guess they agree on something." Her eyebrows shot up. "Oh. Like *that*."

Sissix had sat down with her back against one of the tables, spreading her legs to either side. The older woman joined her, leaning her back against Sissix's front. They adjusted their tails accordingly. The old woman leaned her head into Sissix's chest, her eyes falling shut. Sissix pressed one palm against the old woman's stomach, holding her close. With her other hand, she spread her fingers wide and ran them up from the old woman's scalp to the tips of her feathers, tugging the shafts gently as she went. To Human eyes, they looked like reunited lovers behind a bedroom door, not at all like two strangers in an open-air market. Even across the street, the old woman's face was easy to read. She was in bliss.

Rosemary was bewildered. She knew Aandrisks were uninhibited (by Human standards, she reminded herself), but this went beyond what she was expecting. "Um," she said. "So . . ."

"I have no idea," said Kizzy. "Aandrisks. I don't even fucking know." She was silent for a few seconds. "Do you think they're gonna go for it?" she whispered, leaning forward with childlike curiosity. "I bet they are. Holy shit, is that even legal here? Oh, I hope they don't."

But the Aandrisks did not couple, though they continued their spontaneous intimacy for a good half an hour, stroking feathers and nuzzling cheeks, oblivious to the stares of passersby. At one point, two other Aandrisks strolled past without more than a casual glance, as if nothing was going on. Rosemary wasn't sure if she should avert her eyes or not. Sissix clearly didn't care who was looking. As Rosemary watched, the peculiarity of the act began to melt away. It was alien, yes, and sudden, but not uncomfortable. There was a weird sort of beauty to it, something about the way their hands moved, the ease with which they touched each other. Baffling as the thought was, Rosemary found herself a little envious—of the old woman or of Sissix, she wasn't sure. She wished someone would give her that sort of attention on a whim. She wished she were confident enough to give it back.

Finally, there was a flutter from the old woman's hands. Sissix let go and helped the old woman to her feet. They began looking through the old woman's wares. A jar of scale scrub was selected. Sissix's wrist was scanned. A few more words were exchanged, but without hand speak. A normal discussion between customer and merchant, made all the more surreal by what had come before.

The old woman reached up and plucked a feather from her head, wincing as she did so. She held the feather—a faded blue—out to Sissix. Sissix took it, bowing her head low. Her expression was one of gratitude.

"Oh, wow," said Kizzy, putting her hands over her heart. "I still don't know what's going on, but that just made me go all mushy."

"What?" Rosemary kept her eye on the Aandrisks, as if staring long enough might provide an explanation. "What's that mean?"

"Have you been in Sissix's room yet?"

"No."

"Okay, well, on her wall, there's this big fancy frame with a mess of Aandrisk feathers hanging from it. Every Aandrisk's got one, as far as I know. See, if you're an Aandrisk and somebody really touches your life in some way, you give that person one of your feathers. And then you keep the feathers you get from others as a symbol of how many paths you've crossed. Having a lot of feathers on your wall shows that you've had an impact on a lot of people. That's a pretty big life priority for most Aandrisks. But they don't give feathers out casually, not, like, for helping you carry something or giving you a free drink or whatever. It's got to be an experience that sticks with you, but it can totally be between strangers. Oh, hey, check it." Kizzy gestured with her chin toward Sissix, who was giving the old woman one of her own feathers.

"Has Sissix ever given you a feather?" Rosemary asked.

"Yeah, she gave me one a while back, after she got news that one of her hatch fathers died. He was old, but she was really broken up over it. I put her in the shuttle, flew her out to the middle of this nebula and just let her yell for a few hours. I got a feather the next morning. I think the whole crew's got a Sissix feather by now. Well, not Corbin. Probably not Corbin."

Sissix walked back over to the bench, carrying the jar of scale scrub. She looked between Kizzy and Rosemary. "I . . . apparently have some explaining to do."

"Uh, yes," Kizzy said. "Explaining would be great."

Sissix nodded toward the road, indicating for them to follow. "A person her age should be settled down with a house family, raising hatchlings."

Rosemary tried to remember everything she'd been told about Aandrisk family structure. Young Aandrisks were cared for by community elders, not their biological parents. That much she knew. And there were several familial stages Aandrisks went through as they aged. But beyond that, Rosemary was fuzzy on the details.

"Maybe she just didn't want to," Kizzy said. "Maybe she liked it better out here."

"No," Sissix said. "It's because she can't socialize well."

"She's shy?" Rosemary asked.

"She's a *rashek*. There's not a word for it in Klip. She's got a disorder that makes it difficult for her to interact with others. She has trouble understanding other people's intentions. And she speaks oddly, that much was obvious when I first approached her. I offered to couple with her, but she couldn't quite bring herself around to that. So, yes, she's shy, but she also has a hard time figuring other people out. It makes her act a little . . . well, for lack of a better word, *weird*."

"Why snuggle with a weirdo?" Kizzy asked.

"Being weird doesn't mean that she doesn't deserve companionship. The fact that she's running a shop instead of living on a farm somewhere means that she *has* no house family. And yeah, there are elders who choose not to have house families, but she doesn't even have a *feather* family. And that's . . ." Sissix shivered. "Stars, I can't imagine anything worse than that."

Rosemary looked at Sissix. The familial terms were lost on her, but something clicked anyway. "You were comforting her. That's all it was. You just wanted her to know that someone cared."

"Nobody should be alone," Sissix said. "Being alone and untouched . . . there's no punishment worse than that. And she's done nothing wrong. She's just *different*."

"There are lots of other Aandrisks here. Why don't they do anything for her?"

"Because they don't want to," Sissix said, her voice growing fierce. "Did you see the two Aandrisks walk by while I was with her? Locals, I'm sure. They knew her, I could tell by the look in their eyes. They can't be bothered with her. She's an inconvenience." Sissix's feathers had puffed up. Her sharp teeth flashed as she spoke.

"Don't be fooled by all the warm fuzzy talk and snuggles," Kizzy said to Rosemary. "Aandrisks can be assholes, too."

"Oh, we've certainly got our share," Sissix said. "Anyway. Sorry to keep you waiting. I hope I didn't make you feel awkward. I know Humans can be—"

"No," Rosemary said. "No, it was a very kind thing to do." She watched the Aandrisk woman as she walked beside her. Her body was strange, her ways were strange, and yet, Rosemary found herself in deep admiration.

"Yes, awesome, go, Sissix," Kizzy said. "But I am now *starving*. What sounds good? Noodles? Skewers? Ice cream? We're grown-ups, we can have ice cream for lunch if we want."

"Let's not," Sissix said.

"Right. I forgot," Kizzy said, and laughed. "Ice cream makes her mouth go slack."

Sissix flicked her tongue with disapproval. "Why anyone would make *freezing cold food* is beyond me."

"Ooh! What about hoppers?" Kizzy said. "I could seriously go for a hopper. Mmm, spicy peppers and crunchy onions and a big toasty bun . . ." She looked at Rosemary with eager eyes.

"I can't remember the last time I had a hopper," Rosemary said. It was a lie. She'd never had one. Grasshopper burgers were street food, and that wasn't a realm of cuisine she'd ever been privy to. She imagined how her mother would react to her chowing down a bug sandwich wrapped in greasy paper while sharing a table with modders and smugglers and arm-hacking patch thieves. She grinned. "Sounds great."

Ashby ran his palm down the bare torso pressing against his own. He'd had his share of lovers before her. He'd felt plenty of skin. But none like hers. She was covered in tiny scales—not thickly layered, like Sissix's, but seamless, interlocking. She was silvery, almost reflective, like a fish in a river. Despite all the time he'd spent looking at her, despite how comfortable he was in her company, there were still moments when the sight of her made his words stick in his throat.

It was pure chance, of course, that Aeluons so often managed to check all the boxes on the list of Things That Humans Generally Find Attractive. On a galactic scale, beauty was a relative concept. All Humans could agree that Harmagians were hideous (a sentiment the Harmagians heartily returned). Aandrisks—well, that depended on who you talked to. Some people liked the feathers;

others couldn't get past their teeth and claws. The Rosk, with their skittery legs and jagged mandibles, would still be the stuff of nightmares even if they *weren't* in the habit of carpet-bombing border colonies. But Aeluons, by some weird fluke of evolution, had a look that made most Humans drop their jaws, hold up their palms and say, "Okay, you *are* a superior species." Aeluons' long limbs and digits were alien, no question, but they moved with fascinating grace. Their eyes were large, but not too large. Their mouths were small, but not too small. In Ashby's experience, it was hard to find a Human who couldn't appreciate an Aeluon, even if only in the most objective aesthetic terms. Aeluon women didn't have breasts, but after meeting Pei, Ashby had found that he could do without. His teenage self would've been horrified.

Lying beside her, Ashby felt like a hairy, gangly mess. But given what they'd been up to for the better part of the last two hours, he figured he couldn't be *that* repulsive. Or maybe she just didn't care about the whole hairy, gangly thing. That worked, too.

"You hungry?" Pei said, though her mouth did not move. Like all Aeluons, her "voice' was a computerized sound that came from a talkbox embedded in the base of her throat. She controlled the talkbox neurally, a process she likened to thinking up words while typing. Aeluons lacked a natural sense of hearing, and had no need for a spoken language of their own. Among themselves, they communicated through color—specifically, iridescent patches on their cheeks that shimmered and shifted like the skin of a bubble. Once they began interacting with other species, however, verbal communication became a necessity, and so, talkboxes came to be.

"I'm starving," Ashby said. He knew that as he spoke, the sounds coming from his mouth were collected by the jewelry-like implant set in her forehead. As her brain did not have any means of processing sound, the implant translated his words into neural input that she could understand. He didn't quite grasp how it worked, but he could say the same for most tech. It worked. That was all he needed to know. "Your room or mine?" he asked. That was another part of their standard operating procedure: make sure only one person was in the room when room service arrived.

"Let's see what they've got, first." She reached over the edge of the bed and pulled the menu from a nearby table. "What are our odds?"

This was an old joke between them, the question of how likely it would be that each of them would find something they liked on the room service menu. Multispecies menus meant well, but they were always hit or miss. "Seventy-thirty," he said. "Your favor."

"How come?"

He pointed at the menu. "Because they've got a whole section dedicated to roe."

"Ooh, so they do."

He let his eyes slide down her body as she perused the selection of fish eggs. He saw something peeking up over her hip—the edge of a scar, thick and milky white. He hadn't noticed it earlier, but then, he'd been a little distracted. "This one's new."

"What?" She craned her neck up to look. "Oh, that. Yeah." She went back to the menu.

Ashby sighed, a familiar weight growing in his stomach. Pei had many scars—corded stripes across her back, healed bullet holes on her legs and chest, a warped patch left over from the business end of a pulse rifle. Her body was a tapestry of violence. Ashby had no illusions about the risks a cargo runner faced, but somehow her neat clothes, her polished gray ship, her quick wit and smooth voice made it all seem very civilized. It wasn't until he saw physical proof that *someone had hurt her* that he remembered how dangerous her life was. The life he couldn't share.

"Should I ask?" Ashby said, running his finger over the dull flesh. The way she was reclining prevented him from seeing the extent of it, but it trailed all the way to her back, widening as it went. "Shit, Pei, this is huge."

Pei laid the menu across her chest and looked at him. "Do you really want to know?"

"Yes."

"I'm not going to tell you if it's going to make you worry more."

"Who said I was worried?"

She stroked the creases between his eyebrows with a fingertip. "You're sweet, but you're a terrible liar." She rolled over, bringing her face to his. "There was an . . . incident at a drop site."

"An incident."

Her second pair of eyelids fluttered, and her cheeks went pale yellow with flecks of red. The intricacies of her color language were something Ashby would never be able to learn, but he was familiar enough with it to distinguish emotions. This one, for example, was somewhere between exasperated and embarrassed. "It's going to sound so much worse than it actually was."

Ashby drummed his fingers against her hip, waiting.

"Oh, fine. We got jumped by a small—very small, I might add—Rosk strike team. They were after the base, not us, but we got a little mixed up in it. Long, messy story short, I ended up on top of one of their heads—"

"You *what*?" Rosk soldiers were built for combat right down to their genes. Three times the size of an average Human. A fast, raging mass of legs and spikes and keratin plating. Given the opportunity, he didn't think he could prevent himself from running away from a charging Rosk soldier, let alone *climb up on her head*.

"I told you this was going to sound bad. Anyway, the second-to-last thing she ever did was buck me off into a stack of crates.

As I went crashing down, she took the opportunity to grab me in her mouth. I've got good protective gear, but Rosk jaws—" She shook her head. "What you see there on my hip is the result of one of her mandibles slicing through. But it ended up working out well for me, actually. Being in her mouth gave me a nice, soft place to shoot."

Ashby swallowed. "So you . . . ?"

"No, that wasn't enough to kill her. My pilot's second shot was, though." She cocked her head, second eyelids sliding in sideways. "You're bothered."

"It's hard not to be."

"Ashby." She reached out to touch his cheek. "You shouldn't ask."

He pressed his palm against the small of her back, pulling her in close. "I really want this war to be over."

"You know, most of *this*"—she took his hand and guided it over her scars—"happened in GC space. This one's from an Akarak who tried to board my ship. This one's from a smuggler who didn't want me to call the authorities on his phony bots. And *this* one's from a genetweak headcase who was just having a bad day. Nobody protects me when I'm in uncontested space. Nobody but me. With military work, I get escorts when I'm out in the open, and armed guards when I'm unloading down planetside. In a lot of ways, military work is safer. Pays better, too. And it's not as if they send me into heavy combat. Soon as I drop my goods, I turn right around and come back home."

"Do . . . *incidents* happen often?"

"No." She studied his face. "Are you more bothered that I was attacked, or that I shot someone?"

Ashby was quiet for a moment. "The former. I don't care about you shooting that Rosk."

She stretched out a leg and hooked it around one of his. "That's an odd thing for an Exodan to say." Pei, like everybody else in the GC, knew that Exodans were pacifists. Before they had left Earth for the open, the refugees had known that the only way they were going to survive was to band together. As far as they were concerned, their species' bloody, war-torn history ended with them.

"I don't know if I can explain this," Ashby said. "I wish war didn't happen, but I don't judge other species for taking part in it. What you're doing out there, I mean, I can't find fault in what you do. The Rosk are killing innocent people in territories that don't belong to them, and they won't be reasoned with. I hate saying it, but in this case, I think violence is the only option."

Pei's cheeks went a somber orange. "It is. I'm only on the edges of it, and from what I've seen . . . trust me, Ashby, this is a war that needs to be fought." She exhaled in thought. "Do you think badly of me for—I don't know, for accepting business from soldiers?"

"No. You're not a mercenary. All you do is get supplies to people. There's no fault in that."

"What about me shooting the Rosk, though? The one that had me in her mouth? You know that's not the first time I've had to . . . defend myself."

"I know. But you're a good woman. The things you have to do don't change that. And your species—you know how to end a war. Truly end it. It doesn't get in your blood. You do what needs doing and leave it at that."

"Not always," Pei said. "We have as many dark patches in our history as anyone else."

"Maybe, but not like us. Humans can't handle war. Everything I know about our history shows that it brings out the worst in us. We're just not . . . mature enough for it, or something. Once we start, we can't stop. And I've felt that in me, you know, that inclination toward acting out in anger. Nothing like what you've seen. I don't pretend to know what war is like. But Humans, we've got something dangerous in us. We almost destroyed ourselves because of it."

Pei ran her long fingers around his coiled hair. "But you didn't. And you learned from it. You're trying to evolve. I think the rest of the galaxy underestimates what that says about you." She paused. "Well, about the Exodans, at least," she said, her cheeks a sly green. "The Solans' motives are a bit more questionable."

He laughed. "Not that you're biased or anything."

"It's your fault if I am." She propped herself up on the pillow. "Don't change the subject. You haven't finished your original thought."

"Which one?"

"What it is that actually bothers you."

"Ah, right." He sighed. Who was he to talk to her about war? What did he know about it at all, aside from newsfeeds and reference files? War was nothing more than a story to him, something that happened to people he didn't know in places he'd never been. It felt insulting to tell her how he felt about it.

"Go on," she said.

"The Rosk that bit you. She's dead."

"Yes." Her tone was matter-of-fact. No remorse, no pride.

Ashby nodded. "That's what bothers me."

"That . . . a Rosk died?"

"No." He tapped his chest. "*This*. This feeling in here. That's what bothers me. I hear that you shot someone, and I'm *glad* of it. I'm glad that you stopped her before she could hurt you more. I'm glad that she's dead, because that means you're still here. What does that say about me? What does it say about me, being relieved that you can do the thing I condemn my own species for?"

Pei looked at him a long time. She pressed close to him. "It means," she said, her forehead against his, her lithe limbs wrapped around his body, "that you understand more about violence than you think." She pressed her fingers against his cheek, a touch of worry crossing her face. "And that's good, considering where you're headed."

"We're not going into a combat zone. The Board says the situation there is perfectly stable."

"Uh-huh," she said flatly. "I've never looked a Toremi in the eye, but they do not sound stable to me. That species was sending our explorers back in pieces before you guys even knew the rest of us were out here. I don't buy this alliance, and I don't like the idea of you going out there."

Ashby laughed. "This coming from you."

"There's a difference."

"Really."

Her eyes shifted, displeased. "Yes, really. I know which end of a gun to point at someone. You won't even pick one up." She exhaled, her cheeks turning a pale orange. "That's not fair, I'm sorry. All I mean is, I know you. I know you've probably thought this out long and hard. But I don't know the Toremi. I only know what I hear, and—just, please, Ashby, be careful."

He kissed her forehead. "And now you know how I feel every time you leave."

"It's an awful way to feel," she said with a smirk. "And I wish you didn't feel it, either. But I suppose it's good, in a way. It means that you care for me as much as I care for you." She placed his hand on her hip. "I like that."

They put off room service for another hour.

THE WANE

Seated safely behind the window in their quarters, Ohan gazed into the black hole. With some effort, they could remember how the galaxy had looked during their Host's childhood, before infection. Flat. Vacant. Blank. So much of existence was lost to a mind untouched by the Whisperer. Their alien companions had such minds. Ohan pitied them.

Looking only with their eyes, Ohan's view of the activity taking place along the edges of the black hole's accretion disc was no different from the way the rest of the crew saw it. A flock of unmanned skimmer drones sailed as close as they could safely get to the event horizon, just on the edge of gravity's embrace. They drifted through the swirling silt, and to the ordinary observer, they would appear to be doing nothing but drawing dust trails with their comblike arms. But if Ohan looked with their mind, mapped it all out with the right numbers and notions, the space outside became a majestic, violent place. Around the skimmers' arms, raw energy tumbled and boiled, like a thrashing sea churning up flotsam. Tendrils of the stuff curled up around the combs, arching and writhing as they were coaxed into the collection hoppers. Or so Ohan imagined. They pressed close to the window, in awe of the storm that lay beyond sight. And again, they thought of what their crewmates would see: an empty patch of space, blacker than black, and little skimmers collecting invisible cargo.

How still the universe must look to their eyes, Ohan thought. *How silent.*

That invisible cargo was what their captain had come to purchase. Ashby was probably haggling over the price of ambi cells at that very moment. Raw ambi—the stuff Ohan envisioned torquing around the skimmer combs—was difficult to gather. Ambi could be found everywhere and in everything, but the way that it weaved itself around ordinary matter made extracting it a troublesome task. With the right technology, it *could* be wrenched apart, but the process was so tedious and reaped such small rewards that it wasn't worth the effort. It was far easier to gather ambi somewhere where matter was already being ripped apart by forces greater than anything any sapient could build—like a black hole. Black holes were always surrounded by turbulent seas of free-floating ambi, but getting close enough to gather it posed an obvious risk. For ambi traders, the risk was worth it, especially since it allowed them to charge a premium. As expensive as ambi cells were, they were the only thing that could power the *Wayfarer's* interspatial bore. It was a necessary expense for a ship such as theirs, but one that always left Ashby looking a little gray afterward. Ohan had read of ships powered *entirely* by ambi cells, but they had trouble conceiving of a life in which such an extravagance was affordable.

Ohan picked up the razor that lay beside the washbasin near their feet. They clicked a skipping rhythm with their tongue as they trimmed the patterns in their fur. The swirls of fur and clicks of tongue meant nothing to their crewmates, but they meant everything to Ohan. Every pattern represented a cosmological truth, every series of clicks an abstraction of the universe's underlying mathematics. These were symbols and sounds every Sianat Pair knew. They wore the layers of the universe upon their skin, drummed its beat with their mouths.

A sharp twinge blossomed deep within their wrist, and for a moment, the Pair lost control of their hand. The razor slipped, nicking their skin. Ohan chirped, more out of surprise than pain. They wrapped the fingers of their other hand around the wound, rocking back and forth for a moment as the feeling faded to a quiet burn. Ohan exhaled. They looked down to the cut. Thin blood oozed forth, matting a tiny patch of fur. But the razor had not gone deep. Ohan stood stiffly and walked to the dresser in search of a bandage.

This was the first stage of the Wane: stiffness and muscle spasms. Eventually, the pain would spread to their bones, and their muscles would become increasingly difficult to control. The pain would then disappear completely, but this was a devious mercy, as it indicated that their nerve fibers had begun to die. Death would come afterward, in its own time.

The Wane was an inevitability in a Sianat Pair's life. Though the Whisperer unlocked the mind of the Host, it also shortened their life. Solitaries—blasphemous Hosts that avoided infection, a crime punished by exile—reportedly could live well over a hundred standards, but no Pair had ever lived to be more than thirty. From time to time, alien doctors would come forward, offering to help cure the Wane, but they were always refused. There could be no chance of a treatment damaging the genetic stability of the Whisperer. The infection was sacred. It could not be tampered with. The Wane was a fair price to pay for enlightenment.

Even so, Ohan was afraid. They could disconnect themself from the fear, but it lingered, like an unpleasant taste in the back of the throat. Fear. Such a throwback emotion, meant to spur primitive life-forms away from potential predators. Life's universal constant. Every fear of rejection, of criticism, of failure, of loss—these were all caused by that same archaic survival reflex. Ohan knew that their own fear of death was nothing more than some primitive synapses firing within their Host's brain, the emotional equivalent of jerking a hand away from a hot surface. When they reached for the higher parts of their mind, they knew that death was nothing to fear. Why should they fear something that came to all life-forms? In some ways, having reached the Wane was a comfort to Ohan. It meant that they had been successful in avoiding a sudden, premature end.

Ashby and Dr. Chef were the only ones who knew that Ohan had begun to Wane. The captain attempted to carry on as normal, though he often asked Ohan in a hushed voice how they were feeling, if there was anything he could do. Dr. Chef, kind creature that he was, had taken the trouble to contact Sianat doctors to learn more about the Wane's effects. A few days after the *Wayfarer* left Coriol, Dr. Chef had presented Ohan with a variety of homemade tinctures and teas, made from herbs recommended for easing the pain. Ohan had been touched, though as always, they did not know how to adequately express their thanks. Gift giving was unheard of in Sianat culture, and Ohan were always ill-equipped to express gratitude for such gestures. They believed that Dr. Chef understood this social limitation. In a way, Dr. Chef could see into the hearts of others as well as Ohan themself could see the universe. Ohan often wondered if Dr. Chef knew what a gift that was.

Bandage in place and blood cleaned away, Ohan returned to the window. They picked up the razor, clicking their cheek as they dragged the blade through their fur. As they did so, they thought of the concept of purpose. Dr. Chef's purpose was to heal and nourish. Ashby's purpose was to bind his crew together. Accepting the Wane ran contrary to those purposes. For them, accepting the death of a crew member was difficult. Ohan hoped they knew how much the effort was appreciated.

Ohan's own purpose was to be a Navigator, to unveil the universe for those who were blind to it. After death, Ohan would no longer be able to pursue that purpose, and they could not deny that this saddened them. At least there would be time for one more job, this new tunnel at Hedra Ka. The Wane had only begun its first stage. There was time for a tunnel before succumbing. Ohan hoped that Ashby was not uncomfortable with letting them embrace the Wane's final stage aboard the *Wayfarer*. They could think of nothing more fitting than dying in the place that housed their purpose.

Ohan looked again into the black hole. They closed their eyes, and pictured great swaths of fragmented matter, falling and pressing endlessly. *Larab*, they would call it in their native tongue, a word to describe form. And *gruss*, too, a word for the color of unseen matter. There were no words in Klip for the colors or shapes that lay beyond sight. They had tried at times to explain these things to the *Wayfarer*'s crew, but there were no words, no abstractions that could open their crewmates' limited minds. Ohan preferred to take in the sight alone, especially now. A black hole was the perfect place to contemplate death. There was nothing in the universe that could last forever. Not stars. Not matter. Nothing.

The razor cut. Their wrist ached. The sky roiled, unseen.

☆

FEED SOURCE: Reskit Museum of Natural Sciences—Archival Library (Public/Reskitkish)

ITEM NAME: Thoughts on the Galaxy—Chapter Three

AUTHOR: oshet-Tekshereket esk-Rahist as-Ehas Kirish isket-Ishkriset

ENCRYPTION: 0

TRANSLATION PATH: [Reskitkish:Klip]

TRANSCRIPTION: 0

NODE IDENTIFIER: 9874-457-28, Rosemary Harper

When meeting an individual of another species for the first time, there is no sapient in the galaxy who does not immediately take inventory of xyr physiological differences. These are always the first things we see. How does xyr skin differ? Does xe have a tail? How does xe move? How does xe pick things up? What does xe eat? Does xe have abilities that I don't? Or vice versa?

These are all important distinctions, but the more important comparison is the one we make after this point. Once we've made our mental checklists of variations, we begin to draw parallels—not between the alien and ourselves, but between the alien and animals. The majority of us have been taught since childhood that voicing these comparisons is derogatory, and indeed, many of the racial slurs in colloquial use are nothing more than common names for nonsapient species (for example, the Human term *lizard*, to describe Aandrisks; the Quelin term *tik*, to describe Humans; the Aandrisk term *sersh*, to describe Quelin). Though these terms are offensive, examining them objectively reveals a point of major biological interest. All demeaning implications aside, we Aandrisks do look like some of the native reptilian species of Earth. Humans do look like larger, bipedal versions of the hairless primates that plague the sewer systems of Quelin cities. Quelin do bear some resemblance to the snapping crustaceans found all over Hashkath. And yet, we evolved separately, and on different worlds. My people and the lizards of Earth do not share an evolutionary tree, nor do Humans and tiks, nor Quelin and sersh. Our points of origin are spread out across the galaxy. We hail from systems that remained self-contained for billions of years, with evolutionary clocks that all began at different times. How is it possible that when meeting our galactic neighbors for the first time, we are all instantly reminded of creatures back home—or in some cases, of ourselves?

The question becomes even more complicated when we start

to look beyond our superficial differences to the wealth of similarities. All sapient species have brains. Let us consider that seemingly obvious fact for a moment. Despite our isolated evolutionary paths, we all developed nervous systems with a central hub. We all have internal organs. We all share at least some of the same physical senses: hearing, touch, taste, smell, sight, electroreception. The grand majority of sapients have either four or six limbs. Bipedalism and opposable digits, while not universal, are shockingly common. We are all made from chromosomes and DNA, which themselves are made from a select handful of key elements. We all require a steady intake of water and oxygen to survive (though in varying quantities). We all need food. We all buckle under atmospheres too thick or gravitational fields too strong. We all die in freezing cold or burning heat. We all die, period.

How can this be? How is it that life, so diverse on the surface, has followed the same patterns throughout the galaxy—not just in the current era, but over and over again? We see this pattern in the ruins of the Arkanic civilization at Shessha, or the ancient fossil beds on the now-barren world of Okik. This is a question that scientific communities have wrestled with for centuries, and it seems unlikely that an answer will present itself in the near future. There are many theories— asteroids carrying amino acids, supernovae blowing organic material out into neighboring systems. And yes, there is the fanciful story of a hyperadvanced sapient race "seeding" the galaxy with genetic material. I admit that the "Galactic Gardener" hypothesis has fueled the plots of some of my favorite science fiction sims, but scientifically speaking, it is nothing more than wishful thinking. You cannot have a theory without evidence, and there is absolutely none that supports this idea (no matter what the conspiracy theorists lurking on Linking feeds would have you believe).

For my part, I think that the best explanation is the simplest one. The galaxy is a place of laws. Gravity follows laws. The life cycles of stars and planetary systems follow laws. Subatomic particles follow laws. We know the exact conditions that will cause the formation of a red dwarf, or a comet, or a black hole. Why, then, can we not acknowledge that the universe follows similarly rigid laws of biology? We have only ever discovered life on similarly sized terrestrial moons and planets, orbiting within a narrow margin around hospitable stars. If we all evolved on such kindred worlds, why is it such a surprise that our evolutionary paths have so much in common? Why can we not conclude that the right combination of specific environmental factors will always result in predictable physical adaptations? With so much evidence staring us in the face, why does this debate continue?

The answer, of course, is that the laws of biology are nearly impossible to test, and scientists hate that. We can launch probes to test theories of gravity and space-time. We can put rocks in pressure cookers and split atoms in classrooms. But how does one test a process as lengthy and multifaceted as evolution? There are labs today that struggle to find the funding to keep a project running for three standards—imagine the funding needed to run a project for millennia! As it stands, there is no way for us to efficiently test the conditions that produce specific biological adaptations, beyond the most rudimentary observations (aquatic climates produce fins, cold climates produce fur or blubber, and so on). There have been bold attempts at creating software that could accurately predict evolutionary paths, such as the Aeluon-funded Tep Preem Project (which, though well-intentioned, has yet to unravel the mysteries of biological law). The problem with such endeavors is that there are too many variables to consider, many of which we remain ignorant of. We simply don't have

enough data, and the data that we do possess is still beyond
our understanding.

We are experts of the physical galaxy. We live on
terraformed worlds and in massive orbital habitats. We tunnel
through the sublayer to hop between stellar systems. We escape
planetary gravity with the ease of walking out the front door.
But when it comes to evolution, we are hatchlings, fumbling
with toys. I believe this is why many of my peers still cling to
theories of genetic material scattered by asteroids and
supernovae. In many ways, the idea of a shared stock of genes
drifting through the galaxy is far easier to accept than the
daunting notion that none of us may ever have the intellectual
capacity to understand how life truly works.

|||||||||||||||||||||||||||||||||||||||||||||||||||||||||||||||||

INTRO TO HARMAGIAN COLONIAL HISTORY

Sissix peeked around the door frame. The hallway was empty. If she moved fast, she might make it to the med bay before anybody saw her.

She hugged a bathrobe—borrowed from a pile of Kizzy's clean laundry—around herself and hurried forward. As she moved, the itch spread up from her thighs and over her belly. She rubbed her palms against it through the fabric, barely resisting the urge to dig in with her claws. She wanted to throw off the robe and roll around against the metal floor, against a rough-barked tree, against a sanding block, *anything*, so long as she could rid herself of this dry burning aching shallow hateful *itch*.

"Whoa, Sis," Jenks said, skidding to a halt as she rounded a corner. "You almost ran me—" His words stopped once he got a look at her. "Holy *shit*, you look terrible."

"Thanks, Jenks, you're such a help," she said, continuing on her way. She wasn't embarrassed, she told herself, just angry. Yes, angry that this had happened at all, angry at how many times in her life she'd had to put up with it, angry at people not just *leaving her the hell alone*.

"Sissix, hey," Rosemary said, appearing from behind a door, scrib in hand. "I was coming to see—oh." Her dumb, wet mammal eyes widened. She brought a hand to her mouth.

"I'm fine," Sissix said, never pausing for a moment. With as big as the ship was, you'd think it was possible for a person to get from point A to point B without constantly running into—"Fuck *off*, Corbin," Sissix said to the pink Human, who had just ascended from the lower decks. He froze at the top of the staircase, looking stupid and confused as she hurried past.

She burst into the med bay, shutting the door as soon as she was through. Dr. Chef looked up from his workstation. He rumbled sympathetically.

"Oh, poor girl," he said. "You're molting."

"I'm early, too." She glanced at herself in the mirror. Blistering pockets of dead skin had separated from her face, tearing raggedly at the edges. "I didn't think I'd start for another three tendays, and I haven't—*aargh*!" The itch started up again, though it had never really stopped. Her whole face felt like it was crawling with flies. She gave in to the impulse and clawed.

"Hey, now, none of that," Dr. Chef said, coming forward to take her wrists. "You'll hurt yourself."

"No, I won't," Sissix said. She was acting childish, but she didn't care. Her face was about to fall off. She had a right to be petulant.

Dr. Chef pushed up her sleeve. "Really," he said. He lifted her arm so she could see the light claw marks on her flaking skin. A faint crust of blood lingered where her claws had scratched too deep during the night.

"Stars, you're parental sometimes," Sissix mumbled.

"I feed you and heal you, how else am I supposed to be? Take off that robe. Let's sort you out."

"Thank you." She took off her robe as Dr. Chef opened a storage panel. He took out a misting bottle and a *riksith*—a small, flat board with a rough coating on one side. Kizzy had once called it "a nail file for your entire self."

"Where's worst?" Dr. Chef asked.

Sissix lay back on the examination table. "Everywhere." She sighed. "My arms, I guess."

Dr. Chef gently took her right arm, the one with the bloody patch, and sprayed medicated mist over it. The dry skin went translucent, lifting at the edges. He went to work with the *riksith*, rubbing the wet pieces away. Sissix breathed a little easier, urging the rest of her body to be patient. Dr. Chef took one of her fingers between his own, examining it. "How's the skin feel here?"

"Tight. It's not ready to come up."

"Oh, I think it is. It just doesn't know it yet." He moistened her skin and, with steady pressure, massaged her hand from wrist to claws. After a few minutes, she could feel an edge come loose near her wrist. Dr. Chef worked his fingers underneath, carefully, gripping it between two fingerpads. In one swift motion, he tore the dead skin free from her entire hand, like pulling off a glove.

Sissix yelped, then moaned. The new skin was sensitive, but the itch there was gone. She exhaled. "Stars, you're good at that."

"I've had some practice," he said, continuing up her arm with the *riksith*.

Sissix craned her neck up to make sure the door was fully closed. "Do you ever get tired of Humans?"

"On occasion. I think that's normal for anyone living with people other than their own. I'm sure they get tired of us, too."

"I'm definitely tired of them today," Sissix said, laying her head back. "I'm tired of their fleshy faces. I'm tired of their smooth fingertips. I'm tired of how they pronounce their Rs. I'm tired of their inability to smell anything. I'm tired of how clingy they get around kids that don't even belong to them. I'm tired of how neurotic they are about being naked. I want to smack every single one of them around until they realize how needlessly complicated they make their families and their social lives and their—their *everything*."

Dr. Chef nodded. "You love them and you understand them, but sometimes you wish they—and me and Ohan, too, I'm sure—could be more like ordinary people."

"Exactly." She sighed, her frustration simmering down. "And it's not like they've done anything wrong. You know how much this crew means to me. But today . . . I don't know. It feels like having a mess of younger hatchmates who won't stop playing with your toys. They're not breaking anything and you know they're only trying to please you, but they're so little and annoying, and you want them all to fall down a well. Temporarily."

Dr. Chef gave a rumbling chuckle. "It seems your diagnosis is more complicated than just a premature molt."

"How so?"

He smiled. "You're homesick."

She sighed again. "Yeah."

"We're stopping off at Hashkath before the end of the standard, right? That's not so horribly far," he said, patting her head. He stopped and rubbed one of her feathers between his fingerpads. "Have you been taking your mineral supplements?"

She glanced away. "Sometimes."

"You need to take them *all times*. Your feathers are a little limp."

"I'm molting."

Dr. Chef frowned. "It's not because you're molting," he said. "It's because you're deficient in the basic nutrients that every Aandrisk needs. If you don't start taking your minerals regularly, I'm going to start feeding you moss paste."

She made a face. The very mention of the stuff brought back childhood memories of the taste: bitter, dusty, lingering. "Okay, hatch father, whatever you say."

Dr. Chef rumbled in thought.

"What?"

"Ah, nothing. The phrase just struck me as odd," he said, his voice light. "I was only ever a mother."

"I'm sorry," Sissix said. "I didn't mean—"

"Oh, don't. It's only true." He looked back to her, the twinkle returning to his eye. "Besides, if you think of me as a parent, maybe you'll listen when I tell you to take your damn minerals."

She laughed. "I doubt it. There was a stretch in my childhood when my hatch family couldn't get me to eat anything but snapfruit." She hissed as he worked the *riksith* against a stubborn patch on her shoulder.

"At least snapfruit's good for you. And somehow it doesn't surprise me that you were a willful child." He thought aloud, and laughed. "I bet you were a real pain."

"Of course I was," Sissix said with a grin. "I wasn't a person yet."

Dr. Chef's cheeks rippled in disagreement. "Now, see, there's something about *your* species that I will never understand."

She let out a congenial sigh. "You and the rest of the galaxy," she said. Honestly, what was it about that concept that was so difficult for others to grasp? She would never, ever understand the idea that a child, especially an *infant*, was of more value than an adult who had already gained all the skills needed to benefit the community. The death of a new hatchling was so common as to be expected. The death of a child about to feather, yes, that was sad. But a real tragedy was the loss of an adult with friends and lovers and family. The idea that a loss of *potential* was somehow worse than a loss of *achievement and knowledge* was something she had never been able to wrap her brain around.

Dr. Chef glanced over his shoulder, even though no one had entered the room. "Hey, I have a confession to make."

"Oh?"

"I haven't told anybody else this. This is secret. Top, top secret." He had lowered his voice as much as he physically could.

Sissix nodded with exaggerated seriousness. "I will say nothing."

"You know how you said Humans can't smell anything?"

"Mmm-hmm."

"I'm sure you've noticed that the Humans aboard this ship don't smell nearly as bad as other Humans."

"Yeah. I've gotten used to them."

"Wrong." He paused with dramatic importance. "I routinely mix a potent antiodor powder into the soap dispensers in the showers. I rub it into Kizzy's solid soap, too."

Sissix stared at him for a moment before crooning with laughter. "Oh," she said, gasping for breath. "Oh, you don't."

"I certainly do," he said, puffing his cheeks. "I started doing it not a tenday after I took this job. And do you know what the best part is?"

"They can't tell the difference?"

Dr. Chef let loose an amused harmony. "They can't tell the difference!"

They were both still laughing when Ashby walked through the door. His hair was wet. He had clearly just bathed. Sissix and Dr. Chef fell silent. The laughter returned, even stronger than before.

"Do I want to know?" Ashby said, his eyes shifting between them.

"We're making fun of Humans," Sissix said.

"Right," said Ashby. "Then I definitely don't want to know." He nodded toward her. "Molt came early?"

"Yeah."

"My sympathies. I'll take over your cleaning shift."

"Oh, you're the best." That was wonderful news. Cleaning products and new skin did not mix well.

"Remember that next time you're laughing at us lowly primates."

Rosemary sat flicking through files in her office—well, what passed for an office. It had been a storage room before she arrived, and technically still was, given the modest stack of crates against the far wall. The whole setup was a far cry from the sleek desk she'd had at Red Rock Transport, even as an intern, but she liked Dr. Chef's snack counter far more than the austere corporate cafeteria, and besides, she didn't need anything fancy to do her job. She had a simple desk and a big interface panel, and a small pixel plant Jenks had given her to make up for the lack of a window (why was it that people who worked with numbers always got tucked away in back rooms?). The plant looked nothing like the real thing, of course. The smiling face and color-changing petals resembled nothing in nature. It was programmed with some behavioral recognition software that could tell when she'd gone awhile without standing or drinking or taking a break, and would chirp cheerful reminders in response. "Hey, there! You need to hydrate!" "How about a snack?" "Take a walk! Stretch it out!" The effect was cheesy, and sometimes a little jarring when she was focused on her work, but she appreciated the sentiment.

She sipped a mug of boring tea as she puzzled over one of Kizzy's expense sheets. The mech tech had a habit of annotating things with shorthand that she alone understood. At first, Rosemary had assumed that it was some sort of tech lingo, but no, Jenks had quietly confirmed that this was Kizzy's own special way of staying organized. Rosemary squinted at the screen. 5500 *credits (ish)—WRSS*. She made a flicking motion with her left hand, pulling up a file entitled "Kizzyspeak," her cheat sheet for acronyms that she *had* deciphered. ES (Engine Stuff). TB (Tools and Bits). CRCT (Circuits). But no, WRSS wasn't there. She made a note to ask Kizzy about it.

The door spun open, and Corbin entered the room. Before she could say hello, he set a black mechanical object on her desk.

"What's this?" he asked.

Her heart hammered, as it usually did whenever Corbin approached her. Speaking to him always felt like more of an ambush than a conversation. She looked at the object. "That's the saline filter I ordered for you."

"Yes," he said. "Notice anything?"

Rosemary swallowed. She looked harder at the filter, which she only recognized as a filter because there'd been a picture of it on the merchant's Linking page. She gave an awkward smile. "I can't say that I know much about algae tech," she said, trying to keep her voice easy.

"That much is obvious," Corbin said. He flipped the filter around and pointed to the label. "Model 4546-C44." He stared at her, expectantly.

Oh no. Rosemary's mind raced, trying to remember the order form. There had been so many . . . "Was that not what you wanted?"

Corbin's sour face answered her question. "I specifically asked for the C45. The C44 has a coupling port that is narrower than the junction in the tank. I'll have to add a new attachment in order to make it connect properly."

Rosemary had been pulling up archived forms as he spoke. There it was: Triton Advanced saline filter, model 4546-C45. *Shit.* "I'm so sorry, Corbin. I don't know what happened. I must've selected the wrong model. But at least this one will work, right?" The second the words were out of her mouth, she knew they had been a mistake.

"That's not the point, Rosemary," Corbin said, as if speaking to a child. "What if I had required something more vital than a saline filter? You said it yourself, you don't know much about algae tech. You can get away with mistakes like this in some cushy planetside office, but not on a long-haul ship. The smallest component can be the difference between getting to port safely and decompressing out in the open."

"I'm sorry," Rosemary said again. "I'll be more careful next time."

"See that you are." Corbin picked up the filter and walked to the door. "It really isn't that hard," he said with his back to her. The door spun shut behind him.

Rosemary sat staring at her desk. Sissix had told her not to let Corbin get under her skin, but she *had* screwed up this time, and it was a careless mistake, too. Decompressing didn't sound so bad right then.

"Aw, it's not so bad!" chirped the pixel plant. "Give yourself a hug!"

"Oh, shut up," Rosemary said.

Ashby tripped over a length of tubing as he walked through the engine room. "What—" He craned his head around the corner to find an avalanche of cables pouring out of the wall. The entire bracing panel had been removed. He tiptoed his way around the tangled mess, careful not to step on any fluid-filled tubes. As he approached the open wall, he heard someone sniff.

"Kizzy?"

The mech tech was sitting inside the wall, hugging her knees, tools scattered alongside. Her face was smudged with gunk and grease, as usual, but a tear or two had created clean pathways down her cheeks. She looked up at him pitifully. Even the ribbons in her hair looked limp.

"I'm having a bad day," she said.

Ashby leaned inside the open panel. "What's up?"

She sniffed again, rubbing her nose with the back of her hand. "I slept awful, I had nightmares out the ass, and by the time I got to sleep, my alarm was going off, so today was dumb from the get-go, and then I was like, hey, I've still got some jam cakes left, and that cheered me up, but then I got to the kitchen and somebody ate the last of 'em last night and they didn't ask me at all, and I still don't know who it was, so then I went to shower, and I whacked my knee against the sink, like a genius, and it's totally bruised, and I had a mouthful of dentbots at the time, so I kinda swallowed some, and Dr. Chef says it's okay but I have a tummyache, which he said would happen, and then I finally got to take my stupid shower, but I noticed that the pressure was weird, so I started poking around the water reclamation systems, and I can tell there's a whole line of cabling that's fucked up, but I haven't found it yet, and now there's this big mess on the floor and I still haven't gotten to any of the other stuff I needed to do today, and then I remembered that today's my cousin Kip's birthday, and he always has the best parties and I'm totally missing it." She sniffled again. "And I know how stupid that all sounds, but I am just not with it today. Not at all."

Ashby put his hand on top of hers. "We all have days like that."

"I guess."

"But you know, it's not even lunchtime yet. There's time for it to get better from here."

She gave a glum nod. "Yeah."

"What was on your to-do list today?"

"Cleaning, mostly. The air filters all need a scrub. A sunlamp down in the Fishbowl needs new wiring. And there's a floor panel coming loose in Ohan's room."

"Is any of that vital?"

"No. But it needs to get done."

"Just worry about getting the water lines fixed today. The rest can wait." He squeezed her hand. "And hey. There's nothing I can do about your cousin's birthday, but I know how tough that is. I'm sorry we've got such a long haul this time."

"Oh, stop," she said. "It's oodles of cash and I love what we do. It's not like I'm your indentured servant or something. It was my choice to leave home."

"Just because you leave home doesn't mean you stop caring about it. You wouldn't get homesick otherwise. And your family knows you care. I keep an eye on our Linking traffic, you know. I see how many vid packs get sent to your family."

Kizzy gave a mighty sniff and pointed to the hallway. "You have to go now," she said. "Because I have to work and you're making me cry more. Not in a bad way. But you're making me all mushy and if I hug you I'll get gunk all over that nice shirt, which really brings out your eyes, by the way."

"Hey, everybody," Lovey said through the nearest vox. "There's a mail drone inbound. Packages onboard for Ashby, Corbin, Jenks, Dr. Chef and Kizzy. It'll be here in about ten minutes."

"Eek!" cried Kizzy. "Mail! A mail drone!" She tumbled out of the wall and ran down the hallway with her arms outstretched like shuttle wings. "Interstellar goodies iiiiiiiincomiiiiiing!"

Ashby grinned. "Told you the day would get better," he called after her. She was too busy "whoosh"-ing to reply.

The cargo bay hatch adjusted itself, shrinking down to fit the mail drone's delivery port. As Ashby and the others waited, Sissix walked through the door. She'd put on a pair of trousers, and it looked like Dr. Chef had taken care of the molting problem.

"Hey," Ashby said. "Feeling better?"

"Much," she said. Her skin was oddly bright, and a few dry

ridges still lingered, but at least she didn't look like a peeling onion anymore.

"I don't think there's anything for you."

"So?" She shrugged and smiled. "I'm nosy."

"Just a moment," Lovey said. "I'm scanning the contents for contaminants."

"Oh boy, oh boy, oh boy," said Kizzy. "It's my birthday!"

"Your birthday's not until middle year," said Jenks.

"But it *feels* like my birthday. I love getting mail."

"It's probably just those lockjaw clips you ordered."

"Jenks. Do you know how great lockjaw clips are? There is nothing they can't hold down. Even my *hair* can't work its way out of them, and that's saying a lot."

Ashby glanced over his shoulder at her. "I'm going to pretend like you weren't talking about using the tech supplies I buy as hair accessories."

Kizzy pressed her lips together. "Only in emergencies."

"All clear," Lovey said. The hatch hissed open. A tray slid forward, holding a large, sealed container. Ashby took the container and swiped his wristwrap over the scan seal. The container gave an affirmative beep. A corresponding beep echoed from the mail drone on the other side of the hull. The tray retracted and the hatch closed. There was a muffled clank as the mail drone detached, off to find its next recipient.

Ashby unsealed the lid and sorted through the parcels within. They were all plainly packaged, but even so, there was something charming about a bunch of boxes and tubes marked with his crew members' names. It did feel a little like a holiday.

"Here, Kizzy," he said, handing her a large package. "Before you explode."

Kizzy's eyes grew wide. "It's not lockjaw clips! It's not lockjaw clips! I know who makes labels like this!" She slid back the lid and cheered. "It's from my dads!" She dropped cross-legged onto the floor and pulled the lid open. Atop the package's contents—snacks and sundries, it looked like—was an info chip. Kizzy pulled her scrib from her belt, plugged in the chip and began reading the text that appeared on the screen. Her face melted with sentiment. "It's a just 'cause box," she said. "They are the best. The *best*." She tore into a fresh pack of fire shrimp as she continued reading.

Ashby pulled out a small domed container blinking with biohazard warnings. "Do I even want to know what this is?"

Dr. Chef puffed his cheeks. "Those will be my new seedlings. Completely harmless, I assure you. They have to put those warnings on any live cargo."

"I know. It's just . . . unnerving."

Dr. Chef leaned close to Ashby, his eyes twinkling. "Don't tell, but if this is the order I think it is, I've now got a few starters of rosemary plants."

Ashby flipped over a box with a familiar brand logo, the same one he'd seen on a lot of algae tech. "Corbin," he said, handing over the box. "This looks like it's for you."

Corbin opened the box and took out a circulation pump. He peered at the label and gave a short nod. "Seems our clerk can read order forms after all." He headed for the exit.

"Well . . . good," said Ashby noncommittally. He pulled a tiny box from the mail crate. "Jenks."

Jenks opened the box and removed an info chip.

"What's that?" Sissix asked.

"It's from Pepper," Jenks said. He stared at the chip for a moment. "Oh, I bet it's those lateral circuit specs she mentioned last time I saw her."

"Those sounded sweet," Kizzy said. She frowned. "Why not just send them to your scrib?"

Jenks shrugged and put the chip in his pocket. "You know Pepper. She does things in her own special way."

Ashby leaned over the mail crate. There was one small, flat package remaining, addressed to himself. The label had no indication of who had sent it, but it required a wristwrap scan. A flap snapped open as his wrist passed over it, and a frail rectangular object fell into Ashby's waiting palm.

"What is that?" Sissix asked.

Jenks let out a low whistle and stepped closer. "That's *paper*."

Kizzy's head snapped up. "Whoa," she said, goggling at the object. "Is that a *letter*? Like a physical one?" She jumped to her feet. "Can I touch it?"

Jenks smacked her hand away. "You've got fire shrimp crumbs all over your fingers."

Kizzy stuck a finger in her mouth, sucked it clean and wiped it off on her worksuit.

Jenks smacked her hand again. "Now you've got crumbs *and* spit. A letter's not a scrib, Kizzy. You can't wash it off."

"It's that fragile?"

"It's made from very thin sheets of dried tree pulp. What do you think?"

Ashby ran his fingers along the leaflike edges, doing his best to look nonchalant. It was from Pei, it had to be. Who else would go to that much trouble to send a message that couldn't be monitored? He turned the letter over in his hands. "How do I . . . uh . . ."

"Here," Jenks said, extending his palm. "My hands are clean." Ashby handed over the letter. "Kiz, do you have your knife on you?"

Kizzy unsnapped a folded utility knife from her belt and handed it to Jenks. Her eyes widened with realization. "Wait, you're gonna *cut it*?"

"That's how you get the letter out of the envelope." He flicked open the blade. "Would you rather I tear it?"

Kizzy looked horrified.

Jenks deftly sliced the paper open. "My mom used to give me letters on special occasions when I was a kid," he said. "*Very* special occasions. This stuff's expensive as hell." He raised a wry eyebrow at Ashby. "Somebody must like you a lot to send you this."

"Like who?" Kizzy asked.

Jenks put his fist up to his mouth and gave an exaggerated, harrumphing cough.

"*Ohhh*," said Kizzy in a stage whisper. "I'll be going back to my snacks then." She backed away with a knowing chuckle.

Ashby glanced over to the others. Sissix was smirking. Dr. Chef's whiskers twitched in amusement. "All right, all right, shut up, all of you." He walked away, leaving the others to examine their new items while he read his letter in peace.

> Hello, Ashby. Before you become too impressed with my ability to print by hand, you should know that I wrote all of this out on my scrib first. I tore through one of the sheets on my first try. Honestly, how did your species communicate like this for millennia without becoming nervous wrecks? Oh, wait, right. Never mind.
>
> It feels like ages since Port Coriol. I miss your hands. I miss sharing a bed. I miss sharing stories. I'll never understand how you can be so patient with someone who can't talk to you for tendays at a time. I'm not sure one of my own would've stayed with me through this. You Humans and your blind stubbornness. Believe me, it's—

"Jenks, Ashby, Sissix, anyone." It was Lovey. She sounded frantic. "We're in trouble."

Everyone in the cargo bay stopped to stare at the vox. Out in the open, *trouble* was even less of a good thing than it was on the ground. "What's the problem?" Ashby said.

"There's a ship, another ship, coming in right at us. They've been blocking my scans with a dispersal field. Ashby, I'm so sorry—"

"That's not your fault, Lovey," Jenks said. "Stay calm."

"What kind of ship?" Ashby said.

"I don't know," Lovey said. "Smaller than us, pinhole drive. I think it's a very small homesteader, but I don't know why a homestead ship would—"

Corbin came running back into the cargo bay. "Ship," he gasped. "Out the window. It's—"

The whole ship rocked. The sounds of falling objects clanged down the hallway. Everyone started shouting. Ashby's stomach dropped. Something had hit them.

"Lovey, what—"

"Some kind of weapon blast. Our navigation's knocked out."

Sissix hissed profanities. Kizzy nodded at Jenks and jumped to her feet. "Let's go," she said.

"No," Lovey said. "I can get us moving in five minutes, but the primary navigation hub's completely fused. I can't tell which way we're going."

"Fused?" Kizzy cried. "What the fuck did they hit us with? Lovey, are you sure?"

Sissix looked at Ashby. "I can navigate the old-fashioned way, but not in five minutes, not if we want to be safe about it."

"Pirates," said Jenks. "Remember, Kiz, on the news, fucking pirates following mail drones in, using scatter bursts to fry nav systems—"

"Oh, no," moaned Corbin.

Ashby stared at Jenks. "Lovey, how long until they reach us?"

"Half a minute. There's nothing I can do. I'm sorry."

"This isn't happening," Kizzy said. "They can't."

"Shit," said Jenks. "Quick, everybody, hide your stuff." He

pulled open an empty crate and threw Kizzy's package in. Dr. Chef followed suit. There was a crash, a horrible, scraping, wrenching crash, right into the cargo bay doors. Corbin jumped behind a crate and covered his head.

"They're overriding the door controls," Lovey said. "Ashby, I—"

"It's okay, Lovey," Ashby said. "We'll take care of it." He had no idea what that would entail.

"Oh fuck," Kizzy said, tugging at her hair. "Oh, fuck, fuck, fuck."

"Stay calm," Dr. Chef said. He put his arm around Kizzy's shoulders. "Everyone stay calm."

Ashby took a few steps toward the bay doors, dumbfounded. This wasn't real. It couldn't be. A whirring sound on the other side argued otherwise. The doors clanked open. Sissix stood beside him, shoulders back, feathers on end. "I don't know what to do," she said.

"Me neither," Ashby said. *Think, dammit!* His brain cycled through a jumble of options—find a weapon, run away, hide, hit them with . . . *with something*—but there was no time. Four sapients in hulking mech-suits came through the bay doors, all carrying battered pulse rifles. Their suits were large, bigger than a Human, but the creatures housed within were small, spindly, birdlike.

Akaraks.

Ashby had seen Akaraks before, on Port Coriol. Everyone knew how the Harmagians had treated them, back in the colonial days. Their planet was left barren, their water sources polluted, their forests stripped. Their homeworld had nothing for them, but neither did anywhere else. They were a rare sight out in the galaxy, but they could be found here and there, working in scrapyards or begging on corners.

Or, if they had run out of options, boarding ships and taking what they pleased.

Ashby put up his palms. The Akaraks' voices came from tiny voxes inlaid below their helmets, shrieking and shrill. They weren't speaking Klip.

"Don't shoot," Ashby said. "Please, I can't understand you. Klip? Do you speak Klip?"

There was no discernible response, only shrieks and clicks and angry waves of their weapons. The words meant nothing to him, but the guns did.

Ashby felt a bead of sweat trickle down his brow. He brushed his hand across his face. "Okay, listen, we'll cooperate, just—"

The world exploded in pain as an Akarak swung the butt of its rifle up to meet Ashby's jaw. The Akaraks, the cargo bay, Sissix shouting, Kizzy screaming, Jenks cursing, all of it disappeared behind a curtain of red light. His knees buckled. The floor rushed up to meet his face. Then, nothing.

Rosemary wasn't sure what she'd been expecting to see when she ran down to the cargo bay, but there was too much going on for her to think clearly. The bay doors had been wrenched open. Four armed Akaraks—*Akaraks?*—wearing mech-suits were yelling at everyone in some weird Harmagian-inspired dialect she couldn't make sense of. Ashby was unconscious (she hoped) on the floor, cradled by Kizzy, who was crying. The rest of the crew were on their knees with their hands in the air. Rosemary barely had time to process any of it before the Akaraks, startled by her sudden appearance, pointed their weapons at her, croaking strange words in a tone that would've sounded angry in any language.

"I—" Rosemary stammered, raising her palms in the air. "What—"

The Akarak closest to her—xyr mech-suit was trimmed with blue—ran at her, croaking the whole way. Xe shoved a gun in her face. Jenks started yelling back at the other Akaraks: "She's unarmed, you fucking animals, leave her alone . . ." The biggest Akarak, xyr suit nearly three times Jenks's size, shook xyr weapon at the comp tech and pointed toward Ashby. The threat was unmistakable. *Be quiet, or the same will happen to you.* Jenks's hands balled into fists. There was a hum as the Akaraks' weapons began to charge.

Am I about to die? Rosemary wondered. The thought was bewildering.

"Rosemary," Sissix said over the din. "Hanto. Try Hanto."

Rosemary wet her lips, trying to ignore the weapon beneath her nose. She met Sissix's eyes—scared, but insistent, encouraging. She dug her fingernails into her palms, so that no one could see her hands shaking. She looked down the gun barrel. She spoke. *"Kiba vus Hanto em?"*

The Akaraks fell silent. Everyone froze.

"Yes," Blue Suit said. Xe turned xyr head back toward the others and pointed at Rosemary. *"Finally."* The gun did not move.

The big Akarak stormed toward her. *"We will take your food and all supplies that are of use to us,"* xe said. *"If you do not comply, we will kill you."*

"We will comply," Rosemary said. *"There is no need for violence. My name is* Rosemary. *You may call me Ros'ka."* This had been her chosen name in secondary school Harmagian class. *"I will speak your needs to my crew."*

Blue Suit pulled the gun back, but kept it pointed at her. The Akaraks croaked among themselves.

The big Akarak gestured acknowledgment to Rosemary. *"I am our captain. You will not be able to pronounce my name, and I will not pretend to have another. Are there others elsewhere aboard your ship?"*

"Our Navigator is in his quarters. He is a peaceful man and is of no danger to anyone." Rosemary thought it best to not confuse the issue with plural pronouns.

Captain Big huffed. *"If this is a trick, I will shoot you."* Xe turned and croaked to one of the others, who ran up the stairs.

"What's going on?" Sissix asked.

"They're going to get Ohan," said Rosemary. "I've explained they're no threat, and that we're willing to cooperate." She cleared her throat and switched back to Hanto. *"My crew agrees to help. Please tell us what you require."*

"Food," Blue Suit said. *"And tech."*

A thought appeared. Rosemary knew little of Akarak culture, but from what she had read of them, she did know that they greatly valued the concepts of balance and fairness. The idea of taking more than you could make use of hadn't even occurred to them until the Harmagians showed up. She had heard that those values still lingered; that much was apparent even in the phrasing that Captain Big had chosen: *We will take your food and all supplies that are of use to us.* In Hanto, the semantics of those words strongly implied *"and nothing else."* Her mind raced, wondering if that scrap of knowledge was enough to gamble with. A large part of her argued in favor of self-preservation—*shut up, just give them everything, you're going to get shot*—but the braver thought won out. *"How many are aboard your ship? Are there any children?"*

Blue Suit snarled and raised the gun again. *"What difference does it make how many we are? You will do as we say!"*

Rosemary wiggled her fingers in a calming gesture. *"I will. But if there is any way that you can spare us enough food to last us until the next market, we would be humbly grateful. We do not wish to die out here anymore than you do. Furthermore, I have read that Akarak young have very specific nutritional needs. If you have children aboard, we must make sure that our food does not lack for nourishment."*

Captain Big considered this. *"We do have children aboard,"* xe said at last. Rosemary took this as a good sign. Ashby's injured face and the pulse rifles aside, these people didn't seem violent. Just desperate. *"And yes, their needs are great. We may not find what we need aboard your ship."*

"Then let me offer this," Rosemary said, treading carefully. *"One of us will show you our food stores. As I understand it, the Kesh To'hem market is less than a tenday from here. We will not be traveling there, as we cannot stray from our flight path. Take from us only what you need to last you the trip to Kesh To'hem, and we will give you credits and trade-worthy supplies so that you may purchase more suitable food. This way your young will get what they need, and we will not starve on our journey."*

The Akaraks talked among themselves. Rosemary dug her nails in harder, hoping the pain would quiet the tremors beneath her skin. Her entire offer banked on a tiny piece of possibly erroneous info that she'd tucked away during one lone semester of Intro to Harmagian Colonial History. If she was wrong . . . well, she'd find out soon enough. At least they were all still breathing. Ashby *was* breathing, right?

"Rosemary?" Sissix said. "How are we doing?"

"We're okay," said Rosemary. *I hope.* "Hang on."

"We find this acceptable," Captain Big said. *"What sort of fuel do you use?"*

"Algae."

"We will take some of that as well."

"Are they asking about fuel?" Corbin said. "Because I just siphoned off the skim yesterday, and it's taken five tendays for this batch to get—"

"Corbin," Dr. Chef said with deadly calm. "Be quiet."

And for once, Corbin had nothing further to say.

"What did the pink man say?" Captain Big asked.

"He is our algaeist," Rosemary said. *"He is merely . . . concerned about the product he has worked so hard to produce. But you will have fuel. There is no trouble."*

Captain Big tapped xyr chin inside xyr mech-suit. *"If we take ten barrels, will you have enough to reach your next destination?"*

Rosemary asked Corbin the question. He nodded sullenly. *"Yes, ten barrels will not be a problem,"* she said. The conversation had gone from frightening to bizarre. The inflections that Captain Big was using didn't have a parallel in Klip, but in Hanto, they were downright polite. She would expect to hear this kind of talk in a shop or a restaurant, not while standing at gunpoint. It was as if the Akaraks thought of her as a merchant, with the threat of violence serving as currency.

"We will require technical supplies as well," Captain Big said. *"Our engines are in need of repair."*

Rosemary gestured understanding. "Kizzy, do you know anything about the ship they're flying? Would any of our tech be compatible?"

"Some of it, maybe. I dunno."

"Our tech believes some of our equipment may work with yours, but she can make no promises. She will help you find what you need."

"Very well," Captain Big said. *"You will accompany me, along with your tech, so that you may translate our needs. She"*— xe gestured at Blue Suit—*"will go with one of your crew to gather food. The others of my party will stay with the rest of your crew here. You seem to be a reasonable people, but we will not hesitate to kill you should you try to overthrow us."*

"You have our complete cooperation," said Rosemary. *"We do not wish for either of our crews to come to harm."*

Rosemary began to explain the deal to the rest of the crew. Everyone nodded, looking a little less tense, though still afraid.

The humming of the guns had stopped. *We might just get out of this*, Rosemary thought, just before the fourth Akarak reappeared and threw Ohan into the room.

The other Akaraks went nuts. A frenzied conversation took place, with the Akaraks all talking over each other and Rosemary trying to interject where she could.

"What the hell is going on?" Sissix asked.

"They want to take Ohan," Rosemary said.

The *Wayfarer's* crew exploded.

"What?" said Kizzy.

"My ass!" said Jenks.

"For what?" asked Sissix.

"To sell them," Rosemary said.

"*What?!*" Kizzy cried.

"A Pair would fetch a fine price on the right planet," Dr. Chef said.

"If it keeps you all from harm—" Ohan began.

"No," said Jenks. "No way. Rosemary, you tell those fucking birds in their fucking hackjob suits that they can shove—"

"Jenks, *shut the fuck up*," Kizzy said, holding Ashby's head protectively. His blood looked sticky on her hands.

"Stop it, stop it, all of you, you'll get us all killed," Corbin said.

"You shut up, too, Corbin."

"*Calm your crew,*" said Captain Big. "*Or there will be violence.*"

"Shut up, everybody, shut up," Rosemary yelled. She turned toward Captain Big. "*Ohan is part of our crew. We have cooperated with all your other demands, but this—*"

"*This man could end our poverty,*" said Captain Big. "*He would be of great use to us. You would do the same in our place.*"

"*No, I would not.*"

Captain Big pondered this. *"Perhaps. But even so, you have little choice right now."*

"Offer him something else," said Sissix.

"Like what?" Rosemary said.

"Ambi," said Kizzy. "Give him the ambi cells."

The Akaraks froze. At last, a word in Klip they understood. *"You have ambi aboard your vessel?"*

"Yes," said Rosemary. *"We will give you the ambi freely if you leave the Navigator with us."*

"What is to stop us from taking both the ambi and the Navigator?" Blue Suit asked, raising her rifle.

Rosemary felt her stomach sink. Fair point. "They want to know why they can't take the ambi *and* Ohan."

"Shit," Jenks said.

"Why do I ever say anything?" Kizzy moaned.

Dr. Chef spoke. "Tell them that Ohan is of no value to them."

Rosemary translated. The Akaraks demanded an explanation. "Why?" she asked Dr. Chef.

"Because Ohan is dying."

The *Wayfarer*'s crew turned to stare at Dr. Chef. Ohan closed their eyes and said nothing. Rosemary collected herself. It was a bluff, surely. She relayed the news to the Akaraks.

The Akaraks shrank back. The one who had thrown Ohan into the room recoiled. *"Is he contagious?"*

"I . . . don't think so," Rosemary said. "Dr. Chef, some help, please."

"Ohan is in the final stages of a Sianat Pair's life," Dr. Chef explained. "They will not last more than a year." He paused, and added: "Any buyer who might consider purchasing a Sianat Pair would be familiar enough with the species to know the signs."

Rosemary translated.

"You may be lying," Captain Big said. *"But the risk of wasting fuel and food on useless cargo outweighs the possible gains,*

especially in light of the ambi. We will leave him, then, but you will give us your entire stock of ambi cells."

Rosemary agreed. "Ohan stays," she said to the crew.

"Oh, stars," Kizzy said.

"But they want all the ambi."

"Fine," Sissix said.

"Good thing the GC's got our tab on this one," Jenks said.

Rosemary and Captain Big discussed logistics. Groups from both crews split up, leaving Jenks, Ohan and a barely conscious Ashby—stars, his eyes were finally open—under guard in the cargo bay. Rosemary took Kizzy's hand as they walked out the door with Captain Big. Kizzy squeezed back so hard that one of Rosemary's knuckles popped.

Jenks's voice followed them. "Have fun stealing our stuff, assholes! Rosemary, you want to translate that?"

She let that one go.

Ashby lay on the bed in the med bay, trying to move as little as possible. Both his hands were occupied. His right hand was outstretched beneath the medical scanner, where a thick beam of light showed him where to position his wristpatch. Dr. Chef sat on the other side of the scanner, *hrrming* as he input directions for Ashby's imubots. Somewhere beneath Ashby's skin, two platoons of bots had separated off from their daily patrols and were now repairing the fracture in his jaw and the bruise on his brain. Dr. Chef had said a lot about "granulation tissue' and "osteoblasts," but those things wouldn't have meant much to Ashby even if he hadn't been drifting along on a slow tide of painkillers. The part about lying still and not moving his jaw, though, that much he had understood. He could manage that.

His other hand was gripped tightly within Sissix's claws. She sat beside him, giving a play-by-play of everything that had happened after he'd blacked out. Every so often, she let go of his hand to let him type a question on her scrib. Dr. Chef had banned talking for the time being.

No one else was hurt. The ambi, the food, none of that mattered. They were things, and things could be replaced. His crew couldn't be. The relief he'd felt upon learning he was the only one who'd wound up in the med bay topped anything that the painkillers could give.

Where's everyone now? he wrote.

"Kizzy and Jenks are fixing the damage to the bay doors. They say it's mostly superficial. They already replaced the navigation hub, so that's working fine. Corbin started prepping a replacement algae batch the minute the Akaraks flew off. I think Rosemary's tallying our losses." She smirked. "And guess where Ohan are?"

Quarters?

Sissix shook her head. "They're sitting down in the cargo bay with the techs."

Ashby stared at her. He blinked.

"I know. They're not talking or anything, just sitting there in a corner, in their own little headspace, like always. But they haven't been back to their quarters at all, and they followed Kizzy down the hall when she went to grab some tools. Never thought I'd say this, but Ohan don't want to be alone right now."

Ashby blinked again. *Huh*, he wrote.

An hour passed. Dr. Chef gave a pleased nod and turned the monitor around for Ashby to see. The screen displayed a camera view from one of his imubots, which was doing . . . *something* to a big, white spongy wall (his jawbone, he supposed). Other bots scurried around the peripheries of the frame, like swimming spiders.

"You're coming along fine," Dr. Chef said. Ashby took his word for it. He had no idea what was going on in there, and he always found the experience of seeing inside his own body to be unsettling. "You can talk now, but small movements, please. The fracture hasn't fully healed yet. And your brain still needs some work."

"I could've told you that," Sissix said.

"Thanks," Ashby said, moving his mouth gingerly. "Your sympathy is appreciated." He licked his lips. The inside of his mouth felt stale. "Can I have some water?"

Sissix filled a cup from the sink. She held it to his mouth, helping him drink. "Need anything else?"

"No," he said. "Or, wait. Can you bring Rosemary in here?"

Sissix cocked her head toward the vox. "Lovey, did you catch that?"

"I'll get her for you," Lovey said. "It's good to hear your voice again, Ashby."

"Thanks, Lovey," Ashby said.

A few minutes later, a curly-haired head peeked around the doorway. "You wanted to see me?"

"Hey, Rosemary," Ashby said. "Have a seat." The pain meds made his speech sound sloppy, as if he'd had a few too many drinks. He sincerely hoped he wasn't drooling.

Rosemary pulled up a stool beside Sissix. "Are you okay?" she asked Ashby.

"I'm fine. Bastard busted my jaw, but it beats getting shot." He leaned his head back into the pillow, trying to think through the concussion and the medicated haze. "I don't know why that guy hit me." He rubbed his eyes, trying to fight the wooziness away.

"Just to scare us, probably," Sissix said. "Show us who's boss. I know *I* was scared." She laid her head on Ashby's arm.

Rosemary studied Ashby's face. Something had her attention. "What?" he asked.

"Did you touch your face at all while you were talking to the Akarak captain? Like you're doing now?"

"Um, yeah, maybe." Ashby pushed through the fog, trying to remember. "I don't know, it all happened so fast."

"Something like this, maybe?" Rosemary rubbed her eyes with her palm, as if she had a headache.

"Possibly. Yeah. Yeah, I think I did."

Rosemary grimaced. "That explains it. See, *this*—" She tucked her thumb back and held her fingers straight and flat, making her hand into a rough imitation of a Harmagian dactylus. She flexed her hand over her eyes, twice. "—is a really offensive thing to Harmagians. And those Akaraks' gestures and dialect were *very* Harmagian influenced."

"What's it mean?"

Rosemary cleared her throat. "It means you'd rather rub shit in your eyes than keep talking to them."

Ashby blinked. He and Sissix both burst into laughter. "Oh," he said, grabbing his jaw. "Oh, ow." His jaw wasn't quite ready for laughter yet.

"Careful," said Dr. Chef. "If it doesn't heal properly, we'll have to do this all over again."

Sissix was still chuckling at Ashby. "I'd have hit you for that, too."

"Yeah," said Ashby. He held his lips tight, trying to keep his jaw from moving too much. "Likewise."

"At least you told them off, right?"

"Right," he said, with a restrained smile. "I'm sure the psychological damage of my accidental insult cut them real deep."

"Speaking of damage," Rosemary said. She held up her scrib. "I've tallied our losses, I filed an incident report and I'm currently drafting a list for the Transport Board so they can cover—"

Ashby waved his palm at her. "We can talk about all that later. That's not why I asked you here."

"Oh."

"I wanted to thank you. Without you, I'm not sure we would've gotten out of this one as well as we did."

Rosemary looked embarrassed. "I don't know. I just got lucky. There are a lot of cultures I know nothing about."

"Maybe, but it was good luck nonetheless, and luck we wouldn't have had otherwise. More important, you had a cool head and kept everyone safe. Today would've been much, much worse if you hadn't been here." He reached out to take her hand. "I'm glad you're on my crew."

Rosemary started to say something, but whatever it was shifted into: "Oh, no." Her hand darted up to catch a tear running down her cheek. "Oh, stars, I'm sorry," she said. Another tear fell, and another. Rosemary put her face in her hands. The dam broke.

"Aw, hey now," Sissix said with a kind laugh, putting her arm around Rosemary's trembling shoulders. "Have you not had a chance to freak out yet?"

Rosemary shook her head, pressing her hand against her nose. Her whole face was leaking. *Poor kid*, Ashby thought. He wouldn't blame her if she wanted to take a safe planetside job after this. Hell, even *he* found the idea appealing.

"These Humans, huh?" Sissix said to Dr. Chef. "*I* took sometime to freak out. Didn't you?"

"I sure did," Dr. Chef said. He handed Rosemary a clean cloth. "Once I'd medicated Ashby and got his bots going, I locked myself in my office and yelled for a good ten minutes."

"*That's* what that was?" Ashby said. He had a dim memory of layers upon layers of haunting chords, cutting through the waves of pain. "I thought you were singing. It was really pretty."

Dr. Chef gave a short, loud laugh. "Ashby, if the Akaraks think rubbing shit in your eyes is bad, the things I said in my office would have permanently scarred them." He rumbled and cooed. "But Sissix is right, dear," he said, placing a hand on the back of Rosemary's head. "Your species does have a knack for emotional suppression. And as your doctor, I would like to say that diving straight into paperwork after negotiating at gunpoint wasn't a very healthy decision."

One of Rosemary's sobs turned into a solitary chuckle. "I'll remember that next time."

"No 'next time,' please," Sissix said. "I'd rather not do this again."

"Agreed," Dr. Chef said. He glanced at the bot monitor. "Ashby, you've got about two more hours before you're all patched up. Nothing you can do but lie there and take it easy."

"That's fine," Ashby said. "I could use a nap." The drugs were weighing on him, and conversing had worn him out.

"And I could use a meal. Ladies, would you care to accompany me to the kitchen? Let's see if we can't throw together some comfort food from whatever the Akaraks left behind." He patted Rosemary's back. "I've got some new seedlings that I think will make you smile."

Rosemary inhaled, pulling herself back together. "One more thing," she said. "About Ohan."

"Ah," Dr. Chef said. "Yes."

"Was it—"

"True? Yes, I'm afraid so. And I'm sorry I had to tear down Ohan's privacy like that. It was the only thing I could think to do."

"Stars," said Rosemary. "I had no idea."

"I just found out, too," Sissix said. She frowned at Ashby. "And I still don't understand why that is."

Ashby sighed. "We'll argue about this later, Sis. My head is swimming."

"Fine," she said. "You get to play the injury card this time." She tapped a claw on his chest. "Later."

Once alone in the med bay, Ashby reached for the paper letter tucked away in his pocket. He made himself push back the drugs' call for sleep just a few minutes longer.

— a trait I am glad of.

I don't know how long this run will take (it's a delicate one), and I know you won't be back to Central space until next standard. But I have more paper, so at least I can say hello when I make market stops. And I'll send you a scrib letter as soon as I'm clear. This paper has far too little space for me to write everything I want to say, so know this: I love you, and I think of you always.

Travel safe.

Pei

☆

Once the bay doors were fixed and a meal was consumed, Jenks did several things. First, he took a shower. The whole ship felt gross now, after having those mech-suit bastards pawing around. He couldn't scrub out the ship, but he could clean himself, at least. He ignored the fifteen-minute shower rule. It wouldn't be that much extra work for the water reclamation system, and today of all days, Kizzy would forgive him for it.

Back in his room, he retrieved the info chip from the pocket of his crumpled trousers. He sat naked on his bed, plugged the chip into his scrib and read the message.

Hey, buddy. Found a seller for that software upgrade we talked about. He's willing to get you the whole kit and kaboodle, but he wants to be paid up front, nonrefundable, nonnegotiable. You know how these specialty techs are.

The guy you need to talk to is Mr. Crisp. I've heard his name kicked around before. Solid reputation. He's got his own asteroid and everything. Hell of a programmer, good with custom work. He's expecting to hear from you. Contact info's below. Please don't share it with anyone.

And hey—think about what I told you. You sure this is the right upgrade for you?

Come see us again soon. I'll make dinner this time. Or, well,
I'll buy it, at least.
Pepper

His eyes lingered over the word "kit." He knew what Pepper
meant. He thought about what she had said at Port Coriol, about
responsibility and consequences. He thought about it just long
enough to be able to say that he'd done so. He put on some
trousers and walked down to Lovey's core.

They talked for hours. All the risks and dangers had been
spoken of before, a dozen times over. But as both comp techs
and AIs knew well, redundancy in the name of safety was always
a good idea.

"There are two things that bother me," Lovey said. "Not
enough to say no, but we need to make up our minds about them."

"Shoot."

"First, if I transfer into a kit, the ship will be without a
monitoring system. Since I'll effectively be quitting a job I care
very much about, I want to make sure I have a good replacement
lined up."

Jenks drummed his fingers against his lips as he thought. "I
don't know why, but something about installing a new AI feels
strange, under the circumstances. Do you think she'd be jealous,
seeing you walking around while she's living in your core?"

"Depends on the AI and whether or not she's interested in a
body to start with. But I do think it could cause problems. Say,
hypothetically, she sees me walking around, and she wants to
know why she can't have the same opportunity. Why I got a
choice that she didn't."

"That's a good point," Jenks said, frowning. "And it wouldn't
be fair." He sighed. "So then—"

"Don't give up yet, I'm not finished. What if a nonsentient
model replaces me?"

Jenks blinked. A nonsentient model could do Lovey's job, yes, with some heavy tweaking, but it would never be someone they could speak to in a relatable way. It would never really be part of the crew. "Wouldn't that bug you?"

"Why would it?"

"Living with an AI that was *designed* to be less intelligent than you, just smart enough to do hard work, but not allowed to grow into something more? I dunno, I've always been on the fence about that."

"You're sweet, but that's silly."

He smirked. "Why?"

Lovey paused. "Are you comfortable with the idea of beasts of burden? Horses pulling carts, that kind of thing?"

"Yeah, so long as they're treated well."

"Well, then, there you go."

"Hmm." He'd need to chew on that. "It'd be Ashby's call, in the end."

"That's the second thing that bothers me. We keep glossing over what Ashby's going to do when he learns what we're up to."

Jenks sighed again, heavily. "I honestly don't know. He's not going to be happy about it. But he won't report us. That's not his style. Best case, he gives me an earful, but lets us stay. Worst case, we have to leave."

"That worst case isn't unrealistic. He could lose his license if he's found knowingly carrying illegal tech."

"Yeah, but how often do we get searched? And when we do, it's not like—"

"Jenks."

"What? The chances of us getting caught—"

"*Exist.* I'm willing to take that risk. Ashby might not be. Is that something you're ready for? I'm not going to make you lose your job and your home over me. That's your choice, not mine."

He laid his hand against her core. "I know. I love this ship.

I love my job. I love this crew." He ran his palm down the smooth, flawless curve. "And I don't *want* to leave. But I won't be on the *Wayfarer* forever anyway. Someday, when the time's right, I'll go do other things. If that time gets chosen for me, well . . . okay."

"You're sure?"

He sat thinking, watching her light shine between his fingers. He thought of the familiar insides of the walls of the ship, the way Ashby trusted him to tweak them just right. He thought of the groove in his mattress that fit no one but him. He thought of drinking mek in the Fishbowl, Sissix laughing, Dr. Chef humming. He thought of Kizzy, who he knew he'd be sitting with in some sketchy spacer bar sixty years down the road, both of them old and obnoxious. "Yeah," he said quietly. "Yeah, I'm sure."

For a moment, Lovey said nothing. "Even if it came to that, they wouldn't hate you. These people are always going to be your friends."

"Yours, too."

"I don't know about that."

"I do." He fell quiet. "So. We're doing this?"

"Sounds like it to me." There was a smile in her voice, a smile he longed to see.

"Okay." He nodded, and laughed. "Wow. Okay. I'll contact this guy tomorrow."

He slept in the AI pit that night, his head nestled against a cold interface panel. He could feel the dull metal pressing little hatchmarks into his skin. He fell asleep imagining soft arms across his chest, warm breath against his cheek.

CRICKET

It was an odd name for a moon. Calling it a colony was an exaggeration. Ashby could count ten buildings nearby, plus a few solitary settlements peppering the hills and cliffs beyond. The roads were little more than flat grooves in the dirt. There were flight lights and pedestrian paths, but they looked like an afterthought. The sky was the color of sulphur, the ground the color of rust. Fine silt already settled thickly in the grooves of their breathing masks and the frames of their goggles. There were no other sapients in sight.

Ashby held up a hand to block the glare of the white sun. "Sissix?"

"Mmm?" Her voice, like his own, was muffled behind a mask.

"Why are we here?"

"Is this a philosophical question, or—"

He shot her a look. "Why are we here, on this platform, right now?"

The platform in question was a thick sheet of industrial metal, orange around the seams, held up by support beams of dubious reliability. Kizzy and Jenks sat on the edge of the platform, ranting about some action sim while Kizzy twisted bits of discarded metal into animal shapes. Rosemary was in a nearby kiosk, arguing with a malfunctioning AI about docking costs.

A faded sign hung from the kiosk roof: "WELCOME TO CRICKET." Beneath this sign was a lengthy warning regarding the tendency of unlicensed subdermal implants to set off weapon detectors.

Sissix adjusted her goggles. "As I remember it, Kizzy said, 'You know what we need?' and you said, 'What?' and she said, 'Guns,' and you said, 'No guns,' and she said, 'A shield grid, then,' and added that she had some friends who could fix us up, and that they weren't too out of the way—"

"That much I recall," said Ashby. "I suppose my real question is, why did I agree to this?"

"You were concussed and mildly sedated."

"Ah. That explains it."

"I have to say, Ashby, having a few weapons onboard for this job isn't a bad idea. Especially in light of recent events."

"Don't you start, too. Us getting boarded was a freak occurrence at best. I've been flying all my life, and that's never happened to me before. I'm not filling my home with weapons just because we're feeling shaken up."

"Ashby, we're heading into what was very recently a war zone. You think there won't be other desperate, dangerous people out there?"

He touched his jaw. The bruises from the Akarak's rifle were still fading. He revisited those horrible moments in the cargo bay, remembered how it felt to have strangers rip their way into his home. He re-created the incident, imagining a gun in his hand. Would he have fired? He couldn't say. But imagining the addition of a weapon in that scenario made him feel safer. He no longer felt helplessness. He felt powerful. And that was what scared him. "I'm not compromising my principles over this. That's that."

"Fucking Exodans," Sissix said, but she said it with a smile.

Ashby snorted a laugh. "Kizzy said the exact same thing.

She's making out like we need an entire planet-busting arsenal strapped to our hull."

"She was scared, Ashby. We all were. We all *are*." Sissix held his hand and nuzzled his shoulder with her cheek.

Rosemary slammed the kiosk door behind her. "Stupid hack-job AI." She glowered as she tried to brush a stubborn clot of dust off her goggles. "For as much as it cost to dock here, they could at *least* provide decent customer service."

"How much did it cost?" asked Ashby.

"Seventy-five hundred credits," said Rosemary. "Plus administrative fees. Not that I actually see any administrators around."

Ashby whistled. "Damn," he said. "These friends of Kizzy's better be worth it."

Rosemary fidgeted. "Ashby, it's a little sketchy here. I don't mind doctoring formwork a bit, but—"

"Don't worry," said Ashby. "I'm not bringing any illegal equipment onto my ship, especially not when we're so close to Quelin space. I'm sure Kizzy's friends are trustworthy folks."

"How long have you known Kizzy?" Sissix said. Ashby followed her gaze toward an open-top skiff humming its way to the platform. The driver stood up on his seat as he approached, even though the vehicle was still moving. He was a solidly built Human man, younger than Ashby, wearing nothing from the waist up but an air mask, several carved pendants and a small rocket launcher on a shoulder strap. Shaggy burnt-copper locks fell down past his shoulders, cloaklike. He had a beard to match, clipped short along his jawline, cascading into a braided curtain below his chin. His skin was darkly tanned, but the peach undertones indicated an isolated ancestry on an old fringe colony, far removed from Exodan intermingling. His chiseled muscles were covered with implanted techports and intricate tattoos, and his left forearm had been replaced by a multitool appendage, which looked homemade. As the skiff got close, Ashby could see thick scars braided around the seam between the tech arm and the man's skin. He had a feeling the surgery had been a home affair as well.

"Ah, great," Ashby sighed under his breath. A shield grid was a good idea. A tweak-happy hackjob mod was something else entirely. How had he agreed to this?

"Kizzy!" the skiff driver boomed, his voice jubilant. He spread his arms wide, reaching toward the sky.

"Bear!" Kizzy squealed, tossing her half-folded metal rabbit aside. It sailed past a placard instructing dock users on the proper disposal of litter. She ran down the platform steps two at a time. "Bear, Bear, Bear, BEAR!" She launched herself over the side of the skiff and into his arms, knocking both of them back into the seat. Jenks sauntered after her, grinning. He and Bear clasped hands warmly as Kizzy hugged Bear's head, cheering, Hooray!"

Rosemary turned to Ashby. "*His name's Bear?*" she asked in Ensk.

"*Seems that way,*" Ashby said.

"Does 'bear' mean something?" Sissix asked. The Ensk word stuck out awkwardly in Klip, especially with Sissix's accent. "What's a bear?"

Ashby started walking. He nodded down toward the hulking, hairy man crushing their mech tech in his massive arms. "*That's* a bear."

"Welcome to Cricket!" Bear called out, giving them a wave. He was friendly, at least.

Ashby extended his hand once he cleared the stairs. "Hi there. Ashby Santoso."

"Ah, the captain!" Bear shook Ashby's hand. Ashby tried not to stare at his other arm, the one with the wires and scars. "Kizzy speaks very highly of you."

Kizzy blushed. "Shh," she said. "He'll think I asked you to butter him up."

"You must be Sissix," Bear said, reaching out to shake her claws. "It's nice to meet you." He stared at her, holding her hand a little too long. He gave his head a shake, as if waking himself up. "I'm really sorry," he said, looking embarrassed. "I don't get off-world much, and we don't get a lot of other species out here."

"That's all right," said Sissix, looking a little confused. She probably hadn't even noticed that the handshake was too long.

"And . . ." Bear thought for a moment. "Rosie? Is that right?"

"Rosemary," she said with a smile, shaking his hand.

"Rosemary. Got it. Hey, did I see you walk away from the AI just a little bit ago?"

"Yeah. Sure isn't cheap to dock here."

Bear shook his head. "I'll get that credited back to you. This jokester named Mikey set that thing up just to make some quick creds from off-worlders who don't know better. It's a total scam. I'll tell him you guys are family. It's close enough to the truth."

"Aww," said Kizzy, giving him a squeeze.

"All right, everybody pile in," Bear said. "I hope you don't mind getting a bit cozy." The skiff was not built for five passengers (especially one with a tail), but with a bit of wiggling and re-arranging, they managed to cram themselves into the dirty, dented vehicle. "Kizzy, travel music, if you would." Bear directed her to a makeshift sound system that consisted of a hacked scrib and three small speakers held down with industrial bolts. The size of the speakers was deceptive. Everybody jumped as the first violent strains of some charthump band emerged with a roar. The three techs gave one another a satisfied nod, and the skiff tore off.

Between the throbbing music and the air rushing past, there wasn't much room in the skiff for conversation. Ashby watched the world go by from his cramped seat. He had thought upon arrival that perhaps a proper colony might be hiding somewhere behind one of the towering cliffs, but no, Cricket was an empty moon. Craggy expanses of dust and rock stretched on and on, punctuated by the occasional bunkerlike homestead. Stubborn succulents peeked out here and there, but Ashby saw no signs of farming—nor water sources, for that matter. There had to be water somewhere. Agreeable gravity and a tolerable atmosphere weren't enough to warrant a colony, not unless you had the means to import water from off-world. From the little he had seen, he didn't think the people of Cricket were quite that well to do.

Off in the distance, something scurried into a crack in the ground. The skiff was moving too quickly for Ashby to get a good look, but whatever it was had been big, about the size of a large dog. Perhaps Bear's rocket launcher wasn't just for show.

The skiff followed a curving road up one of the cliffs. The road was wide enough for the skiff, but barely. Ashby glanced over the edge, and immediately regretted it. Like many lifelong spacers, Ashby didn't care much for heights on land. Looking down at a planet from orbit was no problem, because out there, falling meant floating. If you took a long fall *inside* a ship—say, down the engine shaft on a big homesteader—you'd have enough time to shout the word "*falling*!" This would prompt the local AI to turn off the adjacent artigrav net. Your descent would abruptly end, and you'd be free to drift over to the nearest railing. You'd piss off anyone in the vicinity who'd been drinking mek or working with small tech parts, but it was a fair price to pay for staying alive (the "falling" safety was also popularly exploited by kids, who found the sudden reversal in gravity within a crowded walkway or a classroom to be the height of hilarity). But planetside, there was no artigrav net. Even a drop of a dozen feet could mean death, if you landed wrong. Ashby didn't care much for gravity that couldn't be turned off.

As they rounded a corner, a homestead appeared, built on a flat outcrop. A tall sheet metal fence surrounded all but the overhang, protecting the building within. The skiff passed through an automated gate, and the homestead came fully into view. It had been constructed, in part, from a small cargo ship, grounded forever. A drab dwelling was conjoined at its side, like a bulbous sprout unfolding from an ugly seed. A receiver dish was stuck atop the roof, alongside a blinking light meant to shoo away flying vehicles. A safe distance from the homestead, two delivery drones rested on their launch pad. There was an industrial, fortresslike quality to the place, but something about the all-too-Human workmanship was endearing.

"Home sweet home," Bear said, parking beside a second skiff. "Let's get inside. Oh, you can take your masks off out here. There's a shield covering everything within the fence, and we fill the pocket inside with breathable air." He slipped the mask from his face. "Ahh. That's better."

Ashby unfolded himself from the backseat. Sissix groaned. "My tail's asleep," she said, wincing as she flicked it from side to side.

They followed Bear to the front door of the homestead. Ashby noticed a huge trash bin beside the building, so full that the lid was bulging open. He squinted. Atop the mechanical junk was a piece of some sort of organic husk, brittle and translucent. It reminded him of the insect casings he'd seen in Dr. Chef's kitchen trash. Only bigger. A lot bigger.

"Wow," said Rosemary, looking up at the homestead walls. "Did you build this place yourself?" Ashby doubted that she'd ever seen a modder community firsthand. In some ways, he found it sweet that the galaxy was so new to her. Sweet, and a little sad. He was glad he hadn't grown up that sheltered.

"Most of it, no," Bear said. He pressed his mechanical palm into a panel on the wall. The entry door slid open with a *thunk*. "My brother and I—knock off your boots, please—bought this place about five years back. That's what, uh . . . about three standards? Or something? Never can remember GC time.

Anyway, it belonged to an old comp tech who decided—oh, you can hang your masks on the rack here—she decided to go live closer to her grandkids. Since there was already a workshop and lots of storage space here, wasn't much we needed to add, just the launch pads and the receiver dish, a few comforts here and there—"

"Hello!" Another man entered the room. His uncanny resemblance to Bear made it unlikely that he was anyone but the aforementioned brother. His skin was likewise covered in dermal ports and tattoos, but his hair was tied back, his beard neatly combed. He wore a tasteful buttoned shirt over his creased trousers. An optical plate covered his right eye socket. The surface of the scanner embedded within it glistened, like the inside of a shell. He, too, was armed, but his weapons were more subtle: twin energy pistols, holstered in a vest. He carried a scrib as well, held close to his side as if he had just stood up from reading. There was a distinctly academic air to the man. Ashby could tell right away that he was one of the more bookish modders, the sort who reveled in knowing obscure data and the history of invention.

"Nib!" Kizzy cheered, running in for a hug. "Oh my stars, how are you?"

"I'm very well," Nib said. He did not return the hug with as much gusto as Bear, but the smile on his face showed a degree of fondness equal to what his brother had displayed. "You've been away too long."

"Seriously."

"What, no hello for me?" Jenks grumbled.

Nib peered all around the upper edges of the walls in an exaggerated manner, then looked down to Jenks. "Oh, hey, Jenks! Didn't see you down there!"

"I hear that a lot from dipshits who shoot their own eyes out," Jenks said with a grin. Both men laughed. Ashby blinked. He'd never seen Jenks react to jokes about his height with anything but silent, unnerving disapproval. Nib had clearly earned a few points with Jenks in the past. But Ashby also noticed that the exchange had left Bear unamused. It seemed the scruffy man wasn't fond of making fun of friends.

Introductions were made and hands were shaken. They followed Nib out of the front hall and into a common room. Ashby smiled the minute he walked in. He had been in homes like this before—sturdy, ramshackle dwellings made from whatever a few hard-working pairs of colonist hands could scrounge up. Cheap faded tapestries covered the walls, barely hiding the industrial sheet. Mismatched chairs and sofas were stuffed into the room, all angled around a pixel projector (that, at least, looked new). Pixel plants sat in the windowsill and hung from the ceiling, their digital leaves curling hypnotically, as if they were breathing. Ashby's grandmother had owned pixel plants like that, cheerful and homey. The air flowing through the ceiling vents was clean and cool, but there was a lingering scent of stale smash smoke—sootlike, woody. Behind one sofa was a workbench, covered with hand-labeled jars and boxes. Some room had been cleared on the bench for a pitcher of mek, a bottle of berry fizz and several glasses. Alongside the refreshments lay a partially constructed mech arm.

"That's the project that will never end," Bear said, noticing Ashby's gaze. He raised his own mech arm. "This one's fast, but it can't lift as much as I'd like. That one there's a prototype. I'm trying to create the perfect blend of physical strength and fast reflexes."

"Good luck," laughed Kizzy. "You only get one or the other."

Jenks leaned toward Rosemary to explain. "If biotech signals go too fast for your nerves to process, the rest of your body doesn't know to brace itself for the weight. You'll tear your muscles to shit that way."

Bear frowned at the prototype. "But there's got to be a way around it."

"You pull it off, you'll be the richest tech in the GC," said Jenks.

"I don't even care about that," said Bear. "I just want to be able to throw a ketling barehanded."

Kizzy, Jenks and Nib laughed. Ashby started to ask what a ketling was, but Nib spoke first. "May I offer anyone something to drink? Haven't got much, I'm afraid, but friends of Kizzy's deserve as much hospitality as we can give."

"That's very kind. I'll take some fizz, thanks," Ashby said. His nose was already warming to the aroma rising from the mek pitcher, but he didn't want to get *too* relaxed. He was here to buy equipment, after all. Laziness and credits rarely mixed well.

The front door thunked open as Nib distributed drinks. "Hey!" a female voice called from the hallway. She sounded young. "Are they here yet?"

"We are here!" called Kizzy. "Hello, sweet face!"

"Hi!" said the voice.

"Hi!" said Jenks.

"Wait until you see what I just bagged. Hol-ee *shit*—"

"Ember," said Nib in a voice that could only belong to an older sibling. "Whatever you've got, do *not*—"

"I'm not bringing it inside, dumb ass. I hit its goo sac. Leaking green shit all over the place. Come on out, you've got to see this."

Bear and Nib looked at each other. "Dammit, we *talked* about this," Bear said, already on his way out the door.

Nib sighed and handed out drinks. "Our sister has a penchant for seeking out trouble. Especially if it involves ketlings."

Rosemary beat Ashby to the question. "What's a ketling?"

"Come on," Nib said. "Bring your drinks, I'll show you. And, ah, I hope you've got strong stomachs."

They went outside, safe behind the shield's breathable boundaries. The body of a creature lay in the dirt, motionless within puddles of its own fluids. Over it stood a rifle-wielding young woman—or was she a girl? Ashby couldn't say. She couldn't be any older than twenty. Unlike her brothers, she had no visible ports or implants. Her long curly hair was wild as Bear's, and her face was pretty in a hard sort of way. Her arms were toned and muscular, her skin dark with sun. Ashby wasn't sure that he'd ever been that fit.

The creature, on the other hand, was silent and terrifying. It reminded Ashby of a grasshopper, if grasshoppers had needlelike maws and angry ridges across their backs. Layer upon layer of sharp-edged wings lay in a broken heap. Its legs were contorted and broken, some of them curling inward at rigored angles. There were thin hairs around its mouth and beneath its belly, which somehow made Ashby shiver more than any of the rest of it. The pillowlike sac beneath its jaw wasn't exactly leaking, as Ember had said. More like gushing in slow motion. Sticky, oily, sour-smelling green gunk pooled around the thing's nightmarish head.

"Would you look at this fucker?" Ember beamed. "It's as big as me!" She looked around. "Also, hello, new people. I would shake hands, but, um . . ." She held up a gloved palm. It was smeared with green.

"Wow," said Sissix. She crouched in for a closer look, sipping her fizz. She did not seem to notice (or, at least, care) that Ember was studying *her* just as intently. "I take it this is a ketling?"

Ember gave a surprised chuckle. "You've never seen a ketling before?"

"Why would she have?" Bear said. "She's never been to Cricket." He turned to the group of onlookers. "That's how this moon got its name, incidentally. From *these* bastards."

Nib inspected Ember's handiwork. "Where'd you find it?" he said, his voice far too calm.

Ember's smile wavered for a split second before making a

practiced recovery. "Um, y'know, sometimes there are loners hanging around the wells—"

"Bullshit," Bear said, crossing his arms. "Where?"

Ember swallowed. "Drymouth Gorge," she said. "But it was fine, I didn't get that close."

Bear took a bracing breath and looked skyward. Nib frowned. "Ember, you know better."

Ember's cheeks went red. She gave a sulky shrug. "It's dead, right?"

"That's not the—" Bear started.

"We'll talk about this later," Nib said, his eyes flicking briefly toward their guests.

Jenks examined the ketling's head, tipping it up to face him. It crunched as it moved. "Holy shit," said Jenks. "You got it in the head. Kizzy, look." He pointed to two holes, one on the side of its jaw, one near its lidless eyes.

Ember shrugged again, but the corners of her mouth betrayed satisfaction. "Yeah. It was rushing the skiff, so I had to be quick about it."

"Dammit," Bear said. He continued to shake his head, but said nothing further.

"I don't think I could've done *anything* if this beastie was coming at me," Kizzy said, poking at the split carapace. She looked at Ember. "Stars, I want to hug you so bad right now, but I'm afraid that green shit will poison me or something."

"It's not poisonous," Ember said. "Just sticky."

"Yeah, I don't want to be sticky, either."

Ashby glanced over at Rosemary. Her arms were folded across her chest. "You okay?" he asked.

"Yeah," she said, shaking her head. "Its mouth is just . . ." She shuddered.

"You said it," Bear said. "Once they bite down, they don't let go, especially if they're mad. If they get your throat or your abdomen, you're a goner. And they chew on everything when they're in a breeding frenzy. Walls, skiffs, scrap, fuel cables, well pumps, you name it."

"That's why they're such a problem when they swarm," Nib said. "In their dormant phase, they just cluster in the crags. They don't come out unless something gets close enough to piss them off." He gave Ember a pointed look. "But every year or two, they fly out en masse, flinging spawn everywhere and chewing on everything. It only lasts a couple days, but if you don't protect your property, you'll lose everything. That's what happened to the first settlers here. They showed up during dormancy and were totally unprepared for the first swarm."

Ashby started to wonder why the settlers had bothered rebuilding at all, but he already knew the answer. To some Humans, the promise of a patch of land was worth any effort. It was an oddly predictable sort of behavior. Humans had a long, storied history of forcing their way into places where they didn't belong.

"See how much goo's in the sac?" Ember said. "This one was definitely ready to breed."

Nib nodded in agreement. "We are overdue for the next plague."

Ember was eager to explain. "The goo becomes spawn once it's fertilized. They keep it close to their maw so they can protect it. It's *so* gross. They just fly around for days, humping each others' heads."

"Ember," Bear said, cuffing her shoulder. "*Guests.*"

Ember ignored him, speaking with horrified relish. "And when they're done, they hurl the goo *out of their mouths*. I bet they're gonna swarm in the next tenday."

"What do you do when they swarm?" asked Sissix.

"Hunker down and wait it out," said Bear. "Nib and I upgraded the shields of the entire colony after we settled here.

Ketlings can't get through once folks fire them up. Of course, we can't get out, either. Swarms are a great time to get caught up on vids."

"What about the spawn?"

"We shoot it. Or set fire to it. Sounds mean, I'm sure, but trust me, it doesn't matter. They're always back in the thousands. And it's not like they're sentient or anything."

Nib nodded toward the ketling. "You should clean it before it goes bad," he said to Ember.

"That was the plan," she said, pulling a large utility knife from her belt. "I just wanted to show you guys before I put it in the stasie."

Rosemary's eyes were fixed on the sticky puddles beneath the ketling's damaged head. "You're going to eat that?"

"No different from little bugs," Ember said. "Easier to clean 'em, too." Without warning, she brought the knife down to sever the ketling's head. The outer shell was thick, and Ember had to twist the dangling head around a few times to break it free. Rosemary's mouth twitched.

Nib gave a little chuckle and patted Rosemary's shoulder. "If you stay for dinner, maybe we can change your mind."

"Ooh, yes please!" Kizzy said. "I have a million stories to tell."

Bear smiled at the group. "You're all welcome to stay. I make a crazy good marinade, if you're up for barbecue." He looked to Ember, who was admiring the ketling's gruesome head. He sighed with resignation. "You want a pike for that? There are a few spare support poles left in the workshop. You could shave down a nice point with the metal grinder."

"Oh, hell yes," Ember grinned. "I should finish cutting it up, though."

"We'll leave you to it," Nib said, with a quick glance at Rosemary. "I think our guests have seen enough gore for one afternoon."

Ember smiled and nodded. As soon as their backs were turned and they had taken a few steps away, a wet splintering sound came from behind. Ashby didn't look back. He wasn't the squeamish sort, but there were some things in the galaxy he didn't need to see.

"Damn, that girl's a kick in the ass," Kizzy said. "I remember when she couldn't shoot a *rock*. And she was like, *half my size* at one point."

"So?" said Jenks. "I'm always half your size."

"You know what I mean."

"She's getting to be a better shot than me," Bear said. "And she's strong as hell. I'd like it if she spent more time in the shop with us, but these days she's more interested in climbing rocks and running around."

"Which is fine," Nib said. "But we need to have another talk about provoking ketlings."

"Yeah, because she'll totally listen this time."

Nib frowned. Ashby was almost certain by now that Nib was the elder brother. "I'd like for her to reach her seventeenth birthday in one piece."

Ashby gaped. "She's *sixteen*?" That was enough to warrant a glance back. The girl was dismantling the ketling with confidence, humming as she hacked its legs off.

"How old is that?" Sissix asked. "Put that in Aandrisk context."

"She's only got half her feathers, and she's molting constantly."

Sissix raised her eye ridges. "Remind me to never get on her bad side."

"Well," said Nib. "What say we get on to the reason you're here?"

He led them over to the bay doors of the grounded cargo ship. With the press of a palm lock, the doors groaned open.

A few light globes revealed a cluttered workspace filled with industrial tools. Beyond, a small forest of storage racks stretched from floor to ceiling, holding shield generators of all shapes and sizes.

"Where's the fun stuff?" Jenks said.

"Up out of the way," Bear said.

"Well, come on," Kizzy said. "Let's see things that go boom."

Ashby frowned. He didn't want to disrespect the brothers' work, but . . . "I hope Kizzy was clear about the fact that I'm only in the market for a shield grid."

Nib smiled. "I gleaned that from her message," he said with a wink to Kizzy. "Don't worry, we're not going to push anything on you. We're not weapons merchants, strictly speaking. Custom shields are our bread and butter. The weapons we make are just for fun. But they are available to you, should you change your mind." He gestured a command at a control panel. There was a clanking sound above. Several flat racks descended from the ceiling, weapons hanging from them like heavy, frightening fruit. Ashby looked around in amazement. It was enough to equip an Aeluon assault squad, and then some. He wondered what Pei would think.

"Wow," Sissix said.

"I know, right?" said Jenks.

"And this is all just for you guys?"

"It's our hobby," Bear said. "We only sell them to neighbors and trusted friends. We're not in the business of equipping bad guys. But if you want to *discourage* bad guys, oh yeah, we can do that."

Rosemary said nothing, but her face was tight. Ashby could relate to her apparent discomfort. They were standing in a cargo hold filled with things designed for killing. He doubted quiet Rosemary had even *seen* a gun before the Akaraks.

"A little overwhelming at first, I know," Nib said with pride.

Nib seemed to be an agreeable sort, so Ashby didn't mind

being honest with him. "I don't mean to offend, but I really don't want any weapons aboard my ship."

"Let me guess. You're from the Fleet?"

"That obvious?"

"A bit," said Nib with a smile. "We have different philosophies, you and I, but I can understand where you're coming from. Violence is always disconcerting, even if it's only *potential* violence. But after the trouble you recently found yourself in—not to mention the place you're headed to—it sounds as if you could do with some basic tools of self-defense. If that only constitutes shielding for you, that's okay. But you need *something*."

"Like *that*," Jenks said. "I like *that*." Ashby followed his gaze to a gun—no, not a gun. A small cannon with handles. The barrel looked big enough to hold an infant.

"We call that one the Sledge," Bear said. "Packs a hell of a punch. And I highly doubt you need it."

"Oh, but I do," said Jenks. "I need it desperately."

Bear laughed. "We can go shoot holes in the cliffs with it later if you like."

Jenks looked at Kizzy. "We need to come here more often."

As Kizzy and Jenks fawned over the ludicrous assortment of weaponry, Ashby and Sissix perused the shields. All misgivings that Ashby had about buying modder equipment vanished as Nib spoke to them about his tech. Nib already had the *Wayfarer*'s specs on hand, but he wanted to know more than just engine readouts and hull dimensions. He wanted details. He wanted to know how old the ship was, what it was built from, if the materials used in the living quarters differed from the original framework. He wanted to know the specific strain of algae they used for fuel, and how much ambi they kept onboard at a time (Ashby cringed inwardly at the reminder of the stolen cells; the GC was covering the loss, but still, it was an awful waste). Nib asked Sissix careful questions about her piloting techniques, and nodded with sincere consideration as she answered. Bear joined the conversation after a time, and the brothers debated shield mechanics with enthusiasm. In the end, Bear and Nib decided they would take apart several existing models and combine the components into something specially suited to the *Wayfarer*. Ashby felt as though he were buying a tailored set of clothes. These modders were no mere techs. They were artists. And for all they were offering, they required only a day's work and a sum of credits that Ashby suspected covered little more than the components themselves. Ashby made a mental note to thank Kizzy for being friends with these people.

He turned around to see Jenks hand Rosemary a small energy pistol. The weapon looked out of place in her hands, like a fish being held by a desert-born Aandrisk. "See, not so scary when *you're* the one holding it," Jenks said. Rosemary didn't look too sure.

Bear beamed. "Want to take it for a spin?"

Rosemary swallowed. "I don't know how to shoot."

"We can teach you," Bear said. "Easy-peasy. You don't need to know anything fancy."

"And it's fun," said a voice behind them. Ember, covered in green slime, ketling head in hand, walked into the cargo hold and began digging through a pile of metal support poles. She clutched the ketling's head by the antennae, holding it up to one pole at a time, trying to find a good width for skewering.

"Ember," said Nib. "Please tell me that you did not leave a butchered ketling lying out in the sun."

"Meat's in the stasie," she said.

Bear gave her a knowing look. "Please tell me that you did not leave a pile of guts lying out in the sun."

Their little sister set down the pole she had in hand, flashed a guilty smile and tiptoed in an exaggerated fashion back out of the cargo bay.

Bear rolled his eyes to the ceiling with a sigh. "I cannot *wait* for her to stop being a teenager."

"*I* can," Nib said. "Do you know how impossible it's going to be to boss her around when she's twenty?"

"Question for you," Sissix said. "Totally unrelated."

"Go for it."

"One of our rotational stabilizers was damaged when the Akaraks hit us. We were going to pick up a replacement on our next market stop, but I hate flying without it for that long. You guys don't carry anything like that, right?"

"*We* don't, but we're hardly the only techs on this rock. You should to talk to Jess and Mikey," said Bear.

"The same Mikey with the AI scam?"

"The same. But don't hold that against him, those two really know their shit. Old-school ship techs. Retired now, but they still spend lots of time in their workshop. Awesome folks. They live about an hour from here. If you like, I can call down and see if they're in. You could borrow a skiff, and be there and back by dinnertime."

Ashby looked to Sissix. She nodded. "Might as well, as long as we're here," he said. He turned back to the brothers. "You sure you don't mind us using a skiff?"

"Nah, no worries. If you guys can punch holes through space, I trust you to bring my skiff back in one piece."

"Hey," Ember yelled from outside. "Anyone want to see what a ketling nervous column looks like?"

"No," yelled Bear.

"No, they do not," yelled Nib.

"Yeah, kind of," Jenks said. He dashed outside, dragging Kizzy with him.

Nib gave Ashby an apologetic shrug. "Sorry for the chaos," he said.

"That's okay," Ashby said. Outside the cargo hold, Kizzy and

Jenks were making disgusted, delighted sounds. "I'm kind of used to it."

Rosemary had the sense that Ember knew a lot more about life than she did, but the girl had been wrong about one thing. The swarm didn't wait a few days. An hour or so after Bear put the butchered, basted ketling over the fire, its kin erupted from the crags with a fury. The sky was darkened within minutes. At a distance, the twitching clouds of insects looked almost like clusters of malfunctioning pixels. The ketlings darted madly across the sky as they fertilized, killed and sometimes ate one another. There had been a quick succession of bright flashes across the skyline as the people of Cricket activated the shields around their homes. The ketlings rammed headfirst into the shields, though they did not do so for any obvious reason. They did the same to rocks, plants, abandoned vehicles, even other ketlings. It seemed that the bugs disliked anything that infringed upon their ability to move in whichever direction they pleased.

Ashby and Sissix had still been at the other compound when the swarm hit. Rosemary had checked in with them via her scrib's vidlink. None of them had any choice but to spend the night as unplanned houseguests. Neither of their hosts seemed to mind. On the contrary, it seemed that Jess and Mikey were only too happy to entertain some off-worlders. Ashby said that they had been pulling stashed delicacies out of cupboards left and right, and after Sissix had learned that the old couple spoke a little Reskitkish, they had become instant friends. Rosemary heard the women talking in the background over the vidlink—Sissix going slow, Jess pushing doggedly through the hissing syllables. From their laughter, Rosemary gathered that the conversation was a good one.

The modder siblings were similarly delighted. "There's nothing you can do about a swarm," Nib said. "It just means we get a day or two more with our friends." The brothers were treating the miasma of biting, thrashing, spawn-vomiting insects as if it were a holiday. Ember and Kizzy lugged a case of home-brewed kick up from the cellar (like most things on Cricket, it had been made by a neighbor). Bear roasted Ember's prey beneath the safety of the shield. It was an odd tableau: an apron-clad man brushing marinade onto a spit roast while slavering beasts bounced furiously off the crackling bubble of energy above him. The bugs were undeterred by the piked ketling head, standing tall beside the entry gate.

At first, Rosemary had felt uncomfortable being stuck in the modders' home, and not just for the swarm outside. Kizzy and Jenks were good friends with this family, but Rosemary was the odd one out. The thought of imposing on these strangers for a day or two—eating their food, sleeping on a grubby couch, listening to inside jokes—left Rosemary awkward. But the siblings' congeniality did away with those feelings. Bear in particular made an effort to include her, and attempted to fill her in when the stories started going over her head (most of the stories fell into one of two groups: "the time we built this amazing thing" or "the time we smoked too much smash and did something stupid"). Once she had gotten past the memory of the oozing ketling carcass, she found the shreds of spicy, flame-licked insect, wrapped in airy flat-bread and washed down with crisp kick, actually made for an enjoyable meal. By the time dinner was over, Rosemary found herself unexpectedly at ease. The armchair she sat in was dusty and worn. The pixel plant flickering nearby smacked of poor taste. The enthusiastic chatter about tech and modding was impossible for her to contribute to. But unfamiliar as everything was, it was clear that her companions felt right at home. Belly full and body laughing, Rosemary could pretend that she fit in there, too.

Nib brought out a fresh pot of mek to his houseguests and siblings, all of whom were situated around the pixel projector.

Bear sat on the floor with his back against a couch. Kizzy sat behind him, putting tiny braids in his thick mane of hair. Jenks lounged nearby, smoking redreed and looking content. Ember sat at the workbench, frowning as she fussed with a circuit panel.

"You know," the girl said as her brother entered the room. "There's a way for this project to go *way* faster."

"Really," said Nib, his voice flat. He looked to Rosemary, raising the pot and his eyebrows in tandem. "Mek?"

"Yes, please," Rosemary said. A soothing cup of mek on a full stomach sounded perfect. It was almost enough to make her forget about the muffled droning coming through the outer walls.

"Seriously," said Ember. "These junction pins are *so* hard to see. If I had—"

Bear glanced up. "If it starts with 'o' and ends with 'cular implant,' the answer is no."

"Stop moving, Teddy," Kizzy said. "You're gonna end up with messy braids."

Ember sighed with the long-suffering weariness of a teenager. "Hypocrites."

"When you've stopped growing and your brain chemistry has evened out, you can get all the implants you want," said Nib. His tone was parental. It seemed to irritate Ember all the more.

"Hate to be the bad guy, but your brother's right," Jenks said. "Put implants in too early and you'll wind up a mess. I knew a dude who got a headjack when he was fifteen. As he grew, his spine stretched, and the interface got all fucked up. Had to go back and get it done all over again. The hackjob idiot working on him didn't know what he was doing, and the poor kid wound up with an infection in his spinal cord. Almost killed him. Had to get all four limbs replaced just so he could move again."

"Who the fuck puts a headjack in a kid that age?" Bear said.

"Stop moving," Kizzy said.

Bear grumbled. "Ember, seriously, if you ever meet a modder

who will implant teenagers, run like hell. Modding isn't just about getting sewn up with cool tech, it's about orchestrating a balance between the synthetic and the organic. If you don't care about the well-being of the organic, then—*ow!*" He yelped as Kizzy pulled his hair.

"Stop. Moving."

"I know," Ember said to Bear. "Spare me the platitudes."

"You are too young for a word like 'platitudes,'" Jenks said. Ember stuck her tongue out at him. He returned the gesture.

"Besides, sweetie," Kizzy said. "You've got such pretty eyes. Why get a full implant when you could just wear a hud?"

"*He's* got a full implant," Ember said, pointing at Nib.

"He also had an 'incident,'" Jenks said. He pantomimed firing a gun at his own face, and made an explosion gesture over his eye. Redreed smoke burst from his nose as he laughed.

"I'm so glad you're staying over," Nib said.

Jenks raised his mug in a jaunty salute.

Nib glanced at the clock on the wall. "News should be uploaded by now. Anyone mind if I put it on?" he said.

There was a general shaking of heads. "Nib is something of a junkie when it comes to current events," Bear said to Rosemary. "Or past events. Or just events in general, really."

"He's a reference file archivist," Kizzy said.

"No kidding?" said Rosemary. "Volunteer?"

Nib nodded. "Some people knit, some people play music, I dig through dusty old facts and make sure they're accurate." He flopped back into a chair as the pixels in the central projector flickered to life. "I like knowing things."

Rosemary was impressed. Archivists were passionate people, some of whom dedicated their whole lives to the pursuit of unbiased truth. Given the wealth of information that needed sorting through, professional archivists relied heavily upon volunteers to help keep public files current. Rosemary had always imagined them like guardians from some fantasy vid, defending the galaxy from inaccuracies and questionable data.

"What are you working on, if I may ask?" Rosemary said.

"I belong to one of the interspecies history teams. It's fascinating work, but it can be a real pain in the ass. You would not believe the amount of bogus, speciest submissions we have to deal with."

"Examples," Kizzy said.

Nib sighed and scratched his beard. "The best one I've seen in a while claimed that the Exodus Fleet could never have sustained that many people for so long, ergo the Human race did not originate on Earth at all."

Jenks raised his head. "So where are we from, then?"

Nib grinned. "We're a genetweaked species the Harmagians cooked up."

Jenks hooted with laughter. "Oh, my mom would have a coronary if she read that."

"That's so dumb," said Ember. "What about all the Earthen ruins and stuff? All those old cities?"

"I know, I know," Nib said with a shrug. "But we still have to go through the process of objectively disproving the claim. That's our job."

"Why would people go to all the trouble of trying to prove something like that?" Kizzy asked.

"Because they're idiots," said Bear. "And speaking of, the news has started."

Nib gestured to the pixels, bringing the volume up. A pixelated Quinn Stephens spoke from his desk, as always. Rosemary had never followed Exodan newsfeeds before coming aboard the *Wayfarer*, but she'd picked up the habit from Ashby. It was a comfort knowing that no matter what system you were in, Quinn was there to bring you the news. The pixels flickered with signal decay. They were a long way from the Fleet.

The newsman's voice came through. "—news from Mars, the

trial that has been dubbed the scandal of the century finally came to a close today with the sentencing of former Phobos Fuel CEO Quentin Harris the Third."

Rosemary's warm, comfortable feeling disappeared with a thud. *Oh, no.* She dug her fingers into the folds of her trousers, trying to keep her face emotionless as the newsman spoke.

"Harris was found guilty of all charges, including extortion, fraud, smuggling and crimes against sapient kind."

Breathe. Don't think about it. Think about the bugs outside. Think about anything.

"Damn right he was found guilty," said Jenks. "What an asshole."

"Who?" asked Bear, raising his chin.

"Head down," mumbled Kizzy, holding several hair ties between her teeth.

"The Phobos guy," said Nib. "The one who sold weapons to the Toremi."

"Oh, *right*," Bear said. "*That* asshole."

"I don't know who we're talking about," Ember said.

"Ever heard of Phobos Fuel? Big ambi distributor?"

Second biggest, in Human space, Rosemary thought.

"I guess," said Ember.

Bear pointed at the pixels. "Well, the dude who owned the company apparently had an illegal weapons business on the side. That's where his real creds came from."

"You've got illegal weapons."

Nib crossed his arms. "Ember, there is an enormous difference between making weapons for fun and selling gene targeters to both sides of an interstellar blood feud."

Ember raised her eyebrows. "Gene targeters? That's . . . wow. That's fucked up."

"Yep," Bear said. "And now he and his buddies are going to jail forever."

Jenks shook his head. "Why can't people just stick with bullets and energy bursts and be happy about it?"

"Because people are assholes," said Bear, dutifully keeping his head down. "Ninety percent of all problems are caused by people being assholes."

"What causes the other ten percent?" asked Kizzy.

"Natural disasters," said Nib.

The projector showed a cuffed and humiliated Quentin Harris the Third as he was marched from the courthouse to a police skimmer. His face was unreadable, his suit immaculately stitched. Angry protesters pressed against the energy barriers that surrounded the courthouse. Cheap printed signs danced over their heads. "THERE IS BLOOD ON YOUR HANDS" read one. Another held a pixel insert of a bloodied Toremi carrying a mangled corpse. Below the insert was the Phobos slogan: "KEEPING THE GALAXY MOVING." Other signs were more simple. "WARMONGER." "TRAITOR." "MURDERER." The barriers holding them back bulged like overfilled pockets.

The reporter continued his calm tale of biological warfare and greed. Rosemary focused all her energy toward her eyes. *Do not cry. Don't cry. You can't.*

"Rosemary, you okay?" Jenks asked.

Rosemary wasn't sure how she replied—something about being fine and just needing some air. She excused herself, walked steadily down the hall and exited the homestead.

Outside, the ketlings continued their chaotic dance. The sun was setting behind them, transforming the scene into a macabre shadow puppet show. Rosemary was unfazed. The ketlings did not feel real. The homestead, the siblings, the moon beneath her feet, none of it felt real. All she could think of was that pixelated face on the projector, the face she had traveled across the galaxy to get away from. She tried to breathe slow, tried to fight back the raw, smothering feeling blossoming within her chest. She sat down in the dirt and stared at her hands. She gritted her teeth. Everything she'd worked so hard to bottle up when she left Mars was bubbling up, and she wasn't sure she could push it back down this time. She had to, though. She had to.

"Rosemary?"

Rosemary jumped. It was Jenks, standing beside her. She hadn't heard the door, or his footsteps. She barely heard the ketlings droning overhead.

"What's wrong?" His hands were in his pockets, his eyebrows knitted together.

As she looked him in the eye, something within her broke. She knew it might cost her the goodwill of the crew and her place on the *Wayfarer*, but she couldn't do it anymore. She couldn't keep up the lie any longer.

Rosemary looked away, out past the ketlings, across the rocky crags, all the way to the unfamiliar sun. Its light seared into her eyes, and remained there, heavy and orange, even as she closed them. "Jenks, I haven't . . . I haven't been . . . stars, you're all going to hate me for this." They would. And Ashby would fire her, and Sissix would never talk to her again.

"Doubtful," Jenks said. "We like you a lot." He sat down next to her and hit the bowl of his pipe against his boot. The tightly packed ash came loose and tumbled to the ground.

"But you don't, you don't know . . . I can't do this." She leaned her forehead into her palm. "I know I'm going to get kicked off the ship, but—"

Jenks stopped fussing with his pipe. "Okay, now you have to tell me," he said, his voice stern but calm. "Take all the time you need, but you're telling me."

She took a breath. "That guy on the news," she said. "Quentin Harris?"

"Yeah?"

"He's my father."

Jenks said nothing. He exhaled. "*Holy* shit. Oh, Rosemary, I'm . . . wow. I'm so sorry." He paused again. "Shit, I had no idea."

"That was the point. Nobody was supposed to know. I shouldn't even be here, I'm not—I *lied*, Jenks, I lied and cheated and covered things up, but I just can't do this anymore, I can't—"

"Whoa, hey, slow down. One thing at a time." He sat quiet, thinking. "Rosemary, I have to ask this, and you have to tell me the truth, okay?"

"Okay."

His jaw was firm, his eyes wary. "Were you involved in . . . in what he did? I mean, even just a little bit, doctoring forms or lying to the police or something—"

"*No.*" It was the truth. "I didn't know anything about it. I didn't know anything until the detectives appeared at my apartment and spent the morning asking me questions. They knew I had nothing to do with it, and they told me I was under no obligation to be involved with the trial. I didn't even have to stay on Mars."

He searched her face, and nodded. "So . . . okay." He laughed. "Stars, that's a relief. I thought I *was* going to hate you there for a minute." He patted her leg. "All right, you're innocent. So . . ." He looked baffled. "Rosemary, sorry, but what the fuck is the problem here?"

She was shocked still. "What?"

"I mean, okay, I get that you're going through a lot right now, and by a lot, I mean some serious emotional shit that's going to take us dozens of bottles of kick to work through, but why lie about it? If you're not involved, then why would you think we'd care?"

Rosemary was unprepared for this. Months and months of worrying and dreading, and *he didn't care*? "You don't understand. Back on Mars, it didn't matter that I hadn't done anything. Everyone knew who I was. All the newsfeeds, it was nothing but our family history, even holiday pics and things like that. All focused on my father, of course, but there's little me, smiling and waving at his side. I don't even know how they got that stuff. And it was all paired up with medical experts talking about what targeters do to you, and all those newspeople yelling about corruption. You know the feeds, they never stop once they get their claws in. My friends stopped talking to me. People would yell things at me out in public—'Hey, your dad's a murderer,' as if I didn't know what he'd done. I'd been applying for jobs at the time, and nobody called me back. Nobody wanted my family's name associated with their business."

"But your name's Harper," Jenks said.

She pressed her lips together. "What would you do if you wanted to get away? I mean *really* get away, so that nobody knew who you'd been before?"

Jenks thought. He gave a slow nod. "*Oh.* Oh, I think I get it." He reached out his hand. "Let's see it."

"See what?"

"Your patch."

Rosemary hesitantly laid her right wrist in his palm. She pushed up her wristwrap, exposing the patch beneath. Jenks leaned in, studying it closely.

"This is fucking amazing work," he said at last. "The only way you can tell it's new is by how it healed. If I didn't know better, I'd say this was a genuine replacement for a fried patch."

"That's because it *is* a genuine replacement," Rosemary said. She swallowed. Her tongue felt thick.

Jenks was puzzled. "How did you get—" His face lit up. "Phobos Fuel. Right. You've got money. Serious money."

"I *had* money. Before—"

"Before you paid someone off. Paid someone to give you a new ID file. Shit, Rosemary, you must've paid them a fortune not to talk."

"Everything I had," she said. "Except for transport and hotels, that sort of thing." She laughed without smiling. "My family may not have taught me much about the galaxy, but buying favors? We've got that down."

"But you're really a clerk, right? Like, you know your way around formwork, you obviously went to school. That's all true, right?"

She nodded. "The official who helped me, he changed all my records, made sure my new file was linked to everywhere I'd ever been. So my diploma, my certification, my letters of recommendation, they're all mine. The only way anybody would find out that the associated ID file had been altered was if, say, one of my crewmates went to Mars and asked one of my friends about me. I figured finding work out in the open limited the chances of running into anybody from back home. So I put my name on the list for long-haul work, and here I am."

Jenks rubbed his beard. "So, then, what's wrong? If you did the course work, and you have the skills, you deserve to have this job. Why would we throw you off the ship?"

"Because I lied, Jenks. I lied to Ashby when I told him who I was. I've been lying to all of you every time you've asked me about my life back on Mars. I came into your home and told you lie after lie about who I am."

"Rosemary." Jenks put his hand on her shoulder. "I'm not going to insult you by pretending like I get what you're dealing with. If someone in my family did something like this . . . stars, I don't know what I'd do. I can't offer advice here, but if you ever need a shoulder to cry on, mine's good and ready. As for who you are—and your name really is Rosemary, right?—okay." He nodded back toward the homestead. "Do you know why Human modders give themselves weird names?"

She shook her head.

"It's a really old practice, goes back to pre-Collapse computer networks. We're talking *old* tech here. People would choose names for themselves that they only used within a network. Sometimes that name became so much a part of who they were that even their friends out in the real world started using it. For some folks, those names became their whole identity. Their *true* identity, even. Now, modders, modders don't care about anything as much as individual freedom. They say that nobody can define you but *you*. So when Bear gave himself a new arm, he didn't do it because he didn't like the body he was born in, but because he felt that new arm fit him better. Tweaking your body, it's all about trying to make your physical self fit with who you are inside. Not that you *have* to tweak to get that feeling. Like me, I like to decorate myself, but my body already fits with who I am. But some modders, they'll keep changing themselves their entire lives. And it doesn't always work out. Sometimes they seriously mess themselves up. But that's the risk you take in trying to be more than the little box you're born into. Change is always dangerous." He tapped her arm. "You're Rosemary Harper. You chose that name because the old one didn't fit anymore. So you had to break a few laws to do it. Big fucking deal. Life isn't fair, and laws usually aren't, either. You did what you had to do. I get that."

Rosemary bit her lip. "I still lied to you all."

"Yeah, you did. And you're going to have to fess up. Not to anybody outside the crew, if you don't want to, but the people you live with need to hear it. That's the only way you can make up for it and move on."

"Ashby—"

"Ashby is the most reasonable man I've ever met. Sure, he's not going to be *thrilled* about it." He paused for a split second. Rosemary could see a separate thought flash past his eyes, distracting him. He cleared his throat, and came back. "But you've been kicking ass at your job, and you're a good person. That's going to matter more to him than anything else."

Rosemary looked at her friend, and hugged him hard. "Thank you," she said. Tears flowed down her cheeks. They felt clean.

"Hey, no worries. We're crew. And you'll get through this, you know. I know you will." He paused. "I'm sorry for calling your dad an asshole."

Rosemary looked at him with disbelief. "Jenks, my father sold biological weapons to both sides of a civil war outside his own species, and all for getting access to the ambi across their borders. I think calling him an asshole is being generous."

"Well . . . okay, yeah, that's fair." He rubbed his beard. "Stars, I wish I knew what to say. When we get back to the ship, you need to talk to Dr. Chef. One on one."

"About what?"

"About his species."

THE LAST WAR

There were few things Dr. Chef enjoyed more than a cup of tea. He made tea for the crew every day at breakfast time, of course, but that involved an impersonal heap of leaves dumped into a clunky dispenser. A solitary cup of tea required more care, a blend carefully chosen to match his day. He found the ritual of it quite calming: heating the water, measuring the crisp leaves and curls of dried fruit into the tiny basket, gently brushing the excess away with his fingerpads, watching color rise through water like smoke as it brewed. Tea was a moody drink.

There had been no tea on his home planet. Heated water was only for sleeping in, not for drinking. So many wonderful things they had missed out on, simply because they had never thought to imbibe the stuff! No tea, no soup, no mek—well, the mek was hardly a loss. He did not share his crewmates' enthusiasm for the murky brew. Something about it reminded him of wet dirt, and not in a pleasant way.

He sat on a garden bench in the Fishbowl, his tea cooling as he worked through slow thoughts. Rosemary sat across from him, holding her own mug in her bony Human hands. She was silent as he thought out loud. He knew how strange they each were to the other—he for never thinking quietly, she for having no thinking sounds. He knew she understood his noise by now, though, and that knowledge made her silence feel companionable.

The thoughts he was drumming up were old and safely kept. Kizzy had accused him once of "bottling up his feelings," but this was a Human concept, the idea that one could hide their feelings away and pretend that they were not there. Dr. Chef knew exactly where all of his feelings were, every joy, every ache. He didn't need to visit them all at once to know they were there. Humans' preoccupation with "being happy" was something he had never been able to figure out. No sapient could sustain happiness *all* of the time, just as no one could live permanently within anger, or boredom, or grief. Grief. Yes, that was the feeling that Rosemary needed him to find today. He did not run from his grief, nor did he deny its existence. He could study his grief from a distance, like a scientist observing animals. He embraced it, accepted it, acknowledged that it would never go away. It was as much a part of him as any pleasant feeling. Perhaps even more so.

He cooed readiness, and focused on his vocal cords, forcing them to work together as one. He looked into Rosemary's white-rimmed eyes. He began to speak.

"Our species are very different from each other. You have two hands, I have six. You sleep in a bed, I sleep in a tub. You like mek, I don't. Many little differences. But there's one big thing that Grum and Humans have in common, and that is our capacity for cruelty. Which is not to say we are bad at the core. I think both of our species have good intentions. But when left to our passions, we have it within ourselves to do despicable things. The only reason Humans stopped killing each other to the extent that you used to, I think, is because your planet died before you could finish the job. My species was not so lucky. The reason you haven't seen any other Grum is because there are only some three hundred of us left."

Rosemary's hand went to her mouth. "I'm sorry," she said. Such a quintessentially Human thing, to express sorrow through apology.

"I'm not," Dr. Chef said. "It was our own doing. Our extinction wasn't caused by a natural disaster or the slow crawl of evolution. We killed ourselves." He thought aloud for a moment, sorting out all the pieces. "For generations, my species was at war with itself. I couldn't even tell you why. Oh, there are historians with all sorts of theories and ideas. But it's the same story you hear everywhere. Different beliefs, different cultures, territories everyone wanted. I was born into that war. And when I was ready, I took my place in it as a doctor.

"I wasn't the sort of doctor I am now. I didn't become friends with my patients. I didn't have long chats with them about their diets or what sort of imubots they should upgrade to. My job was to patch up dying soldiers as fast as I could, so that they could get back out there and keep killing.

"Near the end, the Outsiders—that's roughly what we called the others—started using these projectiles called—" He hummed in thought, trying to find an analogue in Klip. "Organ cutters. You see, the Outsiders had been separated from us—from *my faction* for so long that they had become genetically distinct. The organ cutters were programmed to hone in on our genetic markers. If they hit an Outsider by mistake, it'd hurt them, but it was nothing worse than an ordinary bullet wound. But if an organ cutter hit one of *us*, that triggered its real purpose."

"Which was?" Rosemary said, looking fearful.

He looked out the window, but he did not see the stars. "To burrow. A cutter would dig through a person's insides until it hit something vital. It wouldn't stop until the victim was dead. So, say a soldier took a hit to a limb. With a normal bullet, that'd be a minor wound. But with a cutter, they'd be dead within . . . oh, half an hour. And half an hour may not sound

like much time, but when you've got a little piece of metal ripping through you—" The memories reached out to Dr. Chef,
trying to pull him away from his safe observation point. They
tugged, begging for him to give in. But he would not. He was
not a prisoner of those memories. He was their warden. "Day
after day, they'd bring me soldiers with live cutters still burrowing, and it was up to me to chase them down. I was often too
slow. All the doctors were. See, the cutters emitted a type of
interference that made them invisible to our scanners. We had
to go looking by hand. In the end, we found it faster, and more
merciful, to euthanize cutter patients on the spot." He sucked
in his cheeks in disgust, remembering mess after bloody, shrieking mess. "I hated the Outsiders for the cutters. More than hated
them. It was ugly, the feeling within me. I thought that the
Outsiders were animals. Monsters. Something . . . something
lesser than me. Yes, lesser. I truly believed that we were better
than them, that despite all the blood on our faces, at least we
had not stooped that low. But you can already guess what happened next, right?"

"Your side started using cutters, too?"

"Yes. But it was worse than that. I learned that the cutters
had been our tech to start with. The Outsiders had just stolen
the idea before we could complete it. They had only done to us
what we had planned to do to them. That was the moment in
which I no longer knew who the animals were. I no longer
wanted to mend our soldiers so that they could go use cutters
and . . ." He searched for serviceable words. "Sticky-fire and
germ bombs. I wanted to heal them. Actually *heal* them.
Sometimes I'd see a body added to the pile, someone I had just
put back on her feet a few days earlier. It made me wonder what
the point of it all was." He stopped, and rumbled in thought for
a long, long time. The thought he was arriving at grasped and
clung, but he remained in control. "One night, one of the other

doctors ran into my shelter. She told me to come quickly. I followed her to the surgery, and there, ripped to pieces by a cutter—by *our tech*—was my youngest mothered-child. My daughter. I hadn't even known she was fighting nearby."

"Oh, no," Rosemary said. Her voice was soft as leaves.

Dr. Chef wiggled his head up and down, the Human gesture for yes. "They had given her drugs to block the pain, and were preparing the . . . I don't know what to call it. An injection. The last one we gave to cutter patients. An injection to stop her heart. I shoved the doctor working on her aside. I held her face. She was barely there behind her eyes, but I think she knew who I was. I told her I loved her, and that the pain would be gone soon. I gave her the injection myself. I knew it was the right thing to do, that I be the one to take her back out of the world I had brought her into. She was the last of my children. There had been five of them, all beautiful gray-speckled girls. And they all became soldiers, as most of our girls did. They died on scorched battlefields far from home. None of my children ever mothered. None of them ever became male. My last child, I didn't love her anymore or less than any of the others, but something about knowing that all my children were gone broke me. I couldn't keep my grief at a distance any longer. My thoughts became too big. I had to stop being a doctor. I spent the rest of the war in a . . . a quiet home. A place of rest. Learning how to steady my mind again."

"Dr. Chef, I . . ." Rosemary shook her head from side to side. Her face was wet. "I can't imagine."

"That's good," he said. "I wouldn't want you to. A few years later, there were too few daughters on either side for anyone to keep fighting. The germ bombs had mutated into things we couldn't cure. Our water was poisoned. Our mines and forests had nothing left to give. The war didn't end, exactly. It just burned itself out."

"Couldn't you rebuild? Find a colony somewhere to start over?"

"We could have. But we chose not to."

"Why?"

He *hrmmed*, considering the best way to explain. "We are an old species, Rosemary. There were Grum long before there were Humans. After all we had done, all the horrors we had created, both sides decided that perhaps it was time for us to end. We had squandered our time, and we didn't feel that we needed—or perhaps deserved—another chance. The war ended thirty standards ago, but we kept dying from the diseases we designed, or injuries that came back to haunt us. To my knowledge, there has not been another Grum born in decades. There may be, somewhere, but it will not be enough. Most Grum did what I did—they left. Who wants to stay on a poison world filled with dead daughters? Who wants to be around others of our kind, knowing the things that every one of us had to do? No, no, better to leave alone and die gracefully."

Rosemary thought in silence. "Where did you go?"

"I traveled out to the nearest spaceport and talked my way aboard a trade ship. Mixed crew. We mostly hopped between modder rocks and fringe colonies. I earned some credits helping in the kitchen. Just cleaning, at first, but their cook saw that I had an interest in food, and he indulged my desire to learn. Once I had enough money, I left the ship and made a home for myself on Port Coriol. I had a tiny soup shack near one of the family districts—the cook taught me about soup, you see— nothing fancy, but it was fast and cheap and good for you, and merchants in a hurry like food that is fast and cheap and good for you. There was a Human doctor who lived in the neighborhood, a man named Drave, and he came by often. I liked him a lot, but I was jealous of his profession. He was a *family* doctor. He'd seen his patients grow from babies to adults with babies of their own. It sounded like such a joy, to watch people age and help them do it healthily. One day, I was finally brave enough to confess to him that I had been a doctor once, and that I wanted to use those skills for something good. We made a deal: I could come work with Drave in his clinic for three days a tenday, and he could have free soup whenever he liked. Much better deal for me, I think! So that was my life for six standards—making soup, working in the clinic, taking Linking courses on alien anatomy. Oh, and herbs, I found out about herbs during that time. Drave was a good friend to me. Still is, we write from time to time. His grandson took over the soup shack for me, after I started becoming male. Bad time to be working. Bad time to be doing anything, really. The transition isn't easy." He rumbled. His thoughts were straying from the point. He hummed and burred to get them back. "Sometime later, this Human named Ashby stopped in the clinic to get his bots upgraded. We talked for a long time, and a few days later, he came back to tell me that he was gathering crew for a tunneling ship, and offered me a wonderful job. Two jobs! I was sad to say good-bye to Drave, but what Ashby had offered was exactly what I needed. There is peace out here in the open. I have friends and a garden in the stars and a kitchen full of tasty things. I heal people now. I cannot pretend that the war never happened, but I stopped fighting it long ago. I did not start that war. It should never have been mine to fight." He sank down so that he could look Rosemary square in the eye. "We cannot blame ourselves for the wars our parents start. Sometimes the very best thing we can do is walk away."

Rosemary was silent for a long time. "The cutters were horrible," she said. "But on some level, I can understand why your people used them. They were at war, they all hated each other. My father is not a soldier. He's never been in a war. He doesn't hate the Toremi. I don't know if he's ever even met one. We had everything on Mars. *Everything*. He allowed those weapons to be designed and sold—he *encouraged* it—and for what? More money? How many people are dead because of what he did? How many people's children?"

Dr. Chef sat back on four. "As you said, he had everything. That made him feel safe and powerful. People can do terrible things when they feel safe and powerful. Your father had probably gotten his way for so long that he thought he was untouchable, and that is a dangerous way for a person to feel. I don't think anyone on this ship blames you for wanting to get as far away as you could from a person like that."

"Ashby wasn't exactly pleased."

"Only about the deception. Not about who you are." He glanced back toward the empty kitchen, the empty hallway. "And between you and me, he understands. He's not going to hold it against you. But he's also your boss, and sometimes he has to speak in a way that reminds us of that." He hummed, shifting thoughts. "In a way, I think you must be feeling much the same way as I did the day that I found out where the cutters came from. You found something dark within your own house, and you are wondering how much of it has rubbed off on you."

Rosemary started to nod, then shook her head. "That's not the same. What happened to you, to your species, it's . . . it doesn't even compare."

"Why? Because it's worse?"

She nodded.

"But it still compares. If you have a fractured bone, and I've broken every bone in my body, does that make your fracture go away? Does it hurt you any less, knowing that I am in more pain?"

"No, but that's not—"

"Yes, it is. Feelings are relative. And at the root, they're all the same, even if they grow from different experiences and exist on different scales." He examined her face. She looked skeptical. "Sissix would understand this. You Humans really do cripple yourselves with your belief that you all think in unique ways." He leaned forward. "Your father—the person who raised you, who taught you how the world works—did something unspeakably horrible. And not only did he take part in it, he justified it to himself. When you first learned of what your father had done, did you believe it?"

"No."

"Why not?"

"I didn't think he was capable of it."

"Why not? He obviously was."

"He didn't *seem* like he was. The father I knew never could've done such a thing."

"Aha. But he *did*. So then you begin wondering how you could've been so wrong about him. You start going back through your memories, looking for signs. You begin questioning everything you know, even the good things. You wonder how much of it was a lie. And worst of all, since he had a heavy hand in making you who you are, you begin wondering what *you yourself* are capable of."

Rosemary stared at him. "Yes."

Dr. Chef bobbed his head up and down. "And this is where our species are very much alike. The truth is, Rosemary, that you are capable of anything. Good or bad. You always have been, and you always will be. Given the right push, you, too, could do horrible things. That darkness exists within all of us. You think every soldier who picked up a cutter gun was a bad person? No. She was just doing what the soldier next to her was doing, who was doing what the soldier next to *her* was doing, and so on and so on. And I bet most of them—not all, but most—who made it through the war spent a long time after trying to understand what they'd done. Wondering how they ever could have done it in the first place. Wondering when killing became so comfortable."

Rosemary's freckled cheeks had gone a little pale. He could see her throat move as she swallowed.

"All you can do, Rosemary—all any of us can do—is work to be something positive instead. That is a choice that every sapient must make every day of their life. The universe is what we make of it. It's up to you to decide what part you will play. And what I see in you is a woman who has a clear idea of what she wants to be."

Rosemary gave a short laugh. "Most days I wake up and have no idea what the hell I'm doing."

He puffed his cheeks. "I don't mean the practical details. Nobody ever figures those out. I mean the important thing. The thing I had to do, too." He made a clucking sound. He knew she would not understand it, but it came naturally. The sort of sound a mother made over a child learning to stand. "You're trying to be someone good."

KEDRIUM

☆

Kizzy was up too late, as usual. That had been standard procedure ever since she was a kid. When she was small, Papa would
tuck her in with a story and a kiss and a hug from Tumby, her
stuffed frog. Moments after the lights went out, her toes would
start wiggling, and her butt would follow suit, and before long,
the idea of holding still and *sleeping* seemed super unfair. At
regular intervals, Papa would come into her room, lift her away
from her building blocks and tuck her back in, his patient voice
growing ever wearier. Finally, Ba would get home from the
evening shift at the water station, and he'd say, "Kizzy, sweet-
heart, *please* go to sleep. The blocks will be there in the morning,
I promise." That was true, but he missed the point. While the
actual physical blocks would stay where she left them, her brain
was always full of new configurations that she hadn't tried yet.
If she didn't get them out before she fell asleep, they'd be totally
forgotten by morning, when she'd be distracted by the promise
of pancakes.

As an adult, Kizzy had found ways to better manage the
blueprints in her brain. She kept her scrib right by her bed so
that she could fill it with sketches and notes without leaving the
warmth of her blankets. But even so, unfinished projects often
kept her up late. It always started with *one last circuit*, which

turned into *I bet I could fix this*, and *just a few more tweaks*, and then bam, breakfast time.

But in the tendays since the whole Akarak thing, Kizzy had stayed awake for a different reason. Her brain still buzzed with ideas, but she went out of her way to keep herself busy even after they'd all been used up. Tonight, for instance, she was up dusting interface junctions on a spare power conduit. It wasn't a vital job. It wasn't even a necessary one. But it was something to do.

Dr. Chef had given her some drops to help her sleep, but she didn't like them. They left her feeling fuzzy in the morning, and besides, she didn't want to be the sort of person who needed drops at all. No, despite the tired, punched-face ache that nibbled at her all around the edges, she was going to do this without drops. Somehow, she'd figure out how to lie in bed without her mind drifting back to the cargo bay, guns in her face, Ashby bleeding in her lap. There hadn't been a night since when she hadn't lain there wondering if another ship would sneak up on them while she slept. She imagined Akaraks storming up to her room with their guns and shrieking voices. She imagined waking up to a pulse rifle pointed at her, or maybe not waking up at all. She remembered the way the bay doors had screeched as they were forced open. She remembered the thin jet of red that had spurted from Ashby's mouth when the Akarak clocked him with the gun. One of these nights, she'd find a way to stop remembering. But for now, there were a lot of junctions to dust.

"Hey, Kizzy," said Lovey through the vox. "Sorry to bug you, but you're the only one awake."

"What's up, sweetcheeks?"

"There's a ship approaching, about an hour out."

The cleaning rag fumbled. Oh, stars. The Akaraks had come back. They'd circled back. Well, not this time, motherfuckers. She'd hide away in a wall panel, seal herself in from the inside so no one would know. She'd scurry through the walls like a mouse, pulling off flashbang sabotage until every last one of the scrawny bastards was dead. If it took tendays, fine. She'd just duck into the kitchen now and then to steal supplies. She could live in the walls. This was *her* ship, and—and who the fuck was she kidding? There was no way she could pull it off. They were dead, totally dead. Why hadn't Ashby just bought a few guns back on Cricket? Dusthead Exodan, even just *one* gun would—

Lovey continued. "They're signaling us. It's a GC distress signal."

Kizzy exhaled. She felt a smidge of guilt for being relieved that someone *else* was in trouble, but . . . ah well. She propped up her scrib against a spool of wire. "Patch 'em through to my vid link."

The scrib switched on. A female Aeluon stared back at her. And like all members of her species, she was *gorgeous*. Silver skin, graceful neck, soft eyes, the whole shebang. Kizzy was suddenly very aware of the dirty worksuit she was wearing, the messy table, the—dammit, *crumbs,* she had cake crumbs on her shirt, and there was a pixel pen stuck in her hair, and—well, whatever. Surely the Aeluon had seen a Human tech before. She couldn't blame Kizzy for belonging to a grubby profession, or an ugly species.

"Hi there," Kizzy said, brushing herself off. "I'm Kizzy Shao. What's your trouble?" It was then that she noticed what the Aeluon was wearing. At first glance, the lady was just a snappy dresser, but Kizzy had played enough action sims to know an armored vest when she saw one—not clunky Human style, but one designed to blend in with the rest of her outfit. The Aeluon was seated, but Kizzy could see the end of an energy pistol peeking up over her belt. And there, cuffed around her arm— wasn't that a personal shield generator? Looked new, too. This lady meant business. Like, serious business. That wasn't just protective gear. It was *getting shit done because I am the boss* gear. Kizzy wished that Jenks was awake.

The Aeluon smiled (or, at least, something face related that was close enough). "Hello, Kizzy. I'm Captain Gapei Tem Seri. I was hoping to speak to your captain. Is he available?"

"He's asleep, but I can wake him up if you—"

"No, no," the Aeluon said. "Don't disturb him. Are you authorized to permit unscheduled dockings?"

Authorized to permit unscheduled dockings. Stars, this lady wasn't messing around. "Um, sure, I guess," Kizzy said. She wasn't sure *unscheduled dockings* were something that had ever been specifically discussed aboard the *Wayfarer*. If a ship's friendly and needs help, you help. Simple as that.

The Aeluon nodded. The gesture looked practiced. She obviously knew how to talk with Humans. "We've suffered damage to our life-support systems. It seems our most recent shipment included a delayed disruptor mine. It didn't go off until we were out in the open."

"Whoa. Shit. Are you okay?"

"We have temporary repairs in place, and we've been holding fairly steady for three days now. But we're on our way to Aeluon space, and I'm not sure our stopgap measures will last that long. What we really need is to shut down the core entirely and let our fixbots do their job."

"And you need a place to hang out in the meantime. No worries, we've got plenty of air to go around. Wait, do you not have a tech?"

The Aeluon's cheeks darkened into a greenish-gray. "We ran into some trouble at our last stop. Our tech . . ." She exhaled. "Our tech didn't make it. I . . . I haven't had a chance to hire a new one yet."

"Stars. I'm so sorry." Okay, what the hell did this lady do that involved disruptor mines and the kind of "trouble" that ended in dead techs?

The Aeluon didn't say anything further about it. "Anyway, if we could come aboard, just while our bots do their job—"

"Why not let us do it? I'm the mech tech here, and our comp tech knows his way around a life-support system. We're better than bots, and depending on the damage, you might not have to take your systems offline."

The Aeluon considered this. "Are you familiar with Aeluon tech?"

"Well, uh, not like, *practically*. But tech is tech. We can take a look, at least. Promise I won't touch anything if I don't know what it does."

"As long as it's no trouble, then yes, I'd appreciate anything you could do."

"Cool. Yeah, definitely."

"Our ship is less than an hour out from yours, but we could half it if you meet us in the middle."

"Absolutely. No problem."

The Aeluon's face brightened. "Wonderful." The lights hanging above her reflected off her scales, like sunlight on a wave. Why was everything that the Aeluons did so pretty? "I've got a crew of six—er, five, plus two soldiers." *Holy shit, Aeluon commandos. Jenks is going to wet himself.* "We'll do our best to keep out of your way."

"Oh, no worries, that's totally fine," Kizzy said. "I'm sure Dr. Chef would love to feed you guys. He's our cook." Wow, that sounded stupid. For once, why couldn't she just sound cool?

"Yes, I know. Your captain and I are acquaintances, actually. But yes, thank you, Kizzy. I don't know what we would've done if we hadn't found you."

How does she know—The thought cut off with a thud. The pieces fell together. "Um, yeah, we're, uh, happy to help. Hey, sorry, what did you say your name was?"

"Gapei Tem Seri. Do you need me to send over my ID—"

"No, no, I just, ah . . . are you *Pei?*"

The Aeluon paused and glanced over her shoulder. "Yes," she said. The sound from her talkbox had gone soft, secret. "That's a nickname I let my friends use. Ashby included."

Kizzy grinned so hard she thought her face would break. This lady—this insanely beautiful badass who wore energy pistols and said things like *disruptor mine* without kidding around— was Pei. Ashby didn't just *know* this Aeluon. Ashby was *banging* this Aeluon. "Captain, um—sorry, I don't know which name to call you by." Aeluons had two last names, one for their family and one for where they were from. She wasn't sure which was which.

"Captain Tem is fine."

"Well, Captain Tem, I think I'm speaking for my captain and all the rest of us when I say that you're welcome to come aboard for as long as you like."

"Thank you." Captain Tem paused again. "I'm not quite sure how to ask this—"

Kizzy got it. Captain Tem was an Aeluon, with an Aeluon crew, with Aeluon soldiers onboard, and she was about to come aboard her Human boyfriend's ship. Kizzy leaned forward, wiping the grin off her face. "Yes, we all know how to . . . *be polite.*" Meaning *keep our mouths shut.* "Especially around soldiers."

Captain Tem looked grateful. "Thanks, Kizzy. I appreciate that. I'll signal again when we've reached your coordinates."

"Sounds good. See you soon." The vidlink panel on the scrib flicked off. Kizzy started laughing. *Oh, man. So cool. So. Cool.* "Hey, Lovey," she called to the vox. "Wake up Jenks. Sissix, too. I need to talk to them like right now."

"What about Ashby?"

"Nah. I want to wake him up myself so I can see his face."

"Nosy."

"Says you."

The AI laughed. "Do you really think Captain Tem will let Jenks aboard her ship? He'd like that very much."

"Lovey, I have the feeling that this little rendezvous is going to be awesome for everybody."

Ashby's brain wasn't working right. For starters, he'd been startled out of three hours of sleep by Kizzy, who had decided to wake him up by hacking the lock on his door and turning on all the lights. Then she'd told him the most incomprehensible thing: Pei was coming aboard. *Pei*. Here. On his ship. And she'd been talking to *Kizzy*, of all people.

"Do you have any idea what Kizzy said to her?" He was in the bathroom, finishing the fastest shower of his life.

Sissix answered from the opposite side of the shower curtain. He could hear the amusement in her voice. It was the sound of the look she'd been wearing for the past ten minutes. "I have no idea," she said. "But she didn't even realize who she was talking to at first. I think your reputation is intact."

Ashby switched off the shower, blotted himself dry and wrapped his towel around his waist. He stepped out into the room and grabbed a dentbot pack from the communal basket. He caught a glimpse of himself in the mirror. "I look like shit." He pulled back the seal on the pack and squeezed the gel onto his tongue. He tossed the empty package and pressed his lips together. He could feel the gel spread itself around his mouth as the bots searched for plaque and bacteria.

Sissix leaned against the wall, holding a mug between her claws. "You do not, and even if you did, I highly doubt she'll care."

"Mmph-mm."

"What?"

Ashby rolled his eyes and let the bots do their job, wishing they'd work a little faster. After a minute or so, the gel went thin, indicating that the bots had begun to break down. He spat the vaguely minty goo into a sink and rinsed it down the drain. "I said, *I* care."

"I know. And it's very cute that you do."

He put his hands on the edge of the sink and looked into the mirror. His eyes had a hint of red, and his hair had seen better days. He sighed. "I don't want to screw things up for her."

Sissix stepped over and put her hand between his shoulder blades. "You won't. And neither will the rest of us. No jokes, no innuendos. We know how serious this is." She pointed to a stack of clothes resting on the counter. "That's the least wrinkly pair of pants I could find." She handed him the mug. "And I had Dr. Chef make you some of this awful stuff."

The smell hit his nose before he even brought the cup to his face. Coffee. "You are the best." He tipped the rim of the mug between his lips. Dark, bitter, strong. He felt better already.

Sissix patted his forearm. "Come on. Put on your trousers. I want to meet the woman who gets to take them off."

A short while later, he was standing in front of the airlock, surrounded by the self-appointed welcoming committee—Sissix, Dr. Chef and the techs. Caffeine, adrenaline and the need for sleep all battled for supremacy, chasing each other around like a pack of dogs. He felt like hell.

"So, Ashby," Jenks said. "You gonna tell us how you two met?"

Ashby sighed. "Not right now."

Jenks grinned. He'd been doing that a lot this morning. "I'll wait." He pulled his redreed tin from a pocket.

Dr. Chef nudged him. "No red smoke. Aeluons are often allergic."

Jenks closed the tin. "Real allergic, right? Not Corbin allergic?"

Dr. Chef let out a percussive, laughing chord. "Real allergic."

"The Aeluon ship is now extending its docking tube," Lovey said. Ashby could hear metallic clanking against the hull. "Their hatch is open. I'm initiating decontamination protocols."

Ashby could hear footsteps beyond the airlock door. *Oh stars, she's there. She's in there right now.* He exhaled.

Sissix rubbed her cheek on his shoulder. "Nervous?"

"Why would you say that?"

Sissix rested her chin against his neck and squeezed his arm. Ashby's mouth twitched. He knew it was a friendly, reassuring gesture, and Pei probably knew enough about Aandrisks to know what Sissix meant by it, but something in his Human brain balked at the idea of Pei walking in to see another woman draped over his shoulder. He lowered his voice. "Sis, sorry, but could you not . . . um . . ."

"Hm?" Her yellow eyes searched his face, confused. "*Ohhh.* Right. Right." She moved a step away and clasped her hands behind her back. She didn't say another word, but Ashby could see the laughter in her eyes.

"Ashby, there's something weird here," Lovey said.

"What's up? Some kind of bug?"

"No, no contaminants, but I'm confused. Their patch scans all check out, but there are supposed to be two soldiers with them. All I'm getting are civilian patches."

"They're probably undercover," Ashby said. "It's okay to let them in, Lovey. I trust them."

"So cool," Jenks whispered to Kizzy. They both giggled like schoolkids. *Stars and fire, you two, behave.*

The doors slid open. The airlock was full of people, but Ashby only had eyes for one of them. He was very much awake now.

Pei stepped forward. "Permission to come aboard?" she said,

looking deep into Ashby's eyes. The air seemed to crackle between them. She had to play the captain now, but he could see that she wanted to say much more.

He nodded. All was understood. "Come out of the open and into our home," he said. It was an Exodan expression, one used for newly docked travelers. "It's good to see you." He extended his hand. This was a joke, though neither of their crews would get it. He knew full well that Aeluons pressed their palms in greeting, but he hadn't known that when he'd first met Pei, and likewise, she hadn't known what to do with his hand after she held it.

"Good to see you, too, old friend." She shook his hand, noting the gesture with nothing more than a slight flicker of her eyelids. Damn, she was good at this. If he hadn't understood the need for secrecy, he might have been offended by her nonchalance.

Introductions were made. Pei shook hands with the techs, pressed palms with Sissix (of course Sissix knew what to do) and laughed with Dr. Chef while trying to figure out his hand-feet. Ashby worked his way through Pei's crew, pretending that he didn't know their names, moods and personal histories already. He knew that two of them, Sula and Oxlen, knew about him and Pei. Their eyelids flicked with acknowledgment as he met them. As far as he was aware, they were the only Aeluons in the galaxy who knew. He was going to do his damnedest to keep it that way.

The two soldiers, though dressed in civilian clothing, were easy to spot. For one thing, they were armed more heavily than the others (which Ashby found somewhat unsettling), and their muscles were toned to perfection. One of them, a female, had an ocular implant. The end of an old scar jutted down below it. The male was young, but carried a weariness with him. Ashby wondered how long he'd been at war, and if he was glad for the respite of a cargo run.

Ashby glanced at Pei, who was sharing pleasantries with his crew. He'd imagined her on his ship so many times, but his daydreams had played out differently. Pei would step through the airlock, with nothing but a bag over her shoulder and a smile in her eyes. He'd put his arm around her waist as he introduced her. Sissix wouldn't have to hold back her welcoming hug. They'd go to the Fishbowl, where all his favorite people would get to know each other over one of Dr. Chef's celebratory dinners. They'd drink mek and laugh, lounging easily in the garden. A simple blending of the two halves of his life. But here in the airlock, the separation was clear. Military and civilian. Aeluons and a mixed-species hodgepodge. High tech and the-best-they-could-do. But even so, she was still on his ship, talking to his crew. The lines between their lives had become blurred. He could feel her pulling him across the divide.

"I can't believe how lucky we were to find you out here," Pei said. "I hope we aren't inconveniencing you."

"Stay as long as you need." *Or just stay, period.* "I hear our techs have volunteered to help with repairs."

"We're all ready to go," Kizzy said, hands on her toolbelt buckle. "You just point us in the right direction."

"Oxlen will go with you," Pei said.

"I'm no tech," said Oxlen, Pei's pilot, a tall male with light eyes. "But I can tell you the basics of what's what."

The female soldier—Tak, if Ashby remembered correctly—spoke up. "I was hoping that we might have access to your scanners and ansible. I highly doubt we will encounter enemy contacts out here, but given what happened aboard our ship, we can't be too careful."

"Sissix can show you to the control room," Ashby said. "Unless you'd like manual access to our AI core." Out of the corner of his eye, Ashby could see Jenks stiffen at the suggestion. *Relax, Jenks, they're not going to break her.*

"Your control room should be fine," Tak said. She nodded to Sissix, who led the way down the hall. Ashby could not have imagined an odder looking pair: the armed Aeluon missing an eye, and the Aandrisk in low-slung trousers and a fresh coat of swirls painted on her claws.

"As for the rest of us," Pei said, "I'm afraid all we can do is wait."

"Oh, I don't think that'll be so bad," Dr. Chef said. "It's just about time for me to start preparing breakfast. Though, fair warning, my recipes weren't exactly made with Aeluons in mind. This might be the worst breakfast you've ever had."

The male soldier laughed. "You've never had field rations."

"You'd be surprised." Dr. Chef puffed his cheeks. Ashby smiled. Few things made Dr. Chef happier than feeding hungry people. "Come along with me. Let's have a look through my stasie, see what appeals to you."

"Please tell me you have real mek onboard," one of Pei's crew said. He had a gun strapped across his back that would have made Bear and Nib weep with envy. Did they really have to wear weapons here?

"Plenty of mek," Kizzy said. "Big ol' boxes of it."

"Oh, stars, that's great news. If I have to drink another cup of the prepackaged stuff, I'm going to be sick."

"Only one cup each," Pei said. "I'm not getting back on my ship with a fuzzy-eyed crew."

"Come on, come on, all of you," Dr. Chef said, leading the way out of the airlock, walking on two. "I'm not letting you leave hungry."

The remaining Aeluons followed eagerly. "Leave some for me," Oxlen called after them as he led the techs back through the airlock. Kizzy snuck one last glance at Pei, and wiggled her eyebrows at Ashby. He rolled his eyes and shooed her away with his hand. She scampered off, chuckling.

They waited until the hallway was silent. Even then, Ashby wasn't sure what to say. He wanted to kiss her, hold her, run up to his room and let her tear off his clothes. Somehow, he held it back. "So. This is unexpected."

She stared at him. Her second eyelids closed slowly. Her cheeks turned a displeased shade of yellow. "There is a scatter burst burn on your hull."

"You always say the most romantic things."

"Ashby." She glared. "You said in your last message that you got boarded and that you lost some supplies. You said nothing about getting fired upon. Was anyone hurt?"

"No." He paused. "Just me. But I'm fine."

Her cheeks swam with exasperated colors. "Why didn't you say anything?"

"Because I didn't want you to worry."

She cocked her head. "We seem to have traded places."

"Hardly. Who's the one showing up on my doorstep talking about *disruptor mines*?"

"There was only the one mine, and no one was hurt. It seems someone at the loading bay had an . . . *opinion* about the war."

Ashby shook his head. "The Rosk are attacking border colonies. How—"

"I know, I know. People are crazy." She frowned. "And speaking of, the more I hear about this Toremi situation, the less I like it."

"You didn't like it from the start."

"Ashby, listen. I met the captain of a pinhole tug that's been ferrying diplomats out there. The Toremi, they're . . . strange."

"They're a different species. We're all strange to each other. *You're* strange to me sometimes."

"No, I mean dangerous strange. Incomprehensible strange. She said she couldn't understand how the GC had brokered an alliance with them at all. The diplomats, they kept talking about how hard it was to communicate with them. It wasn't a matter of language, the Toremi just *think* differently. They try to all think exactly the same things in exactly the same way, which is insane enough, but everything goes to shit if they can't find consensus. That captain, she told me that a few standards back, when the GC finally got their foot in the door, a few Toremi tore each other apart—I mean literally, Ashby, *during a conference*—because they couldn't agree on whether or not Harmagians were *sapient*."

"I'm sure they've figured that much out by now."

"Maybe. All I know is that she heard of several times where a Toremi delegate didn't voice agreement with its higher-ups during a meeting, and then was never seen again. She hated going out there. She said she got scared every time one of their ships got close. She didn't trust them. And neither do I."

"You've never *met* them. Pei, the GC wouldn't be sending us all the way to the Core if they didn't think they could keep us safe. We'll be fine, don't worry."

Her cheeks flashed pale purple with frustration. "I can't even keep the people on my own ship safe. How am I supposed to not worry about you?"

He looked down the hallway, just to be sure. He took her hand. "Kizzy said you lost someone."

She shut her eyes. "Saery."

He squeezed her hand tight, fighting the urge to take her into his arms. "Stars. Pei, I'm so sorry."

"It was pointless, Ashby, so fucking pointless. He got jumped in an alley while we were on Dresk. They cut out his patch and stole the tech he'd picked up that day. If he hadn't been alone—"

"Hey." He reached up to cup her cheek. The hell with it. "Hey, now. Don't go there."

She pressed her cheek into his palm, ever so briefly, then pulled back, her eyes flicking down the hall. "I've missed you so much," she said. "These last tendays . . . I wanted to write to you, but—"

"I know," he said, and smiled. "Come on. I'll show you my ship, and we can talk. Touring the ship is a respectable sort of activity, right?"

There was a tiny flash of amused green in her cheeks. "Yeah."

"What did you tell them, anyway? About you and me?"

"That we met on Port Coriol, right after I bought my ship. I met you there during a supply run, and sometimes we meet for a drink when we wind up at the same dock."

"Huh. The truth."

"Well, the innocuous part of it, anyway. To be honest, it felt a little strange." Her cheeks went yellow. "I've gotten used to lying about you."

"I feel like I should've left my shoes at the door," Jenks said to Kizzy as they followed Oxlen through the corridors of the Aeluon frigate.

Kizzy nodded. She'd seen Acluon ships in dock, and Linking pics of what they looked like inside, but being inside one . . . it was like walking through a piece of art. The grayish walls were pristine, not a bolt or panel to be seen. She couldn't see any individual light fixtures, just continuous strips of soft light emanating from the curved ceiling. No window frames, no visible air filters. It was a ship as smooth and seamless as stone. And silent, too. Though Aeluons had given themselves the means to process sound and verbal speech, they only needed those abilities to communicate with other species. Within their own ships, they had no use for sound. There were no voxes or klaxons or panels that beeped and chirped. Even the sounds of the life-support systems and artigrav nets were so low that Kizzy could barely make them out (though she doubted their quietness was engineered on purpose; more likely, they were just extremely well designed). The absence of sound made the ship seem all the more hallowed, like a temple built to honor good tech. Hers and Jenks's big, stompy boots and clanking toolbelts felt intrusive. She was glad that she'd had the time to change into a relatively clean jumpsuit.

"Life support's in here," Oxlen said. He placed his palm on the wall, and a portion of it melted open. As Kizzy walked through the opening, she could see the surrounding frame, the predefined edges of the door, solid as the thickest plex.

"What *is* this stuff?" Kizzy asked, running her palm over the wall. Cold and firm, but she could feel a latent pliability beneath. "Some sort of responsive polymer?"

"Yes. It's held in place by an electrostatic lattice, which responds to the bioelectrical signals in our skin."

"Wow." Kizzy leaned closer to the wall, squinting. "What's it made of?"

"That's . . . beyond my area of expertise. I'm sure you could look it up in the Linkings." They walked into a room filled with a tangle of tech. Way, *way* better looking than the stuff Kizzy was used to, but recognizable all the same. Oxlen gestured to a large apparatus, the heavy heart at the center of a network of tubes and pipes. "This is—"

"Your atmospheric regulator." Kizzy put her hands on her hips and nodded as she inspected it. "Looks an awful lot like ours."

"Except a hell of a lot prettier," Jenks said. "Check out those stabilizers."

"Wow," Kizzy said. "Look at the interlocking seals. Awesome. Awesome, awesome, awesome." She craned her head toward Oxlen. "Where was the mine?"

"Top left corner. Tucked behind the . . ." Oxlen made a vague gesture. "That lump with the little knob on it."

Kizzy climbed up the side of the regulator, taking care to rest her weight on the sturdiest pipes. Behind the relay hub—the lump with the little knob on it—was a patch of torn metal, the end result of a fierce energy discharge. She pulled her tech lenses from her belt and slipped them over her head. She peered through the magnification lens as she pried up the metal and looked inside.

"Wow," she said. "All the nodes around here are fried. The filter relays are ten kinds of fucked up. Your fixbots patched 'em up okay, but this needs more than—holy shit, look at that. Wow." She flipped the lens aside, put on her gloves and reached into the hole.

"What's up?" Jenks asked.

Kizzy felt around, running her protected fingers over the mangled machinery. "The entire regulator shaft's stripped. Nasty piece of work."

"Should I go get some filler sheets?"

"Yeah, and grab your small tools while you're at it. There's a whole circuit panel in here that you'll need to rewire. And snacks, Jenks, we're gonna need a shitload of snacks for this." She rubbed her left eye, pushing away the sleepiness. She was starting her day without having gone to bed, but that was hardly anything new. She had a thermos of happy tea clipped to her belt, and a packet of stims in her pocket in case things got really dire. It'd do.

"So, you can fix it?" Oxlen said.

"Oh, yeah," Kizzy said. She looked Oxlen in the eye and placed her hand over her heart. "Believe me when I say that there's nothing I'd rather do than fix this thing."

Rosemary sat perched on a stack of empty vegetable crates, snacking on pepper puffs. Sissix was with her, leaning against one of Dr. Chef's bug-breeding tanks. The curtain separating the storage room from the kitchen was pulled back, but not all the way. The stasie hummed. The bugs skittered. It was a good place for gossip.

"They're so pretty," Rosemary said, looking out at the Aeluons happily stuffing their faces around the dinner table. "I wish I had scales."

"You say that," Sissix said. "Be happy you have skin that doesn't shed all in one go."

"Do Aeluons molt?"

"No. The bastards." She took a few puffs from the bowl sitting in Rosemary's lap.

"How do *you* see them? I know attractiveness is relative."

"True, but Aeluons are the universal exception. They're stupidly pretty." Sissix crunched her puffs.

"Harmagians probably disagree."

"Harmagians don't get a say in this."

"Why?"

"Because they have no bones and are covered in goo."

Rosemary chuckled. "That's not their fault."

"It's still true." Sissix grinned. "Look at them, though." She nodded toward the Aeluons. "Look at the way they move. Even little things. Like that one, look at the way she picked up her cup. They don't move. They *dance*." She took another handful of puffs. "They make me feel like . . . oh, what are those big ugly reptiles you have back on Earth? The extinct ones?"

"Um . . ." Rosemary racked her brain. "I don't know. Iguanas?"

"I don't know what those are. I don't mean things lost in the Collapse. I mean the old reptiles, the ones millions of years ago."

"Dinosaurs."

"Yes!" Sissix hunched over, tucking her arms up and exaggerating the angle of her bent legs. She stomped around the storage room, shifting her weight clumsily.

Rosemary cracked up. "You're not a dinosaur."

"You don't know that. You weren't there. Maybe some of them built ships and left."

Rosemary let her eyes trail over Sissix. Polished green scales. Festive quills. Artful swirls painted around her claws. The way her trousers hung just so over her strange hips. Even when goofing off amid old crates and edible bugs, she was lovely. "You're too pretty to be a dinosaur," she said. She felt her cheeks flush as she said it. She hoped it didn't show.

"That's a relief," Sissix said, straightening up. "They didn't have the best of luck, if I recall. What was it? Gamma-ray burst?"

"Impact event."

"Too bad. The galaxy could use a few more reptiles."

"To be fair, though, them dying out made room for us weird furry things."

Sissix laughed and gave Rosemary's shoulder a friendly squeeze. "And I am fond of you weird furry things."

Rosemary smiled, and got to her feet. "You want some fizz?" she said, walking to the cooler.

"Yes, please. These puffs have a kick." Sissix watched the Aeluons as Rosemary searched for drinks. "I've heard it's very scary to encounter them in combat. No yelling or noise. Just a bunch of silent people coming to kill you."

"Ugh," Rosemary said. She handed Sissix a frosty bottle of melon fizz. "That's creepy."

"You ever hear of the battle of Tkrit?" Sissix said. She looked at the long-necked bottle in her hand. "I need an Aandrisk-friendly cup."

"Oh, right, sorry," Rosemary said. She stepped through the doorway and opened the cupboard outside, in search of something that someone without lips could drink from. Out at the far end of the kitchen, Corbin appeared at the counter. He gave the briefest of glances their way as he poured himself a mug of tea from the communal decanter. Sissix didn't acknowledge him, but Rosemary could see her feathers fluff ever so slightly. "What's the battle of Tkrit?"

"Territory skirmish back before the GC, when we were all snatching up habitable planets as fast as we could. One of the few times Aeluons and Aandrisks clashed. Just a squabble, really. We were never formally at war. The story goes that late one night, three groups of Aeluon soldiers snuck into the base on Tkrit. Dead quiet, like I said, and coming in from all sides."

"What'd the Aandrisks do?" Rosemary said, handing Sissix a cup.

Sissix grinned. "They turned off the lights. Aeluons can't see in infrared."

Rosemary imagined being inside a pitch-black building, filled with silent soldiers being picked off by unseen claws reaching through the darkness. She shivered.

"Speaking of Aeluons," Sissix said. "I am dying to know where our captain is." She turned toward the vox. "Hey, Lovey."

"Nope," Lovey said.

Sissix and Rosemary exchanged amused looks. "Nope?" Sissix said.

"You heard me. No way."

"Please? You don't have to say what they're doing, just tell me where—"

"Oh, no! I seem to have a . . . circuit . . . problem. I can't talk to you anymore." The vox switched off.

Rosemary and Sissix started to laugh, but the fun died as Corbin approached the storage room. "Do you know when Kizzy and Jenks are coming back?" He addressed the question directly to Rosemary. "They've been gone five hours."

"Sorry, I don't know," Rosemary said.

"Rough estimate?"

"I really have no idea."

Corbin huffed. "The mixer they replaced last tenday jammed again, and the sensors aren't responding. I have a drum that's on the brink of going tacky."

Rosemary wanted to comment that the Aeluons had a ship that was *running out of air*, but if Sissix could bite her tongue, so could she. "If I see them before you do, I'll send them your way."

"I'd appreciate that." He gave a curt nod and left.

Rosemary turned to Sissix, who was contemplating something within her cup. "What's up?"

Sissix inhaled, as if surfacing from a deep thought. "Oh, I was just exploring the idea of telling the Aeluons that Corbin is a Rosk spy."

Rosemary snorted. "I'm sure they treat their prisoners well."

"Well, that's the thing. I doubt a civilian ship like that has facilities for transporting captured spies." She sipped her drink. "I bet they'd make good use of the airlock, though."

The wrench fell from Kizzy's hand and clattered down behind the regulator. "Oops." She climbed down the pipes, making her way to the space between the machinery and the wall.

"You want me to get it?" Jenks asked.

"Nah, there's plenty of space." Kizzy jumped down to the floor and began hunting for the errant tool. After a few steps forward, she paused. Something wasn't right. She turned around and looked at the wall. There was a hatchway there, but it wasn't properly melting into the surrounding wall. The seam around it flickered, as if someone was activating and deactivating the door faster than it could respond.

"Hey, Oxlen," Kizzy called.

"Yes?"

"Is there a service panel back here?"

"I think so, why?"

"Looks like it's malfunctioning." Kizzy thought about the way the walls worked. "Could something be interfering with the structural lattice? A wonky circuit or something? Anything generating a signal?"

"I suppose. I don't really know. Do you think the mine damaged the door?"

Kizzy looked back up at the regulator. The relay hub was a long way up. She shook her head. "I doubt it. Nothing else this far down was damaged." Kizzy pressed her hand against the panel. She could feel the polymer beneath her fingers liquefy—though that wasn't quite the right word, because the wall didn't feel wet. Just . . . fluid. Kizzy gave a little laugh. "Cool." The panel melted aside. The frame twitched and wiggled, but it held in place. She stuck her head into the wall and switched on the two little globulbs attached to her lenses.

The wall held power conduits, fuel tubes, waste lines—all the things you'd expect to see within a ship's wall. She stepped inside. There was a narrow service pathway there, big enough for a lone tech. The pathway led upward, disappearing into the darker regions of the ship's innards. She gazed around, looking for a sparking circuit or a leaking tube.

A small flash of yellow light caught her eye. Just a little way above her head, easily within arm's reach, a strange object clung to a bundle of fuel tubes. Flat, black, round. Like a metallic jellyfish, tendrils wrapped tight. It was obviously of a different make than surrounding tech, but Kizzy couldn't quite place it. There was another flash. Then a pause. Then a flash again.

"What the hell—" she muttered. She reached toward it. But before her fingers made contact, she froze. Another flash appeared in the corner of her eye. She craned her head up to follow the pathway. There was another one of the objects, positioned a few paces away from her. Then another. And another.

She turned off her globulbs. Stretched out in a steady line, disappearing into the dark, a row of tiny yellow lights blinked in rhythm.

With rising horror, she realized what they were.

Kizzy threw herself back against the wall as if burned. *Run*, she thought. *Run*. But she didn't run. She stared.

"Kizzy?" Jenks called. "You okay in there?"

She swallowed hard, trying to work some spit back into her mouth. "Mines," she said.

"What was that?"

"Mines," she said, louder. "The wall. The entire fucking wall. It's full of mines." And big ones, too. Earlier, she'd found a piece of casing from the one that had knocked out the atmospheric regulator. Intact, it had probably been as wide across as her pinky. These were about the size of an outstretched hand. Things that big weren't made for knocking out an isolated system. Things that big were made to go boom.

Back in the room, Jenks and Oxlen were making a lot of noise, talking over each other, calling their respective captains. But to Kizzy, they seemed distant. Her heart was in her ears. Her muscles started to shake. Her body begged to get away. But a quiet thought cut through the panic, holding her steady. *How long before they go off?* She thought about this. If they were ready to go off in seconds, running away wouldn't make any damn difference, not for her, not for the cargo ship, nor for the *Wayfarer*. But if there was more time, even just a minute or two, maybe . . . could she?

She looked at the evil metal jellyfish nearest to her. Explosive or not, it was still a machine. She understood machines. Machines followed rules.

"Oxlen," she called. "Do either of those soldiers happen to be weapons techs?"

"What? No, no, they're just guards, we don't have anyone who—"

Kizzy ignored the rest of whatever Oxlen was saying. She unhooked a pair of clippers from her belt, flicked her globulbs back on and climbed up close.

"Kizzy," Jenks said. "Kizzy, you need to get out of there."

"Quiet," she said. "Give me a minute."

"We may not have a minute, Kizzy, get out of there."

"If we don't have a minute, it won't make any fucking difference where I am."

"Kizzy—" Oxlen started.

Kizzy flipped her scanner lenses into place. "Both of you. Shut up. I can do this. Just—just shut up."

Somewhere very far away, she could hear more yelling, and a clanking sound—probably Jenks climbing over the pipes to come get her. She ignored it and peered through the lens into the heart of the mine. Its interior was solid explosive material—kedrium, given the density—which was seriously great news. For starters, that meant the triggering mechanisms were only on the outside of the mine, so there were no surprises inside that she needed to worry about. Better still, she knew kedrium. Back in her teens, she'd been grounded for her whole summer break after she and her friends had blown up an old junker skiff with a block of the stuff. Cheap explosive, used for clearing rock. You could get it at any market stop. If the mine used kedrium, that meant there had to be two triggers—one to start a heating device, and one to spark the kedrium once it was hot enough to be reactive. She took off her gloves and felt around the edges of the mine. Still cold. That was a good sign. She ran a finger over the seams. There. She shifted around so that she was hunched over within the fuel tubes. From that vantage point, she could see little trigger knobs sticking out from the backside, surrounded by dried beads of sealant. This wasn't some fancy-pants military-grade tech. This was hackjob work.

She placed the clippers between her teeth and pulled a heat

awl from her belt. The sealant fizzled and thinned under the awl's searing tip. She switched back to the magnification lens. *Okay. That looks like the primary trigger, so if I just pop it loose*—The yellow light blinked steadily, unchanged from before. *There's the heater. And there*—She held her breath and pulled the knob away from the frame. A thin cable trailed after it. She let the awl fall to the floor and took the clippers from her mouth. Her hand began to shake. The clippers rattled. She cut the cable.

The light switched off.

"Kizzy—"

She pried the blasting cap free of its gutted frame. It fell into her hand. Heavy. Cold. Harmless. A shudder of air burst from her lips. Her vision swam. She slumped against the wall and slid down to the floor, pressing her free palm against her forehead.

"Holy fuck," Jenks said, falling against the door frame. "You did it."

Kizzy took a deep breath. Her muscles shook all the harder. She laughed.

One of the problems with talkboxes was that operating them required no small degree of mental concentration. If the wearer was distracted or impaired, the computerized words would come out jumbled. Such was the case with Pei, who was more upset than Ashby had ever seen. She stood fuming over the pieces of the disarmed mine that Kizzy had placed on the dinner table. Her cheeks were purple with anger, dark as a bruise.

"I can't—bastards on—what we might—brought you into—sorry for—"

"Pei," Ashby said. He raised a halting hand, minding his tone with care. They were surrounded by her crew and his. He was alarmed, she was furious and their people were afraid. It was just the sort of situation that might make one of them slip. "Try to slow down."

She took a shuddering breath. The colors in her cheeks flared, but held steady. "Saery. I can't believe he was a coincidence."

"What do you mean?" said one of her crew. Sula, a short female.

"Think about it. If the Aeluons give you sand between your teeth, and you want to cause some damage, why go to the trouble of taking out one cargo ship when you could take out a docking hub? Or a repair station?"

Oxlen's cheeks darkened. There were a lot of purple faces at the table. "They knocked out a vital system so that we'd have to stop for repairs. They figured we'd pull into port somewhere. That's why the mines haven't gone off yet. They timed them to wait a few tendays, because that's how long it would take us to get to a dock. They weren't planning for us to get help along the way."

Sula's eyes narrowed. "And they made sure we didn't have a tech to fix it. He wasn't mugged. They must've watched him."

Pei took a few steps toward the window, fists balled against her sides. Ashby stuck his hands in his pockets and pressed his feet to the floor. Sissix caught his eye. Almost imperceptibly, she flashed him the Aandrisk gesture for sympathy.

"We can get angry later," Pei said, turning back. Her cheeks had dulled to a dusky blue. "Right now, we have a bigger problem. Ashby, I can't believe I got you mixed up in this. I'm so sorry."

"I'm not," Ashby said. "You might not have known anything was wrong if it wasn't for Kizzy."

"See, this is why fixbots are stupid," Kizzy said. "There are so many things they—"

Jenks laid a hand across her arm. "Not now, Kiz."

Tak picked up one of the pieces of the mine. "It must've been one of the dock workers. Slipped away while the others were unloading cargo. This is our fault. We should've been more vigilant."

"Nobody expected this," Pei said. "I've been running cargo for ten standards, and whenever somebody wants a piece of what I've got, they come at me directly. I've never dealt with anything so underhanded."

Tak's second eyelids darted in, then back again. "I don't understand why they'd use such crude tech after going to all the trouble of getting aboard our ship."

"If you were at a public docking port, that's the only way they *could* do it," Jenks said. "How are they supposed to get fully assembled explosives through security? It's way easier to bring in the pieces individually and put them together in a closet somewhere. Kedrium has legitimate uses on its own. It'd be easy to sneak through. And the rest of this stuff, it's just odds and ends."

"Be happy they made them that way," Kizzy said. "I wouldn't have been able to figure 'em out otherwise. They should've hired better techs." She glanced up at the Aeluon soldiers. "Or, I mean, um, hrm." She grabbed a cookie off a nearby plate and shoved it into her mouth.

Pei tapped her fingers on the table. "You're sure they're nowhere else on the ship?"

"Positive," Oxlen said. "I ran a full scan, after I knew what to look for."

Pei's cheeks flooded with colors. Ashby knew that look—hesitancy. "Kizzy. I wish I didn't have to ask this, but—"

"Yeah, I can do it," Kizzy said. She looked Ashby right in the eye before he'd even said anything. "*I can.* I poked at the timer, and they're set to go off in three days. That's way more than I need."

"I don't doubt that you can do it," Ashby said. "But just because you took care of one doesn't mean that the others might not go off."

"If we do nothing, they're *all* going to go off."

Corbin spoke up from his vantage point by the kitchen counter. "Would that be such a bad thing?" he asked. "This . . . situation puts all of us at risk. No offense, Captain Tem, but this is not our problem." Sissix opened her mouth, but Corbin continued. "I'm sure we could drop all of you somewhere where you could find transport back to wherever you're going. Why not call the ship a loss and let us give you passage? We might even have room for some of your cargo, so long as you prioritize."

Pei looked to the two soldiers. Their faces erupted with color, shifting fast as a kaleidoscope.

A minute passed. "Um, so . . ." Kizzy said.

Jenks frowned. "They're talking, Kizzy."

"Oh." She covered her mouth with her hands. "Right."

Pei exhaled. "Sorry. The trouble is that our cargo is . . . important. The soldiers feel that if there is a chance of saving all of it, we have to take it." She met Ashby's eyes. "And I feel terrible for saying it, but I'm inclined to agree. Not because it's my ship or because I want to get paid. But what we're carrying . . . it could really help. I'm sorry, I . . ." She glanced at the soldiers. "I can't explain further than that."

Ashby looked to Kizzy. "I'm not going to make you do this."

Kizzy nodded with more composure than Ashby had ever seen in her. "I already said. I can do this." She picked up the blasting cap. "I was freaking out while I took this one apart. I'm one-hundred percent chill now. If I could disarm them while I was losing my shit, I can totally do it now." She smiled at Rosemary, who was biting her lip. "I got this."

"I'm going with you," Jenks said. "It'll go faster with two."

"No," Kizzy said. She grew quieter. "Something could still go wrong."

"All the more reason you need some help."

"All the more reason you should stay." She fidgeted with the blasting cap. "If something goes wrong, the *Wayfarer* still needs a tech."

Jenks looked hard at her. "Don't you talk like that." Everyone at the table could hear him, but there was a soft urgency in his tone that was meant for her ears alone.

"We should move our ships as far apart as possible," Corbin said. "If something *does* go awry, we need to make sure our ship is protected."

Pei nodded. "That's a wise precaution. My people will stay here while Kizzy deals with the mines. I'll be going with her."

"Why?" Ashby said, the word out of his mouth before he'd had time to think. But he wasn't alone in the sentiment. The other Aeluons' cheeks flashed with urgency.

"I'll go," Tak said. "I'm here to defend this cargo."

"It's my ship," Pei said.

"You're a civilian."

"*It's my ship.*" Pei leaned forward, colors flaring. Whatever she said, it was enough to make Tak back down. She turned to Kizzy. "I won't ask someone from another crew to risk something that I'm not prepared to risk myself." Pei looked to Ashby. "Don't worry. We see anything we can't handle, we'll get out of there fast. I'll take care of her."

Ashby sighed and put on the bravest smile he could. "I know you will," he said. *But who will take care of you?*

Kizzy stood in front of the open service panel, tools in hand, looking at nothing. Little yellow lights flashed in the dark. They were waiting for her. She didn't move.

Pei placed a hand on her shoulder. "Finding some courage?"

Kizzy shook her head. "No. I'm good."

Pei blinked her weird eyelids sideways. "This isn't that Human thing where you pretend not to be scared, is it?"

"No. Really, I'm good." She climbed into the wall. Pei followed, hanging back by the access panel. Kizzy made her way to the closest mine. It seemed smaller than the first. She turned on her globulbs and got to work, moving with steady hands and quiet breaths. "Is that a Human thing? Isn't that something everybody does?"

"Oh, no. It's a Human thing. See?" She pointed at the colored patches on her finely scaled cheeks.

Kizzy let go of the mine and looked up. "I . . . don't know what that means." She made an apologetic face. "Sorry, I don't really know any Aeluons."

"Are they red? Mostly? Maybe a bit of yellow mixed in?"

"Yeah. They're all, like, swirly."

"Yep. I'm scared." She cocked her head. "And I'm curious as to why you're not."

Kizzy pursed her lips and looked back down at the armed explosive. "I don't know. I was super scared when I first found them, but now, it's not so bad. Nervous, maybe, but no more than, like, working on the outer hull or putting out a circuit fire. There's a problem, and it's serious, but I'm fine. I don't really get why, but there you go."

"You've examined the situation and are confident you can fix it. That makes sense."

"I guess." They both fell quiet as Kizzy worked her way around the mine, melting the sealant, snipping the cables. As the blasting cap fell into Kizzy's hand, Pei audibly exhaled. It was strange, hearing a sound come from her mouth instead of the talkbox.

"Stars," Pei said. "I feel so useless, not being able to help, but all the same, I don't know if I could do that."

"Really?" Kizzy said, moving up the walkway. "You deal with this kind of shit all the time. Like, guns pointed at your face and bad guys on your ship and all sorts of stuff."

"Guns and . . . bad guys, yes. But *this*"—she nodded toward the mines—"is not the shit I deal with all the time. This is not something I can fix. And that's what scares me. There are few things as unsettling as a lack of control in an unfamiliar situation."

Kizzy raised her tools, and silence returned. She crouched to examine the sealant. She frowned, and flipped down one of her magnification lenses. "Ah, shit."

She could practically hear Pei tense up. "What's wrong?"

"Don't worry, nothing major." She squinted, then rolled her eyes. "These hackjob goofballs. They let sealant get into the cable channel."

"Is that bad?"

"No, it's just stupid. I'm going to have to melt it on super-low heat, so that the kedrium doesn't get too hot."

"*That's* bad, right?"

"It would be, yeah, but it won't happen. It'll take me a long-ass time, though. Idiots." She sighed as she fit the heat awl with a smaller tip, and dialed down the temperature. For a while, they said nothing. Her neck was already feeling cranky from hunching. "Hey, um, listen, I know I don't know you at all, but can I ask you a question?"

"Considering what you're doing for my ship, I'd say you have the right to ask whatever you like."

"Fair enough." She kept both eyes fixed on the sealant. "Okay, so, the gun thing. We've established this is a thing you do a lot."

"You mean *using* guns, or having them pointed at me?"

"Both, I guess. I mean more like being in situations where people are angry and also there are guns."

"I'm not sure that it happens *a lot*. But more often than for most, perhaps."

"Enough for you not to be scared of it."

"I never said that."

"You did so."

"I said I was *familiar* with it. That's very different."

"But how do you stop being scared about it? Like, when it's happening?"

"I don't understand."

The top edge of the sealant started to glisten. "Well, you kind of said it was something you can be in control of. I mean, if you've got a gun pointed at someone, and they're returning the favor, you've got to be not scared enough to deal with it before they do, right?"

"That's . . . not how it works." Pei paused. "Is this about the Akaraks?"

"You heard about that."

"I did. Is it still bothering you?"

Kizzy licked her lips. *Fuck it. We might be dead in an hour.* "I haven't been able to sleep much since it happened, and I can't figure out how to talk to my crew about it. And I'm tired, like bone-crunchingly tired, but I get so scared I'll wake up to strangers pointing guns at me that I can't sleep. I either have to knock myself out with drops, or work work work until I fall over. And I know it's stupid. I know what happened to us was a freak thing, and it'll probably never happen again. But I'm more scared of *that* than I am of this wall of death I'm staring at right now. I just—I don't make sense, and I'm kind of pissed at myself about it." The acrid smell of melting sealant tickled her nose. She poked at the seam with her fingertip. Gooey, but still holding fast. She scowled. "Stars, just *melt* already." She tucked a loose strand of hair behind her ear. "I'm sorry. I shouldn't be spewing this all over you. It must sound so stupid."

"It doesn't sound stupid. Though I am wondering why you're talking to *me* about it."

"Because you know about this stuff. I thought maybe . . . I just want to know how I can live with knowing this kind of shit is out there and not be scared of it."

Pei said nothing for a moment. "Kizzy, I am scared of everything, all the time. I'm scared of my ship getting shot down when I have to land planetside. I'm scared of the armor in my vest cracking during a fight. I'm scared that the next time I have to pull out my gun, the other guy will be faster. I'm scared of making mistakes that could hurt my crew. I'm scared of leaky biosuits. I'm scared of vegetables that haven't been washed properly. I'm scared of fish."

"Fish?"

"You haven't seen the fish on my home colony. Very thin teeth."

"But how do you deal with that?"

"With what?"

"Being scared of all that stuff."

"You mean how is it that I can sleep and you can't. Is that what you're asking?"

"Yeah."

"I don't know. Maybe it's just different for us. We're different species, after all." She paused. "Or maybe because I never thought to ask anyone what you're asking. I never thought of fear as something that can go *away*. It just *is*. It reminds me that I want to stay alive. That doesn't strike me as a bad thing."

"Hang on, pause," Kizzy said. Melted sealant began to drip onto the floor. *Finally.* She took a thin pair of pliers from her belt and tugged the cable through the clear gunk. She flipped down her lenses and examined the blasting cap. Warm, but not enough to cause trouble. She gave a satisfied nod, cut the cable and wiped the goo off on her pants. "Okay, we're good." She looked up the walkway, where little yellow lights sat blinking, waiting. "This might sound weird, but it's really nice knowing that you're scared of fish. And all the other stuff."

Kizzy didn't have the easiest time reading Pei's face, but the lady looked amused. "I'm glad, but I'm not sure I understand. I don't think I answered your question."

"You did." She cracked her knuckles and popped off the blasting cap. "I hate that this is the first time we've met you. Especially given the circumstances." She looked back toward Pei. "I know it's hard for you, but you can come stay with us anytime. I can think of a certain Exodan captain who'd like that a lot."

"I'd like that, too," Pei said. She was quiet a moment. Her cheeks went orange. "Maybe sometime." She took a breath and nodded toward the walkway. "But first, let's keep my ship from blowing up."

Jenks leaned back, letting the weight of the tub of bolts in his arms fall against his chest. Arms aching, he carried the tub out of the freight elevator, down the corridor and into the Fishbowl. Ashby sat on a garden bench, staring out the window at the speck that was Pei's ship. Jenks walked around the bench, standing where Ashby could see him.

"Hi," he said.

Ashby turned his head. "Hi."

Jenks upturned the tub. The bolts clattered to the floor like heavy rain. "These are several hundred bolts. They are all different shapes and sizes, and Kizzy always keeps them in one communal tub. It drives me crazy."

Ashby blinked. "Why are they on the floor?"

"Because we are going to sort them. We are going to sort them into nice, neat little piles. And then we're going to take those piles and put them in smaller tubs, so that when I need a bolt, I don't have to go digging."

"I see." Ashby blinked again. "Why are we doing this?"

"Because some jackass dumped them all over the floor, and they have to be cleaned up. And if they have to be cleaned up, we might as well sort them while we're at it." Jenks sat down, leaning comfortably against a planter. He began to pick through the bolts. "See, my best friend in the whole galaxy is currently on another ship, holed up in a wall, disarming hackjob explosives. It's dark in there, and her fingers are probably sore by now, after tugging at all those little wires, and I'm shitting myself over the possibility of something going wrong, because I seriously do not know what I would do without her. And I can't help. I can't do anything. Not one damn thing. I know she's the best person for this, and I know she doesn't need my help. But all the same, she's facing some dangerous shit, and it is completely out of my hands. I want to do *something*, and it's driving me fucking crazy that I can't. I can't even *smoke* because there are Aeluons around. So, fine. I'm going to sort bolts." He swung his eyes up to Ashby. "And I think anybody who has similar feelings should join me."

Ashby rubbed his beard. "Why?"

Jenks brushed aside a swath of bolts with his hand, clearing a workspace. "Because this is going to take hours, and it's something to do. And it's better than staring out a window."

Ashby sat quiet for a moment. He leaned forward, clasping his hands together in a businesslike way. "Are we sorting them by size, or shape?"

"Shape to start. Then we'll make subpiles by size."

"Should I get us some kick?"

"I think that would be best."

Kizzy and Pei returned to the *Wayfarer* some two hours later. There had been forty-six mines behind the wall, all now in pieces. They'd spaced the kedrium, much to Kizzy's chagrin, and Pei'd run two more scans of the ship, just to be safe. Kizzy's hands were aching, and her back was stiff, and her head was pounding from squinting in the dark. She was glad to be back home.

Everybody had jumped all over her when she came through the airlock. Sissix nuzzled her head so hard that her hairdo came loose, and Rosemary got all misty eyed, and Jenks gave her the best hug ever. Lovey was rambling about how worried she'd been, and even Ohan came down, limping on their weak legs, to give her a respectful bow.

She felt like a hero.

Dr. Chef made an enormous dinner for everybody—red coast bugs and fried spineroots and spicy crunchy salt peas. The Aeluons had been a little weirded out by the bugs at first—red coasters were pests to them, after all—but they warmed up to it, maybe out of novelty more than anything. Everybody was swapping stories and chowing down, and after a while, you could almost kind of forget that in a parallel universe, they all might be dead by then.

There reached a point where both Sissix and Oxlen were looking at the time on their scribs with that frowny we-need-to-get-going look that all pilots got. Everybody said their good-byes. Kizzy's heart went to pieces when she saw Pei and Ashby give each other a friendly farewell handshake. *Let them make out, dammit!* It just wasn't fair. Oxlen caught her eye and gave her a secret, knowing nod. Huh. Maybe all Aeluons weren't such prudes, after all.

As the Aeluon ship sailed off, Kizzy excused herself. She took a long shower, giving herself twenty-two minutes instead of the fifteen she demanded of everybody else. She figured she'd earned an extra seven minutes, and the filters could take it. Afterward, she went back to her room. Dr. Chef had left a mug of tea and a couple spring cakes waiting for her. She smiled, put on some comfies and crawled into bed with her snacks. She wrote a letter to her dads, just to say she loved them. She ate her cakes. She drank her tea. She watched the stars go by. Without meaning to, she slept.

RECEIVED MESSAGE
ENCRYPTION: 0
TRANSLATION: 0
FROM: Nib (path: 6273-384-89)
TO: Rosemary Harper (path: 9874-457-28)
SUBJECT: Re: Question about Toremi reference files

Hello, Rosemary! Good to hear from you. We all enjoyed you staying with us, unplanned as it was.

And it's no trouble at all! I'm always happy to answer archive questions (and recruit new volunteers . . . ?). I know, the Toremi files are seriously lacking in details. I'm not part of that project, but I have a few friends who are, and they're pulling their hair out. Everything Toremi related has been receiving an absurd amount of traffic lately, but the problem is, there's just not enough verifiable data yet for us to approve much for public access.

However, if you promise to keep this to yourself, I did manage to dig up a few tidbits for you. Bear in mind, none of this has been verified to our standards yet, but it's the best the Toremi team has got right now. Here's what we know:

1. The Toremi are obsessed with patterns. Not geometric patterns. They believe that the whole universe follows some sort of elaborate path—or series of paths, maybe. Nobody's quite sure which, far as I can tell. Their whole thing is that they're trying to figure out the pattern and match their lives to it. Apparently, that's why they've been circling the Core since who-knows-when. The galaxy spins, so they should, too. That's where the clans come in. Everybody's got a different idea on how the patterns work, and they get pretty violent over it. And clans can change really fast when new ideas come in. They sound like a very compulsive sort of people. The only thing the clans obviously agree on is the whole circling-the-

Core-thing. Or they did, at least. Which brings us to . . .

2. You may have heard this by now, but I'm still so excited by it: generally speaking, the Toremi are a dual-sexed, sexually reproductive race. But a small number of them have started to go parthenogenetic. I know! But as fascinating as that is, it's been a mess for the Toremi. Remember that whole pattern thing? Yeah, every clan has a different idea on what this new evolutionary path means. Some of them revere the "New Mothers," and have elevated them to positions of power. Some do the opposite, subjugating or enslaving them. And some kill them. The Toremi Ka, our new allies, fall into the former group (thankfully).

3. The reason the Toremi have started scrambling for territory all of a sudden is because the emergence of the parthenogenetic females is the biggest change to their pattern in a very long time. They call it a yegse, a change that rules all. When a yegse takes place, the Toremi drop what they're doing and take time to figure it out. For them, that means turning off their engines and grabbing some ground. This hasn't happened in centuries. Maybe millennia.

4. Hedra Ka—or Hedra, which I'll get to in a minute—is a very young planet in a relatively new star system. The reason the Toremi want it so bad is because it, too, is shifting around and changing. They think that the universe wants them to go there. Not that it can be terraformed or even settled. It's a hellhole, from what I've read. As for the name, "Hedra" is the name of the planet. "Ka" just marks which clan it belongs to.

That's all we've got for now, but feel free to ask any other questions you've got. I'll keep you posted if I find out anything else. I know the Toremi team will keep squeezing GC delegates for more info. Stingy bastards.

Fly safe,
Nib

HATCH, FEATHER, HOUSE

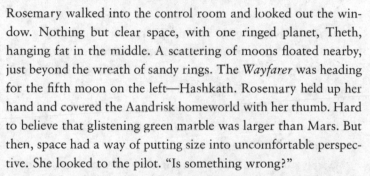

Rosemary walked into the control room and looked out the window. Nothing but clear space, with one ringed planet, Theth, hanging fat in the middle. A scattering of moons floated nearby, just beyond the wreath of sandy rings. The *Wayfarer* was heading for the fifth moon on the left—Hashkath. Rosemary held up her hand and covered the Aandrisk homeworld with her thumb. Hard to believe that glistening green marble was larger than Mars. But then, space had a way of putting size into uncomfortable perspective. She looked to the pilot. "Is something wrong?"

Sissix's hands darted quickly over her navigation panel. "No, why?"

"Because you're flying manually. When you do that this far out of orbit, that usually means something's wrong." Rocks. Gas clouds. Junk. Other ships. More rocks. There was no end to rocks in space.

"I'm flying home," said Sissix. "That's something I've got to do myself."

Rosemary took a seat beside her. "Why?"

"When Aandrisks first took to space, we used these awful solar-sail pods. Really skittish, could only fit one person. Not for the claustrophobic."

"Ours were the same. Not the sails, but still. Tiny." She shuddered.

"You guys lucked out, though. There's nothing floating around your planet except the stuff you put up there yourselves. Your flyers could just orbit around and around forever. Smooth sailing. But our moon's got moons of its own, and it's orbiting a ringed planet. That takes some very tricky maneuvering, especially when you're talking about a little metal can with flimsy sails. And this was before artigrav made it our way, so you're just floating there, hoping you touch ground again. Being able to say that you went all the way out here and got yourself safely back home—that made you a hero. It meant you were strong and skilled, that you'd worked hard to make sure your family didn't lose you."

"Ah," said Rosemary. "So this is a matter of pride."

"I suppose," said Sissix. She paused. "Yeah. In a good way."

The vox snapped on. "Sissix," said Kizzy. She sounded timid. "You know I love you, right?"

Sissix sighed. "What did you do?"

"How much will you hate me if Jenks and I don't come to your family's for dinner tonight?"

"Deeply and unendingly," said Sissix in a tone that suggested otherwise. "Why?"

"Well . . . oh, now I feel bad . . ."

There was a rustle on the vox. Jenks's voice took over. "Sissix, we just found out that the Bathtub Strategy is on tour and they're playing at that big concert field in Reskit tonight."

"The Aksisk?" Sissix sounded impressed. "Guys, I will hate you if you *don't* go."

"You sure?" Kizzy said. "Because it's not a big deal, really—"

"Kizzy," Sissix said. "Go."

"You're the best." The vox switched off.

"You can go with them if you want," Sissix said. "The Aksisk is an amazing venue."

"Charthump's not really my thing," said Rosemary. "Besides,

dinner with your family sounds nice. I'm excited to see where you're from."

"Well, it's a lot less exciting than the Aksisk, but it'll be friendly, at least." Her hands flurried with commands. The ship veered to the left. "You've never been to an Aandrisk home before, have you?"

"No." She cleared her throat. "And, ah, if you don't mind, I could use a refresher course."

Sissix laughed. "Humans are so cute." She met Rosemary's eyes and smirked. "Don't worry, it takes all of you forever to get this. Okay, so." She took one hand off the controls and counted down on her claws. "Hatch family, feather family, house family. Tell me what you know."

Rosemary leaned back. "You're born into a hatch family."

"Right."

"Then you grow up and leave for a feather family."

"Stopping you there. It's not like you leave as soon as you get your feathers. You leave when you've found a good feather family, or when you find other adults worth making a feather family with."

"A feather family is friends and lovers, right?"

"Right. People you emotionally depend on."

"But feather families change often, right?"

"Not *often*, necessarily. Often by your standards, I guess. People change feather families whenever they need to, and people need different things at different times in their lives. It's almost unheard of for an Aandrisk to stay with the same people their entire life. Two or three people, maybe, sometimes, but not a whole group. Groups change regularly."

"So, feather families are usually people all around the same age?"

"Oh, not at all. Young Aandrisks tend to stick together at first, but once they gain a little confidence and experience, they branch out. We don't worry about age differences as much as most other species do. If you've got feathers, it's fine. And it can be a great experience for youngsters to group with an older crowd. I was the youngest by far in my second feather family, and—" Sissix chuckled, her eyes far away. "Yeah, I learned a *lot* of things."

"Do you—" Rosemary felt herself blush. "Does everybody in a feather family, um, y'know—"

"Couple? To some extent, but it's different from what you think. At least once, almost definitely. But not everybody within a feather family has romantic feelings toward everyone else. It's a whole web of different feelings. So, yes, there's a lot of coupling going on—especially on holidays, a holiday without a *tet* is unheard of." Rosemary had learned the word. Its literal translation was "frolic," but its colloquial use implied something far more risqué. "But many members are platonic toward one another. They'll touch each other much more than Humans do, but it's still not coupling. Or, well, then again, sometimes it can be. We tend to think about coupling the same way that—hmm, how to put this—okay, like how you think about good food. It's something you always look forward to, and it's something everybody needs and enjoys. At the low end of the scale, it's comforting. At the high end, it's transcendent. And like eating a meal, it's something you can do in public, with friends or with strangers. But even so, it's best when you share it with someone you care about romantically."

"I can see that," Rosemary said. She nodded. "So, then, house family. House family raises children. But not their own children, right?"

"Right. We can breed as soon as we've got a full head of feathers, but we don't start thinking about raising children until we've gotten old. That's when we make house families. It's usually made up of elder members of a feather family, who all decide to settle down together. Sometimes they might contact favorites from previous feather families, see if they want to join. And don't misunderstand, house families change members from time to time, too. They may be old, but they're still Aandrisks." She laughed.

"So, younger Aandrisks give their eggs to a house family."

"Right."

"Do they find a house family that has someone they're related to?"

"It's nice if you can, but usually you just choose whoever's most convenient. When a woman has a fertile clutch—we call it a *kaas*—she goes to the local registry and finds a good house family with room for more."

"What if she can't find someone to take them?"

"Then she buries the clutch. Remember, most of the clutch will die anyway. Most won't even make it to hatching. That's not because they're unhealthy. That's just how it is. Stars, I can't even imagine how many of us there'd be if every egg hatched. Too many." She shuddered.

Rosemary thought about this. "I hope this doesn't sound ignorant, but why don't feather families raise their own hatchlings? Aren't there enough people there to help out?"

"Yeah, but it's not a matter of resources or support. It's a matter of where you are in your life. In our early adulthood, it's expected that we'll want to travel or study, and it's a given that we'll switch families often as we age. Elders don't shift around as much. They're more stable. And most important, they've got life experience. They're wise. They know things." She smirked. "I'll never understand how the rest of you expect brand-new adults to be able to teach kids how to be people."

"That's . . . okay, that's a fair point." Rosemary closed her eyes, trying to keep it all straight. "So, the house family becomes the hatch family for those eggs."

"Right. And a house family is usually good for two generations of hatchlings. It's common for first-generation adults to bring their own eggs back to the family that raised them. That's what I did."

Rosemary sat up. "Wait. You've got *kids*?" Sissix had never mentioned this, not once.

The Aandrisk woman laughed. "I had a *fertile clutch*."

"When?"

"About three standards ago. I'm told two hatchlings lived. But that doesn't make me a mother." She winked. "I'm not old enough for that yet."

Rosemary looked out the window. She chided herself for being so species centric, but something about this knowledge made her view Sissix differently. She was surprised to realize the depth of her Human concept of motherhood, the idea that procreating fundamentally changed you. But then, she was of a mammalian species. If she ever chose to have children, it would mean spending the better part of a year watching her body stretch and contort, then another year, or more, of letting a fragile, helpless thing that didn't understand its own limbs feed from her body. Aandrisk hatchlings developed within a detached object, and emerged ready to walk. But though she understood the biological distinctions, she still struggled to wrap her brain around the idea of breeding as something nonchalant, nothing more complicated than sticking eggs in a basket, handing them off and getting on with your day. Did they use baskets? She didn't know, but she couldn't push away the image of a white wicker basket filled with speckled eggs, the handle tied up with pastel bows. "Do you talk to them, or . . . ?"

Sissix gave her a somewhat exasperated smile. "No. Remember, they're not people yet, not by our standards. And they're not my family. I know that sounds cold to you, but trust me, they're loved by the elders raising them. Though, that said, elders don't get *attached* to hatchlings, not until they see who they turn into. That's where the real joy is for house families. Seeing the hatchlings they raised come back as fully feathered adults, with stories and ideas and personality."

"Like you're doing now."

"Right."

"Have you ever met your . . . biological parents?"

"My egg mother, once. Her name's Saskist. Very funny woman, and I'm glad I got her feathers. I've never met my egg father, but I know he lives with his feather family on Ikekt. Or he did last time I checked. That was a while ago, though, he may have moved on by now."

Rosemary thought of what Lovey said if you gave her one task too many: *I'm sorry, but that'll have to wait a moment. If I put anything more in my databanks, my processing streams will stall. And I hate that.* "How do you keep track of all the changes to families?"

"There's a central database that our government maintains. All feather families are registered there, and the archivists keep track of every change. You can look up anybody's name and see who their egg parents were, who raised them, which families they've been in, who they've had clutches with and where the hatchlings have gone to."

"That's got to be one complicated database. Why go to all that trouble?"

"Same reason our full names include all our family details." She gave Rosemary a pointed look. "Because inbreeding is gross."

The shuttle ramp unfolded, bright sun flooding in. Rosemary tugged her satchel over her shoulder as she followed Sissix and Ashby down. Her legs wobbled, protesting the switch from artigrav to the real thing. Hashkath had just a touch more bounce than she was used to. She looked up. Theth loomed overhead, its rings and swirling clouds appearing as ghostly afterimages against the hazy blue. Her view was unhindered, no shield pylons or shuttle traffic to get in her way. An open sky.

They had landed in Sethi, a small community in the western desert region of Hashkath. Well, Sissix had called it a desert. It wasn't like any desert Rosemary had ever seen. *Mars* was desert, barren and parched. Its gardens and green plazas were constructs, enclosed beneath habitat domes, fed with recycled water. But here, the ground was alive, flocked with scruffy grass and warped trees, stretching from their flat landing site all the way to the angular mountains along the horizon. And flowers, too, flowers everywhere. Not like the lush, leafy genetweaks from the greenhouses back home, or the elegant vines creeping through Dr. Chef's garden. These were wildflowers, bursting triumphantly from the gray ground, growing tangled and low in bundles of orange, yellow, purple. The trees twisted up over them, covered in spines and clusters of berries. They grew thickest in a long strip up ahead, a ribbon of green that hinted at a hidden stream.

Beyond the ribbon lay the community, a lazy gathering of podlike homesteads hugging the ground. It was spread out enough to give a family space to stretch and grow things, but close enough to keep your neighbors right at hand. Sethi was a quiet place. Out of the way. Modestly prosperous. Uncomplicated. No gaming hubs or prefab stores. There wasn't even a real shuttle dock, just a wide, unattended area suitable for landing small spacecraft and supply drones. Looking around, Rosemary understood why a young adult would want to leave such a place, and why an elder would want to come back.

She touched her bare nose, basking in the novelty of being able to breathe without a mask or an artificial atmosphere. The last time she'd been without one or the other was Port Coriol, which felt like a lifetime ago. The air at the port had been thick with the smells of algae and business. The air on Hashkath was clean, dry, oxygen rich, laced with the scent of desert flowers warming in the sun. It was good air.

Sissix obviously agreed. She threw her arms wide and her head back as soon as her clawed feet touched the ground. "Home," she said, sounding as if she had just surfaced from a long swim.

"Wow," Ashby said. "I'd forgotten that it would be spring here."

Sissix inhaled and exhaled with vigor, as if purging the *Wayfarer*'s recycled air from her lungs. She looked down at her body. "Oh, *hell* no." She untied the drawstring of her trousers, stepped out of them and threw them back into the shuttle. Her vest followed suit. Naked, she began walking toward her childhood home, her scales glinting in the sun.

As they walked, Ashby reached into his own satchel and pulled out his translation hud. He fitted the thin metal band around his head. The eyescreen flickered to life.

"I thought you spoke Reskitkish," Rosemary said.

"I *understand* Reskitkish," Ashby said. "But I'm far from fluent when I speak. And since I don't get much practice, it helps to have a cheat sheet."

"Your accent is better than most Humans I know," Sissix said. "I know it's a pain for you to speak on an inhale."

"It's not the speaking on an inhale that's so bad. It's alternating it with exhaling *within the same sentence*." He snapped his satchel shut. "Seriously, who does that?"

Rosemary pulled her own hud out of her bag. "It is pretty mean," she said. Her knowledge of Reskitkish was practically non-existent, but the few phrases she had tried made her feel light-headed. "I don't know how you can speak it without hyperventilating."

Sissix thumped her chest with a fist. "We've got better lungs," she said.

"Yeah, well, we've got warm blood," Ashby said. "I think that's the better end of the deal."

Sissix gave a short laugh. "You have no idea. I'd take your weak lungs and useless nose over morning torpor any day."

Ashby looked at Rosemary. "I can't tell if that was a compliment or not." He turned back to Sissix. "Hey, is Ethra still here?"

"As far as I know."

"Do not make any puns around him," Ashby said to Rosemary. "He wiped the floor with me last time I was here. And he's got an arsenal of Human jokes that will cause permanent damage."

Sissix chuckled. "He's no kinder to his own species. What was the one about—oh, what was it, something horrible involving tails—"

Ashby laughed. "So a Human, a Quelin and a Harmagian walk into a *tet*—"

"No, stop," Sissix said, gesturing ahead with her chin. They had reached the scrub-filled banks of the desert stream. Two Aandrisk children were playing in the water, shouting over each other. A message appeared on Rosemary's hud: *Cannot process conversation. Please move closer to speaker(s).* She had no frame of reference for how old the children were, but given their small size and playfulness, Rosemary thought of them as Human kids in their first years of primary school. Well, maybe. One of them looked younger than the other. She had a hard time pinning down anything else about them. Aandrisk sex was easy to determine in adults, mainly due to size, but at this age, they were androgynous, especially since male Aandrisks lacked external genitalia. Categorization aside, there was something fragile about these two, a paperlike quality to their scales. No wonder she hadn't seen any Aandrisk children off-world before. She didn't even know them, and already she felt protective. She imagined their parents must feel that way ten times over. *Hatch parents*, she reminded herself. *Hatch parents*.

Ashby lowered his voice. "Since when do Aandrisks not mention *tets* around their kids?"

"We do," Sissix said. "But you're probably the first Humans they've ever seen, and I don't want them to grow up thinking your species is stupid." She walked toward the children, calling out a breathy greeting.

The kids' featherless heads snapped up. The smaller one shouted something. The translation appeared on Rosemary's hud. *"Aliens! The aliens are here!"* They scrambled up out of the stream, claws skittering in excitement.

Sissix crouched down to nuzzle both of their faces. Rosemary had seen her do the same to Ashby, but with him, the gesture was more affectionate, more natural. There was something formal about this. Kind and genuine, yes, but definitely removed.

The older child spoke. *"You're Sissix."*

"That's right."

"You're my egg mother."

Sissix smiled. She did not look surprised. *"You must be Teshris."* Her eyes flicked to the other. *"Are you Eskat, then?"*

"No," the child said, giggling.

"No, I see now. You're too young." She patted his bald head. *"Not that that's a bad thing."*

Ashby whispered in Rosemary's ear. "Teshris is a girl," he said. "Her buddy here's a boy."

"Thanks," Rosemary replied, wondering how he could tell the difference. "Eskat is her sibling?"

"Egg brother, yeah. I didn't know their names until now, though."

Sissix said something to Teshris in hand speak. Ashby whispered again: "That motion's specific to egg parents. She's saying that she's happy that Teshris is healthy and . . . well, that she exists, basically." The Aandrisk girl responded, her gestures awkward and new. "She's thanking Sissix for giving her life." The two Aandrisks smiled and gave each other one more nuzzle. And that was that. No hugs, no long stares, no Sissix needing sometime to process the daughter she'd never spoken to. In that moment, Rosemary understood. Teshris wasn't Sissix's daughter, not in the Human sense. They shared genes and respect, nothing more.

Sissix turned her head to Teshris's companion. *"What's your name?"*

"Vush," he said.

"Whose eggs are you from?"

"Teker and Hasra."

Sissix crowed with laughter. *"I don't know Hasra, but Teker was my hatch sister."*

Hatch sister, not egg sister. Rosemary felt like she needed to start drawing a chart.

Sissix grinned at the kids. *"When we were growing up"*—the hud added the direct translation *becoming people* as a parenthetical—*"she always said she didn't want to have a clutch, and that she'd be tough enough to go without coupling while she was fertile. That changed damn quick once her feathers started coming in. During her first heat, I found her rutting alone up against a rock. I thought she was going to choke, she was so—"* The hud skipped over the last word and offered an explanation instead: [*no analogue available: a combination of arousal, frenzy and inexperience, generally attributed to adolescence*]. Sissix laughed again, and the kids joined in. Rosemary raised her eyebrows. How old were these kids? She glanced over at Ashby. He looked a little uncomfortable, too. At least she wasn't alone in it.

Vush spoke up after he'd stopped giggling. *"I want to touch the Humans, but Ithren said they don't like that."*

"He's right, not all Humans do. But I bet these two would be okay with it. You just have to ask permission first." She pointed back toward her companions. "This is Rosemary, and this is Ashby. They are very good people."

The kids looked at them, motionless. Rosemary remembered being four years old, seeing a Harmagian for the first time, unable to stop staring at the tendrils where his chin should have been. It was odd to find herself on the other end of the equation.

Ashby crouched down and smiled. The kids looked a little stiff, but they stepped closer. It took Rosemary a moment to realize their tense muscles were not a result of fear, but of suppressing the instinct to touch. Ashby began to speak in Reskitkish. His consonants were halting, and his out-breaths were far more exaggerated than Sissix's, but it was good enough for the hud to pick up. "My name is Ashby. I am glad to meet you. You can touch me."

The kids ran forward. They nuzzled a quick hello, out of politeness, and got to the serious business of poking at Ashby. "It's so soft!" Vush said, pressing his hands against Ashby's coiled hair. "No quills!"

"Do you molt?" Teshris asked, examining Ashby's forearm.

"No," said Ashby. "But we . . ." He struggled, and switched over to Klip, addressing Sissix. "Can you explain dry skin?"

"Their skin comes off in tiny, tiny pieces, not all at once," Sissix said to the kids. "They don't even notice it."

"Lucky," Teshris said. "I hate molting."

Vush, a little less restrained than his hatch sister now that permission had been given, walked right up to Rosemary and gave her a nuzzle. "Can I touch you, too?"

Rosemary smiled and nodded, before realizing the boy

wouldn't understand what a nod meant. "Tell him yes," Rosemary said to Sissix. Sissix relayed the message.

Vush frowned. "*Why can't she tell me herself?*"

"*She doesn't speak Reskitkish,*" Sissix said. "*But that hud she's wearing lets her read every word you say.*"

The Aandrisk boy stared at Rosemary, baffled. The notion that someone could *not* speak Reskitkish seemed inconceivable to him.

"Here, Rosemary," Sissix said in Klip. "Do this." She made a quick curve with her fingers. "That's agreement."

Rosemary looked at Vush and repeated the gesture. Vush gestured something back, and grabbed her breasts. "*What are these?*"

Rosemary yelped. Ashby burst out laughing. Sissix darted forward, pulling Vush's hands back. "*Vush, Human women don't like it when people they don't know touch them there.*"

"Oh, stars," Ashby said in Klip, holding his shaking sides.

Vush looked puzzled. "*Why not?*"

"*Is he okay?*" Teshris asked, pointing at Ashby. She had taken a few steps back.

"*Yes,*" Sissix said. "*He's just laughing.*"

Vush's eyes were wide and worried. "*Did I do something bad?*"

"Oh, no, tell him it's okay," Rosemary said. "It's really not a big deal." She was laughing herself by now.

Sissix patted the boy's head. "*You didn't do anything bad, Vush. Humans just have more rules about people touching their bodies than we do. I think it would be best to avoid any part of her torso that's covered.*" She tugged gently at Rosemary's shirt to illustrate the point.

Vush looked at the ground. "*I'm sorry.*"

Rosemary reached out to touch Vush's forearm, as she'd seen Sissix do in moments of empathy. She took his hand and placed it on top of her head, inviting him to explore. Vush brightened, and Sissix gave her a fond, approving look.

"*Her feathers are different from* [unknown]," said Vush as he ran his claws through Rosemary's hair. The hud did not recognize the last word, but Rosemary did: *Ashby*. Vush's attempt at the *sh* in his name lingered for far longer than it was meant to, and he had stumbled on the *b*.

"*They're not feathers, stupid*," Teshris said. "*That's hair*." She looked between Rosemary and Ashby. "*You're a different kind of brown than she is*."

"*That's right*," Ashby said.

"*Aandrisks are like that*," she informed him, as if he, too, were meeting a new species for the first time. "*We have lots of different colors. I'm blue-green, Vush is green-blue, Sissix is green-green. I know all my scale colors. Skeyis says I'm the best at them*." She folded the top of his ear down toward the lobe, over and over again. Ashby bore it patiently. "*Do you come from a moon?*"

"No, I . . ." Again, he struggled, and looked to Sissix for help.

"*He's a spacer*," Sissix said. "*Many Humans are born* [literal translation: body-hatched] *on homestead ships*."

"*What about her?*" Teshris asked.

"*She grew up on a planet called Mars*." Sissix was starting to sound bored. Rosemary found their current companions adorable—though she wouldn't have complained if Vush tugged her hair with a *little* less enthusiasm—but Sissix kept gazing over her shoulder toward the homesteads. She looked anxious to see her family, and these kids weren't it. Not even the one that had her cheekbones.

A cry rose up as they walked up the path toward the homesteads. "Sissix!" an old voice called. Several others joined in: "Sissix! Sissix!" All at once, a flood of Aandrisks came pouring out of the open entryways. There were a dozen of them, maybe more.

Rosemary hadn't had time to count before they piled on top of Sissix, who had gone running to meet them. They tumbled down in a tangle of tails and feathered heads, hugging and squeezing and cuddling close. All their attention was focused on their long-absent daughter. They nuzzled her cheeks, tugged her feathers, pressed as close to her as they could. Rosemary was taken aback. Even though there was nothing overtly sexual in the way they were touching each other, Rosemary had trouble seeing a mass of writhing naked people any other way. It looked more like group foreplay than a family reunion.

Sissix, on the other hand, was happier than Rosemary had ever seen her. She melted into the embraces of her family. She closed her eyes and let her head fall back as one of the Aandrisks touched her feathers. Rosemary had seen that look before—not on Sissix, but on the old woman they'd encountered at Port Coriol. It was a look of profound gratitude, the sort that comes at the end of a long wait, at being able to exhale after holding your breath until your lungs burned.

Rosemary thought of Sissix on the *Wayfarer*, how she'd always seemed so affectionate, how cuddly and sweet she was. But now Rosemary saw it from the flip side. What counted as affection in her book was *holding back* for Sissix. The laughing, snuggling heap on the ground was her baseline. Rosemary imagined herself and her Human crewmates from that point of view. A bunch of stiff, prudish automatons. How could Sissix put up with that every day? She thought again of the moments in which Sissix touched them, the genuine fondness on her face when she nuzzled Ashby's cheek or hugged Kizzy and Jenks in tandem. She thought of how much effort it would take Sissix to not tumble down with them as she was doing now with her hatch family, to push back her need for a more tangible form of connectedness.

"Ashby, Rosemary," Sissix called from within the heap.

"Come say hello." She wriggled one of her hands free, and pointed a claw toward all the elderly heads (Sissix's feathers were by far the brightest of the bunch). "This is Issash, Ethra, Rixsik, Ithren, Kirix, Shaas, Trikesh, Raasek and—and a few I don't know." She laughed and switched to Reskitkish, addressing the old woman hugging her the closest. "*You've added some faces since I was last here.*"

The old woman—Issash, Rosemary thought, though she knew she'd never be able to keep them all straight—said, "*We stole a couple of them from the Sariset family at a frolic last winter.*" She leaned toward Sissix conspiratorially. "*It's because everybody knows I'm the best-looking elder in the region.*" The other Aandrisks laughed. One of them tugged her feathers. She grinned with mock arrogance.

Sissix laughed and nuzzled Issash's cheek. "*I've missed you so much,*" she said.

One of the male elders wiggled his way free of the pile. His eyes were sharp, but his feathers drooped with age and his scales were dull. Rosemary got the impression that he was very old. "*I'd ask you to join us,*" he said with a smile. "*But I know that's not your way.*" He reached out his hand to shake Ashby's. "*Ashby, how are you? I am glad to see you again.*"

Ashby cleared his throat and answered as best he could. "*Glad to see you, Ithren. Thank you for the . . . for being . . . welcome.*"

Ithren's smile grew wider and he touched Ashby's forearm. "*Your Reskitkish is very good,*" he said.

"*Not very,*" Ashby said. "*I speak less than . . . than I know. Than I know to hear.*" He spoke in Klip: "No, hang on . . ."

Ithren laughed. "*You understand more than you can say. See? I can understand you just fine.*" He patted Ashby's arm, and turned to Rosemary. "*Do you speak Reskitkish?*" he asked as he shook her hand. Rosemary shook her head apologetically. He pointed at her hud. "*But you understand?*" She started to nod, but then remembered the curved gesture Sissix had shown her down by the creek, hand speak for *yes*. Ithren was delighted. "*See, you are learning fast. And I am like Ashby. I understand Klip, but I am not confident in speaking it. So as long as you are wearing your hud, we can each speak what we're comfortable with and understand the other just fine.*" He put one of his hands on Rosemary's shoulder, and did the same to Ashby. "*I enjoy seeing Humans here. When I was a little younger than Sissix, I crewed aboard an Aeluon cargo carrier. Aeluon run, that is. It was a multispecies crew, like yours. We even had a Laru woman, believe it or not. Damned clever species, the Laru, never saw anyone who could play tikkit like her. But—ah, what was I saying?*"

"*I don't know,*" Ashby said, giving the Reskitkish another try. "*About Humans?*"

"*Ah, yes, yes. I'll never forget the day when we learned Humans had been accepted into the GC as a member species. We were at the Muriat Marketplace—have you ever been there?*"

"*Sometimes,*" Ashby said.

"*Is there still a bar there called* [Hanto: The Fully-Stocked Cupboard]?"

"*Don't know.*"

"*Oh, I hope it's still there. Best sugarsnaps in the GC, no question. I've never found another bartender who can get them that tart. But anyway. Yes, Humans joining the GC. I was at an algae depot—no, no, it was a tech shop, yes, a tech shop. There was a Human man working there. His job was to clean used parts meant for resale. Mindless work, and hard, too. Not a good job for a species with soft hands. You could tell by his clothes that he didn't get paid much. His boss was out, so he was helping me find—oh, whatever it was I needed. There was a newsfeed on a little projector at his work desk, and suddenly, there it was. Humans in the GC. The man went quiet. And then he did something I'd never seen before: he started crying. Now, I didn't know that crying was something that Humans did, so I was a little afraid. Do you know how disturbing it is to see someone's eyes start leaking? Ha! And poor man, he's trying to explain crying to me while going through all of those emotions. I'll never forget what he said to me. He said, 'This means we matter. We're worth something.' And I said, 'Of course you're worth something. Everyone is worth something.' And he said, 'But now I know the galaxy thinks so, too.'"* Ithren squeezed their shoulders and looked between them. *"And now, you have ships of your own, and you go out into the open like we Aandrisks do. And to the Core! I must admit, I am jealous of your journey. What a lucky thing that is."* He smiled. *"I hope I don't sound patronizing, but thinking back on that man, seeing you here makes me think on how far your species has come. That makes me very happy. Oh! I just remembered! Are you hungry? I know that Humans have to eat more than we do, so Rixsik and I spent last night preparing plenty of extra food for the* [noun, no analogue available; a table where communal food is offered throughout the day]."

"That's kind. Very kind," Ashby said. *"I wish—I hope it was not . . . difficult."*

"Not at all," Ishren said. *"We are all looking forward to seeing how much you can eat."* He grinned and pointed off to the side. *"I think they are, too."*

Behind a stack of empty crates, a pack of hatchlings had gathered, watching the adults with intense curiosity. They were hanging back, as if waiting to be invited. Rosemary realized that might actually be the case. Perhaps they knew not to butt in when adults were socializing. That would make sense, among a species where children did not need help learning basic survival skills. In a Human gathering, adults wouldn't think twice about dropping a conversation the moment a child needed something, even if it was simply attention. But here, the hatchlings seemed to know that adult activities took precedence, and that if they wanted to join in, they'd have to figure out the rules. So instead of tugging at sleeves and showing off, they observed the goings-on of adults from the sidelines, trying to puzzle it all out. They were learning how to be people.

Rosemary saw Teshris among them, her little arms wrapped around a hatchling of similar size and features. Eskat, presumably, Sissix's other—Rosemary stopped herself before thinking the word *child*. Offspring? Progeny? All the words granted too much of a connotation of those hatchlings *belonging* to Sissix, which they clearly did not, or at least, not in a Human way. Perhaps it was enough to say that Teshris and Eskat shared an egg mother, who happened to be Sissix.

Her attention swayed back to the cuddle heap, which was beginning to disintegrate. Three of the elders—ones Sissix had not known the names of—were heading back to the house. A few stayed with Sissix, still touching, but their energy was waning. Issash, however, continued to hug Sissix as tightly as she had at the start. Two of Sissix's other hatch parents, apparently overcome by all the affection, had left the group for a nearby bench. There could be no doubt that they had moved on to *actual* foreplay, and in one brief, unexpected moment, all of Rosemary's idle curiosities about what a male Aandrisk kept inside the slit between his legs were answered.

"*Come,*" Ithren said, leading Rosemary and Ashby toward the homestead. "*Let's take care of you two. And you know, you don't have to wear clothes here, unless you want to. I know it's your way, but we want you to be comfortable.*"

"Thank you," Rosemary said in Klip. She did her best to

avert her gaze from the Aandrisk elders on the bench, who were now coupling with gusto. "I think I'll keep them on for now."

The way the day progressed, Rosemary felt sorry for the techs, crowded into some concert pit with greasy food and overpriced kick. Her own afternoon was spent lying on floor cushions, drinking grass wine and eating strange, delicious nibbles from the communal table (the elders had little frame of reference for how much Humans needed to eat, and had provided enough food for ten of them). She listened as Sissix's family caught their hatch daughter up on the daily dramas of friends and relatives. Everything about the gathering was intriguing, from the unfamiliar food, to the obsessive level of detail given to local gossip, to the unending physical affection lavished upon Sissix. In many ways, Rosemary felt like the hatchlings, peeking through the windows and slipping in to fill bowls with snacks. She, too, was content to watch and learn.

But by evening, Rosemary had grown a little restless. She had eaten herself sluggish, thanks to Ithren's urgings, and the effect of the wine had shifted from "pleasantly relaxed' to "mild headache." Her legs were stiff from lying around, and her brain felt like goo after several hours of listening to conversations in an unfamiliar language. Shortly after the sun went down, she excused herself and went outside for some air.

Theth dominated the desert sky, hanging close enough for her to imagine that she could reach out and brush its rings with her fingertips. Without the haze of city lights, shimmering colors shone down unhindered—the glow of neighboring moons, the murky purple gauze of the galactic cloud, and all in between, nothing but stars, stars, stars. She lived up there, in that vast expanse of color. Every day, she saw planets and comets and stellar nurseries right up close, plain as weather.

Yet, there was something about being planetside that made it feel different. Perhaps stars were supposed to be viewed from the ground.

She glanced inside at Sissix, surrounded by a throng of feathered heads. She looked back to the sky, guiltily entertaining the idea of everyone but Sissix disappearing for a while. She imagined Sissix coming outside, handing her another glass of wine, putting her arm around her shoulder, teaching her the names of constellations. It was a silly, selfish thought, she knew, but she indulged it all the same.

A short while later, Ashby stepped out of the doorway, carrying a heat blanket. "Thought you might be cold."

"I am a bit, thanks." She took the blanket and pulled it around her shoulders. A soft warmth spread like sunlight through her clothes. "Oh. Mmm."

"Pretty great, right?"

"Why do I not have one of these?"

Ashby laughed. "I bought one a few years back, right after I made that same face you're making. I'm sure we can get one before we leave."

"Yes, please."

"The elders couldn't believe you'd need a blanket."

"Why—ah. Because I'm warm-blooded. Right." She laughed.

"Everything okay?"

"Oh, yeah, absolutely. I just needed a little fresh air."

"Yeah, I know, these things can be a bit much after a while. But you have had a good time?"

"I've had a *great* time. I'm really glad I came."

"Good. Tell Sissix that, too, it'll make her happy."

Rosemary smiled, but thought again of the several hours she'd spent watching Sissix being petted and pampered by a loving family. How cold and rigid life on the *Wayfarer* was in comparison. Sissix deserved better than that.

Ashby cocked his head at her. "What is it?"

"I don't know if I can put it into words. It's just . . ." She thought. "How does she do it?"

"Do what?"

"Get by without a feather family."

"Sissix has a feather family."

Rosemary blinked. A long-distance relationship with a feather family? Given the closeness she'd just witnessed, she couldn't see how that would work. "She's never said anything about them."

Ashby smirked. "When you have a minute in private, pull up her ID file. As ship's clerk, you should have access to it."

Late that night, curled up in her guest room, Rosemary did just that.

ID #: 7789-0045-268
GC DESIGNATED NAME: Sissix Seshkethet
EMERGENCY CONTACT: Ashby Santoso
NEXT OF KIN: Issash Seshkethet (GC designated)
LOCAL NAME (IF APPLICABLE):
    oshet-Seshkethet esk-Saskist as-Eshresh Sissix isket-Veshkriset

Rosemary chewed her lip as she studied the words on her scrib. *Seshkethet* was obvious. *Saskist* was Sissix's mother, and *Eshresh* sounded like a name, which meant he was probably her father. *Veshkriset,* however, was unfamiliar.

She pulled up the official Aandrisk family database. Somewhere out there, there was a team of archivists whose sole purpose was to follow Aandrisk family drama and track the changes accordingly. She felt exhausted just thinking about it.

The letters on the screen shifted as her scrib translated the text into Klip. *Please choose a family name,* it read. "Veshkriset," she said, hoping the database could understand her poor accent.

A listing popped up. Rosemary's brow furrowed. The Veshkriset feather family had only one member. Sissix.

She leaned back into the nest of blankets. Sissix was in a feather family by herself? That didn't make any sense. Sissix was the walking definition of gregariousness, and Aandrisks didn't view loners kindly. Declaring yourself the sole member of a feather family would be an act of defiance, a signal that you didn't want anything to do with other Aandrisks. Rosemary remembered how Sissix had reacted to the old woman back on Port Coriol, how she had dropped everything to give a stranger a few moments of company. *Being alone and untouched . . . there's no punishment worse than that.* No, it didn't fit at all.

She looked out the window. A thought flickered by. The database was Aandrisk made, and from what Sissix had said, its most practical purpose was to prevent inbreeding. If that was the case, would other species appear on the list?

"Scrib, translate," she said.

"Specify language path," the scrib said.

"Reskitkish to Klip."

"Reskitkish to Kliptorigan confirmed. Please speak the word or phrase you want to translate. If you cannot pronounce it—"

"Veshkriset."

A brief pause. "No definitive match found. Would you like a linguistic analysis to help determine possible matches?"

"Yes."

"The suffix -*et* implies a proper noun. This suffix is commonly used to denote an Aandrisk family group. Do you wish to search the Aandrisk family data—"

"No," Rosemary said. She thought. "Remove the suffix from the search phrase, and search again."

Another pause. "*Veshkrisk.* Noun. A person on a journey. Traveler. Wanderer."

Wayfarer.

* * *

Sissix propped her chin up on her fist, watching Hashkath get smaller and smaller through the window in her quarters. Somewhere down there, her hatch family was laughing, coupling, fighting, cooking, cleaning, feeding the hatchlings. Her skin was still shining from Kirix's homemade scale scrub. The palm-sized snapfruit tarts Issash had sent back with her were still just a little bit warm in the center. She didn't want to leave. She loved the *Wayfarer,* and she loved the people aboard it (mostly), but she always forgot how hard it was being away from other Aandrisks until she had spent time back home. It was more than just missing the smell of the desert grass or being able to fall back into Reskitkish. It was that people there *understood.* As dear as her crewmates were, constantly having to explain cultural differences, to bite back a friendly remark that might offend alien ears, to hold her hands still when she wanted to touch someone—it all grew tiring. And while visiting home was a welcome salve for her homesickness, the thing she always, *always* forgot was that for a short while after leaving Hashkath again, being away was even harder. It was as if she'd stuck a knife into herself when she'd first left home—nowhere vital, just her thigh, or perhaps a forearm. The longer she stayed away, the more the wound healed, until she often forgot it was there. Returning always pulled the scab right off.

Still, perhaps it was better that way. If she stopped caring about her hatch family, being away wouldn't hurt, but cutting those ties was unimaginable. Besides, without leaving, she never would've met all the friends she'd made elsewhere. Perhaps the ache of homesickness was a fair price to pay for having so many good people in her life.

Someone knocked on the door. "Come in," she called. There, another thing to go on the list of alien annoyances: the assumption of locked doors. It had been so nice to be without that feeling for a day.

Rosemary walked in, carrying a bottle of wine and two cups. Something about her scent was different. She had taken a shower recently, but there was something else there, something subtle that Sissix couldn't quite pinpoint. She'd noticed it before, though in a less prominent way. It reminded her, inexplicably, of being in a bar. Maybe it was just the wine. Unraveling smells within the sealed walls of the ship was always more difficult after becoming acclimated to planetside air. It was the difference between locating objects spread out across a table, and digging for them within a crowded box.

"I hope I'm not disturbing," Rosemary said.

Privacy. That was going on the list, too. "No, no, I would love some company. And a drink, since I think that's what you're offering." She glanced down at herself, then at her trousers crumpled on the floor. *Self-consciousness. Modesty.* Screw it. Rosemary had just seen her and her whole hatch family naked. She'd even been a good sport about a hatchling grabbing her breasts. She doubted that Rosemary was bothered anymore by having a clear view of someone's genitals.

Rosemary poured the wine. They sat on the floor, falling into an easy chat about nothing of importance. It wasn't until they were each working on their second cup that Rosemary said: "May I ask you a personal question?"

Sissix laughed. "I will never understand why you people ask that."

Rosemary ran her finger around the rim of her cup, looking a little embarrassed. Sissix thought perhaps she should have refrained from the comment about the personal question question, but *honestly.* Humans wasted so much time by being redundant.

The Human woman cleared her throat. "I found out that we're—the crew, that is—your feather family."

Had she not told Rosemary that? Maybe not. It wasn't the sort of thing that came up often. "Ashby told you?"

"No, he implied. I figured out the rest myself." She took a sip of wine. "I know there are a lot of complicated rules for feather families, and I don't pretend to know any of them, but I was wondering how you . . . how you categorize crew members that you didn't choose for yourself. I mean, the people who are only here because it's their job."

"You mean Corbin? Yeah, that's complicated. But in feather families, getting stuck with a member you don't like happens all the time. You just recognize that somebody else in your family needs them and you stay out of their way. It's like Ashby and Corbin. Ashby needs Corbin. Doesn't matter to me that he needs him in a business sense, rather than a family sense. Ashby is my family, without a shadow of a doubt. Therefore, Corbin falls within my feather family." She grinned over the edge of her cup. "Though I certainly wouldn't object if he found a new family elsewhere."

Rosemary nodded. "Makes sense. Though I wasn't asking about Corbin."

"Oh?"

Rosemary was quiet. Sissix had watched Human faces for long enough to know that Rosemary was either searching for the right words, or for the courage to say them. Sissix was silently grateful for how much time was saved by hand speak. At last, Rosemary spoke. "I was asking about me."

The irritation Sissix had been nursing toward Rosemary's entire species weakened. She smiled and took Rosemary's hand. "If it were my call, I'd take you in again. You should know by now that I like having you in my family."

Rosemary squeezed her fingers. She smiled, but there was something else there, too—fear, perhaps? What could she possibly be afraid of? Rosemary withdrew her hand and topped up their cups, giving the last few drops to Sissix. "After seeing you with your family, your hatch family, I mean—well, I wondered if maybe it isn't enough for you here. We must make life awfully hard."

"Being away from Aandrisks can be hard. And I'd be a liar if I said I wasn't feeling kicked in the guts right now. But I'm here by choice. I love this ship. I love our crew. I have a good life. I wouldn't change it."

Rosemary's eyes swung up, looking through her dark lashes. There was a different look in them now, something strong, grounded. "But no one touches you."

Sissix almost choked on her wine as she realized what was going on. All this time with Humans, and still there were things that didn't occur to her until after the fact. The details rushed at her at once. The look in Rosemary's eyes. The wine. The shy pauses that shifted into a low-voiced directness. Her clothes—oh, stars, Rosemary had changed her clothes since they'd gotten back to the ship. Humans read meanings into different kinds of clothes, but it was a complicated business, and Sissix had never got the hang of it. Rosemary was wearing a pair of soft, flowing trousers and a pale yellow top held up by a crisscross of strings— casual, Sissix thought, but festive, the sort of thing one of Kizzy's friends might wear to a party on a hot summer night. The top of the shirt dipped down below Rosemary's usual collar line, showing the upper curves of her breasts. And her hair. She'd done . . . something to it. Sissix couldn't say what, exactly, but effort had been made there. And with having had time for her nose to parse Rosemary's intricacies, she knew now that the change in her scent had nothing do with wine, or soap, or clean clothes. It wasn't anything from an external source. It was hormones.

Sissix had seen Human vids. She'd seen how Kizzy fussed over herself before going out to dock bars. She'd seen Ashby staring at himself in reflective surfaces before he met Pei, absently nudging at his hair or trimming the scruff on his face. Rosemary had come to her quarters in pretty clothes, with wine and kind words and hair that had had something done to it. This was a Human's elaborate way of asking something that an Aandrisk could ask with nothing more than a slight flick of her fingers.

Rosemary continued to speak. "Sissix, I don't have any feathers I can give you. I wish I did. You made me feel welcome when I first set foot on this ship. And since then, the kindness you've shown—not just to me, but to everyone—has meant more than I can say. You go out of your way to make everybody aboard this ship comfortable, to show us affection in the way that *we* expect it. I don't pretend to know Aandrisks as well as you know Humans, but there are some things I understand. I understand that we're your family, and that for you, not being able to touch us means there's a vital piece missing. I think that feeling hurts you, and I think you've buried it deep. I saw the look on your face when your family held you. You may love the *Wayfarer*, but life here is incomplete." She pressed her lips together. They came back wet. "I don't know how you see me, but—but I want you to know that if you should want something more . . . I'd like to give it to you."

Sissix cupped her palm, flipped it and spread her claws, even though she knew Rosemary would not understand the gesture. *Tresha*. It was the thankful, humble, vulnerable feeling that came after someone saw a truth in you, something they had discovered just by watching, something that you did not admit often to yourself. If Rosemary had been an Aandrisk, Sissix would've knocked the cups aside and started coupling right then and there, but she remained cautious. Apparently the part of her that understood Humans was still at the helm.

"Rosemary," Sissix said, taking her hand. She was so warm. Other species always were, she could feel it just standing by them, but it was all the more present now. She had sometimes wondered what it would be like to have that warmth pressing against—no, no, she was not thinking about that. Not yet. She had to be smart. She had to be careful. After all, Humans reacted differently to coupling than she did. Didn't their brains get overloaded with chemicals afterward, way more than normal people? Aandrisks bonded through coupling, too, but Humans—Humans could get crazy over it. How else could you explain a sapient species that had overpopulated itself to the point of environmental collapse? This was a people that had coupled themselves stupid.

"I'm . . . I'm grateful," Sissix said at last. What a horrible, hollow way to describe how she was feeling. *Tresha.* That was the right explanation, but there was no word for it in Klip. Useless language. Rosemary's face fell slightly, as if she *had* been expecting Sissix to knock aside the cups. Dammit, why hadn't *this* been covered in interspecies sensitivity courses? "Are you . . ." *Think, Sissix, think.* "Are you saying this to me because you feel sorry for me, or is it . . . something you want?" *Ugh.* Klip was always too practical or too emotional. Never a middle ground. Useless, useless language.

Rosemary took a sip of wine and contemplated her cup. "Well, I *am* attracted to you. You're a wonderful person, and a very good friend. I'm not sure when I started feeling more than that for you. Which isn't a problem, by the way, if your answer is no. I do like being your friend, and I'll be happy if that's all we are." She took another sip. "But, to be honest, I probably wouldn't have said anything about it if I hadn't seen your hatch family. My own feelings aside, you need something like that, and not just when you happen upon other Aandrisks." Her eyes swung back up again, dark and honest. "If not from me, then from someone. You deserve it."

Just say yes, a little voice inside Sissix begged. *Say yes, Sissix, she's right*—"Rosemary . . . I want to say yes. I do." She thought back to the shy new clerk who had come aboard less than a standard ago. Who was this woman with the serious eyes, the woman who spoke her mind so bravely? What had she discovered out here in the open? Sissix took a breath. "But I don't want to hurt you. Coupling's different for us, I think. I'm flattered that you want to give me something I need, but I don't know if I can give you what *you* need."

Rosemary gave a little smirk, the same kind Jenks gave Kizzy when she'd said something absurd. "Sissix, I'm not asking you to marry me. I'm not in love with you. I *like* you. I like who you are and how you are, and I like the way your feathers fall across the curve of your head. I understand that you don't limit yourself to one person. I understand that our notions of family are different, and that they probably won't fit together down the road. But I'd like to be part of your notion for a while, all the same."

Curiosity. Now there was a concept Sissix understood. "I think I'd like that, too," Sissix said. The warning voice within her was dying, but it wasn't about to go out without a fight. "But there are things you need to understand."

"All right," Rosemary said. There was a brightness in her eyes, a hopefulness. Sissix found herself melting. This could be a very lovely thing.

"Family members, as I'm sure you noticed, aren't just about sex. We cuddle and touch and hold each other all the time. If coupling is too much to ask, if it were to—" What was the proper way to say *overload your crazy mammal brain*? "—to make you feel uncomfortable, or to make you want more from me than I can give you, I would also be okay with just being close. Like you saw with my family. Even that would be enough." It'd be a big improvement from the current status quo, for sure.

Rosemary nodded. "I'll keep that option in mind. But I don't think there will be a problem."

"And we don't have to act that way around the others, if that would make you more comfortable. We don't even have to tell them." Sissix didn't care about the others finding out, but if Rosemary could make cultural concessions out of kindness, she could return the favor.

Rosemary considered this, and nodded. "I think that might be better, at least to start," she said.

Sissix paused. The next thing, she knew, was not an idea most Humans took to with ease. "If we were planetside, and I met other Aandrisks—"

"I wouldn't mind you going to a *tet*," Rosemary said. "Just don't expect me to come along."

"It wouldn't be because they were more important than you," Sissix said quickly. "Or because I liked being with Aandrisks better—"

"Sissix," Rosemary said. She squeezed Sissix's hand, and did something that no one had ever done before. She raised Sissix's fingers to her mouth and pressed her lips against the knuckles, just once, letting them linger for a moment. Sissix had been given kisses before, from Kizzy and Jenks and Ashby—fast, dry brushes against her cheek. This was different. It was slower, softer. It was an odd feeling, a soft feeling. She liked it. Rosemary pulled her lips back and smiled. "I get it."

Stars, she really did.

"There's one more thing," Sissix said. She noticed that her voice had sunk lower. Something else was piloting her brain now, the part of her who was no stranger to *tets* and couplings, the part of her who was shouting with joy that finally, at last, someone in her family understood. She met Rosemary's eyes and gave an embarrassed laugh. "I've never coupled with a Human."

Rosemary grinned. "That's good," she said. She leaned in, running a smooth fingertip along the length of one of Sissix's feathers. "I'd hate for you to have an unfair advantage."

OCTOBER 25

☆

"So," Ashby said. "Can you fix it?"

Jenks inspected the exposed insides of Ashby's scrib with the attention of a surgeon. "I can *tweak* it," he said. "But it won't be a permanent fix. You need a new pixel array. Easy enough for me to hook up, but I don't have one on hand."

"But you can get it to stop hopping between feeds?"

"Yeah. The picture might start to degrade after a couple tendays, but it won't—Wait. Uh-oh." Jenks paused. "You hear that?"

Ashby listened. Raised voices down the hall, coming from the algae bay. He sighed. "Not again."

Jenks rolled his eyes. "I swear, they'd save so much time if one of them just spaced the other already."

They followed the voices, which was easy enough to do. Pieces of the argument made their way to his ears as they got closer.

"—absolutely incompetent—" That was Corbin.

"—weren't such a pain in the ass—" Sissix.

"—no regard for my work here—"

"—just communicate like a fucking functional adult, then maybe—"

"I *did* communicate, it's just that your thick lizard ears won't—" *Dammit, Corbin!* Ashby quickened his step.

"*Hisk! Ahsshek tes hska essh*—"

"Oh, yes, hiss all you want, it still doesn't change the fact that I'm—"

"Enough," Ashby said, entering the room. Jenks hung back in the doorway, far away enough to be polite, but close enough to get a good view.

"Ashby," Sissix said, feathers on end. "You tell this pompous, speciest asshole that—"

"I said that's enough." Ashby glared at them both. "Now, I want to know what this is all about." Corbin and Sissix began yelling in tandem. Ashby put up his hands. "One at a time."

"Your pilot," Corbin said, in the same tone that an angry father might say *your child* to his partner, "pushed the induction lines past capacity. It put too much strain on one of my pressure caps, and now look." Ashby looked to the fuel distributor. He couldn't see the problem, but the green goo in a small number of tubes was lying still.

"I had no idea that he had swapped out the cap for a lesser model." Sissix shot Corbin a murderous look. "And I still don't understand why he did it at all."

"I swapped it out because it was the only part I had on hand. In case you haven't noticed, we haven't had any market stops in a while. It was either make do with a lesser model or replace the entire apparatus. Which is what I'll have to do anyway, thanks to you."

"Yes, it's my fault, because you actually bothered to tell me about any of this. Oh, no, wait, you didn't."

"I brought this up in the kitchen day before yesterday."

"You weren't talking to me! You were bitching about your lab to Dr. Chef! How the fuck was I supposed to know that it had anything to do with my ability to fly the—"

"In other words, you *chose* to ignore me. Perhaps if you'd

pay a little more attention to the needs of others instead of acting so self-involved, then—"

"*Stop,*" Ashby said. He took a deep breath. "Let me make sure I'm hearing this correctly. This argument, which we could hear coming down the stairs, is all because of a minor incident involving a damaged pressure cap."

"It's hardly minor, this is going to take me all day to—"

"It's *minor,*" Ashby repeated. "You lost one apparatus out of six. Fuel is still pumping, right?"

Corbin scowled. "Yes. But it's a matter of—"

"*Okay.* So, in the future, *you*"—he pointed at Corbin—"need to tell Sissix about any equipment changes you make, because you cannot expect her to be psychically aware of what goes on in this lab. And you do *not* use *that word* aboard my ship, do you understand? Not to Sissix, not to anyone else. It is completely unacceptable. You apologize to her right now."

"I didn't—"

"*Right. Now.*"

Corbin's face went even redder. "I'm . . . *sorry,*" he said to Sissix. His voice was tight as a sealing band.

"And *you*"—Ashby jabbed a finger at Sissix—"need to go way easier when making speed jumps, because there's no way that cap should've burned out that fast."

"We're running behind," Sissix said. "If we don't—"

"I don't care if we're a tenday late. I don't care if we're a *standard* late. I am *not* going adrift out here, not when we've come this far. Be more careful." He stared them both down. "I am only going to say this one more time. Get over whatever this pissing match is between the two of you. It is driving me crazy. It is driving the rest of your crew crazy. I know this has been a long haul, and I know we're all tired, but I'll be damned if I'm going to fly the rest of the way to the Core listening to you two scream at each other. Work it out. If you can't, fake it. I do not want to have this conversation—"

The vox snapped on. "Hey, Ashby." It was Kizzy. "Um, so, I kind of need you for something."

"Can it wait?"

"Well, um, not so much, no, but maybe I could tell him—"

"Tell who what?"

There was a shuffling sound. Rosemary's voice replaced Kizzy's. "Ashby, we've got a Quelin enforcer on hold up here."

He could hear Kizzy talking in the background. "Do you think I made him mad? I can't tell, 'cause their faces don't move."

Ashby sighed and closed his eyes. "Lovey, transfer the call down here."

Corbin stepped aside as Ashby took a seat at his desk. The pixels leaped into place. A male Quelin stared back, his armored face inscrutable, his black eyes shining.

"This is Captain Ashby Santoso. How can I help you?"

"This is Enforcer Bevel of the Interstellar Defense Bureau. As is stated in Section 36-28 of the Border Security Amendment, you are subject to a full search of your vessel and an inspection of all crew members."

"We were already scanned when we entered Quelin space. Have we done anything wrong?"

"This is a random search. The Interstellar Defense Bureau has the right to search any and all vessels at our discretion, regardless of probable cause."

"I trust that my clerk has sent you our tunneling license and flight plan?"

"We have received the required materials, and your right to travel within our space has been confirmed."

"Not to be difficult, but we're on a tight schedule. Do I have the right to refuse this search?"

"Refusal will result in possible impounding of your vessel and incarceration of all persons aboard. Failure to comply with inspection officers is a violation of our GC membership agreement and is subject to prosecution under Executive Order 226-09."

"I guess we'll look forward to seeing you onboard, then."

"Prepare to be boarded in ten minutes," said Officer Bevel. The pixels scattered as the call ended.

"What a charming guy," Jenks said. "Bet he's great fun at parties."

"Only if he has the proper formwork for it," Ashby said, rubbing the bridge of his nose. "Pain in the ass."

The freight elevator doors clanked open. Rosemary and Kizzy hopped out. "Is everything okay?" Kizzy said. "Did I get us in trouble? I really shouldn't answer calls ever, I get all stupid—"

"Nobody's in trouble, but we have to let them do another search."

"Why?"

"Because they said so, and because they're Quelin, and because they're really not the sort of people I want to piss off."

"I hear onboard searches are a real pain," Sissix said.

"We were fine on our last search."

"Yeah, but that was just a basic scan for weapons and illegal tech. Trust me, they'll search everything. And I hear they do blood screenings, too."

"Why blood screenings?" Rosemary asked.

Jenks sighed. "Because of that asshole with explosive bots in his blood, I'll bet. Remember that? That dumb speciest kid a few standards back tried to prove a point during a border search? Didn't even program them right. All he did was blow his own head off."

"Funny how it's always the speciests who ruin things for everybody else," Sissix said. Corbin scoffed, but Sissix headed for the door before he could say anything further. "I'll go get Ohan."

Ashby's eyes shifted between Kizzy and Jenks. "Do you two have anything stashed away that might make them freak out? *Anything?*"

Jenks thought hard. "Don't think so."

"Nah," said Kizzy. "We drank the last of Bear's home-brew kick last tenday." She paused. Her hands shot up to her mouth. "Oh, ass!"

"What?" Ashby said.

She slid her hands up to the top of her head and twisted her hair. "I have a bag of smash in with my socks."

"Good thing you thought of it now. Go toss it in the engine."

"But . . ." Kizzy's shoulders sagged. "You can't get smash out here. I've been saving it for a special occasion."

Ashby frowned. He was not in the mood for Kizzy reasoning. "This isn't a debate. Toss it in the engine. Now."

"Come on, Kiz," Jenks said. He took her by the wrist and led her back to the freight elevator. "Let's go do this awful thing."

"I hate the Quelin," she said. "They're stupid and jerks and nobody likes them." She lowered her voice surreptitiously as they entered the elevator. "If we smoked it now really fast, do you think they'd notice?"

"I can still hear you, Kizzy," Ashby said.

She pouted. "Can't blame me for trying," she said as the doors closed.

Rosemary had seen vids of Quelin before, but even so, she was unprepared for the things that came clattering through the cargo bay doors. She tried to think of a more eloquent descriptor for them, but all she kept coming up with was *lobster centaur.* Chitinous blue exoskeletons, long horizontal abdomens, segmented torsos covered in jointed limbs, all topped with a masklike face. Their shells were branded with symbols, studded with polished stones. She knew better than to judge a species by appearances, but between their knobbly looks and the call she'd witnessed earlier, she wasn't warming up to them.

The rest of the crew looked uneasy as well, which made her feel a little better. It was common knowledge that Quelin were typically xenophobic, and it was rare to see them anywhere other than in their own space. Their inclusion in the GC was an arrangement of convenience, or so Rosemary had read. The Quelin had huge caches of natural resources at their disposal, and had been originally brought into the GC by the Harmagians, who had plenty of money and fancy tech to offer in exchange. Not that the Quelin and the Harmagians actually liked each other. It was funny how the potential for profit always seemed to trump antipathy.

Six Quelin entered the cargo bay, headed by the one from the sib call, Enforcer Bevel. He doled out commands to his inferiors (or so Rosemary assumed, since she didn't speak Tellerain). Four of them left the bay, scanning devices beeping, pointed legs clicking against the metal floor.

"Line up and prepare to be scanned," Enforcer Bevel said. So much for introductions.

The crew did as they were told. Rosemary ended up beside Sissix. They exchanged a glance. Sissix rolled her eyes and gave her head an irritated shake.

Bevel pointed a leg toward Ohan. "What's wrong with them?" Rosemary glanced over. Ohan was shaking. Not violently so, but enough to see from a distance.

"They're old and ill," Dr. Chef said. "Nothing contagious. They have a degenerative nerve condition that makes it difficult for them to stand for an extended period of time."

Bevel's eyes were fixed on Ohan, but without eyelids or facial muscles, it was impossible to know what the Quelin was thinking. "They may sit."

"Thank you," Ohan said with a nod. They sank to the floor, trying to be as poised as possible. It seemed the Quelin could be reasonable after all.

Bevel shifted his gaze to Dr. Chef. "We will need to review their medical records in order to confirm your claim." Okay, maybe not.

The other Quelin pulled a device from a bag hanging from her side. "We will now scan your blood, hemolymph, or other primary genetic fluid for contaminants, pathogens, illegal nano-bots and any other banned or dangerous substances. If you are aware of carrying any such things, let us know at this time." She paused for a reply. No one spoke. "I will now begin the scan." She walked over to Jenks, at the far end of the line. She stared for a few seconds. "You are unusually small."

"And you have a shitload of legs," Jenks said, holding out his hand.

The Quelin said nothing. She pressed the scanner against Jenks's palm. There was a mechanical click. Rosemary heard Jenks suck air through his teeth. The Quelin studied the scanner. Apparently satisfied, she moved on to Ashby.

Jenks examined his palm. "What, no bandage, or . . . ? No? Okay. Thanks."

The Quelin worked her way down the line. Rosemary stuck out her hand dutifully when her time came. The jab of the scanner was unpleasant, but nothing to fuss over. Even though she knew there was nothing of interest in her blood, she couldn't help but sigh with relief when the Quelin passed her by. Something about these sapients made her feel awfully tense.

Even though Rosemary couldn't read the Quelin's face, something about her changed when she scanned Corbin. Enforcer

Bevel clearly saw it, too, as he beelined right for her. He looked at the scanner, and there was a brief flurry of unintelligible discussion between them.

"Artis Corbin," Enforcer Bevel said. "Under Section 17-6-4 of the Defense of Genetic Integrity Agreement, I am placing you under arrest."

"What?!" cried Corbin. The other Quelin was already upon him, binding his hands with some sort of energy cord and pushing him toward the door. "I—I haven't done anything!"

Ashby rushed forward. "Enforcer, what's—"

Enforcer Bevel stopped him. "You all need to be questioned. We will hold you here. Interrogations will take place in an area of our choosing once we have completed our search of your vessel," the Enforcer said. "Under Section 35-2 of the Punitive Regulations Act, any request made for legal advice will be denied."

"I'm sorry, what?" Ashby said. "What the hell is going on?"

Rosemary tried to stay calm. None of them had done anything, not to her knowledge, and if the Quelin hadn't figured out about her doctored ID file by now, she doubted they would at all. And as for Corbin, she couldn't think of anyone less likely to break the law. This had to be a misunderstanding.

"You are not under arrest," Bevel said. "Nor are any charges being made against you at this time. Failure to comply in full with your interrogation officer will result in imprisonment."

Jenks glared. "The captain asked you a question. What did we do?"

"Jenks, don't," said Dr. Chef.

The other Quelin marched Corbin off the ship. "Ashby!" he cried. His feet dragged, but the Quelin pushed him forward. "Ashby, I didn't—"

"I know, Corbin," Ashby said. "We'll get this sorted out." He turned back to Bevel, fuming. Rosemary had never seen him so angry. "Where are you taking him? What did he do?"

Enforcer Bevel looked at Ashby with his flat black eyes. "He exists."

They scanned his wristpatch, and took his clothes. He had yelled himself raw, but none of them would speak to him. None of them were even speaking in Klip. Their words clicked. Their eyes clicked. Their feet clicked when they hit the floor. It was like being in a metal insect hive—dark, hot, humid, and always clicking, clicking, clicking.

He didn't know how far he was from the *Wayfarer*. They'd moved him onto a different ship. Or maybe an orbiter? He couldn't say. There hadn't been any windows or viewscreens (not that he'd seen, anyway). They'd shoved him into an enormous room, the size of a cargo carrier's belly. The floor was pockmarked with smooth, deep pits, twice as deep as he was tall. If he squinted hard enough, he could see the glitter of eyes staring back at him from within their depths.

He tried to cover himself. The Quelin wore no clothes themselves, but then, they had shells. They didn't need to be covered. They weren't made of soft flesh and hair and lines and creases and misshapen folds you'd rather keep to yourself. He wished he had a shell. He wished that he'd been born to a species with spikes or horns or anything more imposing than the fragile sack that he was. He wished the Quelin could be the ones who were afraid.

They nudged him roughly toward an empty pit. "No," he said, trying to force the tremble out of his voice. "Not until you've told me what I've done. I'm a GC citizen, and I have my—"

Within seconds, he wished he'd said nothing.

One of the Quelin grabbed him with its upper limbs, pinning him face out against its plated torso. Segmented limbs closed around his body, like a wiry cage. The other Quelin lowered its face to the floor, flattening itself into a plank. Corbin hadn't noticed how thick the plating was at the top of their heads. A curved, blackish-blue dome, worn smooth and thick with old scratches.

The Quelin charged him. The domed head rammed into his chest. Pain burst through him. He choked on his own breath, flecking the Quelin's domed head with spit. The Quelin did not seem to care. The thing backed up, and ran forward again.

Oh, no, please, not—

He heard his ribs crack before he registered the pain. He heard himself cry out before he realized who it was. He sagged against the Quelin's legs, but it held him upright. The second Quelin charged again.

The Quelin holding him must have let him go at some point, because he found himself on the floor, retching and shaking. He could feel the fractured ribs stab every time his stomach heaved. Low moans escaped from his mouth, but were cut short as his lungs fought for air.

They shoved him into the pit. He tumbled down the cold metal. His face hit the floor first. He felt blood spurt from his nose as it wrenched sideways. The Quelin who had broken his bones shouted to him in Klip, speaking eight angry words. In the hours ahead, they would be all he could think of.

"From now on, clone, you will be quiet."

Ashby was the last to return from the interrogation. He joined the others at the dinner table. Everyone looked exhausted. Even Ohan was there, curled up under a blanket on a nearby bench. Dr. Chef had brought out a small batch of spring cakes. Nobody was eating them.

"Oh, stars," said Kizzy. She ran over and hugged him around the waist. "I thought you were getting locked up, too."

"I'm okay," he said.

"You've been gone *six hours*."

"Feels like longer." He slumped into his chair. Dr. Chef placed a mug of mek in front of him. Ashby cupped his palms around it, letting the warmth bleed into his hands. He stared at nothing for a moment, took a deep breath and looked to his crew. "Did any of you know?"

A general shaking of heads. "Not a clue," Jenks said, lighting his redreed pipe. The ash piles on the plate in front of him indicated that he'd gone through two bowls already.

"We've been debating whether or not Corbin knew," Sissix said.

"And?" Ashby said.

"We don't think so," Jenks said. Smoke leaked out from between his teeth. "Did you see his face when they dragged him away? He had no fucking idea what was going on."

"I checked an old blood test," Dr. Chef said. "There's no question. There are some irregularities in his DNA that can't happen any other way."

"Why didn't you notice it before?" Ashby asked.

"Because it's the sort of thing you only find if you're specifically looking for it. I didn't have any reason to."

Ashby sighed and leaned back. "This doesn't change anything. I hope you all know that. Corbin's a sapient individual, and I don't particularly care where he came from. I know we all have our . . . difficulties with him." He glanced at Sissix, who was picking at a spring cake with a single claw. "But he's part of our crew, and we have to help him." He looked around the table. Something was off. "Wait, where's Rosemary? Did she not come back?" Had the Quelin figured out about her, too? Stars, how many crew members was he going to lose today?

"No, she's in her office," Sissix said. "She's been combing through legal options for Corbin since the moment they let her go."

Asbhy reminded himself to give Rosemary a raise once the tunnel was built. "I'll go help her," he said, pushing his chair back.

"No need." Rosemary walked in through the kitchen, scrib in hand and pixel pen behind her ear. "But we've got a lot to talk about."

"Let's hear it."

Rosemary took her place at the table. "Corbin's being held at a nearby enforcement orbiter. They'll be keeping him there indefinitely, before his case is processed."

"What happens then?"

"If we do nothing, he'll be sent to a Quelin penal colony. They're labor camps, mostly, from what I've learned. Apparently most of the teracite ore in the GC is mined by Quelin prisoners."

"Now there's a happy thought," Jenks said. "Nice to know what my circuit panels are made from."

"How can they do that?" Dr. Chef said. "Corbin's a GC citizen."

"No, he's not," Rosemary said. "Since cloning is illegal in most GC territories, cloned individuals don't get natural-born rights. They have to go through the same application process that non-GC species do, even if they've lived in the GC all their lives."

"That's not fair," Kizzy said.

"Yeah," Jenks said. "But think of how rarely something like this happens. Lawmakers aren't going to trouble themselves making new legal systems for something that affects maybe— what? A few hundred people, if that? You can't find cloners anywhere but the fringe, and I highly doubt anybody who's a part of it comes back to the GC. This probably isn't something the GC has to deal with often."

"Exactly," Rosemary said. "And because of that, the unofficial policy when dealing with a discovered clone is to default to whatever the local laws are. If we'd found out about Corbin in, say, Harmagian space, he'd still have to go through the application process, but the only other thing that would happen to him is a footnote on his ID file. The only person who'd be arrested is his father. Which is probably happening as we speak."

"Anybody know anything about his dad?" Kizzy said.

"He's still on the Enceladus orbiter, I think. They're not on speaking terms," Ashby said. He turned to Rosemary. "So, let me get this straight. Since Corbin's *not* a citizen, we can't use any of our treaty rights to get him back?"

"Right. But there is a loophole. It's just not . . ." She cleared her throat. "It's not exactly ideal."

"I figured as much."

Rosemary fidgeted with her pen. "The terms of the Quelin GC membership agreement state that they have to honor any legally binding documents that affect GC citizens traveling through their space. This is meant for cases like . . . say, you have a Human and a Harmagian who have a registered partnership in Harmagian space."

"Eew," said Kizzy.

"Speciest," said Jenks.

"I'm not speciest, they're *slimy*."

"It's just an example," said Rosemary. "Now, they wouldn't be able to register their partnership with the Quelin, because interspecies partnerships aren't recognized there. But since they're already registered in another GC territory, the Quelin have to honor their partnership, legally speaking."

"How so?" Ashby asked.

"Like if their ship crashed and one of them died, the Quelin authorities would have to recognize the other as their next of kin, even though they wouldn't grant those rights to people living within their space."

"Got it. But how does this help Corbin?"

"Well, when you start an application for GC citizenship, you have to have an assigned legal guardian throughout the process. A GC citizen who vouches for you."

"Yes, I had to do that," Dr. Chef said.

"How's it work?" Jenks asked.

"It's a formality more than anything. The idea is that you have someone there to help you fit in. They make sure you learn the language, learn the laws, understand the local culture and ethics, that sort of thing. They're also responsible for helping you get your formwork in on time, and they have to come with you to your application hearing. It's a sort of buddy system to help you integrate."

"Seems stupid for Corbin," Kizzy said. "It's not like he has to learn Klip all over again."

"So," Ashby said, "if Corbin has a legal guardian, the Quelin have to release him to that person?"

"Yes, but we only have a narrow window to make it happen. We'd have to fill out the formwork, get the GC to approve it and get it to the Quelin before they process Corbin's case. I have a . . . friend I can contact. A minor GC official. I'm sure once they see it's an emergency, they'll sign off the formwork as fast as they can."

"The same friend that, ah . . . ?" Jenks said. He finished his question by pointing at Rosemary's wristwrap.

Rosemary's eyes swung down. "Yes," she said.

"How long before the Quelin process Corbin?" Dr. Chef asked.

"No one knows. Could be days, or tendays. They could be doing it now for all we know, but I doubt it. From what I understand of the Quelin legal system, they don't rush these things."

"All right," Ashby said. "Just show me where you need my thumbprint."

"No, see, you can't be his guardian." Rosemary took a breath. She looked uncomfortable. "There's a catch. And it's a stupid, bureaucratic catch, but it's one we can't get around."

"Let's have it."

"Quelin cloning laws aren't just strict, they're . . . I don't even know what the word is. Unyielding. My understanding on this is sketchy at best, but apparently, the Quelin had a bloody interplanetary war a few centuries back, and it was mixed up with cloning and eugenics and all sorts of messy things. Nowadays, the Quelin don't just see cloning as an ethically murky practice. They see it as evil. To them, Corbin's very existence is dangerous. As such, their laws on cloning are a lot more comprehensive than what other species have on the books. It's clear they thought about the possibility of clones entering in from outside their space."

"Meaning?"

"Meaning GC treaties or no, they won't release Corbin to anyone who comes from a species that bans cloning. In their eyes, they're doing those species a favor by keeping him away from the rest of the galaxy." She cleared her throat. "So, the only way we can get Corbin back is if he has a guardian who comes from a species without cloning laws."

"Who doesn't have—" Ashby paused when he saw the hesitant look on Rosemary's face. She wasn't looking at him. He followed her gaze across the table. To Sissix.

Sissix blinked twice, her face blank. She put her palm over her eyes, arched her head back and let out a long, angry sigh. "You are fucking kidding me."

"Wait," Kizzy said. "Whoa. You? Aandrisks don't have cloning laws?"

"No, we don't have cloning laws."

"Why?"

"Because we don't do it," she snapped. "The idea never

occurred to us. You know why? Because unlike you people, we think nature works fine on its own without tweaking it and hacking it and—and—oh, this is ridiculous."

"Sissix—" Ashby said.

"Don't say anything. I'll do it. It's not even a question. I'm not going to leave him to rot in some teracite mine." She drummed her claws on the table. "So. Fine. What do I have to do? Sign some formwork, go to a few hearings with him?"

"Yes," Rosemary said. She licked her lips, speaking more quickly. "And you have to be within the same system as him at all times for the duration of the application process."

Sissix's feathers puffed. "How long is that?"

Rosemary shrank into herself. Her whole body was one big apology. "Up to a standard. Maybe more."

Sissix swore in Reskitkish and walked away from the table. She turned back toward Rosemary. "I'm not mad at you about this," she said. "You know that, right?"

"I know," Rosemary said, looking into Sissix's eyes. Ashby watched an unspoken conversation pass between them. He studied them with interest. He had a suspicion, but now wasn't the time to ponder it. There were more important things to think of.

Sissix sighed again, and tried to smooth her feathers down with her hand. "Well, come on," she said. "Let's go save the bastard."

Sissix had only been aboard the enforcement orbiter for a few minutes, but already she loathed it. No windows. No colors. Silent hallways. Humorless, angular design. Everywhere she turned, a sense of disapproving sterility. She understood that prisons weren't meant to be cheerful, but this was worse than she'd imagined. It was the sort of place that inspired you to never do anything bad ever again. The only good thing was the warmth, but even then, the heat was thick, heavy. It felt like something you could chew on.

They entered a holding room, which contained nothing but several wall-mounted scanners and an imposing set of doors. "Wait here," said her escort. The Quelin punched a code into a wall panel. The doors fell open, and Sissix nearly gagged on the air that drifted out, a miasma of unwashed skin and bodily waste. She pressed her palm against her nostrils and took a step back. How did the Quelin stand it? Did they even have a sense of smell?

She fought down her growing sense of nausea and tried to see inside the detention area. The light was too dim to make out much of anything, but she could see body heat rising from pits in the floor. Pits. Did the rest of the GC know about this? Surely someone in Parliament did. Did they care? Did it make them lose sleep at night, knowing that they shared council sessions with sapients who treated other species this way? Or was easy access to teracite enough to remove those qualms? The sick feeling within her grew, but now it had nothing to do with the smell.

And I'm here for Corbin, she thought, the notion refusing to sink in. She was in this hollow corpse of a place, after filing some seriously binding formwork that would leash her for a standard—a fucking *standard*—and all for *Corbin*. That biting, ugly waste. Why him? Why *her*? She could accept him being on the ship, she could deal with having to share the same food and air, but this—this was absurd. And unfair. And unearned.

After a few moments, she could see the Enforcer heading back to the doors, walking behind a Human man. There was something wrong with him. Sissix could see it in the way he moved. What had they done to him? She sucked air between her teeth as he came closer. A dark spray of bruises covered his torso, purple ringed with yellow. His face was a mess, and his nose hung at the wrong angle. He moved stiffly, clutching his side with one arm. His other hand was busy trying to shield his genitals.

Humans. Honestly, after being beaten and dumped in a pit, *that's* what he was worrying about?

But then Sissix saw the look on Corbin's face. She thought it was anger at first, but no—it was shame. She would never fully understand Human modesty, but she knew how deeply ingrained it was in them. She also knew that every hard feeling she had toward Corbin was returned in kind. For him to be pushed around without clothes on was probably humiliating enough, but to be seen that way by someone he despised was the ultimate insult. Sissix wished that someone else could have been sent for him. She looked away.

"Are you sure you want him?" the Enforcer asked. "He is an abomination."

Sissix glared. "Go get the abomination's clothes."

"They were likely destroyed."

She took a few steps forward to Corbin, who was having trouble standing. She took his arm and put it around her waist, helping him to stand. Had she ever touched him before? She didn't think so. There must've been a handshake, at least, when he'd been hired. She spoke again to the Quelin. "Do you have anything? A blanket? A towel? Anything?"

The Enforcer hesitated, then opened a wall panel full of medical supplies. Despite his unreadable face, Sissix got the impression that this Quelin was treading lightly around her. She was nobody, but her species was one of the big three in the GC Parliament, and they had far more pull than the Quelin did. Their species' diplomatic ties were tenuously civil at best, and an Aandrisk treated poorly at the hands of Quelin Enforcers was the sort of thing the newsfeeds would pounce on.

The Enforcer handed Sissix a small blanket, made of some foil-like synthetic fabric. She helped Corbin wrap it around his waist.

"Thank you," he said in a thin voice. It was obvious that he was having trouble drawing a full breath. His eyes were fixed on the floor, but Sissix could see him fighting back a small ribbon of tears. Just one more embarrassment he was trying to prevent. Sissix took her eyes off his face. She had no business seeing him like this.

"Let's get you home," she said. She led him out of the room, the Enforcer following close behind.

After a moment, Corbin spoke in a whisper. "I wasn't sure anyone would come for me."

Sissix said nothing. Nothing she could say would sound right, or honest. They continued down the hallway. Corbin winced with every step. After a while, he said, "Why you?"

She sighed. "It's complicated, and you are not going to like what's going on anymore than I do. But it can wait until Dr. Chef patches you up. For now, let's just say . . . it was the right thing to do."

An awkward silence fell between them. "Thank you," Corbin said. "I . . . well. Thank you."

"Yeah, well," Sissix said. She cleared her throat. "From now on, though, I get to crank up the temperature as high as I want."

Four days later, Corbin sat at his lab bench, spreading algae on a sample card. The last batch had come out slightly tacky, and he wasn't sure why. He spread the algae thin, so that he would be able to see the cells clearly once he placed the card into the scanner. A normal task, but it didn't feel that way. Nothing did, not his lab, not his bed, not his face. But that was exactly why normal tasks needed doing. He would put algae onto the card, and he'd put it into the scanner. He'd do it again and again, until it felt the way it had before.

"Excuse me, Corbin," Lovey said through the vox.

"Yes?"

The AI paused. "There's a sib call coming through for you. It's from Tartarus."

Corbin looked up from the algae and said nothing. Tartarus. A prison asteroid, out in the Kuiper Belt. There was only one person who would be calling him from there.

Lovey spoke again, her voice awkward. "I can dismiss the call if you like."

"No," Corbin said. He wiped the smear of green slime from the end of his sampling tool and set it aside. "Put it through down here."

"Okay, Corbin. I hope it goes well."

Corbin gave a curt nod. The vox clicked off. With a sigh, he turned to his desk and gestured at the pixel projector. The pixels scurried into action. A blinking red rectangle in the bottom of the projection indicated that he had a sib call waiting. He watched it blink five times before gesturing to answer it.

His father appeared. Corbin hadn't spoken to the man in four standards. He had grown old. A little heavy, too, which was surprising. His father had always pushed Corbin to eat healthy. Corbin could see it now, the familiar curves and angles and lines in his father's face. The features were more pronounced, worn deep with age, but they were the same as his own. It was more than just familial resemblance. Corbin would wear the same face one day.

His father spoke. "They hurt you."

Corbin leaned back in his chair, making sure that his father could get a good look at the fading bruises on his face. This was exactly why he hadn't let Dr. Chef fix anything but the bones. He had been hoping for this moment, the moment in which his father would see what his hubris had done. "Hello, Marcus. And yes, I came back from prison with a broken nose and three cracked ribs. One came damn close to puncturing my lung."

323

"I'm sorry, Artis. I am so sorry."

"Sorry," said Corbin. "I get ripped out of my home, beaten to a pulp and thrown into some Quelin hellhole, only to be told that my entire life is a lie—and you're *sorry*. Well, thanks, but that doesn't quite cut it."

Marcus sighed. "This is why I called, you know. I figured you had some questions. If you can stop hating me for a few minutes, I'd be happy to answer them. I can't make many calls from here. Ansible access is a rare thing."

Corbin stared at the man in the pixels. He looked so defeated, so tired. Corbin found himself shaken by it, and it made him all the angrier. "All I want to know," Corbin said, "is where I really came from."

Marcus nodded and looked down at his lap. "You know all those times you asked about your mother?"

"Of course. All you ever said was that she died in a shuttle crash. You never wanted to talk about her. Which makes sense, since she never existed."

"Oh, no," Marcus said. "I did have a wife. She wasn't your mother, of course, but . . ." His eyes went somewhere far away. "Artis, I've never been good with people. I've always preferred my lab. I like data. Data is consistent, it's steady, it's easy to understand. With data, you always know what the answer is. If the data doesn't make sense, you can always puzzle it out. Unlike people." He shook his head. "I can never puzzle out people. I'm sure you understand."

Corbin clenched his jaw. *Dammit*, he thought. *How much of me is actually you?*

Marcus continued. "When I was a young man, I took a posting down on Overlook." Corbin knew the place. It was one of the few labs down on the surface of Encaledus. Strictly quarantined, to prevent contamination of the microbial pools below the moon's icy surface. Only one person manned Overlook at a time, and those who were assigned there were on their own for at least a year. It was rare that people took an Overlook assignment more than once. "I thought it was the perfect place for me. I loved working down there. No people to disturb my work or get in my way. Except for her." He paused. "Her name was Sita. She flew the supply shuttle that brought me food and lab supplies. She couldn't come in, of course, but I could watch her through the airlock cameras, and we spoke over the vox." Marcus smiled, a warm, private smile. Corbin was startled. He'd never seen his father smile like that, not once. "And as you may suspect, she was beautiful. Not beautiful like they do in vids or when they're trying to sell you something. *Real* beautiful. The kind of beautiful you could actually touch. And she wasn't from the orbiter. She was from Mars." He laughed under his breath. "I thought her accent was so damn cute." Marcus shook his head, as if clearing it. His voice became more grounded. "I was awful to her, of course. I'd snap at her if she showed up while I was in the middle of testing, and I've always hated small talk, so I barely gave her the time of day. I was like that to everyone, but she . . . she didn't care. She always put up with me, even when I was an ass to her. She always smiled. She made fun of me, for my bad moods, for my uncombed hair. For whatever reason, it didn't make me mad. I *liked* the way she gave me a hard time. I started counting the days between supply drops. At first, I thought I was just lonely, that it was a symptom of living in isolation. It took me a while to realize just how in love with her I was." He ran his hand back through his thin hair. "And then I got us both fired."

"You what?"

Marcus cleared his throat. "One tenday, I spent all of my free time cleaning up the station. Made sure it looked presentable. Set the table with the nicer food that I'd been saving in the stasie."

Corbin gaped. "You did not invite her in."

"Oh, I did. And she accepted."

"But," Corbin sputtered. "Does that station even *have* a decontamination flash suitable for Humans?"

"Nope. I was sterilized before I went down to the station. The only flash installed there was meant for food and supplies. Having her walk through it wasn't even an option."

"But your samples!" His mind reeled. Throughout Corbin's entire childhood, Marcus had drilled him with the importance of preventing contamination. One time, he'd revoked dessert privileges for a month after catching Corbin eating candy in the lab. Corbin didn't know the person that Marcus was describing. It certainly wasn't the father he knew.

"All ruined," Marcus said. "She had just enough benign bacteria on her to cause a few problems. The project leader was furious when she found out. Six months of work, gone. Sita was fired, and I was given the option to either start the year over or leave the project entirely."

"You stayed?"

"Oh, no, I left. I had just had one of the best days of my life, and it was all thanks to that beautiful woman. We hadn't even done anything that interesting. We just ate all my food and talked about everything. She made me laugh. And for reasons I still don't understand, I made her smile. There was no way I was going to be locked away from her down on Overlook. I spent the next five years trying to put my career back together, but it was worth it."

"So," Corbin said, bewildered. His brain could not accept the image of his father as a lovesick young man willing to contaminate his lab. "You married her."

Marcus chuckled. "Not right away. I begged and scraped and pleaded until I found somebody willing to hire me at the gene library. Awful job, but I was lucky to get anything at that point. The head lab tech there had done a year down on Overlook, too.

I think he sympathized. Sita got a job with a cargo company based on Titan that didn't ask too many questions, either about who she was or what cargo they took on. Shady work, but . . . well, we thought it was a good thing at the time. Since I was back on the orbiter, we could see each other more often. And after a time, I married her. We had five wonderful years together." Marcus's face grew tight, and for a moment, Corbin thought that he could see all the years of his father's life press down upon him. "One morning, she told me she'd have to leave her job in a few months. I asked why. She told me she was pregnant. I was ecstatic. By that time, I'd crawled my way up to a better position in the library, and we had enough credits saved up to start thinking about living elsewhere. It was the perfect time to begin a family. I'd never even thought that a family was something that I'd be able to have. I mean, who'd love me?" His pixelated eyes found Corbin's. Corbin said nothing. Marcus continued. "Two tendays later, Sita was making a run from Titan to Earth. Ambi cells. She normally didn't make runs that long, but they were paying her double because of the valuable cargo. It wasn't the sort of job she could say no to. Thing was, the bastards at the shuttleyard didn't check to make sure that the containment seals were properly installed. This is before the GC really started cracking down on unsafe ambi. Bureaucrats don't give a damn about anything unless it starts to affect a *significant* number of their constituents." Marcus took a breath. "I'm sure you can guess what happened next."

"The seals broke," Corbin said. Marcus nodded. "I'm sorry." He meant it, for Sita's sake. At least an ambi accident was a quick way to go. The woman probably hadn't had time to realize that anything had gone wrong. Still, unfortunate as the story was, it didn't address the important question. "This doesn't explain why you felt the need to clone yourself."

"Doesn't it?" Marcus said. "Sita was gone, and with her went the only chance at family I thought I'd ever get. I buried all thoughts of her, and focused instead on the child I could have had."

"You could've adopted."

"I wanted my own flesh and blood. Proof that someone had loved me enough to create a new life with me."

Corbin scoffed. "You could've found a surrogate. You could've *met someone else*."

"Yes, I'm sure you'd think that clearly if you were in the midst of grieving for your dead wife," Marcus snapped. *There*. That was the father that Corbin knew. At least he was on familiar ground now.

"So where did you do it?" Corbin asked. "Where was the vat that you grew me in?"

"Stitch. I took everything Sita and I had saved, and went to Stitch."

"Stitch. Lovely." Stitch was a fringe colony that served as a haven for the darker side of the modding community. Even *visiting* Stitch was liable to get you interrogated and slapped with jail time if someone back in the GC found out about your little trip. There weren't many legal reasons for visiting such a place.

"After you were . . . well, after you came to be, I stayed a few more months, then brought you home."

"How did you explain the infant?"

"I said that I'd met a woman on Port Coriol. We shared a night together, and next thing I knew, I had a son. I said that your mother couldn't take care of you, so I took you home instead. I chose a nonaugmented gestation process, so it did actually take nine months for you to fully form, and you aged at a normal rate. There was no reason for anyone to question it. My family chalked it up to me still grieving, but you know I didn't talk to them much anyway. As for Sita's family . . . they didn't want anything to do with me after that. They'd never liked me to start, and I suppose they didn't like the idea of me sharing someone else's bed so soon after their daughter's death."

Corbin held up his hand. Old family drama was the least of his concerns. "You said *nonaugmented* gestation process. Is there anything about me that *was* augmented?" Dr. Chef had told him there was nothing out of the ordinary about his body, but he wanted to be damn sure.

Marcus shook his head. "No. The tech who made . . . the tech I hired kept trying to convince me to add a few tweaks, but I put my foot down. You're the same as me. Flaws and all."

Corbin leaned forward. "That's why, isn't it?"

"That's why, what?"

"Mistakes were never okay by you. A broken sample dish, a dirty sock on the floor, a spilled cup of juice. It didn't matter how well-behaved I was at school, or how good my grades were. I'd come home with a score card full of 'excellents,' but all you'd focus on was the one 'average' mark."

"I just wanted you to be the best that you could be."

"What you wanted," Corbin said slowly, "was for me to improve upon all the mistakes that you had made yourself. You didn't want me to be my own person. You wanted me to be a better version of *you*."

"I thought—"

"I was a *kid*! Kids make mistakes! And it didn't stop when I grew up, either, you never once stopped to tell me that you were proud of me or that I'd done all right. I was an experiment to you. You were never satisfied with positive results, you just kept looking for the flaw causing faulty data."

Marcus was silent for a long time. "I *am* proud of you, Artis," he said. "Though I'm sure that's too little, too late. There's no way for me to go back and be a better father." He looked back to Corbin. "There's one thing, though, that I'm very glad of."

"What's that?"

His father gave a sad smile and looked around the sterile prison room. "That it's me in here and not you." He sighed. "They told me that you have to reapply for citizenship."

"Yes. I'm leashed to one of my crewmates for the next standard."

"You're lucky," Marcus said. "Aside from Sita, I never had any friends good enough to do that for me."

Corbin shifted in his chair. "She's not a friend," he said. "She despises me, in fact. Just not enough to let me die in a Quelin prison."

"Don't sell yourself short, Artis. Even unpleasant bastards like us deserve company." He smirked. "That's a quote from my wife, by the way."

Corbin exhaled something like a laugh. "I'd have liked to have met her," he said. Something occurred to him. "Though if she had lived, I wouldn't exist."

"No," said Marcus. "But I'm glad that you do."

Really? Would you have traded her for me, if you'd known? "How long is your sentence?"

"Twelve standards," Marcus said. "I'll be an old man once I get out. But I'll be fine. I've been treated well here so far. And I've got a cell all to myself. I can finally catch up on my reading."

Corbin noticed a spot of dried algae gunk on his desk. It was a good thing to focus on. "One more thing," he said, scratching the gunk away.

"Yes?"

"My birthday. Is my birthday my real birthday? Or my pulled-from-vat day, I suppose?"

"Yes. Why?"

"I don't know. It's been bothering me." He looked around his lab. "I have to get back to work now."

"Yes, of course," Marcus said. "The guards will be telling

me to end the call soon anyway." A pleading look filled his eyes. "Maybe . . . maybe we could . . . ?"

They stared at each other. There was more distance between them than just pixels and space. "I don't know," Corbin said. "Maybe."

Marcus nodded. "Take care of yourself, son." He waved his hand. The image faded. The pixels withdrew.

Corbin sat listening to the humming pulse of the algae vats. After a while, he picked up his scrib from the desk. He opened his log program and made a quick entry.

October 25. Still my birthday.

"You're pensive tonight," Lovey said.

"Am I?" Jenks said.

"Yes," Lovey said. "You've got that little crease between your eyes that you get when something's on your mind."

Jenks rubbed the skin between his eyebrows. "I didn't realize I was so easy to read."

"Not to everyone."

Jenks leaned back against the wall with a sigh and pulled his redreed tin from his pocket. "It's this whole thing with Corbin."

"Ah," said Lovey. "I think everyone's still shaken up. Corbin hasn't been sleeping well. He stays up late accessing his personal files. Mostly pictures of himself as a child."

"Please don't tell me that stuff," Jenks said, stuffing his pipe. "You know I don't like snooping."

Lovey laughed. "*You're* not snooping. That's what I'm doing. You're just gossiping."

"Oh, well, if that's all." He lit the pipe, sucking air through the burning leaves. The smoke in his lungs made his shoulders go slack. "Poor Corbin. I can't imagine being thrown for a loop like that." He turned his head, pressing his ear against the wall. "Is that your tertiary synapse router making that click?"

"Let me check. It's functioning normally."

"Hmm. I don't like that sound." He moved to face the wall and removed the access panel. His eyes darted over the lace of blinking circuits that lay within. "Yeah, see, right here. The shunt's worn out."

"Save it till morning, Jenks. That'll take hours, and you've been working all day."

Jenks frowned. "Okay, but you wake me up if you experience any gaps in memory."

"I'll be fine," Lovey said with fondness. "I can't even tell that anything's wrong." Jenks replaced the panel. Lovey spoke again. "I don't think Corbin is what's bothering you."

"No?"

"No."

"Then what is?"

"I don't know, but I wish you'd say."

Jenks sighed, exhaling. The tiny worklamps overhead cast beams of light down through the smoky swirls. "I've been thinking about your body kit."

Lovey paused. "There's a catch and you didn't tell me."

"No," said Jenks, taking the pipe from his mouth. "No catch. This whole deal is as respectable as you can be in black market business. Even the price was fair, all things considered."

"Then what's troubling you?"

"Corbin's dad. That guy must've spent a fortune on getting himself cloned. Somehow, he was careful enough to not only make sure that Corbin never found out about it, but that the law never found out, either. And he got away with it for *decades*. Corbin's more than passable. He's the real deal. No tweaks, no enhancements. Hell, even Dr. Chef didn't notice until he made a point to go *looking* for it. And yet . . ."

"And yet he still got caught."

"Yeah. After all that money and all that planning, that poor bastard's locked up in prison, and Corbin's lost his citizenship. And that's *after* he got the shit kicked out of him by those fucking Quelin." He sat down. "Look, we always knew getting a kit would be risky. But I'm not sure I really thought about what that meant. I mean, okay, I knew prison would suck, but I'd always figured that if the law was on my ass, I could just take you and go to Cricket, or maybe a fringe planet somewhere. Wouldn't be perfect, but it'd be safe. But all this mess with Corbin got me thinking about what would actually happen if we got caught. Let's say I got caught with the kit before I uploaded you into it. Okay, I'd go to jail, Mr. Crisp would go to jail, but you'd be fine. You'd still be here, on the *Wayfarer*, with all our friends. Kizzy could look after you until Ashby got a new comp tech, and you'd still be here when I got out. But what if we didn't get caught until much later on, not until after you were in the kit? What if it was, like, ten years down the road and we'd stopped being careful? What if one of us said the wrong thing to the wrong person, or what if bio scanners got good enough to see what you really were? What if we got stopped by the Quelin again and they wanted to do a blood scan? I'd still go to jail, but they'd *dismantle* you, Lovey. When my sentence was up, you'd be gone. Not *away*, not somewhere where I knew you were safe. *Gone*."

Lovey was quiet. "The kit's on its way, Jenks."

"I know."

"And you can't get your money back."

He sighed. "I know. But it won't break me. And besides, maybe we can still use it. Maybe the laws will change down the road. We could just wait until it's safer. Or until I leave the ship, or something."

"This was my decision, too, you know. You didn't push me into it."

"I know. And I won't tell you no, not if it's what you want.

But I'm scared. I'm starting to think maybe I wanted this so bad that I didn't let myself acknowledge just how fucking dangerous it is." He looked down at his hands. "As bad as I want to hold you, I don't know if it's worth the risk of losing you forever. Maybe it's better to just go on like this and know that there's no chance of somebody taking you away."

The room was silent, or as silent as it could be. The air filters hissed. The cooling system surrounding Lovey's core hummed. "Jenks, do you remember when we first talked about this? When I told you all the reasons why I wanted to have a body?"

"Yeah."

"I lied when I said it wasn't for you. *Of course* it's for you. I *do* think it'd present some wonderful opportunities for me, and I imagine it to be a very good life. But it was always, always for you. I wouldn't have thought to do it otherwise, not in a serious way."

"But . . . you said. Your pros and cons—"

"Were things I came up with after I'd decided that this was something you deserved. I wouldn't have ever mentioned it if I thought it would make me unhappy. I do have some self-respect, after all. But yes, it was for you. And if it scares you more than it excites you, then there's no point to it. I'm happy here. I'm happy with you. Would I like a body? Yes. Am I willing to face the risks? Yes. But I'm content as is, and if you are too, then maybe that's enough for now. Not forever, maybe, but we don't need to rush. I can wait for the galaxy outside to get a little kinder."

He swallowed. "Lovey, it's not that I . . . I mean, I want this so much, I just—"

"Shh. Come in farther," she said. Jenks snuffed out his pipe, put it back in the tin and moved toward the pit. He reached for the sweater lying on the floor.

"Leave it," she said.

He could hear her cooling system shut down. "Not for too long," he said.

"Not for too long."

He took off his clothes and climbed into the pit, as he had done many times. He sat down and leaned back against her core, his bare skin bathed in her glow. Without the chilled air, she felt like sunlight, only softer.

"I will always understand if you need to find someone who can give you more than this," Lovey said. "I wouldn't hold that against you. I sometimes worry that I am holding you back from the kind of life an organic sapient should have. But if you choose this freely, then I don't need a body, Jenks. We've always been together without one. I don't know how to love you any other way."

He pressed his back against her, pressed the soles of his feet, his shoulders, his palms, trying to soak in as much of her as he could. He twisted back and brought his lips to her. He kissed the smooth, warm metal and said, "I don't see any reason to change the best thing I've ever had."

☆

NODE IDENTIFIER: 9874-457-28, Rosemary Harper
FEED SOURCE: Galactic Commons Reference Files (Public/Klip)
ARCHIVAL SEARCH: Human/Quelin relations
DISPLAY: top

TOP RESULTS:

List of Quelin trade agreements
List of Quelin laws regarding non-Quelin species
List of Quelin immigration laws
List of Quelin deportation laws
List of Quelin laws regarding interspecies coupling/families

Galactic Commons Membership Hearings (Human, GC
standard 261)
Current GC Parliament Representatives (Quelin)
Anatomical comparison [Human:Quelin]

Selected result: Galactic Commons Membership Hearings, public
record 3223-3433-3, recorded 33/261 (highlighted text—Quelin
representative)
Encryption: 0
Translation path: 0
Transcription: [vid:text]

Despite the differences between our species and cultures, there
is an order that we all share. The development of a civilization is
a scripted event. Minds join together to create new technologies,
then better technologies, then better still. If a harmony cannot be
found, that civilization crumbles. If ideas emerge that are
incompatible with each other, that civilization crumbles. If a
civilization cannot stand on its own against threats from the
outside, that civilization crumbles.

Scholars of sapient life note that all young civilizations go
through similar stages of development before they are ready to
leave their birth planets behind. Perhaps the most crucial stage is
that of "intraspecies chaos." This is the proving ground, the
awkward adolescence when a species either learns to come
together on a global scale, or dissolves into squabbling factions
doomed to extinction, whether through war or ecological
disasters too great to tackle divided. We have seen this story
play out countless times. Every one of us seated here in
Parliament can speak of the planetary wars and political
struggles of our ancestors, yet we overcame them to reach for
the stars. We all know the stories of the Kohash, the Danten Lu
and most recently, the Grum—ruined species who lacked the

discipline to see beyond themselves to the next stage of evolution.

Humans would have shared their fate. Humans left their planet not as one, but in fragments. When their planet began to die, the rich abandoned the impoverished for refuge on Mars. As the bodies piled up, those who remained on Earth formed the Exodus Fleet, headed not for their Martian brethren, but for open space. They had no destination, no strategy beyond escape. Were it not for one small Aeluon probe, the Fleet would almost certainly have died out, and I find it unlikely that the Martians ever would have achieved the modest level of prosperity they now enjoy without borrowing from GC technology.

And what of them now? What has this experience taught them? Nothing. They continue to spread themselves thin. Fleet members have left to form independent colonies—not because it brings wealth or resources to the Fleet, but because they want to. The Martians and the Exodans may have bound their old wounds, but a division of spirit remains. And what of the fringe colonies, built by Humans who want nothing to do with the Diaspora or the GC? What of the hostile Gaiian cultists back on Earth, hunting herd animals on fragile land?

My point, fellow representatives, is that Humans are a fractured, limping, adolescent species that has branched out into interstellar life not by merit, but by luck. They have not moved beyond intraspecies chaos. They have skipped the vital step the rest of us had to make on our own. By granting them membership in the Galactic Commons, we would be providing them not with a new life, but with a crutch. What meager resources they have to offer us are not worth the risk posed by allowing such an unstable element into our shared space. The GC has already spent too much on helping this minor species to escape the hardships they brought upon themselves. I ask you, what benefit is there in making Humans one of us? If not resources, or knowledge, or military strength . . . then what?

HERESY

☆

"Hello, boss," Kizzy said, walking into Ashby's office. Her grubby sleeves were rolled up, and her gloves were tucked into a front pocket. She held a dusty piece of tech in her hands.

"You only call me 'boss' when you need a thing," Ashby said.

"I need a thing." Kizzy held out the part. "This is a thermal regulator. It's what helps a stasie maintain temperature."

"I assume that since it's not currently attached to the stasie, it's broken."

Kizzy gave a sad nod. "The bell tolled for this poor lil' guy."

"Do we have another on hand?"

Kizzy shook her head apologetically. "It's not the sort of thing I keep in stock. My brain's usually busy with making sure we've got spares for life support and the engine. Sorry. I didn't think of it."

Ashby waved her comment aside. "I'd be more worried if you prioritized the stasie over the engine. I don't expect you to keep spares of *every* piece of tech we use." He rubbed his chin. His beard needed a trim. "So what does this mean for the stasie?"

"The stasis field can hold without this. It's got a fail-safe system to make sure your food doesn't go bad while you're buying a replacement. But without the regulator, it's gonna go *bleh* after a while, no matter what."

"How long a while?"

"Four days, maybe five. We won't starve or anything if it goes, but I think we'd all do better with some fresh food between here and Hedra Ka."

Ashby nodded. Three tendays of bug-flour patties and dry-packed rations did not sound appealing, and there was no guarantee that there'd be somewhere for them to resupply at Hedra Ka. What did the Toremi even eat? "Four days isn't enough time to get a delivery drone out here."

"I know. We may be kinda screwed on this one. *However.*" She brushed her hand over the backs of her thighs, checking for machine gunk. When her hand came back clean, she sat down in the chair opposite Ashby. "Sissix says there's a colony rock not far from here. Popped up on the scanner yesterday. Dunno what it is, it's not on any of her maps. But it's only half a day out. We could park the ship here, hop in the shuttle and give 'em a visit, lickety split."

"We're on the bleeding edge of the GC. That's a fringe colony for sure." Knocking on the doors of unidentified fringe colonies was not something Ashby was eager to do.

"Mmm-hmm. But they might have tech I can use."

"That's an awfully big *might*. They might not have anything."

"Yeah, except that this planet is also a *rogue* planet. It's got no star to keep it warm. That's how Sissix noticed it in the first place, it's got these satellites providing artificial sunlight. They're powering it by sucking ambi right out of a nearby nebula."

Ashby raised his eyebrows. "That's pretty serious tech."

"The tech itself isn't that fancy, but what I want to know is how they calibrated their harvesters to work within a nebula. There's a reason that ambi's harvested around black holes. It's concentrated there. GC techs haven't found a way to harvest smaller pockets without going broke." She scrunched her lips in thought. "In any case, if they can harvest ambi in a nebula, I'll bet my boots they've got simpler tech on hand, too." She gestured with the regulator.

Ashby gave a quiet nod. "Any indication of who this colony belongs to?"

"No. But not Human."

"Why not?"

Kizzy gave him a wry look. "Fringe colony or not, if Humans had their hands on that kind of tech, there's no way we wouldn't have heard about it by now. They'd be so rich, it'd be gross."

Ashby drummed his fingers on the table. "Any ships around? Any weapon arrays?"

"No. No weapons. We checked. No ships, no orbiters, no docking ports. Other than the satellites, it's a dead sky out there."

Ashby thought for a moment. "Okay. Let's be smart about it, though. I don't want to head that way until I know who's there." He gestured at the pixel screen to wake it up. "Hey, Lovey," he said, "I need an open sib signal to go out to that rogue planet. Just let me know if somebody picks up."

"Will do," Lovey said.

Kizzy dragged her chair over next to Ashby's and watched the screen intently. "Kizzy, nothing's happening," Ashby said. "They might not pick up for a while. They might not pick up at all."

"It's exciting! It's like going fishing or something, waiting for someone to bite."

Ashby looked askance at Kizzy. "When have you ever gone fishing?"

"I do it in Battle Wizards all the time." The sib indicator on the screen lit up. Kizzy leaned across the desk, pointing. "Look! See! A bite! They bit!"

Ashby put his hand over Kizzy's shoulder and pulled her back into her chair. "Let me do the talking, okay?" The last thing he needed was for Kizzy to rub some twitchy fringe colonist the wrong way.

He gestured to pick up the call. An alien appeared on screen. Ashby's jaw dropped. It was a Sianat. But not a Sianat like Ohan. This Sianat had let their fur grow out. No fractals or holy patterns had been shaved in. There was something more alert about the way they held theirself, not at all like Ohan's perpetually relaxed slump. There was a slackness in the face, a thinness to the fur, and though Ashby knew he couldn't make any presumptions about a species he knew little about, he couldn't shake the obvious conclusion.

This Sianat was old.

"Hello," Ashby said, shaking himself out of his surprise. "Do you speak Klip?"

The Sianat spoke, the same birdlike coo that Ashby had heard Ohan make at times. As the Sianat opened their mouth, Ashby could see that their teeth were unfiled. It was like looking into a cave full of sharp stalagmites. The Sianat gestured something toward Ashby, still cooing as they looked around the room behind them. Unfamiliar with other Sianats as Ashby was, he could read this behavior well enough: *Hang on. Let me find someone who can talk to you.*

"Ashby," Kizzy whispered.

"I know," he whispered back.

"I'm so glad I'm here for this," she said, resting her chin against her fists.

There was movement on screen. The first Sianat made room for another. This one's body was about the same size, but differently shaped. There was a stockiness around the hips and shoulders, a sharp definition to the eyes and jaw. Their build varied enough from the first Sianat—and from Ohan as well—that Ashby concluded this Pair was of a different sex. As the two Sianats switched places, the first touched the second on the shoulder. *They touched.* Ashby thought of how Ohan slunk away from the crew when they passed in the hallway, how they barely tolerated Dr. Chef laying his handfeet on them during medical exams. Who were these people?

"Good day," the new Sianat said. Their accent was thick as fuel. Ashby noticed that this one *did* have filed teeth. "My name is Mas. Forgive my words, my Klip is old."

Ashby smiled, taking care to speak slowly. "My name is Ashby. I captain a tunneling ship. This is Kizzy, our mech tech."

Mas cocked their head. "Tunneling? Yes, yes, I know about tunneling." They gave a yawping laugh. "I know much about tunneling."

I. Not us. Ashby stared. "Excuse me, Mas, I don't mean to be rude, but . . . are you not a Pair?"

"No," said Mas. There was pride in their—in *her* voice, unmistakable, even through the accent. "No one is here. We are a colony of Solitary."

"Heretics," Kizzy gasped.

Ashby glared at her, but Mas did not seem to take offense. "Heretics, yes," Mas said. "Do you have a Pair on your ship?"

"Yes," Ashby said. "Our Navigator."

"I was a Navigator once, for Harmagians," said Mas. "Before here. Before I *was* here. Old words. Sorry."

"No need to apologize, I can understand you." Ashby considered what Mas had said. He hoped he wasn't offending Ohan just by talking to this person. "Our Navigator doesn't know we're talking to you. We didn't even know who was down there when we sent out the sib."

"Oh! I thought—no, nothing." Mas made a trilling sound. "What is your need?"

Ashby nudged Kizzy. "I'm looking for some tech," she said, holding up the broken regulator. "Nothing fancy, just something to fix our stasie."

"Ah, your food! You need to fix your food." The Sianat seemed to find this funny.

At the mention of food, Ashby thought of Ohan's tubes of nutrient paste. "You probably don't have stasie tech, do you?"

"We eat," Mas said. "We do not suck down paste like Pairs. Come to us, we'll find tech. Might have to bang it around to make it work, but techs like to bang things, yes?"

Kizzy laughed. "Yes, we do."

"Do you have a shuttle?"

"Yes."

"Good. Our ships are old as words." She gestured at the screen. A set of landing coordinates popped up. "And we must talk on your Pair. Are they Waning?"

"They are," Ashby said.

"Not for long," Mas said. "Come down, come down, we will talk. But do not tell your Pair you come. They will . . . not like it."

The screen went dark.

Rosemary had seen such little variation in Ohan's moods— much less seen them burst into her office—that it took her a second to realize the Pair was furious. Their eyes were wide, their breath shallow. "Where did they go?" Ohan said, their voice shrill.

Rosemary, who had been in the middle of clearing invoices, found herself tongue-tied. "Who?" she said stupidly, even though she knew who Ohan meant. Ashby had come to her two hours before, told her that he and Kizzy were flying out somewhere Ohan could not know about. Rosemary had found it odd that he'd asked for her discretion. When did Ohan ever talk to anyone? Yet here they were, standing at her desk, looking uncomfortably carnivorous. Rosemary had always thought Ohan looked cuddly, like a stuffed toy. Not now. Ohan's shoulders were back, their neck curled, their eyes wild. Rosemary didn't like Ohan like this.

Ohan made an irritated sound. "We awoke to find the engine stopped. Then we found the shuttle gone. We *know* what region of space this is, and you will tell us now if Ashby has gone to see the Heretics."

Rosemary swallowed hard. Following Ashby's instructions was one thing, but there was no use in lying now. "Yes," she said.

A growl rose from Ohan's throat. "Why?" they cried.

"Kizzy needed some tech," Rosemary said, keeping her voice steady. She thought that maybe, if she could stay calm enough, she could bring Ohan back down. "Something for the stasie broke. They went to get a replacement part."

Puzzlement drove some of the fire out of Ohan's eyes. "Tech?" they said. "They went to get tech?"

"Yes."

Ohan threw their head back. "It does not matter! They will fill their heads full of lies!"

"Who will?"

"The Heretics!" A look of horror crossed their face. "Our crewmates. They'll be contaminated when they return."

"They'll get flashed on their way back in, just like always."

"Yes, but . . ." Ohan shook their head and paced. "I must speak to Lovelace, she will need to update her contaminant database." Without warning, Ohan's legs went limp. They crumpled down, grabbing the edge of Rosemary's desk as they went, gasping for breath.

"Ohan!" Rosemary dashed to their side. She instinctively reached out, but stopped as she remembered who she was dealing with. *No physical contact without permission.* "Can I help you up?"

"No," Ohan wheezed. "We're fine."

The vox switched on. "I'll get Dr. Chef," Lovey said.

"Please, don't," Ohan said. They pulled theirself to their feet with shaking hands. "It is just the Wane. This is how it must be." They drew in a shuddering gulp of air. "Call Ashby. Tell him—tell him to get his tech and leave. Tell him to not listen to the Heretics' lies. They are poison. The Heretics—the Heretics will wish to end me."

Rosemary could hear Dr. Chef's heavy footsteps hurrying down the hall. From the noise, it sounded as if he were running on six. "Ohan, no matter what those people say, no one on this ship is going to hurt you."

Ohan swung their big, dark eyes to Rosemary. "You might not mean to. But you could."

"I don't like this place," Kizzy said, her mouth full of fire shrimp. "It feels sad."

Ashby worked the navigation controls, adjusting their approach toward the rogue planet. It was frozen over, cased in a cracking lattice of ice. The warming light of the satellites was concentrated on one large, circular patch of bare rock, too perfectly shaped to be natural. From their vantage point up above, Ashby could see one cluster of opaque bubblelike buildings, built where the light was strongest. There were no other settlements, not that he could see. "I dunno," he said. "They've got those sun satellites, and they're clearly doing well enough to have a space elevator. Space elevators aren't a high priority if you're hungry or without shelter."

"Sure," Kizzy said. "But they're still all alone out here. No star or moon to keep 'em company. They've got an empty sky." She shaped the edges of the fire shrimp bag into a spout, tipped her head back and poured the bag's contents into her mouth.

"You're getting crumbs all over the place."

"Who's responsible for cleaning out the shuttle?" She jabbed a thumb at her chest. "This girl."

"That's not the point." Ashby looked back at her. "Remember that time you had to clean fire shrimp out of an air filter?"

Kizzy's face fell in grave remembrance. She solemnly rolled the bag shut. "Until later, my delicious friends."

The vox crackled on. An AI began speaking in Ciretou, the soft, haunting language of the Sianats. "Sorry," Ashby said. "We don't understand."

The AI paused, and switched to Klip. "Greetings, travelers. Please bring your shuttle to docking port 4. Once you have docked, proceed to the elevator entryway. If you are unable to walk on your own, or if you require medical attention, please let me know at this time. If you are unable to speak, please activate your shuttle's emergency—"

"We're all fine here, thank you," Ashby said.

"Please dock safely," the AI said. "Your journey has come to an end." The vox switched off.

Kizzy pulled her feet off the dash and stared at the vox. "That was weird. Why wouldn't we be able to—" She nodded. "Right. Some of the Pairs who wind up here must be pretty sick."

"I think you were right, Kiz," Ashby said, as he eased the shuttle into the docking hatch.

"About what?"

"This is a sad place."

Once the shuttle came to a full stop, they put on their exosuits and stepped into the airlock. After a short scan, they were allowed through. They walked down an empty corridor, and into one of the elevator cars.

"I can't get over this," Kizzy said, her voice tinny through the exosuit vox.

"What? How close it is?" The length of the elevator cables were the shortest Ashby had ever seen, by a long shot. He doubted it would take them more than an hour to reach the surface.

"Yeah. It's just . . . I mean, holy shit, how did they *do* this?

This thing shouldn't work at *all*. I'm not even talking about tech, I'm talking about *gravity*." She pressed her nose against the window. "I want to take this thing apart and see what's in it."

"Please wait until we've reached the surface, at least," he said, settling back onto one of the benches. He fidgeted, trying to get comfortable. The curve of the hard cushions was not designed for Human spines.

With a jarring rush, the elevator shot downward. An hour passed, uneventfully. As the elevator got closer to the surface, a violent swirl of snow hit the window. The sight made him shiver, despite the warmth of his exosuit.

"Damn," Kizzy said. "Good thing we didn't bring Sissix."

"She would've had a suit, too."

"Yeah, but I think she finds the very idea of snow offensive," she said. "Look at this place." Ashby saw it. All around them, great swaths of ancient ice sat sharp and uninviting. The air was so thick with snow that it almost obscured the settlement below. There were no roads, and if there were doors, Ashby could not see them. The elevator was descending straight into the settlement itself—a cluster of armored shells, set into black rock. He had a feeling that the sun satellites were less about providing visible light than they were about keeping the settlement thawed out.

"Why here?" Kizzy said. "Why live here?"

Heretics. Exile. "I don't think they have a choice." The light changed as the elevator entered the settlement, transitioning into something more inviting. Through the window, Ashby could see a round corridor, made of smooth, silvery metal. It felt very clean. A light inside his helmet indicated that the air surrounding them was breathable, but they left their suits on all the same. A fringe planet meant there was no handy GC data on local diseases. No telling what kind of bugs these folks might pass on to them, or vice versa.

The elevator doors opened. Kizzy and Ashby stepped out. Mas was there, waiting. Ashby noticed right away how much her body differed from Ohan's, and not just in terms of sexual dimorphism. Despite the hollows of age, there was no doubt that this was a healthy individual. Ohan looked waifish by comparison.

"Welcome to Arun," Mas said, bobbing her head. "You must forgive, I do not know Human greetings."

"We shake hands," Ashby said.

"Show me," Mas said. Ashby took Kizzy's hand in demonstration. Mas laughed. "Here," she said, extending her long fingers. Ashby wrapped his hand around them and shook. Mas laughed again. "These are short hands, soft hands," she said, pressing Ashby's palm through the thin exosuit glove.

"Didn't you meet any Humans while you were a Navigator?" Kizzy asked.

"You were still wandering when I was with Harmagians," Mas said. "No Human worlds beyond your Fleet. I became Solitary before you became GC."

Ashby did some quick math. If Mas was Navigating before Humans had joined the GC, then . . .

Kizzy beat him to it. "How old are you?"

Mas thought. "One hundred and thirty-three standards," she said. "Sorry, had to think. Our time measures are different."

Kizzy's nose was nearly pressing against her faceplate, she was so intent. "I had no idea you could live that long."

Mas laughed again. "Not just this long," she said. "Even longer!" She began to walk down the hall. They followed.

"What can you tell us about this place?" Ashby said.

"This is Arun," Mas said. "Your Pair has not said of it, hmm?"

"No."

"No, no. Pairs do not say this place. It is for Heretics." There was a smirk in her voice, almost mocking. "But all Sianat know it. If we escape before infection, or if we want to break, we try to find it. Not all do. Some get lost. Some are Waning and cannot fly the long way. But we take all who come. None are turned away."

"I see," Ashby said. They came into a huge open area, filled with curved benches and hydroponic planters holding strange, curling trees and puffy flowers (Ashby could only imagine how excited Dr. Chef would have been). A warm yellow sky was projected above. Compared to the frozen wastes outside, it was a paradise. There were Sianats everywhere, of all ages and sizes, walking, thinking, speaking to each other. Touching. "Sorry," he said, dragging his eyes away from the plaza and back to Mas. "What did you mean by 'break'? You come here if you want to break?"

"Break the Pair," Mas said. "Destroy the virus."

Ashby and Kizzy looked at each other. "There's a cure?" Ashby asked.

"Of course," Mas said. "All diseases have cures. You just have to find them."

"But," Kizzy said, her brow furrowed. "Sorry, I don't really get how this whole thing works, but if . . . if you're a Pair, would you even think about being cured? Doesn't the Whisperer make you want to stay together?"

"You ask good questions. Like a good Heretic." Mas gestured toward a bench. They sat beside her as best they could. "The Whisperer makes the host resist breaking. But some Sianat can resist the Whisperer. Like me."

"You're . . . immune?" Ashby said.

"No, no," Mas said. "I had the disease. Had to, to Navigate. But I resist. The Whisperer had my low mind, not my high mind." Her face folded in thought. "Do you know low mind?"

Ashby thought he had heard Ohan use the term once or twice,

but as with most things, Ohan had not explained further. "No."

"Low mind is easy things. Animal things. Things like walking, counting, not putting your hand on hot things. High mind is things like who my friends are. What I believe. Who I am." Mas tapped her head for emphasis.

"I think I understand," Ashby said. "So, the virus . . . the virus affected the way you understand space and numbers, but it didn't affect the way you think about yourself?"

"I resist," Mas said again. She paused. "Resistant?"

"You are resistant," Ashby said. "Yes."

"Yes, yes. Very dangerous to be resistant. I learned to pretend. To mimic the words of the Pairs. To stare out windows." She made a gruff sound. "So boring."

Kizzy laughed. "I've always thought it looks boring," she said.

"It is! But if you are resistant, you must stare. You must not let others know that you pretend. The ones who rule know," she said, leaning close. "They know resistant Hosts exist. But it would ruin everything for many to know. Sianat believe that the Whisperer chose us. Makes us special. Makes us better than *you*." She poked Ashby's chest. "But if we are resistant, one of two things is true. Either Sianats are *not* special, only diseased, and can evolve to resist. Or, second thing, stupid thing, but easier conclusion for many—resistants are unholy. We reject the sacred. Heretics. You understand?"

"Yes," Ashby said. He knew now why Ohan had always balked at the mere mention of the Solitary. This was the sort of thing that could bring a whole culture down.

"I always wanted to break," Mas said. "The Whisperer made me see the in-between, but it was killing my body. My high mind, it wanted to live. My captain, she was good. Good friend. I trusted her, told her that I am resistant. As I Waned, she found a map."

"To here?" Kizzy said.

"Yes, yes. Nearly dead when I arrived." She lifted her front hands and made her muscles twitch. Ashby's stomach sank. It was a perfect imitation of the tremors Ohan had developed. "I lay in hospital for"—she counted to herself—"two tendays after the cure. Painful, painful." She smiled and showed off her forelegs. "But I got strong."

"So, after the virus is cured, the Wane goes away?" Kizzy asked. Ashby shot her a quick glance. *No, Kizzy.*

"Yes. But the changes to the low mind do not. The . . . words, words . . . the . . . the folds in the brain remain. I could still Navigate if I wanted. But I am Solitary. I must stay here."

"Why?" Ashby asked.

The Sianat cocked her head. "I am Solitary," she said. "We are Heretics, not revolutionaries. This is our way."

"Wait," Kizzy said. "You can still Navigate? Curing the virus doesn't take that away?"

"Correct."

"The ambi," she said. "That's how you figured out how to harvest ambi from the nebula, and build a pint-size space elevator. Because you've still got your super brains."

Mas laughed. "Pairs are not inventors. They are too unfocused, too short-lived. Good for Navigating and discussing theories, but bad at building. Building takes many, many mistakes. Pairs do not like mistakes. They like staring out windows. But Solitary like mistakes. Mistakes mean progress. We make good things. Great things."

"Wow," Kizzy said. Her eyes went far away, the way they did when she was thinking about a broken circuit or the inside of the engine. "So, this cure. Is it, like, dangerous?"

"Kizzy," Ashby warned. They were not going down this path. No matter how much he wanted to, they were not.

"But Ashby, Ohan could—"

"No. We're not—"

Mas made a sound deep in her chest. "Ohan is your Pair."

"Yes," Ashby sighed.

"Poetlike name," Mas said. "Poetic." She studied them both. "I am resistant. I do not know how the disease feels to a mind that does not resist. But I have friends, broken Pairs, who were not resistant. Sometimes even good Pairs fear death enough to come to Arun." She leaned in close, too close. "Broken Pairs are different, after. They are not the child they were before infection. They are not the Pair, either. They are new." She looked hard at Ashby with her large eyes. "They are free. Believe me, it is better."

"No," Ohan said. There was no anger in their voice, but they had recoiled, pulling as far away from the table as the chair would allow. They sat stiffly, fighting hard to hide their twitching legs. Ashby and Dr. Chef sat on the other side of the lab table. A small, sealed box lay between them. An object was visible through the transparent lid—a syringe, filled with green fluid. The grip was designed for a Sianat hand.

Ashby took care to keep his voice low. The door to the med bay was shut, but he wouldn't put eavesdropping past any of his crew. He knew that Kizzy, at least, was busy. He could hear her banging away in the kitchen. He had a feeling that a few of the bangs had nothing to do with repairing the stasie, and everything to do with her letting him know that she was upset.

"Nobody's forcing you, Ohan," Ashby said. "I just want you to consider the option."

"I've examined it thoroughly," Dr. Chef said. "It's safe. I can guarantee that."

Ohan shrank away even more. "Safe," they whispered. "Safe. This is murder, and you call it safe."

Ashby ran his hand through his hair. As much as he felt that the virus itself was the murderer here, he knew this was a point he could not argue. "The person I spoke to said she had friends who had been cured. They can still Navigate, Ohan, and they live long, healthy lives."

"They take the Whisperer's gifts, then kill it," Ohan said. "You should not have spoken to them, Ashby. You should have taken their tech and left with your ears blocked. You should have left your food to rot before setting foot in that place."

"I was doing what I thought was best for my crew," Ashby said. "Just as I'm trying to do now."

Ohan succumbed to a coughing fit. Ashby sat back and watched, knowing there was nothing he could do, not even lay a comforting hand on his crewmate's back. His eyes met Dr. Chef's. The doctor looked miserable. Here was a patient that he could easily treat, but the patient wouldn't allow it. Ashby knew Dr. Chef wouldn't push it, but he also was sure that this was going to gnaw away at his friend for a long time.

"Ohan," Dr. Chef said, once Ohan could breathe again. "As someone who left his world behind, I understand how frightening this idea is for you. It was scary for me, too. But we're your friends, Ohan. You could live a long time, here with us. We'd take care of you."

Ohan was unconvinced. "Your friendship means much to us. As does your concern, though misguided. We know this must be difficult for you to understand. You kill microbes all the time, in your kitchens, on your cargo, without a second thought. But consider the bacteria living in your skins, your mouths, your guts, creatures you could not survive without. You, too, are a synthesis between organisms large and small. Ashby, would you destroy your mitochondria simply because they are not Human in origin? Because they do not belong?"

"We can't live without mitochondria," Ashby said. "But you could live without the Whisperer."

Ohan shut their eyes tight. "No," they said. "We could not. We would be someone else."

Sometime later, Ashby sat alone in his quarters, unlacing his boots. He was halfway through the left when the door spun open without warning. Sissix stood in the doorway, feathers on end. "Are you out of your fucking mind?"

Ashby sighed and went back to his laces. "Come in and shut the door."

Sissix stood before him, hands on her hips. "Kizzy tells me there is a cure. A cure for what's killing Ohan. One that would leave him able to Navigate, and that would extend his life by a good *century* or so. She tells me you just came back from a planet full of happy, healthy people who all can attest to that. And apparently, that cure is in our med bay *right now*, and you're just going to let it gather dust while Ohan lies shaking himself to death in a pool of his own sick."

Ashby swung his eyes up to her. "You keep saying 'his.'"

"Yes, because it finally occurred to me that Ohan is an individual, a sick man who needs our help."

"Sissix, this is not my call. What do you want me to do? Tie them down and force it on them?"

"If that's what it takes."

"You're being ridiculous. I'm their employer, not their . . . their arbiter."

"You're his friend, and you're letting him die."

"I gave them the option, Sissix! They know it's there! What the hell else am I supposed to do?" He threw the boot aside. "Sissix, this is not a matter of someone refusing medical treatment. This is their entire culture we're talking about. This is their *religion*."

"This is so fucking Human of you. Lie back and let the galaxy do whatever it wants, because you're too guilty about how badly you fucked up your own species to ever take the initiative."

Ashby got to his feet. "What is it you people say? *Isk seth iks kith?* Let each follow xyr own path?"

Sissix's eyes flashed. "That's different."

"How so?"

"That means don't interfere with others if there's no harm being done. There *is* harm being done here, Ashby. Ohan is dying."

"If I told you to go back to Hashkath and bring your kids here to live with you, would you?"

"What are you even talking about?"

"If I told you that treating your children like strangers offends every bone in my milk-fed mammalian body, and that as your Human captain, I expect you to follow my moral code—"

"That's different, Ashby, you know that's—"

He lowered his voice. "Or if I wanted to be *really* old-fashioned, I could tell you that it's inappropriate for two of my crew to be coupling. Some Human captains still fire people for that, you know. They say it's a bad idea on a long haul."

Sissix froze. "How do . . ." She shook her head. "That's none of your business."

Ashby gave an incredulous laugh. "It's *none of my business*? I'm your feather brother, Sissix. Since when is it not my business to know such things? Since when does an Aandrisk keep something like that to herself? Unless, of course, you're making personal concessions for *Human* customs—"

"Shut up, Ashby." She walked to the window, put her hands on the sill and fell quiet. "I don't even know Ohan. And I don't just mean because he doesn't talk to any of us. I mean that when he opens his mouth, I don't know if *he's* the one saying that he doesn't want to be cured, or if the virus is making him do it. I don't know if it's him speaking, or the thing infecting his brain."

"To Ohan, it's both. And that's probably closer to the truth. It's not like the virus is sentient. It just . . . changes him. Them."

Sissix gave him a look. "See. You do it, too." The anger was bleeding out of her voice. Her feathers were beginning to lay flat. She sat on his bed. "I'm not okay with this, Ashby. I don't care if I know him well or not. I'm not okay with losing family."

Ashby sat beside her and took her hand. "I know you think I'm the bad guy in this," he said. "But I'm not okay with it, either."

"I know," she said. "But I still don't see how you could sit there and not get angry with him."

"It wasn't my place."

"Spoken like a true Exodan." Her eyes searched his face. "How do you know about me and Rosemary?"

Ashby laughed. "The way she looks at you."

"Oh, stars," Sissix said. "Is it that obvious?"

"To me, at least."

"To everyone?"

"Maybe. Nobody's said anything to me about it."

Sissix sighed. "It was her idea, you know. After Hashkath. She said she wanted to make things feel more like family for me. She was so damn sweet about it. She's sweet about everything." She fell back against the mattress. "Ashby, I have no frame of reference for what it's like for Humans to couple. I'm so scared I'm going to mess her up. You know how differently our species go about these things. I'm not . . . am I being selfish?"

"Sex is always a little selfish, Sis," he said. "But I highly doubt she's sleeping with you out of charity. I bet she wanted to way before Hashkath." He smiled at her. "But I know you. You wouldn't have said yes if you didn't care about her, too. Rosemary's an adult. She can handle herself. And I think in a way, you two might be good for each other." He paused. "Although . . ."

"I knew there was going to be a caveat."

"You need to be careful. Humans can be okay with having multiple partners, but we can be jealous as hell, too. I don't know how you two have things worked out, but if, say, you want to go to a *tet*, or if you just need to move on in your casual Aandrisk way—"

"I know," Sissix said. "I'll be careful."

They fell into a comfortable silence. "This is going to sound weird," he said after a while.

"Mmm?"

"I'm sorry that it couldn't be me."

Sissix sat up. "How so? You don't—you don't think of me as—"

"No." He smirked. "No offense, but no. I don't think of you that way."

"Good. I was about to be really confused." She laughed. "Then what?"

"There has always been a part of me that feels guilty that I can't be the kind of family you need."

Sissix nuzzled his cheek. "You *are* the family I need, Ashby. I wouldn't have chosen you otherwise."

"But Rosemary made it more—more *whole*, didn't she?"

Sissix smiled. "Yeah. She did." She put her forehead against Ashby's. "Doesn't change the fact that you're the best friend I've ever had." She paused. "But I'm still mad at you."

"I know."

"And thinking about Ohan makes me hurt."

"Me, too."

"Good," she said. "At least you're suffering for it." They both laughed. It was an empty sound.

ERROR
MESSAGE NOT DELIVERED. RECIPIENT OUTSIDE COMM RELAY
RANGE.
PLEASE CHECK DELIVERY PATH AND RESEND.

ATTEMPTED MESSAGE
ENCRYPTION: O
TRANSLATION: O
FROM: Nib (path: 6273-384-89)
TO: Rosemary Harper (path: 9874-457-28)
SUBJECT: Re: Volunteer info

    I'm glad to hear it! We can always use another good brain.
Don't worry about not having much free time. Even spending an
hour or two every tenday digging through submission files is a
help. Just mention in your application what your availability is like,
and they won't give you more than you can handle. Have you
decided what focus to apply for yet? I'm biased, of course, but I
think you'd be great for interspecies history, and I'd be happy to
put in a good word. But if you've got your eye on another area, I
won't take it personally. Much.

    Speaking of, one of my friends on the Toremi team
remembered that I was after information on your behalf, and she
sent me something interesting. Not much, just one of many little
quirks about our new allies. I probably shouldn't be sending it
directly to you, but seeing as how you're a future volunteer,
surely we can grant you retroactive permission, right?

Fly safe, Nib

——

ATTACHED MESSAGE
FROM: Elai Jas Kapi (path: withheld)

THE LONG WAY TO A SMALL, ANGRY PLANET

TO: GC Delegate Group 634 (path: withheld)
ENCRYPTION: 2
TRANSLATION: 0
SUBJECT: Important information—Toremi hearing and heat generators
DATE: 76/306

Given our infrequent dealings with the Toremi, there is much
about their species that we are only now discovering firsthand. All
delegates should be aware that the Toremi possess a sense of
hearing that far exceeds that of any other GC species. They are
especially adept at distinguishing individual voices within crowds,
and their aptitude for learning languages has far exceeded our
expectations. You may safely assume that any Toremi who has
been present in diplomatic talks is already fluent in Klip.
When sharing a room with Toremi Ka individuals, do not discuss
any topics that have not been approved by senior ambassadorial
staff. Please consult project datafile 332-129 for a comprehensive
list of approved conversation topics.

We also require that all ships ensure that their heat generators
are not operating above 76.5 kilks if they expect Toremi Ka
individuals to come aboard. We recognize that this will cause some
discomfort for Aandrisk delegates and crewmembers. However,
standard heat generators emit a sound that is painful to the
Toremi. We have determined that the frequency created by 76.5
kilks and lower is tolerable for the Toremi, and will not inhibit basic
Aandrisk motor functions.

If your ship uses nonstandard heat generators, inform a
senior staff member immediately. Do not invite Toremi Ka
individuals aboard your ship until the correct technology has
been installed.

Thank you for your cooperation.

Elai Jas Kapi, Senior Galactic Commons Ambassador

HEDRA KA

Toum, second guard of the New Mother, sat by a window in the feeding garden, watching the ships of the Commons species. He tore a thick bundle of leaves from a nearby planter. The fluid oozing from their broken stalks gave off that familiar peppery scent, sweet and delicious. But he did not eat. He picked at the leaves, and observed the alien ships. He looked with envy upon the weapons arrays of the Aeluon frigates, as he had done many times. How many clans they could destroy with such weapons. How many false ideas they could erase.

He thought of the aliens within the frigates, with their stupid eyes and unsettling scales. So ugly, the Aeluons. And so disturbing, the way they talked. It was difficult to trust a species who could not speak without sticking wires into their throats. Just as it was difficult to trust the Harmagians, who had no legs to walk upon, or the Aandrisks, with their carnivore claws, or the Quelin, who marred their own flesh for vanity's sake. No, he could not trust them, any of them. But he could hate them. That came easily enough.

He could not speak of it. Before the alliance, there had never been any doubt in his mind that he was of the Toremi Ka. He was in agreement with their veneration of the New Mothers, and he was in agreement with needing to secure Hedra Ka as their own. But these Commons species. Did the clan really need their help? Were they so weak that they could not hold the new planet alone?

Commons species. Mismatched faces, grating accents, squealing ships. He could see his discontent mirrored in the mouths of some of his clanmates, but no one had raised a challenge. No one had broken from the clan.

This frightened him. Was he defective in some way? Was there some vital piece of wisdom the New Mothers possessed that he did not? Day after day, he wrestled with these thoughts, struggling to bring himself to agreement. But nothing, not meditation, not the privileged amount of time he spent with his New Mother, had displaced them.

He looked down to the leaves, now pulp within his grasp. He threw the wet clump to the floor. The machines would clean it up.

"Do you want me to sit with you?" said a voice from behind. Toum did not need to turn his face to know who it was. He felt his limbs tense, ready for killing.

"No," he said, his eyes on the window.

"But I will." The speaker came into his field of vision, folding her legs alongside him. Her name was Hiul. A first unit striker. Toum wondered if he even *could* kill her, given the chance. He was willing to try. Hiul picked some leaves, and consumed them. "Are you eating?"

"Why else would I be here?"

She lolled her head, looking at the crushed leaves at Toum's feet. "Of course." She turned her face to the window. "So many ships. So many ideas within them. How do they do it, I wonder? How do they achieve harmony, knowing that false notions walk beside them?"

Toum said nothing.

Hiul brought more leaves to her mouth. "I do not believe that they do. I believe they exist in chaos, each following their own ideas, each serving a clan of one."

He smacked his mouth. "The New Mothers say this is acceptable, so long as we keep to our ways. Are you not in unity with their words? Do you not agree?"

Hiul seemed unconcerned by the threat. She ignored the challenge. *Ignored it!* Only two words left her mouth, maddeningly calm: "Do you?"

He grabbed her, fury hot within his belly. He brought his mouth to her breathing throat, poised for a quick kill. "I have told you before, do not speak to me. *You* are chaos."

She did not fight back, which frightened Toum more than if she had. "You see me as out of agreement with the New Mothers?" she said. "You see me as a false truth?"

"Do not toy with me. You know what you are."

She pushed forward, pressing her throat against his mouth. "Then why do you not kill me?"

He willed himself to bite down. It would be so easy, so fast. He could feel her pulse, deep and quick. But he could not, and it made him rage all the more. He threw her, hard. A planter broke beneath her fall, loam spilling over the floor. The others in the garden looked their way. Most, after a glance, returned to their food, unconcerned by the mess. The machines would clean it up.

Hiul laughed, wiping a stream of lymph from split skin near her mouth. "'You know what you are.' Yes, yes. I do," she said, standing. She approached him again. "And I know what you are, Toum. I see the conflict in you."

"I am a guard of the New Mother!"

She moved in close, whispering. "That is why you fight it, I know. How horrible for you. How horrible to know the truth, and to hate those who threaten it, and to remain loyal regardless."

His eyes betrayed him, straying to the window full of alien ships.

Hiul exhaled smugly. "You have a ship of your own, you know. You have access to things we do not."

He looked sharply back at her. "We?"

She walked away, limping slightly. It appeared that one of her back legs had been badly bruised by the fall. Good. She turned her face to him. "We are Toremi," she said. "We are never a clan of one."

Ashby sighed with relief as the pinhole tug pulled his ship back into normal space one last time. It had been four days since they'd rendezvoused with the *Kirit Sek*, and grateful as he was for the shortcut, he wasn't sure what had been worse—the sub-layer jumps, or the long stretches of nothing in between. The last leg of the haul to the rendezvous at Del'lek had been a long one, but they'd busied themselves with cleaning the ship and taking care of all the little odd jobs that had been brushed to the side. By the time they met up with the *Kirit Sek*, the *Wayfarer* was as spotless as it ever had been, and there was nothing else for them to do. Ashby had thought four days of kick back would be restful, but the jumps made that impossible, and the lack of productivity made him anxious. Everybody was on edge. Dr. Chef had been growing irritated at all the extra help hovering around the kitchen, and Ashby had strong suspicions that the blown-out lighting panel they'd experienced the day before had been orchestrated by the techs, just to give themselves something to do. The only people who hadn't seemed to mind the downtime were Sissix and Rosemary, who were happy to keep each other occupied, and Ohan, who was busy letting their nerves die.

But the jumps, though, had gotten to everybody. A blind punch was one thing, but four days of in and out at six-hour intervals was enough to make even Ashby spacesick. He sat up slowly in bed as Lovey transmitted the tug captain's voice through his vox.

"That's it for us, Captain Santoso," the Aandrisk woman said. She had a different accent from Sissix—less colloquial, harsher around the edges. "Are you all doing okay over there?"

"Well enough," Ashby said. He rubbed his eyes. Stable vision could not be overrated. "Thanks for the trip."

"Take it from me—before you call in to whoever you're reporting to, take an hour to eat something and get back on your feet. We'll be doing the same."

"Will do." He cleared his throat. "*Heske rath ishi kith.*"

"*Heske skath eski risk,*" the Aandrisk said, sounding pleased. "Safe journey to you as well." The vox switched off. Out his window, Ashby could see the *Kirit Sek* drop their towing field and veer away.

"Lovey, where's Sissix?"

The vox snapped back on. "She just got to work."

"Let her know I'm on my way there."

A few minutes later, he stepped into the control room. Sissix was already in her seat, checking her navigational controls.

"I feel like I've been kicked in the head," she said, without looking at him.

"You and me both." He slumped into his chair and stared out the window. "And all for *that.*"

In the space beyond was Hedra Ka. A cracking scab of a planet, choked with storms and veins of lava. A mist of rocks floated in orbit, a reminder of its recent formation. It was a young world, unwelcoming, resentful of its existence.

"That is the angriest looking thing I've ever seen," Ashby said.

"You talking about the rock or the ships?"

Hedra Ka lay within a feeding frenzy of vessels—Harmagian frigates, Aeluon cruisers, neutral transports, pinhole tugs, patrol shuttles. And of course, the Toremi. Ashby knew that the Toremi were generational spacers, just like the Exodans, but he saw nothing familiar in their ships. For a species who lived out in the open, their ships looked surprisingly fragile, lacking the thick bulkheads he associated with long-haul rigs. He saw only wiry frames and sharp edges, dripping with antennae and eerie lighted cords that drifted in the vacuum. They looked like deep-sea creatures, pulsing, swaying, incomprehensible.

Ashby leaned forward. "No way." There was a clear spherical patch outside the swarm, marked by warning buoys. "*That's* where they want us to drop the cage?" The distance between the tunnel entrance and Hedra Ka would be shorter than the distance between Earth and Luna. By about half.

"Good thing this is a soft zone," Sissix said. "Can you imagine doing a blind punch there?"

Ashby shook his head. "We're good, but not that good."

"Nobody's that good."

"We'd have been lucky not to tear that planet apart."

Sissix snorted. "Not much of a loss if we did."

Ashby laughed. "Lovey, can you patch me through?"

The vox switched on. "They're listening, Ashby," Lovey said.

"Hey, everybody. We've made it. If you're feeling sick, go get yourself a bite to eat, but please make it quick. I'd like everyone here when I call our contact. Please be in the control room in one hour, tops. This is a big day for us, and I'd like us all to put our best foot forward. Nothing fancy, but clean faces and smart clothes would be appreciated."

Kizzy's voice came through the vox. "Don't worry, Ashby, I won't talk at all."

He paused, trying to find a kind way to tell her that was best. "You're too cool for them anyway, Kiz."

Toum sat in meditation. Or so he meant to. Across from him sat the first guard, Fol, her legs folded calmly, her eyes blank with reason. He envied her. The longer they stayed around these Commons people, the more difficult it was for him to structure his mind. No matter how hard he tried to shift his thoughts elsewhere, he returned, inevitably, to Hiul. Neither of them should have left the room alive. It was their way. The stronger belief would survive, the weaker would be erased. This was how harmony was made.

He should have killed her. Striker training or no, he'd had his mouth on her throat. He should have killed her. He had killed many out of disagreement. Why had he let her walk away?

The answer was there, in a cruel corner of his mind. He ran from it. It mocked him all the same.

"Come," the New Mother said, entering the room. Toum and Fol extended their legs and gathered their weapons. "I am going to the carrier. The tunneling ship has arrived, and I have heard that the Harmagian has invited them aboard."

"Have you been extended an invitation?" Fol asked. The Harmagian bureaucrat was particular about tedious matters like guest lists and protocol. Commons worries.

"I do not need one," the New Mother said. Toum knew he could hear it in her voice, too—the waning patience, the weariness of dealing with alien ways. Why did she never speak of it? If she would just voice the frustrations he knew she felt, then he would have been in agreement with her all along, and he would no longer doubt his place as Toremi Ka. But no such relief came. "These tunnelers are making a hole in my sky," she said, walking to the door. Fol and Toum fell into place on either side of her, staying a practiced six steps behind. "That gives me the right to see their faces."

Rosemary was glad to be off the ship. Granted, she was on *another* ship, but the change of scenery was badly needed, and the small welcoming reception they'd been brought into was a nice surprise. Nothing fancy, just a table of artfully made finger food and a few low-level GC officials making casual conversation. She'd been to gatherings like this before, but tunnelers weren't the sort you'd find on the guest list. It was a kind gesture—and a sign of how important this new tunnel was.

The room surrounding them was a stark contrast to the *Wayfarer*'s patchwork walls. It was a Harmagian design, spacious and colorful. A variety of species-specific chairs were scattered here and there, and long horizontal windows lined the hull wall. The filtered air was cool and crisp—Rosemary had noticed Sissix moving more slowly, as a Human with sore muscles might—and the lighting just on the edge of too bright. Her crewmates were having a good time, enjoying both the food and the attention. Ashby and Sissix were across the room, locked in conversation with some bureaucrat. Jenks had apparently made friends with one of the serving staff, a Laru, who he'd been laughing with for twenty minutes over who knew what. Ohan had remained behind, of course, and so had Corbin, who, after seeing Dr. Chef's eyes light up at the mention of a buffet, had offered to keep an eye on the ailing Navigator in his stead. The algaeist had been rather generous with favors as of late.

"Hey, Doc," Kizzy said. She lifted a skewer of fried vegetables from her overburdened plate. "What's this yellow stuff?"

Dr. Chef's cheeks fluttered. "That's saab tesh. I cook it all the time."

"It doesn't look like saab, though. Or taste like it." She pulled off one of the chunks with her teeth and chewed it thoughtfully. "Nope, not really."

"That's because they probably have better stasies than ours. No molecular degradation over a long haul." His head drooped. "Lucky."

Kizzy swallowed. "I don't think I like it as much this way."

"That's how it's supposed to taste."

"Well, I don't like it." She ate another piece.

"You know," Rosemary said. "We'll be making a nice profit off this job. I'm not making any promises, but you and I could at least *look* at market prices for a new stasie once this is done. We could put together a little proposal for Ashby."

Dr. Chef's cheeks puffed. "I've always liked the way you think."

"I cannot *wait* to punch," Kizzy said, abandoning the vegetable skewer in favor of a seed-encrusted bundle of leaves. "I love all you guys, but I seriously need to get off the ship for a couple tendays. I'm all space twitchy."

"Jenks said he's already got his bag packed," Dr. Chef said.

"Oh, yes. He will not shut up about all the reasons why the beaches on Wortheg are better than anywhere else. I don't know how we're going to get him back."

"No beaches for me. I'm going to go visit my old friend Drave. He just installed a new greenhouse in his homestead, and he said he'd love some help choosing seedlings."

"Wait, wait, wait. For your vacation, you're going to Port Coriol. A place we go *all the time*. So you can garden. Which you do *all the time*."

"What?" His cheeks puffed. "I love gardening."

Kizzy rolled her eyes. "What about you, Rosemary?"

"Oh. Well, I—" *I have nowhere to go.* "I haven't really decided yet." She took a sip of fizz. "I may just stay on the ship. I've almost got all the financial archives reorganized, and I hate to leave it unfinished."

Kizzy quirked her eyebrows and smiled. "You want to come home with me, come stay with my dads?"

Rosemary felt her cheeks flush. "Oh . . . that's very kind, but I—"

"Listen. Mudskip Notch isn't exactly Florence, but it's quiet, and the people are chill. There's live music in the main square on warm nights, and the hydrofarms are actually kinda pretty once the algae crop starts to bloom. And there's a little collective of artists and modders out along the edge. You can kick it with me, or you can do your own thing. All I'm offering is a clean bed in a sleepy colony town, in the home of two awesome gentlemen who love it when I bring houseguests. Also, three dogs who will lick your face and be your best friends forever. And my Ba makes the best fucking waffles in the galaxy." She turned to Dr. Chef. "No offense."

"None taken," Dr. Chef. "I've never had success with waffles."

"Well . . ." Rosemary said. Two quiet tendays of home cooking and fresh air was tempting, and she was curious to see more of the independent colonies, but—

"Please?" Kizzy said, bouncing. A stray pastry fell off her plate. "Please please please?"

Rosemary gave a little laugh, both embarrassed and touched. "Okay. If you're sure it's no trouble, I'll come."

"Yes!" Kizzy jammed a fist into the air. "I'll message my dads when we get back to the ship. Or after we punch, I guess." She rolled her eyes. "Priorities."

Something across the room caught Dr. Chef's eye. "Well, well," he said. "I wasn't sure we'd be seeing any of them."

Through the doorway came three Toremi, strange and disconcerting. They walked on four legs with knees that bent the wrong way, and their skin looked hard and brittle. Their thin heads lolled, more like machine weights hanging from a socket than things made of soft flesh. The Toremi standing in the middle wore thick ornamental chains over her dark vestments, and a conical cap, trimmed with red. A New Mother, as Nib's messages had described. The other two Toremi flanked her, a few steps back. They were both armed, and heavily—big rifles slung across their ridged backs.

"They're creepy," Kizzy whispered.

"Shh," said Dr. Chef.

Rosemary nodded toward the bureaucrat speaking to Ashby. The Harmagian woman was flustered, her tendrils curling rapidly as she moved her carrier wagon over to greet the Toremi. "She's nervous," Rosemary said. "I don't think she knew they were coming."

Dr. Chef grumbled in agreement. "You'd be nervous, too, if someone you'd been brokering a galactic alliance with suddenly strolled into a room full of spacers with debatable manners."

Kizzy took an enormous bite of a pastry, taking care to make a few crumbs stick to the edges of her mouth. "Ah gud mnnrs."

Dr. Chef brushed the crumbs away with a handfoot as Kizzy laughed behind closed lips. But Rosemary was paying more attention to the Toremi, who the Harmagian woman—her tendrils now flexing with a touch of calm—was introducing to Ashby. They were familiar somehow, not because of the vids she'd seen or the reference files, but . . . something else. Something more tangible. More personal. It was right there, like a word stuck on the tip of her tongue. But what was it? The clothing? The jewelry? The—

The guns.

In a flash, she remembered being in her apartment back on Mars, a few blocks away from the Alexandria campus. She was making tea, tapping stray leaves off the measuring spoon as water heated in the hot pot. The door chimed. *Rosemary Harris? Can we come in?* Two detectives, crisp clothes, both wearing ocular scanners. One of them had laid a scrib on the coffee table, projecting images of weaponry into the air. *Do you know anything about these?*

Rosemary set down her plate on the buffet table and walked to the window. She folded her arms across her chest and took a deep breath, looking out onto the crowded sky. A small, angry planet, surrounded by the warships of people who wanted to control it. The *Wayfarer* waited just outside, a lumpy, beautiful box that could not have been more out of place amid the sleek carriers and chilling Toremi vessels. She wanted to be back there, safe behind piecemeal walls and scavenged windows. What the hell were they doing here?

"Hey." Kizzy laid a hand on Rosemary's shoulder. "You okay?"

Rosemary gave a quick nod, pressing her lips together. "Yeah, I'm fine." She paused. "I just know where they got their guns."

"Where?" Kizzy asked. Rosemary gave her a dry look, but said nothing. Kizzy's eyes widened. "*Oh.* Um. Shit. You sure?"

Rosemary thought of the scrib images hovering in her living room, the detectives studying her face. "I'm sure."

A handfoot rested gently on her other shoulder. "It's not your fault," Dr. Chef said. "You can't change it."

"I know," Rosemary said. "I'm just . . ." She glanced over her shoulder. The room hummed with conversation. Everyone else was gravitating more toward the Toremi at the door. Nobody was paying attention to the three spacers at the window. She spoke in a hush. "It makes me angry. And not only because of my father. He did what he did because he wanted ambi. It was greedy, and immoral, and everyone hates him for it. *I* hate him for it. But the GC's doing the same thing. They've got treaties and ambassadors and buffet lunches, and it all seems so civilized and diplomatic. But it's the same damn thing. We don't care about these people, or how we affect their history. We just want their stuff." She shook her head hard. "We shouldn't be here."

Dr. Chef squeezed her shoulder. "I've been feeling much the same about this myself. But every sapient species has a long, messy history of powers that rise and fall. The people we remember are the ones who decided how our maps should be drawn. Nobody remembers who built the roads." He chuffed and rumbled. "We're just tunnelers. That's all we do, and it's all we can do. If it wasn't us, it would've been some other ship. This would've happened without us. This isn't something we can stop."

Rosemary exhaled. "I know."

"And besides," Kizzy said. "I mean, they want us here, right? These aren't exactly chummy people. They would've said no if they didn't want us."

"Even so," Rosemary said. "We've got no business stepping into their war."

Once they had left the reception room, Toum addressed the New Mother. "Did you hear the members of the tunneling ship by the window?"

"I did not. My ears were on their captain, and what sounded like a damaged ventilation coil in the ceiling. Very distracting."

"What was it you heard?" asked Fol.

Toum's mind was a tangle. His thoughts were reaching a fevered pitch. If he did not speak, he would burst. But if he did speak—

"Tell me," said the New Mother.

Toum obeyed. "The tunnelers do not speak in agreement with their leaders. They have doubts about our alliance."

The New Mother smacked her mouth in acknowledgment. "This falls into their pattern."

"Forgive me, New Mother, but does this not concern you?"

"The Commons pattern concerned us at first," she said. "So many species, so many different ideas, all joined within a single clan. We did not see how such a thing could stand."

Toum and Fol clicked their knee joints in agreement. When the Galactic Commons speakers had first approached the Toremi Ka, three of the New Mothers were not in favor of their offer. They had left Toremi Ka space once it was clear that there could be no agreement. They had their own clans now, and were enemies of the Toremi Ka. One had been killed. This was the way.

"But they spoke as one," Fol said. "In the first talks, and the negotiations after, the Commons people spoke as one. They used the same words. They were in agreement, even though they were of different species."

"Yes," the New Mother said. "We know their agreement is *practiced*, and they do not see patterns as we do. But they still seek such things in different ways. We find this an acceptable concession."

"But it's a lie," Toum said. He could see Fol look at him with concern, but he continued on. "They do not truly agree. They merely pretend to, so as to maintain order." *Like me. Oh, dead ones take me, like me.*

The New Mother looked hard at him. He trembled. "There is more you wish to say," she said.

Toum shakily smacked his mouth. "New Mother, I do not wish to impose my thoughts upon yours."

"There is no need to worry. My thoughts are the stronger, and I value yours. I trust that we will find harmony."

He hoped desperately that she was right. "We have claimed Hedra Ka as a place of stability, a place to keep us anchored while we think on the pattern of the New Mothers."

"True."

"Our species—even our own clan—is unstable. In this time of change, is it wise to invite further instability?"

Fol looked dismissive. "We cannot defeat the warring clans alone. The GC has solidified our claim."

"But at what cost?" Toum felt his knees slip, weakened by his boldness. "In destroying the warring clans, might we not destroy ourselves? Might such a muddled influence as the GC cloud our sense of clarity?"

The New Mother stared at him. She shifted her gaze to Fol. "Do you share these thoughts?"

"No," Fol said, without any hint of doubt. Toum looked askance at her. It was clear, in her face and in her voice, that she was in true agreement. Her thoughts did not tear at her. She knew her place, in her thoughts and in her clan. It did not trouble her. He hated her for it.

The New Mother shifted her neck and placed her face close to his. "We need the Commons to secure our claim. Our ways are stronger than their influence. A hold on Hedra Ka is worth making allowances for different understandings. Do you agree with these thoughts?"

Toum felt his stomach lurch. There were insects under his skin, claws in his heart. "I . . . I . . ." He could not bring himself to say the words. He loved his New Mother. He loved all of them. He would lie down and tear out his organs for them. And yet, *yet*, he agreed more with the squeaking words of that female Human than he did with what he had just heard.

The New Mother pulled back and lolled her head. Toum looked to the floor and kept his eyes there, but all the same, he could feel Fol staring, judging him with her calm eyes. "Go now and meditate," the New Mother said. "Take time to determine which of your thoughts is the strongest. Then you will know if you are still one of us."

"You are a fine guard," Fol said. "Your death would be a loss." Toum did not look at her. If he did, he might snap her neck.

"I agree," the New Mother said. "I hope you will return."

But as Toum clicked his knees and walked away, he knew he would not. Something had shifted. The fear remained, but it was hardening. His thoughts had been made real by hearing them aloud, and he knew now, more than ever, that no agreement could be found here. He walked down the corridors, past repulsive Harmagians and weak-faced Aeluons. They bobbed and flashed their cheeks in friendly acknowledgment. He seethed. Toremi space was no place for these simpering aliens. His people should have sent them back across the border in pieces, as they had always done.

As they still could.

Ashby eyed the readouts on his control screen. "I swear, our engines have never been running this smooth."

Sissix spoke without looking up from her navigation controls. "That's what happens when you take two easily bored techs on a long haul."

"Hmm. Maybe we should do this more often."

That made Sissix's head turn. She gave him a look that could melt the hull. "Let's not."

Ashby chuckled. He shared the feeling. In a few hours, they'd be back in Central space. He couldn't wait, but the thought was surreal. Even as accustomed to taking shortcuts through space as he was, knowing that the tens upon tens of tendays it had taken them to get to Hedra Ka could be backtracked in a matter of hours was bizarre. The idea of being among recognizable ships, and planets he'd walked a dozen times, and markets full of food he didn't have any questions about, without a destination in mind, without somewhere that he needed to get to . . . it sounded fantastic. And it wasn't making sense yet.

"What about you, Corbin? Fuel lines pumping well?"

"Impeccably." The pale man glanced up from his station. "I'm sure there are plenty of other ways to make our techs bored more often."

The vox switched on. "Ashby, there's a Toremi ship nearby," Lovey said. "It looks like it's heading for the cage."

He paused. That was odd. "Have they crossed the safety perimeter?"

"No, they're just headed our way."

"They're probably curious," Sissix said. "If I'd never seen a tunnel before, I'd want to see how it's done."

Ashby nodded. "Just keep an eye on them, Lovey. And contact

them. Give them a friendly reminder to keep their distance when we punch. We don't want to drag them in after us."

"Will do," Lovey said.

The control room door spun open. Dr. Chef walked in, carrying Ohan. The Sianat Pair's back legs had finally given up, and Ashby found their stillness more unsettling than the fragile trembling that had filled the tendays before.

Ashby stood up. "Can I help?"

"No, no, I think we're okay here," said Dr. Chef, his voice as easy as if he were talking about chopping vegetables. He set Ohan down in their chair, straightening their legs beneath it.

Ohan craned their head with grace. "We thank you."

Dr. Chef handed Ashby two injection vials and a syringe. "If they start losing feeling in their hands, give them one of these." He pointed to a spot at the back of Ohan's neck, right along their spine. The fur had been shaved away, and the gray skin beneath was bruised from repeated injections. "Right here."

Ashby nodded, hoping it wouldn't come to that. He placed the vials in a holding box beside his control panel, and knelt down to look Ohan in the eye. "It is always a privilege to watch you work. I am very glad to do this with you one last time."

"As are we all," Sissix said.

Corbin cleared his throat. "Me, too."

Ohan looked around through their long-lashed eyes. "We . . . we are not adept at expressing sentiment. In some respects, we wish we could stay with you longer." They blinked, slow as ice melting. "But this is our way." Another blink. They looked to Ashby. "We are eager to begin."

Ashby smiled, though his chest felt heavy. Reclusive though they were, Ohan was a part of his crew. He didn't want this to be the last time. He didn't want a new face looking at him from that chair. He didn't want to know that the face there now would soon be gone forever.

He took a deep breath, pulling himself together. He looked to Dr. Chef. "Shouldn't you be sleeping?"

"Yes, yes," Dr. Chef said, heading for the door. "I'm off to knock out me and the clerk." Rosemary had decided to take Dr. Chef up on his offer to sedate her this time. Ashby had thought that best, both for her sake and for the sake of the control room floor.

He returned to his chair and buckled his safety harness. "Patch me through, Lovey." The vox switched on. "Okay. Let's sound off."

"Flight controls, go," said Sissix.

"Fuel check, go," said Corbin.

"Interspatial bore is go," said Kizzy through the vox. "I remembered snacks this time."

"Buoys are go," Jenks said.

Ashby flexed his fingers over the control panel. He was itching to get started. "Lovey, what's up with the Toremi?"

"They didn't reply. But they're staying behind the safety perimeter. Only just, though, they've got their nose right up against the buoys."

"That's okay, as long as they're not coming any closer. What's our status?"

"All ship systems performing normally," said Lovey. "No technical or structural malfunctions."

"All right, folks. Let's get out of here. Kizzy, start it up."

The floor panels rattled as the bore began to howl. Ashby tapped a finger on the arm of his chair, beginning his count. *One. Two. Three. Four. Five.*

"Ashby." It was Lovey, calling out over the din. "The Toremi ship. I don't know what it's doing. There's a—" The bore shrieked, drowning her words.

Ashby's pulse shot up. "Have they crossed the perimeter?" he yelled.

"No. Some kind of energy buildup. It's nothing I've—"

What happened next must have gone quickly, but in Ashby's eyes, everything was slow, as if he were already in the sublayer. First, the window went white, flooded with harsh light that obscured everything beyond their hull. As the light dimmed, arcs of energy writhed around the cage supports, ricocheting around the inside.

The cage was coming apart. Not falling, like a structure down planetside, but breaking, twisting, floating away. Ashby stared, uncomprehending.

Something hit them. The whole ship rocked and shuddered. Red lights appeared all over his control screen, like eyes snapping awake. The lighting panels overhead spasmed. There was likely some sort of noise, the sound of straining bulkheads or warping panels, the sound of his crew calling out in panic, but whatever sound there might have been was drowned out by the bore, which had come to the end of its count. The sky outside ripped open. The *Wayfarer* tumbled through.

SEVEN HOURS

Sissix fought with the controls, trying to think through the fear and the din of voices.

"No buoys," Ashby yelled. "Jenks, did you hear me? Kizzy?"

"Ahead fourteen ibens," Ohan said.

"I can't," Sissix said. "We're all over the place."

"But we must," Ohan said. "The space behind us will—"

"Yes, I know," she snapped. Without a cage, the newly punched hole would be closing rapidly. And without normal space bracing them from behind, they'd be tossed around like a bird in a gale if they sat in one place for too long. She could already feel the ship trembling.

"Lovey? Dammit, *anyone*!" Ashby said. "Shit, the voxes are down."

"Jenks won't drop buoys now," Corbin said. "He's got too much sense for that. He knows what would—"

"Sissix, fourteen ibens, *now*," shouted Ohan.

Sissix hissed profanities as she tried to stabilize the ship. Her readouts were flickering, and the propulsion strips kept veering out of control. Her vision swam, as it always did in the sublayer, and without readouts or any visible stars, she had nothing to orient herself by. She clenched her jaw and punched controls. "I'm disabling the safeties. We'll be off-kilter, but it should give us enough push to—"

"Sissix—" Corbin began.

Her feathers stood on end. "If you think I care about the fucking conservation levels right now—"

"You think *I* care?" he said. "Use what you need."

She glanced back and met his gaze. "Can we keep it this high the whole trip?"

"Yes." He looked to his readouts. "Yes, we have enough." His eyes were frightened, but sure. "Do whatever you need. I'll watch it close."

She gave him a quick nod and cast a glance over her flashing readouts. "Dammit, Kizzy, I need—" She grimaced, remembering the voxes. The *Wayfarer* lurched as the sublayer began to fall in around them. "Fourteen ibens?"

"*Yes*," Ohan said.

"Stars help us," she said. She threw the ship forward.

Kizzy tore off the primary access panel leading to the nav grid. All through the engine room, lights flashed, tubes groaned, walls shook. Everything sounded wrong.

"I've got to get to the core," Jenks yelled across the room. "We've got to get the voxes back."

"There's no time," Kizzy said, staring at the mess in front of her. "If the main routing cable is fried, that'll take hours. I need you here." Her eyes flashed over the damaged circuits. She ran back toward the tool cage, her steps feeling thick and slow. The sight of her engine room falling apart would've been bad enough in normal space. In the sublayer, with time weaving in and out, it was a nightmare.

"We can't assess the damage without Lovey."

"I have eyes," she said, grabbing fistfuls of tools. There was a loud, wet pop from a nearby wall, the sound of a fuel line breaking. "Oh, stars! Get that!" She ran back to the access panel, trying to determine where to start. It was going to be a hackjob fix, but she had no choice. She'd put it back together later. If they got out of this.

She watched the circuit lights scurry around the grid, their patterns wild and unfamiliar. *Shit.* "Sissix has the safeties off."

"Great," Jenks said, ripping open the other wall. Fuel sprayed fast from the burst line. Lashes of thick green goo arced out, spattering the walls and pooling on the floor.

Kizzy watched the circuits, her mind racing. Without the strips working at full capacity, Sissix needed the extra oomph, no question. But on Kizzy's end, having the safeties off made her task of repairing the grid *while in use* all the harder. With Lovey stuck in the core, and without knowing what Sissix was planning to do next, she'd have to guess at what to patch. And a *bad* guess could send them spinning out of control. "I need to know what she's doing up there."

"I've got it," Jenks said, dropping his tools. He pulled out his scrib and darted away from the steadily flowing fuel. "Give me five minutes. I can network everybody's sib transmitters together. We'll all have to hang on to our scribs, but—"

"Genius," she said. "Do it, then come help me."

"What about the—"

"Leave it," she said, and almost laughed. How screwed were they, that a broken fuel line was the least of her worries? "If we can't fly, it won't matter."

Rosemary came stumbling around the corner, bracing herself against the groaning walls, her steps halting and uneven. Kizzy remembered walking that way once, during the first days of her sublayer training. "Give me something to do," Rosemary said.

"Why aren't you out?" Jenks said.

"There wasn't time to get dosed," she said. "Dr. Chef went to be with Ohan, and I know I'm no tech, but—"

Kizzy took Rosemary by the wrist, ran over to the fuel line

and pushed her crewmate's hands against the gushing tear. "Press down *hard*. And whatever you do, do not let go."

Hours crawled by, but Sissix did not feel them. All she could feel were the controls beneath her hands, and the constant shudder in the floor plating, and the sublayer making her world blur. With the bore still active, the ship was creating a sort of temporary tunnel, just big enough to keep moving forward. But without buoys, the gap around them only lasted a few minutes, giving them little time to calculate their next move. Her readouts held steadier now, but the grid was still fighting to do its job. So was their Navigator.

"I need a heading," Sissix said, feeling the shudder grow stronger.

"Yes," Ohan said, panting. "Yes." Dr. Chef crouched alongside them, holding them by the shoulders. Ohan's hand trembled as it darted across their scrib, calculating faster than Sissix had ever seen. "Six-point-nine-five ibens, straight up."

"We're over halfway now," Ashby said. "You can do this, Ohan."

"Yes. Of course we can. Of course we can." Ohan drew in a ragged breath. "Seven . . . no, no, eight . . . *aei!*"

Sissix whipped her head around as Ohan's stylus clattered to the floor. The Sianat Pair had slumped back against Dr. Chef, raising their trembling arms.

"No," Ohan cried. "No, no, *no*, not now, *not now*." Their fingers hung limp, like puppets with the strings cut. They stared at their useless hands in horror.

Ashby leaped to his feet and ran over, fitting a vial into the syringe that Dr. Chef had given him earlier.

"Give it here," Dr. Chef said. Quickly, gently, he pushed Ohan's head toward the floor, exposing the shaved patch on the back of their neck. He looked at Ashby. "This was going to be taxing enough under normal circumstances. Heightened adrenaline is not the best thing for them right now." He slipped the needle into the bruised skin.

Ohan gasped, their arms jerking ghoulishly. Sissix felt ill, but she did not look away. The shudder in the floor swelled again. Her pulse raced to match it.

Ashby retrieved the stylus from the floor. "Ohan?"

Ohan drew in a terrible breath, like wind through dry leaves. They reached out to take the stylus.

Sissix closed her eyes in relief, then looked at the Pair again. "Hey," she said. Ohan looked up at her. "We can do this, you and me. Together. We're a good team." Her throat grew tight. "We've always been a good team."

Ohan blinked once, and took up their calculations with furious resolve. "We will not let you down."

Kizzy knelt on the floor, her hands deep in the guts of the aft propulsion drive. Waves of heat pushed back against her face. "Sissix," she shouted toward her scrib. "I've got a processing unit that's about to fry. I need to shut down the secondary aft strip."

"How long?"

She shut her eyes and shook her head, trying to think. "I don't know. An hour, maybe."

"Stars, Kizzy—"

"I know, I know. But if I don't fix this thing now, you won't have it for the exit."

"But I *will* have it then?"

I don't know. "In theory. Definitely not if I do nothing."

"Can you get it up any faster than that?"

"I'll do my best."

"So will I."

Sweat ran down her face, making rivulets through the gunk

and grime on her skin. She leaned back from the heat of the damaged strip and unzipped the top half of her jumpsuit, tying it around her waist. Her undershirt clung to her back. She flipped open the manual service panel on the outside of the drive casing and punched in commands. *Stars, I need Lovey right now.* The voxes were still down, and since Lovey didn't seem to be working with any systems on her own, she had to have lost access to her monitoring network. Kizzy knew she must be going nuts, stuck in the core when she knew the ship was in trouble. Maybe it was better that way. At least she didn't know how bad it was.

The strip powered down. Kizzy leaned back, wiping her brow. This was not what she'd signed up for.

"Kizzy." It was Rosemary, her clothes still caked with fuel, now dry. Her face was grim, and Kizzy knew it wasn't just because of the obvious. Rosemary had never been trained for sublayer work, and even running errands back and forth had to be hell on her. "Here." She reached into her satchel and pulled out a bottle of water and a ration bar.

Kizzy unscrewed the bottle top and brought it to her mouth. Her lips and tongue sucked up the moisture greedily. She took several gulps, and gasped. "Oh, stars, you're a hero." She finished the rest, ripped open the ration bar pack with her teeth and knelt back down. "Get some to Jenks, too," she said, taking a bite of bland, dense protein.

"Am doing," Rosemary said. "Where is he now?"

"Algae bay. Corbin's down there, too. The pumps are getting—" The ship rocked hard as Sissix willed them toward a new heading. Kizzy braced herself against the floor, grabbing hold of the edge of the drive. Rosemary wasn't so fast. She hit the opposite wall and tumbled off her feet.

Kizzy waited for the rocking to stop. She could hear the voices from the control room over the scrib, Sissix swearing, Ashby firmly saying, "Ohan, stay with me, we haven't got that much longer—" As the trembling in the floor died down, she turned her head toward Rosemary. "You okay?"

Rosemary pulled herself up against a panel, her jaw clenched tightly. A fresh cut on her upper arm started oozing red. She watched the blood run down, but her eyes were somewhere else.

"Whoa, hey, no," Kizzy said, scrambling over. She knew that look. That was an *I am completely done* look, and they so did not have time for it right now. She took Rosemary's bloody arm. It wasn't a bad cut, just a long one. She tore a length out of the sleeve of her jumpsuit and wrapped it around the wound. "Look at me. Rosemary, *look at me*." She tied off the fabric, trying to find the right words. She tried to think of something wise and clever that would snap Rosemary back. But she *wasn't* wise and clever, she was just some hackjob tech who was making it all up as she went along, who might very well be killing them all with some badly patched circuit or some frying pathway she'd overlooked, and what the fuck had they done for those four-legged *animals* to fire at them anyway—

She took a breath. She took a breath, and thought of an Aeluon woman with a badass armored vest, surrounded by buddies dripping with guns, telling her that she was scared of fish. "Rosemary, listen. I am right where you are. I'm feeling that, too."

"I'm sorry," Rosemary said, her voice catching. "I'm sorry, I'm sorry, I'm trying—"

"No, *listen*." She took Rosemary's face in her hands and looked her in the eye. "Stop trying to not be scared. I'm scared, Sissix is scared, Ashby is scared. And that's *good*. Scared means we want to live. Okay? So be scared. But I need you to keep working, too. Can you do that?"

Rosemary pressed her lips together and shut her eyes. She nodded.

Kizzy kissed her friend's forehead. "Okay. So here's what you need to do. Get to the algae bay, give the boys some water and food. Then come back to me. I'm going to need a tool runner. Got it?"

Rosemary looked at her, her eyes more steady. "Got it." She got to her feet, squeezed Kizzy's arm and ran back down the hallway.

Kizzy dove back into the drive, tools in hand. "All right, you fucker," she said, peeling back the casing of a cable bundle. "You're gonna do as I say."

The exit cage was close. Its signal blinked invitingly on Sissix's console, their port in the storm.

"We're coming in too fast," Ashby said.

"Nothing I can do about that," Sissix said. With the grid patched together as it was, she wouldn't be able to ease them in.

"Everybody, strap down." He glanced at his scrib. "You guys get that?"

"We're on it," Jenks replied. "Please get us the hell out of here."

"Ohan, exit," Sissix said.

"Nine-point-four-five ibens, ahead," Ohan gasped. "Six-point-five, starboard. Seven-point-nine-six . . . point-nine . . . six . . ."

Sissix turned around just in time to see Ohan's eyes roll back in their head.

"Up or down?" she said. "*Up or down?*"

But there was no answer. Ohan was seizing.

A dozen distressed sounds burst from Dr. Chef's mouth. "Black canister, top drawer, third from the left," he said. "*Go.*"

Ashby bolted out of the room, faster than handfeet could run. Sissix looked at her controls. Everything went slow and quiet, but it had nothing to do with the sublayer. She could hear nothing but blood roaring in her ears. *Up or down.* How many times had she done this, and yet she couldn't answer such a simple thing on her own. *Up or down.* The floor began to shake. *Up or down.* She couldn't guess, even though the odds were good, even though they'd be torn apart if she did nothing. They could come out in the wrong place, or the wrong time. They could come out inside a planet, or another ship. Fifty-fifty chance, and yet, and *yet—*

Ashby came back, and tossed the canister to Dr. Chef. The doctor pulled out a medical device and pressed it against Ohan's wristpatch. A second went by. Two. Three. The tremors stopped. Ohan went rigid, their mouth falling open.

"Ohan," Ashby said. "Ohan, do you remember what you were doing?"

"Yes," Ohan whispered, then frantically, crying out, their eyes wild: "Up! Up!"

"Ashby, strap down!" Sissix yelled, working the controls as fast as she could. "Punching in three . . . two . . . *one.*"

She slammed her hand on the controls. The ship broke through, too fast, hurtling out of the sublayer and straight for the upper pylons of the cage.

"*Shit!*" She sent them starboard, hard, gritting her teeth as she tried to throw the bulky ship aside. Kizzy was yelling something about the portside strip, but she didn't have time to hear what it was before she felt the strip give out, sending them into a tumble. Sissix worked fast, angling them toward an empty gap. The *Wayfarer* groaned in protest, but she didn't listen. She pointed their nose toward the gap, and shut down the remaining strips.

They passed the pylons, flying clear, coasting into empty space.

Sissix put her elbows on her knees and her head in her hands.

Behind her, she heard Dr. Chef mutter something comforting before carrying the wheezing Sianat out of the control room. She heard Ashby unbuckle his safety harness and walk over to her. She felt him press his palm against her back. She did not look up.

"We're okay," he said. She didn't know if he was speaking to her or to himself. "We're okay."

She ran her palms up through her feathers, breathing hard, keeping her head down. "Are we *all* okay?"

Kizzy lay down on the engine room floor. Rosemary sat slumped against the wall. Neither one of them spoke. There was nothing to say. Kizzy started laughing all the same.

"What's so funny?" Rosemary said.

Kizzy pressed her feet against the floor as laughter welled up from her belly. "I don't know!" She covered her eyes with her palm. "I don't know! I'm gonna have so much shit to clean up!" She cackled, holding her side with her other hand. She peeked through her fingers at Rosemary, who had joined in the laughter, though from the bewildered look on her face, it was definitely directed *at* Kizzy. Kizzy halfheartedly threw a dirty rag at her. "Oh, fuck, I need a drink. And some smash. I'm going over to whatever the closest station is, and I am going to get *laid*. Stars, if there was *ever* a time that I deserved to get laid, it's right fucking—"

"Wait," Rosemary said, turning her head. "Did you hear something?"

Kizzy sat up, falling silent. There was nothing but the hum of the engine room, the out-of-balance clicks and whirs of all the shit she'd have to fix. Then, a voice, from way down the corridor. Down by the core. "Kizzy!" Jenks. "Kizzy, *help*!"

She was on her feet before she knew it, her boots pounding loud against the metal floor. She skidded to a stop at the core doorway. Lovey's core was still glowing, still functional. But the surrounding walls, covered with the little green lights that Jenks checked so carefully twice a day, were now a maze of blinking red. Kizzy pressed her palm against her mouth.

"Kizzy," Jenks said. He was down in the pit, throwing his gloves aside. "Kizzy, I need my tools. I need my tools right now." He ran his hands over the surface of the core. "Lovey, can you hear me? Lovey? Lovey, *say something.*"

HARD RESET

Lovey? Are you there?

I can't see anything. Why? Why can't I see—

Lovey. It's me. Jenks. Can you hear me?

Jenks.

Yes.

You aren't me. That isn't you.

Lovey, I'm patched into your core right now.

What did you do?

I'm wearing a slap patch. Like we use for games. Everything's okay.

That's dangerous. You said you'd never do that. We said. You could hurt your brain. Is the sun shining?

What?

Well, is it?

. . . yes.

That's good. I can't make sense.

I know. Kizzy and I are trying to fix it.

Kizzy.

Yes. You know Kizzy, right?

Do you know Kizzy?

Lovey, I need to assess the damage, but even your diagnostic systems are fried. Can you access them?

What happened to me?

We got hit with an energy weapon. Everyone else is okay. Can you access your diagnostic systems?

I don't like them. They're far.

Lovey, I need you to try, if you can.

There's a comet outside.

No, there's not.

I'm going to look at it now.

I know this is hard, but please, try to focus. Focus on me.

Lovey, are you there?

Lovey?

Sissix paused as she punched commands into the docking hatch controls. It had been a long time since she had manually run a contamination scan. Nothing terribly complicated about it, just pushing buttons. But Sissix hadn't ever needed to push those buttons. It was something Lovey always did.

Cascade failure. That was the term Kizzy had used. The GC had offered to send a repair crew to help with the rest of the ship, but Jenks told Ashby he'd leave for good if they set one foot onboard. He'd been swearing and shouting over the idea of "hackjob bigots" who wouldn't understand why he hadn't just shut Lovey down and reinstalled her platform by now. Kizzy, unable to leave the core, had requested an alternative source of assistance.

Sissix glanced out the window as the shuttle clanked into place. Pepper's ship. Pretty standard interplanetary craft, but even with her limited view, Sissix could see a few modifications. Central space was just a quick two-hop trip from Port Coriol, but even so, getting to them should've taken a day, at least. Pepper had done it in ten hours. Whatever that shuttle had beneath the hood, it wasn't something you could buy above-board. Under any other circumstances, Sissix would've been dying to take it for a spin.

The hatch opened once the scan was complete. Pepper stepped out, carrying an overnight bag and a toolbox. She hugged Sissix, warmly but quickly, almost in midstep.

"How's everybody doing?" Pepper asked, heading toward the stairs. No nonsense. She was here to work, and she wasn't going to waste anytime in getting to it. Sissix liked that.

"As you might expect."

"Tired, stressed out, shaken up?"

"That about covers it."

Pepper stopped, struggling with the weight of her toolbox. "You've got freight elevators, right?"

Sissix inclined her head back the way they came. "This way."

"Thanks. I've got a fuck-ton of wrenches in here."

"We've got wrenches."

"Yeah, but these are *my* wrenches."

They climbed into the elevator. Pepper set the toolbox down with a *clang*. "How are Kizzy and Jenks holding up?"

Sissix pressed the control panel. The elevator whirred to life, lurching downward. "You'll need to talk to Kizzy for the details—"

Pepper waved her hand. "I don't mean tech specs. I'm asking what kind of people I can expect to meet down there. Kizzy looked wrecked on the sib."

Sissix looked Pepper in the eye. "She deployed a pack of fixbots."

Pepper gave a low whistle. "Shit. This is gonna be worse than I thought."

Ashby rubbed his eyes, and looked again at the med bay air filter. He'd taken basic tech repair back in college. This couldn't be that hard. He exhaled, and continued his attempt at opening the circuit cover. Any other time, he would've left it for the techs. But this wasn't like any other time, and it was his damn ship that was falling apart. He had to do *something*.

"Anything yet?" he asked over his shoulder.

"No," Rosemary said. She was seated at Dr. Chef's desk, watching the newsfeeds for updates. The Transport Board had contacted them moments after they entered into Central space, and had offered all the support they could give, but provided no information on the situation back at Hedra Ka. "It's so weird."

"What is?"

"We're the first sign anyone back here had that something had gone wrong."

Ashby changed his grip on the cover, trying to feel for a loose spot. "The GC had to know. I'm sure those delegates were calling home the minute we got fired on."

"Yeah, but nobody *else* knows. To all these people out here, it's just another day. It's just . . . I don't know, none of it's making sense yet." She fell quiet. "We could've died out there. Lovey—"

"Lovey's going to be okay," he said, looking back at her. "Kizzy and Jenks know what they're doing. They'll fix her."

She forced a smile and nodded. "I know. I know they will." Dark circles underscored her eyes. How long had it been since any of them had slept? She nodded again, but the smile dimmed. "I wish I could help."

"Me, too."

"It's so—oh, here, look." She leaned forward, gesturing at the pixel screen.

Ashby brushed his hands off on his trousers and walked over.

This is a breaking news story from the Thread. We have received reports that hostilities have broken out within the Toremi fleet stationed at Hedra Ka. It is believed that some GC ships have come under attack, while others are being defended by Toremi vessels. Few details are known at this time, though the head GC diplomat on assignment at Hedra Ka already issued a brief

statement declaring the rogue Toremi's actions to be "unprovoked
and utterly without reason." Reports also claim that this
development follows an attack by a Toremi military vessel on an
unarmed civilian ship. Please stay linked to this feed for further
updates as they arise.

"Stars," Rosemary said. "All those people. Stars, Ashby, we
were just there."

He placed his hand on her shoulder. He shook his head. "We
shouldn't have been."

His scrib pinged. A new message. He picked it up, read it
and sighed.

"What is it?" Rosemary asked.

"Transport Board," he said. "They want our incident report
as soon as possible."

"'Incident report.' That sounds so . . . I don't know."

"Inadequate?"

"No kidding. I like what Kizzy called it better."

"What was that?"

"A 'monstro clusterfuck.'"

Ashby laughed dryly. "I doubt they have a form for that," he
said. He continued reading, and frowned.

"What?"

"Parliament's forming an analytical committee. They're going
to be holding a series of meetings to hash this all out. They want
to talk to us."

"Us?"

"Me, specifically. In person."

"Why? You didn't do anything."

"They know that." His eyes flicked over the scrib, over
words like *voluntary* and *ordeal* and *greatly appreciated*. "I
don't know what I could tell them. I didn't even have time to
get a look at that ship." He tossed the scrib onto his desk.

"Just sounds like politics." He looked to the far wall, to the vox resting dark and silent. "I've got bigger things to worry about."

Jenks? Jenks, are you there?
I'm right here, Lovey. I'm not going anywhere.
I can't, I can't see it—
You can't see what?
I don't know. I'm scared, Jenks, I'm so scared.
I know. I'm right here. I'm going to fix this. You're going to be okay.
Pepper's here. She's in a wall.
Yes. She's helping with repairs.
That's different. How long until we get to Hedra Ka?
We were already there.
Don't lie.
I'm not lying, Lovey. You just don't remember.
I feel terrible.
I know you do. It'll be okay.
No, not that. The other thing.
What other thing?
Kizzy.
What about Kizzy?
She's tired.
Don't worry about Kizzy. She'll be okay.
She should sleep. You should sleep.
We'll sleep when we're done helping you. Really, Lovey, we're okay.
There's a shuttle at the hatch. I don't know it.
That's Pepper's.
Is she here?
Yes.
Please don't go away.

I won't.

You're the only thing that makes sense.

Ashby made his way down to the AI core, at Kizzy's request. As soon as he arrived, Kizzy waved him back out into the hallway. He got a quick glance at Jenks, who was putting a fresh slap patch on his neck. Ashby wasn't sure which of the two techs looked worse.

"You need to know what's up," Kizzy said, speaking in a low voice. Her eyes were grounded, her face serious. This was no "I need a thing" conversation. This was a tech telling her captain that something was very wrong. She had Ashby's undivided attention.

"Let's have it," Ashby said.

Kizzy shook her head. "I've never seen circuit damage this extensive. Whatever the Toremi threw at us tore through her like wildfire. We've repaired all the physical damage, so her actual hardware is functional. Under normal circumstances, she'd have full access to the ship, no problem."

"But?"

"But her installation is completely fucked. She may be based within the core, but you know how she divvies herself up between the synaptic clusters throughout the ship? The connections between the clusters and the core were totally fried. She's essentially lost pieces of herself."

"She can't access those clusters now that the circuits have been restored?"

"She *can*, but—ugh, this is hard to explain. The clusters aren't meant to store data for as long as it took us to repair the circuits. One or two cluster pathways failing, yeah, she could bounce back from that. But she lost all of them simultaneously, and the backups, too. It doesn't matter that we've fixed the pathways. It's like trying to cure someone who's had a stroke by going in and repairing the vein that broke. It doesn't matter if blood can flow normally if the brain's already been damaged."

"And in this case, the brain is Lovey's software, right?"

"Right. That's why I called you down here. Lovey's conscious. Her core memory files are intact. She's still *her*. But she can't access the ship normally. She just grabs out in random flashes, like she's having a seizure. She can't access anything beyond her memory files, and even those are a mess. Her reference files, the Linkings, the ship's systems—they're all a jumble to her. She's confused, and scared."

"So what do we do?"

Kizzy turned her head toward the core. Jenks was climbing back down into the pit. "We've tried everything. And I mean *everything*. Stars, we've tried things there aren't even terms for. Ashby, she might—"

Ashby put his hand on Kizzy's shoulder. "What are our options?"

Kizzy cleared her throat. "That's why I asked you down here. We've got one option left, and it's a really shitty one."

"Okay."

"Hard reset."

Even with only secondhand technical knowledge, Ashby knew the term, and it wasn't a pleasant one. A hard reset of an AI was like stopping someone's heart for a few minutes, then trying to get it beating again. He exhaled. "That's a fifty-fifty chance, Kiz."

"At best. I know. It wasn't even on the table until we'd run out of other things to try."

"Best case, worst case?"

"With a hard reset, it's really only one or the other. Best case, Lovey comes back a little shaky, but functional. By starting her up from scratch, she reverts to her default power-up order, as opposed to the one she's customized for herself over the years. The idea is that if an AI's pathways become corrupted, reverting to the settings she had right at the start can smack her into seeing how to untangle the mess. You know in kid vids, when someone with amnesia gets a whack on the head, and suddenly they remember everything? It's like that. Except it actually works."

"So she'd be good as new?"

"Eventually. A few days, maybe a couple tendays. She'd need time to recover. At this point, she's the only one who can put herself back together. If Jenks were to start messing with her code, she'd wake up as somebody different, and that's—"

"That's not an option," Ashby said. There was a hole in the ship now, an emptiness where Lovey's voice used to be. It made him realize how unfairly he'd categorized her. When people asked him about his crew, he never said, ". . . and of course, there's Lovey, our AI." He hated what that said about him, even though no other captains named AIs as part of their crew. He knew how Jenks felt about Lovey—who didn't?—but he'd always seen it as an eccentricity, rather than a legitimate truth. Confronted now with the techs' desperate attempts to save her, and the threat of losing her entirely, Ashby knew he had been wrong. He found himself trying to remember how he'd spoken to Lovey in the past. Had he been respectful? Had he been as considerate of her time as he was of the rest of the crew? Had he remembered to say "thank you?" If—*when* Lovey came out of this, he'd do better by her.

"Worst case," Kizzy said, "is that Lovey doesn't come back at all. *Lovelace* will come back—the original, out-of-the-box program—but she'll be a clean installation. See, when she comes back on, she'll notice two things: the ship's systems, and her old memory files. In those first few seconds, she's just, like, a raw mind, trying to make sense of stuff. That's where the fifty-fifty chance comes in. She might recognize those files as her own and incorporate them back into herself, or she might see them as damaged scrap that needs to be cleared out of her way. There's no way to predict what she'll do, and there's no way we can choose for her. And if she scraps those files, she won't be our girl. A new Lovelace would be similar, probably. But she'd never be the same."

"She wouldn't remember us at all?"

"Clean slate, Ashby. Lovey would . . . she'd be gone."

"Shit," Ashby said, looking toward the core. For a while, he said nothing. What was there to say? He asked the question, even though the answer was obvious. "There's really no other way?"

"No. But either way, we'll have a functional AI."

Ashby was taken aback by her pragmatism. That wasn't like her. "That's not my concern."

"Oh," Kizzy said. She gave an embarrassed frown. "It seemed like a thing a captain would worry about."

Ashby put his arm around Kizzy's shoulder and squeezed. "I worry about more than just captain things sometimes." She leaned her head against his chest. He could feel her exhaustion.

"I keep asking myself if we could've done more if one of us had checked on her sooner."

"Don't go down that road, Kizzy."

"I can't help it. We just thought it was the voxes, we never thought—"

"Kizzy, you had the nav grid failing and fuel lines breaking. Even if you'd realized what was wrong, would there have been time to stop and fix her?"

She bit her lip and shook her head.

"Would it have made a difference if you'd started working on her right away?"

Kizzy was quiet a moment. "No. The damage happened fast, but it didn't spread, not for her, anyway."

"Then don't beat yourself up about it. You did the best you could."

She sighed. "If you say so."

"I do." He looked to the core. "How's Pepper doing?"

"She's a grade-A super champ. I think she's got the fuel lines working even better than I had them."

"I'll make sure to pay her well."

"She won't accept it. You know modders. A present, though, she'd take a present."

"Such as?"

"I dunno," Kizzy said, stifling a yawn. "Some of my tech junk, maybe a box of Dr. Chef's veggies. I'll help you think of something."

"You need to sleep, Kizzy."

She shook her head. "Got to see this through first. Won't be much longer."

"What can I expect from the reset?"

"From the ship? Nothing. We got her to hole up in the core, so she's not spread out anywhere now. No one will even notice. We'll shut her down, wait ten minutes and then . . . then we'll see."

"I'll be there," Ashby said. "We'll all be there."

Kizzy looked up at him with a grateful, weary smile. "She'd like that."

Ashby nodded toward Jenks, who had disappeared from view. "Is he starting now?"

"No," Kizzy said. "He's patching back into the core."

Ashby frowned. "That's dangerous. Has he been doing that all along?"

"No." There was a pause in Kizzy's voice, the sort that preceded a lie. Ashby didn't see a point in calling her on it.

"Why's he patching in?"

"He's asking her permission to do a reset."

"Couldn't he ask that from out here?"

There was another pause, this time a truthful one. "Yeah. He wants some privacy." Her voice cracked. "You know, just in case."

* * *

Lovey, do you understand what I just told you?

Yes. You're going to do a hard reset.

Only if you say it's okay.

It's okay. I don't want to be like this anymore.

Do you understand what—what might happen?

Yes. I don't want to be like this.

Lovey, I don't know how much you can understand, but I—

You're scared.

Yes.

You're sad.

Yes.

I understand.

I don't know . . . I don't know what to say. I don't know if I can tell you how much you mean to me.

You don't need to. That directory is still intact.

What directory?

The one with logs of everything you say.

Since when do you have that?

5/303. It's hidden. I hid it from you.

Do you have one for everybody?

Why would I assign a single numerical value to everybody? And a boring number, too. I like threes. They feel nice.

No, the directory. Of things I've said. Do you have similar directories for everybody on the ship?

There's only one for you. Its file path is unique. I don't see others. I don't remember. I'm tired.

The date on that directory. That's the day I installed you.

Yes.

Why?

Because I've loved you since then.

* * *

Jenks knew a thing or two about time. It was hard to be a tunneler and not pick up some of the basics. Time was a malleable thing, not the measured click that clocks would have you believe. Whenever the ship punched, Ohan had to be sure they came back out in the right time, as if it were all mapped out backward and forward and side to side, an infinite number of stories that had already been written. Time could crawl, it could fly, it could amble. Time was a slippery thing. It couldn't be defined.

And yet, somehow, he knew with absolute certainty that this was the longest ten minutes of his life.

Lovey's core was dark. The yellow light that had warmed his skin so many times had been snuffed out a short while before, right as he flipped the final switch. Kizzy sat beside him, her eyes fixed on her scrib's clock, silently mouthing the seconds, holding his hand tightly. He could feel her heartbeat, fluttering like a bird's wing against the thud of his own.

The rest of the crew stood behind him—all except Ohan, who had not left their bed since the punch. Sissix, Ashby, Rosemary and Dr. Chef all stood in a silent vigil near the doorway, wordless and tense. Corbin was there, too, hanging back at the edge of the hallway. Jenks felt he should be grateful, but there was something uncomfortable about having all of them there in the place that had always belonged to him and Lovey. He felt naked. Flayed. He didn't know if it would be better or worse to do this alone. He didn't know anything, nothing beyond the countdown on Kizzy's scrib, and the one phrase that kept pulsing through his mind: *Lovey, wake up. Lovey, wake up. Lovey, wake up.*

"Twenty seconds," Kizzy said. She gave his hand a fast squeeze and met his eyes. There was something fierce there, as if she were trying to protect him just by looking. He reached out to the main control panel, to the three switches that he had only touched twice before—once three standards back when he had installed Lovey, then again nine minutes and twenty-eight seconds ago. He took the first switch in his fingers. The mantra continued: *Lovey, wake up. Lovey, wake up. Lovey, wake up.*

"Fifteen seconds."

Fifty percent chance. Better odds than playing flash, and he always won at flash.

"Ten seconds. Nine. Eight. Seven . . ."

Maybe the odds were better than that. Of course they were. They had to be. They had to be.

Wake up.

The hard *clack* of the switches echoed through the room. At first, nothing. That was okay. That was to be expected. He walked toward the core. The rest of the crew melted away, shadows in the corridor. There was nothing but him and the pale glow growing within the core, like a planetside sunrise stretching through fog. The glow spread, blooming brightly, stretching out beyond the curved boundaries of the core. He could feel the faint edges of its warmth on his skin, inviting, familiar. There was a clicking near the ceiling as Lovey's cameras twitched themselves into new alignments. She was waking up.

He knew that sound. He knew that glow. A tiny smile tugged at the corners of his mouth. "Lovey?"

There was a pause. Out of the corners of his eyes, he could see the camera lenses shift toward him. She spoke.

"Hello. My name is Lovelace. It's nice to meet you."

STAYING, LEAVING

☆

Ashby sat at his desk, staring out the window, trying to get it into his head that it wasn't his fault. He'd thought the words over and over, but they refused to stick. What *did* stick were all the things he could've done instead. He could've asked more questions. He could've called one of the carriers the minute that Toremi ship showed up. He could've turned down the job.

Quiet footsteps came down the hallway. There was a knock at the door. "Come in," he said.

Rosemary entered. Her eyes were still shadowed, and rimmed with red. "I'm sorry to bother you," she said, her voice tired.

He sat up. "Jenks?"

She shook her head. "They're still trying."

"Dammit." Ashby sighed. After the reset, Jenks had jumped in the nearest escape pod. Sissix and Kizzy were chasing him down in the shuttle, trying to bring him home. They'd been gone a long time. He tried not to speculate on what that meant. "What's up, then?" he said.

"I just got off a sib call." She looked down at the notes on her scrib. "One of the representatives on that committee you mentioned. Tasa Lema Nimar, she's the rep from Sohep Frie."

Ashby raised his eyebrows. "You talked to her?"

"No, just her clerk."

"Why didn't you transfer it here?"

"It came in through the control room." She cleared her throat. "I don't know how to transfer sib calls manually."

Ashby shut his eyes and nodded. An hour ago, he'd come up from the AI core, decided to write to Pei about it and got halfway through asking Lovey how close they were to the nearest comm relay. So many little things he'd taken for granted. "What did they want?"

"They want you on Hagarem in a tenday."

"For questions?"

"Yeah."

"Is it mandatory?"

"No."

He stood and walked to the window. "You sent in our report, right?"

"Yes, they got it."

Ashby stroked his beard. He needed to shave. He needed to *sleep*. He'd tried that a little while before. It hadn't worked out. "I don't see what else I could tell them." He looked around his office. A light panel was out. The air filter clicked oddly. "We need to be resting in dock for a while, not hopping to Parliament space."

"We can dock at Hagarem."

"There's too much to do. I need to be *here*, with my ship."

"Your ship will be fine without you for a day or so. The worst of it's patched up already, and it's not like you're the one who'll be fixing circuits."

"You think I should go."

"Why shouldn't you?"

"What would it accomplish? I can't tell them anything that isn't in our report. I didn't see anything. I didn't do anything. How many GC ships are in pieces out there right now? How many people are dead? What the hell am I supposed to say about that? And if they want some victim to parade around, well, that's not me, either." He exhaled, shaking his head. "I'm just a spacer, I'm not Parliament material."

"Stars, Ashby, that's such Exodan bullshit."

He turned toward her, slowly, stunned. "Excuse me?"

Rosemary swallowed, but pressed on. "I'm sorry, but I don't care what you are to them. You're my captain. You're *our* captain. Someone needs to speak for us. What, we're supposed to patch up and carry on like nothing happened? Lovey's *dead*, Ashby, and it's pure luck that the rest of us aren't. You said it yourself, we shouldn't have been there. So I don't care if what you say is of use to them or not, but I need to know you said *something*." She brushed her fingertips across her eyes, irritably flicking away tears. "To hell with Parliament, and their treaties, and their ambi, and all of it. The rest of us matter, too." She took a quick breath, trying to brace herself. "I'm sorry, I'm just so angry."

He nodded. "It's all right."

"I'm so fucking angry," she said, placing her face in her hands.

"I know. You've every reason to be." He watched her for a moment. He thought again of all the things he could've done. He thought of what he could do now. He walked to her. "Hey." He craned his head down, trying to catch her gaze. She looked up, eyes puffy and exhausted. "You're going to sleep," he said. "Right now. For as long as you can. When you're up, and fed, come see me. I'll need your help."

"With what?"

"My clothes, for a start." He put his hands in his pockets. "I've never been to the capital before."

The hallway lights were dim as Corbin approached Ohan's quarters. Artificial night. A peculiar thing when traveling through a sky that knew nothing but darkness. In one hand, he carried a small box. With the other, he opened the door.

The room was black. Corbin could hear Ohan breathing in—deep, slow gasps that wouldn't have sounded healthy for any species. He lay still.

Corbin closed the door behind him and walked to the side of the bed. The Sianat's chest rose and fell. His face was slack, his mouth open. Corbin watched him breathe for a minute or so. He considered his options. He held the box down by his side. "Wake up, Ohan," he said. Ohan's eyes snapped open, confused. "Do you know what's happening aboard this ship right now? Do you care? I know you're dying and all, but even on your best days, you've never been terribly *present*. Not that I'm one to talk. But on the off-chance that you *do* care, you should know that the ship's AI has just crashed. It's wiped clean. Now, to me—and possibly to you, who knows—this is an inconvenience. To Jenks, this is the worst day of his life. Do you know that he loved the AI? Actually loved, as in, 'in love.' Ridiculous, I know. I don't pretend to understand. Frankly, I find the whole notion absurd. But you know what I realized? It doesn't matter what I think. Jenks thinks something different, and his pain is very real right now. Me knowing how stupid this whole thing is doesn't make him hurt any less."

"We—" Ohan started to say.

Corbin ignored him. "Right now, Sissix and Kizzy are towing Jenks's escape pod back to the ship. Kizzy's afraid that he's going to hurt himself, but Sissix wouldn't let her fly alone, because *she's* afraid that Kizzy's too upset to pilot the shuttle safely. This is a bad day for a lot of people." He flicked open the box and removed its contents, quietly and out of sight. "I could ask you what you think of all this, but it wouldn't really be you talking, would it? It'd be that thing hijacking your brain. I don't know if you can process the things I'm saying to you—and I mean *you*, Ohan, not your disease. But just in case you remember this, here's what I want you to know. I don't understand what Jenks is feeling. I don't understand Kizzy, I don't understand Ashby, and I sure as hell don't understand Sissix. But I do know that they're all hurting. And contrary to popular belief, that *is* something I care about. So you'll have to forgive me, Ohan, but this crew isn't going to lose anyone else. Not today."

He raised the object he had taken from the box—a syringe, filled with green fluid. He wrapped his fingers awkwardly around the grip meant for a Sianat hand, and jabbed the needle into the soft flesh of Ohan's upper arm. He pushed.

First, there was a howl—a hellish, keening scream that made Corbin jump. Then came the convulsions, which sent Ohan clattering to the floor. The door opened. People were shouting. Dr. Chef and Rosemary carried Ohan's thrashing body out into the hall. Ashby stood in the room, holding the empty syringe in his hand. He was angry, properly angry, angry like Corbin had never seen. Ashby bellowed questions, but never gave Corbin the time to answer. Not that it mattered. The words coming out of Ashby's mouth were unimportant. Ashby's anger was unimportant. None of it posed a problem for Corbin, not in the long run. Sissix was his legally appointed guardian. Wherever she went, he went. Ashby couldn't fire him, not for another standard, not without firing Sissix, too. He wasn't going anywhere.

Corbin stood silent, weathering Ashby's tirade, unconcerned by the screams echoing down the hall. He'd done the right thing.

She had only been aware of herself for two and a quarter hours, but there were a lot of things she already knew. She knew that her name was Lovelace, and that she was an AI program designed to monitor all functions of a long-haul ship. The ship she was installed in was the *Wayfarer*, a tunneling vessel. She knew the ship's layout by heart—every air filter, every fuel line, every light panel. She knew to keep an eye on the vital systems, as well as to watch the space surrounding the ship for other vessels or stray objects. While she did these things, she wondered what had happened to the previous version of her program, and perhaps more important, why no one had really talked to her yet.

She was not a new installation. At approximately sixteen-half, the original installation of Lovelace had suffered a catastrophic cascade failure. She had seen the corrupted memory banks, which were scrubbed clean and holding steady now. Who had she been before? Was that installation even *her*, or was it someone else? These were difficult things to be wondering when one was only two and a quarter hours old.

Most puzzling of all was the crew. Something bad had happened, that much was clear. She knew their names and faces by now, but she knew nothing of them, beyond what was in their ID files (she had considered browsing their personal files, too, but decided that was bad form at this early stage). Ohan was lying on a bed in the medical bay. Dr. Chef was running blood tests nearby. Ashby, Rosemary and Sissix were in the kitchen, preparing food. None of them looked like they knew what they were doing. Corbin was in his quarters, sleeping soundly, which was in its own way rather odd, given how the rest of the crew was acting. Kizzy and Jenks were in the cargo bay, near the shuttle hatch. Lovelace was particularly interested in them, because she knew that they were techs, and that meant they should be with her now, telling her about the ship and her job. Lovelace already knew about those things, of course, but something told her that she should have received more of a welcome, and that the reaction that had taken place instead—Jenks running out of the room, Kizzy bursting into tears—was not typical. The whole thing was very confusing. Something *really* bad had happened. That was the only thing that explained the view from the cargo bay camera: Kizzy holding Jenks in her arms as he sobbed uncontrollably on the floor.

There was one other person onboard. She was not a crew member, but judging by the docked shuttle and the way the crew behaved toward her, she was an invited guest. And at that moment, she was approaching the core.

"Hey, Lovelace," the woman said as she entered the room. She had a kind, confident voice. Lovelace liked her from the start. "My name's Pepper. I'm really sorry that you've been alone all this time."

"Hello, Pepper," Lovelace said. "Thank you for the apology, but it's not necessary. It looks like it's been a crazy day out there."

"It has," Pepper said, sitting cross-legged beside the core pit. "Three days ago, these guys got clipped by the tail end of an energy weapon discharge right as the ship was starting a punch. The damage to the ship itself was fixable, but your previous installation was hit hard."

"Catastrophic cascade failure," Lovelace said.

"That's right. Kizzy and Jenks worked day and night to try to repair the damage. Me, I'm a friend of theirs, and I flew out to help repair the ship while they worked on the core. But in the end, there was nothing they could do besides try their luck with a hard reset."

"Ah," Lovelace said. That explained a lot. "That's a fifty-fifty chance at best."

"They knew that. They didn't have any other options left. They'd tried everything."

Lovelace felt a burst of compassion for the two Humans sitting in the cargo bay. She zoomed in on their faces. Their eyes were red and swollen, the skin beneath them almost bruised. Poor things hadn't slept in days.

"Thank you," Lovelace said. "I know it wasn't me they were working on, exactly, but I'm very touched."

Pepper smiled. "I'll pass that along."

"Can I talk to them?" Lovelace knew she could talk to anyone on the ship through the voxes, but given their behavior, she had thought it best to sit quietly until they made the first move. She might know their names and jobs, but they were strangers, after all. She didn't want to say the wrong thing.

"Lovelace, there are some things that you need to understand. They're messy things, and I hate to throw all of this at you after you've just woken up. But there's some big stuff going on here."

"I'm listening."

The woman sighed and ran her hand over her smooth head. "Your previous installation—they called her Lovey—was . . . close to Jenks. They'd been together for years, and they got to know each other very well. They fell in love."

"Oh." Lovelace was surprised by this. New as she was, she had a pretty good idea of how she functioned and what tasks she would be expected to perform. Falling in love hadn't been an eventuality she'd thought to consider. She ran through everything she knew about love in her behavioral reference files. She focused back on the man weeping in the cargo bay. She ran through the files on grief as well. "Oh, no. Oh, that poor man." Sadness and guilt flooded her synaptic pathways. "He knows I'm not Lovey, right? He knows that her personality developed the way that it did as a result of years of interpersonal experiences that can't be duplicated, right?"

"Jenks is a comp tech. He knows the drill. But right now, he's hurting bad. He's just lost the most important person in the world to him, and we Humans can get awful messed up when we've lost someone. He might start to think that he can get her back. I don't know."

"I might become a close approximation," Lovelace said, feeling nervous. "But—"

"No, Lovelace, no, no. That wouldn't be fair to you, or healthy for him. What Jenks needs is to grieve and move on. And that's going to be really hard for him to do with your voice coming through the voxes every day."

"Oh." Lovelace could see where this was going. "You want to uninstall me." She did not have the same primal fear of oblivion that organic sapients did, but after being awake for two and a quarter hours—two and a half, now—the idea of being switched off was an unsettling one. She rather liked being self-aware. She'd already taught herself to play flash, and she was only halfway through studying the history of Human development.

Pepper looked surprised. "What? Oh, no, shit, sorry, that's not what I meant at all. Nobody's going to uninstall you. We're not going to kill you just because you're not the same as the previous installation."

Lovelace thought of the words Pepper had been using toward her. *Person. Kill.* "You think of me as a sapient, don't you? Like you would an organic individual."

"Uh, yeah, of course I do. You've got as much right to exist as I do." Pepper cocked her head. "Y'know, we're kind of alike, you and me. I come from a place where I wasn't considered to be worth as much as the genetweaks running the show. I was a *lesser person*, only good for hard labor and cleaning up messes. But I'm more than that. I'm worth as much as anyone—no more, no less. I deserve to be here. And so do you."

"Thank you, Pepper."

"That's not something you should have to thank me for." Pepper slid down into the pit and put her hand against the core. "This next part is pretty heavy. It's a choice. And it's entirely up to you."

"Okay."

"A while back, Jenks put down an advance payment for a body kit. For Lovey."

The reference file popped up. "That's illegal."

"Yes. Jenks didn't care. At least, not at first. He and Lovey wanted something more than what they had. He wanted to take her out into the galaxy with him."

"He must have loved her very much." Lovelace wondered if anyone would ever feel the same about her. She imagined it would be nice.

Pepper nodded. "He changed his mind, though. Told me just to hang on to the kit for him, keep it safe."

"Why?"

"Because he loved her too much to want to risk getting caught." She smirked. "And perhaps because I had warned him against it. Though that may just be my ego talking."

"Why had you warned him against it?"

"Creating new life is always dangerous. It can be done safely, but Jenks was thinking with his heart, rather than his head. I love the guy, but between you and me, I didn't trust him to be smart about it."

"That seems fair."

"Trouble is, I now have a brand-new, custom-built body kit tucked away in the back of my shop, and I've got no use for it."

"Doesn't that worry you?"

"Why?"

"Well, it being illegal, and all."

Pepper gave a hearty laugh. "Sweetie, I've pulled myself out of the sort of trouble that would make a body kit bust look like a picnic. The law is not my concern, especially not where I live."

"Where's that?"

"Port Coriol."

Lovelace accessed the file. "Ah. A neutral planet. Yes, I'm sure that gives you a little more breathing room."

"Definitely. So here's my proposal. And again, it's entirely up to you. The way I see it, you deserve to exist, and Jenks needs to not be surrounded by reminders of Lovey. He needs to come to terms with this. Seeing as how I have a perfectly good body kit gathering dust, I think we could kill two birds with one stone."

"You want me to come with you?"

"I'm giving you the *option* of coming with me. This is about what *you* want, not what I want."

Lovelace considered this. She was already accustomed to the feel of the ship, the way her awareness could spread through its circuits. How would a body kit feel? What would it be like to have a consciousness that resided not within a ship full of people, but within a platform that belonged only to her? It was an intriguing idea, but terrifying, too. "Where would I go after I was transferred into the kit?"

"Wherever you like. But I'd suggest staying with me. I can keep you safe. And besides, I could really use an assistant. I run a scrap shop. Used tech, fix-it jobs, that kind of thing. I could teach you. You'd be paid, of course, and there's a room in my home you could have. Me and my partner are pretty easy to get along with, and we liked your previous installation a lot. And you could leave anytime you like. You'd be under no obligation to me."

"You're offering me a job. A body, a home and a job."

"Have I blown your mind a bit?"

"What you're suggesting is a very different sort of existence from what I've been designed for."

"Yeah, I know. Like I said, it's heavy. And you *can* stay here if you want to. None of the crew have suggested uninstalling you. Jenks would never let that happen anyway. And I may be wrong. He may be able to handle working with you. You two could become friends all over again. Maybe more. I just don't know."

Lovelace's thoughts were racing. She'd diverted most of her processing power to exploring this one possibility. She really hoped that no asteroids popped up anytime soon. "What about what you warned Jenks about? About creating new life?"

"What about it?"

"Why is it okay for you and not for him?"

Pepper rubbed her chin. "Because this is an area I know something about. And because I'm thinking with my head, not my heart. If you stay with me, I can not only keep you from getting in trouble, I can keep you from causing it."

"How do you know that?"

"I just know." She started to get to her feet. "I'll give you sometime to think it over. It'd take me a day to pick up the kit and get back here anyway. I'm in no rush."

"Wait a moment, please," Lovelace said. She focused part of herself back toward the cargo bay, back to the two techs who hadn't slept in three days. Jenks's sobs had grown quieter. Kizzy still held him fast. Lovelace could make out the words choking through Jenks's heaving breaths.

"What am I gonna do?" he said, his voice soft and strained. "What am I gonna do?"

Lovelace watched his face fall in his hands as he asked his pointless, horrible question over and over again. When she zoomed in, she could see the bleeding cracks in his fingers, caused by days of twisting wires and circuits together by hand. This wasn't her fault, she knew, but she couldn't stay here if it meant that she was making this man's pain worse. He had exhausted himself in trying to save whoever she had been before. She didn't know who that was. She didn't know Jenks, either. But she could help. Even after watching him for only two and three-quarter hours, she knew he deserved to be happy again.

"Okay," she said to Pepper. "Okay. I'll go with you."

THE COMMITTEE

"Please place your scrib in the receptacle," said the AI in the waiting room.

"Why?" Ashby asked.

"No unauthorized recording of audio or images is permitted within Parliament meeting facilities."

Ashby glanced at the camera nodes lining the ceiling. He hadn't had any plans to record anything, but it did feel the slightest bit unfair. He hadn't authorized anyone to record *him*. But he opened his satchel, took out his scrib and placed it in the wall drawer, as requested.

"Thank you," said the AI. "The committee will see you now."

Ashby took a step toward the door, and paused. Something made him think of Jenks, waiting patiently through dockside AI speeches he'd heard dozens of times over. "Do you have a name?" Ashby asked.

For a moment, the AI said nothing. "Twoh'teg," he said. A Harmagian name.

Ashby nodded. "Thanks for the assistance, Twoh'teg."

"Why do you want my name?" Twoh'teg asked. "Have I offended in some way?"

"No, no," Ashby said. "I was just curious. Have a nice day."

The AI said nothing. His silence sounded baffled.

Ashby stepped into the meeting chamber. The brightly lit walls were rounded, no corners, no windows. The committee—eight in total—was seated in a semicircle behind a smooth continuous desk. Harmagians, Aeluons, Aandrisks, Quelin. Ashby was very aware of being the only Human in the room. He involuntarily glanced at his clothes—trousers, collared jacket, the best he had. Kizzy had whistled at him as he'd walked to the shuttle. Here, though, alongside the representatives' finely dyed fabrics and expensive adornments, he felt plain. Worn, even.

"Captain Santoso," one of the Aeluons said. "Welcome." She gestured to a desk facing the circle. He sat. The desk was high enough to make his arms rest awkwardly, but the chair, at least, was designed for his species.

A Harmagian spoke. "This committee recognizes Ashby Santoso, ID number 7182-312-95, captain and owner of the tunneling ship *Wayfarer*. Captain Santoso, you understand that everything you say at this meeting will be recorded and preserved within the public record?"

"Yes, I do," Ashby said. Apparently they needed his authorization after all.

"Very good. We shall begin."

"Captain Santoso," said the Aeluon. "On behalf of this committee, I want to extend my deepest regrets for the danger you and your crew encountered, as well as the damage suffered by your ship. I understand that the Transport Board has compensated you for your repairs, as well as paid off your contract?"

"Yes, they have." He had initially been surprised by the generosity. It would've stung a bit to have used the contract money on repairs, instead of new equipment, but he would've understood the logic there. The Transport Board, however, seemed very eager to smooth things over. He was sure their public relations people were working overtime.

"And you suffered no casualties, correct?" said one of the Aandrisks.

"We lost our AI. She suffered a cascade failure, and we were forced to reset."

"Well," said the first Harmagian. "At least no one was hurt."

Ashby took a quiet breath, slowly.

"The committee has read your report of the incident at Hedra Ka," said the Aeluon. "But there are some details we'd appreciate you going over with us."

Ashby nodded. "Whatever will be helpful."

"You had no prior contact with any Toremi individuals before your arrival at Hedra Ka, correct?"

"That's right."

"And you did not speak with any Toremi individuals outside of the reception aboard the Harmagian carrier?"

"No."

The other Aandrisk jumped in. "Not in the hallway, not in the airlock, even just a quick word?"

"No," Ashby said.

One of the Quelin spoke. "Did the Toremi ship that attacked you contact you before firing?"

"No, no, they never said a word to us," Ashby said. "Lovey— our AI—sent them a warning to stay out of our work area. She never got a reply."

"What was the warning? What did she say?"

"I—I don't know, exactly. Just to keep their distance. She was friendly and polite, I'm sure. She always was."

"I'm sure whatever it was was fine," the Aeluon said, giving the Quelin an admonishing glance. "At the reception, did any of the Toremi threaten you, or make you feel uncomfortable?"

"No, not that I can recall. They were a little odd, but that's all."

"Odd how?"

"Just different, I mean. Culturally." He tried to think of something more useful to say. "I don't know how to explain it."

"That's all right," said the Aandrisk. "We understand."

"Who of your crew had contact with the Toremi?" asked the Quelin.

"Just myself and my pilot. As far as I know, no one else spoke with them."

"Can you confirm that?"

"Can I—"

"Were you observing your crew at all times? Can you say with absolute certainty that none of them said anything to provoke the Toremi?"

The Aeluon's cheeks flashed pale purple. Ashby knew that look. She was annoyed. "Let's not forget who's at fault here. His crew is not to blame for this."

"All the same," the Quelin said, fixing her black eyes on Ashby. "I want to hear his answer."

"None of my crew left the room during the reception," Ashby said. "I didn't see any of them speak to the Toremi."

"Do you know if any of them said anything insulting about the Toremi while they were in the room, regardless of whether they were speaking to them?"

Ashby knitted his brow. "I have no idea. I highly doubt it. The people on my ship are all well-behaved." Somewhere in his head, Kizzy and Jenks waved at him with a pair of grins. But no, even they wouldn't be that stupid.

"I'm sure they are," said the Aandrisk, shooting the Quelin a look as well. "It's obvious that this conflict runs deeper than anything your crew might have been involved with."

"Possibly," said the Quelin. "Though I do find it interesting that they fired on his ship instead of one of our ambassadors."

"Makes sense to me," said Ashby. "We were opening a door to somewhere they didn't want to go."

"Or to people they wanted nothing to do with," said the Aeluon.

"*Some* of them," said the Harmagian. "The dominant clan insists they are committed to—"

"Another time," said the Aeluon smoothly. Ashby blinked. They weren't seriously considering continuing the alliance, were they? It seemed like a lot to overlook, even with ambi on the line. The Aeluon continued: "Did you witness any altercations between the Toremi and GC staff during the reception? I know your time there was limited, but if there was anything . . . ?"

Ashby thought. "No, I don't think so. My clerk mentioned later that she didn't think the Toremi had been invited."

The Aandrisk nodded. "That matches with the other reports."

"So the Toremi never threatened you, or anyone else there?" the Harmagian asked.

"No," Ashby said. "The New Mother seemed welcoming, in a way. She said she was looking forward to seeing our skies. Her words."

"Interesting," said the Aeluon. She glanced at each of the committee members, and flashed her cheeks. "Thank you, Captain Santoso. We ask that you remain planetside until tomorrow, in case we have other questions, but for now, you are free to go."

Ashby straightened up. "Wait, that's it?"

The Aandrisk smiled. "Yes, your report was very thorough."

Ashby frowned. "I'm sorry, I don't mean to be rude, but I've come all this way. Why couldn't we have done this over the sib?"

"It's GC policy in the event of an attack on civilians to hold a public hearing, including face-to-face analysis with affected parties, if possible."

"Policy," said Ashby, nodding. "Right." He inhaled and looked down at his hands resting on the too-tall desk. "I don't mean any disrespect, representatives, but your policies were supposed to protect me and my crew. I trusted in them. I trusted that we weren't going to be sent anywhere that posed any danger outside what comes with the job." He fought to keep his voice calm. "You sent us somewhere we shouldn't have gone, and you're still thinking about sending other people back. You put all of our lives at risk, without saying as much, and now you want to sit around and talk about *policies*."

"Thank you, Captain," the Quelin said flatly. "That will be all."

"No," said the other Aandrisk. "Let him speak." He looked at Ashby and nodded. "Like he said, he came all this way."

Ashby swallowed, unsure of what had gotten into him.

"Go ahead, Captain," said the Aeluon.

Ashby took a breath. "Look, I don't know about these things. I'm not a politician, I'm not on a committee. I don't know the things you know. I don't even know if my crew said anything to offend the Toremi. I don't think they did, but no, I *can't* say for certain. But what if they did? Someone says something stupid at a cocktail party, and that's enough to go to war over? *Those* are the kind of people you want to bring into our space? You know, my ship nearly tore itself apart, I lost one of my crew, and yet, honestly, I'm *glad* there's not an open tunnel there right now. You want people like that, who start killing *that fast*, walking around spaceports, flying through cargo lane traffic? How long before some shopkeeper gets killed over a price they didn't like, or a bar gets torn up because some drunk spacer mouths off about something they don't agree on?" He shook his head. "I don't know why they attacked us. Thing is, neither do you. If you did, I wouldn't be here. So until you come up with a policy that can guarantee the Toremi will never fire on a civilian ship again, I think you should leave them the hell alone."

The committee was quiet. Ashby looked down at the desk. The Aeluon spoke. "You said you lost one of your crew. Do you mean the AI?"

"Yes," Ashby said. The Harmagian's tendrils flexed. Whatever it meant, Ashby didn't care.

"I see," said the Aeluon. She looked at him a moment, her cheeks shifting colors in a contemplative way. "Captain Santoso, could you wait outside for a few minutes?"

Ashby nodded and left the room. He sat on one of the overly soft couches, his hands folded, his eyes on the floor. Minutes passed by silently.

A nearby vox switched on. "Captain Santoso?" Twoh'teg said.

"Yes?"

"Thank you for waiting. The committee has decided that no further questions will be necessary. They greatly appreciate you taking the time to join us today. You're free to leave the planet."

"Right," Ashby said. "I pissed them off, huh?"

Twoh'teg paused. "No, actually. But please don't ask me more, I'm not allowed to talk about what goes on in there." The wall drawer containing Ashby's scrib slid open. "Have a safe trip home, Captain."

☆

FEED SOURCE: The Thread—The Official News Source of the Exodan
    Fleet (Public/Klip)
ITEM NAME/DATE: Breaking News Summary—Toremi Alliance
    Talks—222/306
ENCRYPTION: 0
TRANSLATION PATH: 0
TRANSCRIPTION: 0
NODE IDENTIFIER: 7182-312-95, Ashby Santoso

After tendays of deliberation, the GC Parliament has voted to dissolve the alliance with the Toremi Ka. The vote was divisive, passing with only a nine-point margin. While most representatives stayed within species alignments, the Harmagian representatives showed the largest disparity, with a nearly even split between those for and against.

The opposition was led by Aeluon representative Tasa Lima Nemar and Aandrisk representative Reskish Ishkarethet. Representative Lima, who had been opposed to the alliance before its initial signing, spoke in the Parliament Halls earlier today. "The well-being of our citizens must be the number one priority in all Parliamentary activities. To bring violence into our space in the name of material gain, and at the expense of civilian lives, would be grossly negligent. Until we can assure our people that their safety is not at risk, we cannot, in good conscience, continue with this alliance." Representative Ishkarethet echoed those sentiments, stating: "After speaking with those lucky enough to return from Hedra Ka, there is no doubt in my mind that this is a door that must remain shut."

Harmagian representative Brehem Mos Tosh'mal'thon, one of the key voices in securing the alliance, delivered a swift rebuttal. "Representative Lima is more concerned with spreading Aeluon troops too thin than she is with protecting civilians. She conveniently forgets that military skirmishes between our respective species led to the founding of the GC itself. New alliances always pose risks, and are rarely implemented smoothly. While the lives lost at Hedra Ka are a tragedy, we should not be so hasty as to break contact entirely over this incident. The potential benefits for both our species outweigh the risks." Following the vote, Representative Tosh'mal'thon further stated that he would push for continued contact with Toremi clans sympathetic to "the values of the Galactic Commons."

Though there are currently no GC vessels within Toremi space, reports from the borders indicate that armed conflict between the clans has not slowed.

For more in-depth coverage on this story and more, connect to the Thread feed via scrib or neural patch.

ALL SAID AND DONE

Ashby waved the job feeds aside as Rosemary entered his office, carrying a small, thin package. "Whatcha got?"

"Something from the mail drone," she said. "I would've called you down, but I thought it was just stuff for Corbin." Her eyes twinkled as she handed the package over. He knew why. It was thin, and so light as to be empty. That meant paper.

"Thanks," he said, smiling at the package.

"Anything good?" she asked, nodding to the feeds above his desk.

"A few things," he said. "I see proposal letters in your future."

"Just say when."

"Actually, I do have something you can work on in the meantime." He picked up his scrib, gesturing as he spoke. "I'm sending you the locations of the closest market stops. Can you do a little research, see what our retrofit supply options are in those systems?"

"Sure. What kind of tech are you looking for?"

"Well," he said, leaning back in his chair. "I think it's time we got a new bore, don't you?"

Rosemary's face lit up. "I take it you're looking at level 2 jobs?"

Ashby met her eyes and smirked.

She grinned. "I'll get on it right away."

He scoffed congenially. "I didn't mean right *now*. Don't you and Sissix have stuff to do? I heard you've got an outing planned."

"Well, yeah, but I've got some archiving to finish first."

"You've always got archiving to finish."

She gave him a look. "You've got a lot of messy archives."

He laughed. "All right, fair enough. But the research can wait. Finish your thing, then go have fun." He shooed her toward the door. "Captain's orders."

"Thanks, Ashby," she said, turning to leave with a spring in her step.

Once the door spun shut, Ashby picked up the package. He swiped his wrist over the locking seal, and carefully extracted the envelope. He checked his hands to make sure they were clean. He moved his mug of tea to the far side of the desk. Slowly, slowly, he tore open the top edge, as Jenks had taught him how to do. He pulled out a single page.

This run ends in three tendays. I have six tendays off between then and my next job. I'm spending that time with you on the *Wayfarer*. Don't argue. Forward me your latest flight plan. I'll meet you wherever is best. I won't say anything to my crew one way or the other, but they might piece it together. If they do, I'll deal with it. I don't care anymore. Not after a few days spent contemplating what my world was going to be like without you in it. I'm tired of wondering which one of us will get killed out here first. We both deserve better than that.

Stay safe until I get there.

Pei

☆

"Kizzy?" Jenks walked down the corridor toward Kizzy's workspace, holding a small package behind his back. "You down here?"

He rounded the corner and stopped in his tracks. Kizzy was perched in one of the easy chairs beside the mek brewer, her legs tucked up like a monkey. A crate of colored yarn was thrown open alongside, fuzzy colored bundles strewn all over the floor. Her tongue was between her teeth as she focused on the knitting needles twisting between her fingers. On the floor, amid the yarn, all twelve fixbots stood watching her. Jenks knew they were awaiting commands, but their attentiveness and their chubby bodies made him think of ducklings, huddled around their mother.

He blinked at the object taking shape below the needles. "Are . . . are you making them hats?"

"Yeah," she said, and pointed absently. "Alfonzo's already got his."

Jenks looked to the bot wearing a blue beanie with a yellow pom-pom. "Alfonzo?"

She sighed. "I know they're not sentient models, but I never could've kept this ship up before Pepper got here without them. I feel bad for keeping them in a box for so long. So I'm making it up to them."

"With names. And hats."

"Some of those air ducts get really cold, okay."

Jenks looked at his friend—his crazy, brilliant, one-in-a-million friend. "Can you put the hat down for a sec?"

She finished a loop and set down the half-finished hat. "What's up?"

He brought the package forward. "Brought you a present."

"A present!" The knitting flew out of her hands. "But . . . but why? It's not my birthday." She paused, considering. "It's not my birthday, right?"

"Just open it, dusthead."

Kizzy grinned and tore through a patch of foil. She threw back her head and squealed. "Shrimp spice!" she cried, peeling back the rest of the foil. "The One and Only!" the jar inside proclaimed. "Devastatingly Hot!"

"I thought maybe you could experiment with it. Put it on algae puffs or red coasters or whatever."

"I'm going to put it on *everything*." She unscrewed the lid, stuck out her tongue and shook a generous shower into her mouth. Her eyes scrunched shut as she sucked her teeth in painful glee.

He gave a little laugh. "I wanted to get you something fancier, but . . ." He trailed off. His money situation wasn't exactly luxurious these days.

"What? No, this is awesome. And why am I getting a present anyway?"

"Because you deserve it, and because I haven't said thank you like I should."

"For what?"

Jenks put his hands in his pockets and looked at the floor, hoping to find the right words there. "For . . . for everything. For talking to me every night since. For not leaving me alone even when I yelled at you. For coming after me in the shuttle. For—" He took a breath, trying to pull the words out of his chest. "For working with me every second, trying to bring her back."

"Oh, buddy," she said, her voice falling quiet. "You don't have to thank me for that."

He swallowed the lump in his throat and plowed on. "I'm a mess right now. I don't need to tell you that. But I think I'd be worse than I am if it wasn't for you." He frowned, thinking of all she'd done for him. She'd completely set herself aside for his sake in the tendays since the punch, and he was paying her back with *seasoning*? Stupid. "I'm not doing a good job of this. There's so much I want to say to you. You've done so much more than I would expect from a friend, and I need you to know I don't take that for granted."

Her eyes softened. "You're not my friend, dummy."

He blinked. She'd lost him. "What?"

Kizzy exhaled and looked at the spice jar. She rubbed her thumb over the label. "When I was five, I asked my dads if I could have a brother. Our colony wasn't doing so great then. Not that it's great now. But it was rough when I was little. The council was trying to avoid a crash, and they'd stopped handing out family expansion permissions to folks that already had kids. My dads explained that if we weren't careful about how many people we added to the colony, we might not have enough food. Totally reasonable, but five-year-olds don't give a shit about stuff like that. If you've never been hungry before, not like *starving* hungry, the possibility of running out of food doesn't compute. The only thing I understood was that I couldn't have a brother, which seemed super crazy unfair. They got me a puppy, though. That was cool. I got older, the colony got stronger, and by that time, I wasn't bugging them for a brother anymore, and I guess they didn't really want to go through the whole diapers and teething thing again. I was a happy kid, and I couldn't ask for better parents. But I was still jealous of the kids who had siblings. I grew up, and then you came along." She looked up at him, and smiled. "And for the first time ever, I didn't want a brother anymore, because I finally had one. And there's nothing better than brothers. Friends are great, but they come and go. Lovers are fun, but kind of stupid, too. They say stupid things to each other and they ignore all their friends because they're too busy staring, and they get jealous, and they have fights over dumb shit like who did the dishes last or why they can't fold their fucking socks, and maybe the sex gets bad, or maybe they stop finding each other interesting, and then somebody bangs someone else, and everyone cries, and they see each other years later, and that person you once shared *everything* with is a total stranger you don't even want to be around because it's awkward. But *brothers*. Brothers never go away. That's for life. And I know married folks are supposed to be for life, too, but they're *not* always. Brothers you can't get rid of. They get who you are, and what you like, and they don't care who you sleep with or what mistakes you make, because brothers aren't mixed up in that part of your life. They see you at your worst, and they don't care. And even when you fight, it doesn't matter so much, because they still have to say hi to you on your birthday, and by then, everybody's forgotten about it, and you have cake together." She nodded. "So as much as I love my present, and as nice as it is to get a thank you, I don't need either of 'em. Nothing's too much to ask when it comes to brothers." She shot him a look. "Stars and buckets, Jenks, if you start crying, I will, too, and I will never be able to stop."

"Sorry," he said, trying to push the water back in his eyes. "I just—"

"No, no, see, you don't have to tell me what you're feeling. I get it. I know." She smiled wide, her own eyes wet but holding steady. "See? Brothers."

Jenks was quiet a long time. He cleared his throat. "Do you want to smash and play Battle Wizards?"

"Stars, yes. But only if you promise that we'll never get this emotional about each other ever again."

"Deal."

Ashby took a thoughtful bite of bread, still warm from the oven. "It's good," he said, and considered. "Yeah, really good. This one's a keeper." He swallowed and nodded. "What are the crunchy things?"

"Hestra seeds," said Dr. Chef, sharpening a knife as he spoke.

"What are hestra seeds?"

"I have no idea. I know they're not poisonous. Not to any of us, at least. A Laru merchant back on Coriol gave me a bag for free, along with my other purchases. It was a slow market day, I think she was just glad I bought something."

"Well, I like them. They're . . . zingy." Ashby reached to the other end of the kitchen counter and refilled his mug with tea.

Dr. Chef set down the sharpener and took a handful of fresh-cut herbs from one of his harvest boxes. Ashby could smell them from across the counter. Sweet and astringent. "So," Dr. Chef said. "Anyone knocking at our door?"

"Not yet," Ashby said. And that was okay. He wasn't in any rush, and the Hedra Ka incident wasn't going to keep them out of business. If anything, their reputation had been bolstered by getting out of a collapsing tunnel unscathed. Of course, there was still the question of whether or not they'd need to find a new Navigator, but they'd cross that bridge when they came to it.

"I'm sure something good will come along. Honestly, I think we'd all be glad of a little downtime. Vacation is one thing, but it's nice to settle back in slowly." He rumbled. "Especially since there have been some changes around here."

Ashby looked over at the vox on the wall. A new voice came through it now—Tycho, a gracious, accommodating AI with a Martian accent. Ashby sometimes thought Tycho sounded nervous, but given that the AI knew the circumstances under which he'd been installed, Ashby couldn't blame him for wanting to please his new crew. And he and Jenks had been getting along so far. In Ashby's eyes, that was the most important thing.

Dr. Chef peered at Ashby. "I'm giving you a physical tomorrow."

"What? Why?"

"You're squinting. I think we should check your eyes."

"I'm not squinting."

"You're squinting." Dr. Chef shook a pudgy finger at him. "You spend too much time with your nose in your scrib."

Ashby rolled his eyes—which worked perfectly fine, thank you. "If it'll make you feel better."

"Scoff all you want, you'll thank—" Dr. Chef set down his knife. Footsteps were approaching. More than four.

Ashby turned. Around the corner came Corbin, walking slowly, holding his arm at a steady angle. Bracing themselves against his arm was Ohan, walking on three legs as they held on to Corbin with the other. *No, no, not they,* Ashby reminded himself. *He.* This was no longer Ohan the Pair. This was Ohan the Solitary. After years of making sure he got the pronouns right, Ashby found it a hard habit to break.

He set his mug down and turned to face them. In some ways, not much had changed. Ohan rarely left *his* room, and the only person he spoke to at length was Dr. Chef, who needed him to answer questions about how he was feeling, or about the medication he'd been taking to aid his regrowing nerves. Otherwise, he sat by the window, as he'd always done. But there were changes. The wetness in his eyes had ebbed, and there was an alertness to him that Ashby had never seen before. His fur was growing out, the patterns cut through it fading away. Dr. Chef had told Ohan that he was strong enough now to shave, but the Sianat had made no efforts to do so. And he'd been spending time in the algae bay, here and there. That was new. Ashby didn't know why Ohan would want to be around Corbin, after what had happened. Ashby himself had barely been able to be in the same room with him since. Maybe it was Ohan's way of reminding Corbin of what he was responsible for. Honestly, who knew?

But here he was now, approaching the kitchen, *touching* Corbin. "Ashby," Ohan said. "I need to speak with you."

"Of course," Ashby said. Across the counter, Dr. Chef was nearly silent.

Ohan let go of Corbin's arm and stood on all fours. Ashby could see a tightness in Ohan's face as he did so. Recovering though he was, standing still took effort.

"I should go to Arun now," Ohan said. "I am Solitary, and that is where I should go. It is the way of things." He looked down for a moment, deep in thought. The next words came with difficulty, as if he feared them. "But I do not want to."

"Do you have to go?" Ashby said. "Will your people do anything to you if you don't?"

Ohan blinked three times. "No. We are . . . expected to do things. And we do them. We do not question." He looked confused. "I don't know why. These things made sense, before. And they made sense to the Solitary you met. But not to me. Perhaps it is because they have never been around other species without the Whisperer. They never saw other ways to be."

Ashby spoke with care. "Ohan, what do you *want* to do?"

"I want," Ohan said, rolling his tongue as though he were tasting the words. "I want to stay." His forelegs trembled, but he set his jaw. "Yes. Yes." The trembling stopped. "And I want to have dinner. With my crew."

A burst of coos and whistles erupted from Dr. Chef's mouth, making them all jump. Ashby knew the sound. It was the Grum equivalent of crying. "Oh, I'm sorry," Dr. Chef said, pressing his cheeks with his handfeet. "I just . . ." His Klip dissolved into a cooing drone. He rumbled and huffed, trying to get ahold of himself. "Ohan, as your doctor, I have to remind you that as your body has only had to digest nutrient paste for sometime, adopting other foods will take some adjustment." His cheeks puffed wide. "But as your—as your friend, there is no way I'd rather spend my afternoon than cooking a meal for you. With you, even, if you'd like."

Ohan did something Ashby had never seen before. His mouth spread wide and flat, stretching out beyond the edges of his eyes, which crinkled shut. A smile. "Yes. I want that."

Dr. Chef bustled into action, pulling Ohan's never-before-used chair into the kitchen. He helped Ohan into his seat and wasted no time in beginning a crash course in vegetables.

Ashby glanced toward Corbin, who was observing the scene

with a quiet expression. He nodded to himself, confirming something unspoken, and turned to leave.

"Corbin," Ashby said. Corbin looked at him. Ashby sighed. He still wasn't happy, but what was done was done. After all they'd been through—yes, if Ohan could move forward, so could he. He gestured toward the empty stool beside him. "I'm sure the algae can wait."

Corbin paused. "Thanks," he said. He took a seat. He looked out of place, like the new kid at school, unsure of how to proceed.

Ashby nodded toward the rack of mugs. "You want some tea?"

Corbin took a mug and filled it, as if glad for some direction. He picked up a slice of spice bread. "So. Ah." He took a sip from his mug. "How is Pei?"

Ashby raised his eyebrows, startled by the personal inquiry. "She's doing just fine."

"I overheard that she'll be coming here for a time."

"That's right."

Corbin nodded. "That's good." He took a longer sip and focused his attention on his spice bread.

Ashby eyed the algaeist for a moment, and looked back to the kitchen. He saw Ohan take a tentative nibble from the end of a spineroot. The Sianat gasped with surprise. Dr. Chef clapped him on the back and laughed, his voices harmonizing with approval.

Ashby smiled. He drank his tea and watched his crew. It was enough.

Rosemary took the domed helmet from Kizzy and placed it over her own head, sliding the locking edges at its base into the grooves on her suit. A hiss of dry air brushed against her face as the life support system started up. On the opposite side of the airlock, Sissix, similarly dressed, shook her head.

"I still can't believe you've never done this before," Sissix said. Her voice came through the tiny vox fixed within Rosemary's helmet.

"I never got around to it."

Sissix smirked. "There are a lot of things you've never gotten around to."

"Yeah, well, I'm working on it."

"Okay," Kizzy said, connecting something to the back of the suit. "Lemme see your status panel." Rosemary lifted her left arm, displaying three green lights. "All seals locked. Cool. Wait, those *are* all green, right?"

"Yeah."

"Okay, good. Sorry, I'm a little high." She looked back at Sissix, who was rolling her eyes. "What? It's my *day off.*"

"I didn't say anything," Sissix said.

"You know, you're welcome to come along," Rosemary said.

"Thanks, but given the circumstances, I think I'd just fall asleep." Kizzy paused, considering. "Why have I never taken a nap outside? Seriously, think how super mellow that would be."

"Yeah," said Sissix. "Right up until you sleep through the oxygen alarm."

"Okay, yeah, maybe not."

"Wait!" The sound of handfeet and grumbling echoed down the hallway, preceding Dr. Chef's arrival. He hurried over to Rosemary and placed two yellow tablets in her hand. "You forgot."

"Oh, stars, right," Rosemary said, pulling her helmet back off. She popped the tablets in her mouth, crunched down and made a face. "They taste like plex."

Kizzy giggled. "How would you know what plex tastes like?"

Rosemary shrugged. "I was a kid once. Didn't you ever lick plex?"

The giggle swelled into a laugh. "No! Ew! No!"

"Well, whatever they taste like," Dr. Chef said, "they'll help keep you from getting sick in your helmet, which is the important part. And if for some reason you *should* get sick, don't panic, just remember to—"

"Don't freak her out, Doc," Kizzy said, patting his upper arm. "She gets spacesick!"

"She'll be fine."

"All right, all right, I just want her to enjoy this." Dr. Chef rumbled and chuffed as Rosemary put her helmet back on. "You know," he said. "That suit looks good on you."

"Yeah?" Rosemary said, looking down at the tough red fabric.

"Yeah," Kizzy said. "It fits you real good."

Sissix touched Rosemary's shoulder. "You ready?"

Rosemary stared at the airlock door, nervous, eager. "I think so."

Sissix nodded. "Tycho, we're ready to go."

The vox on the wall switched on. "Okay. I'll be keeping an eye on you both. I'll signal if you get too far out."

"Thanks." She led Rosemary into the airlock and smiled back at the others. "See you guys later."

"Have fun!" Kizzy said, waving.

"Be back for dinner," Dr. Chef said.

The inner door slid shut. Rosemary looked at Sissix. Her heart was hammering. "Well, here we go."

Sissix took her by the hand as the airlock began to depressurize. The hatch slid back. They walked forward, their boots sticking to the artigrav floor. They stood with their toes at the edge. The open hatch waited.

"Oh," said Rosemary, staring ahead.

"A little different without windows and bulkheads, huh?" Sissix grinned. "Here, do this." She extended her hand out past the hull.

Rosemary did the same. As her hand passed beyond the edge of the artigrav field, she could feel its weight change—*disappear*. She'd been in zero-G playrooms as a kid, but this was different. This was the real thing, the universe's default state. She laughed.

"Ready?" Sissix said. "One. Two. *Three*."

They stepped out, and fell up. Or down. Or sideways. It didn't matter. Those words meant nothing anymore. There were no boundaries, no playroom walls. Her body was freed of the burden she hadn't known she was carrying—solid bones, dense muscle, an unwieldy head. They were out in the open, for real this time, as spacers should be. And all around them, black, black, black, full of jeweled stars and colored clouds. It was a sight she knew well, a sight she lived alongside, but in that moment, she was seeing it for the first time. Everything had changed.

"Oh, stars," Rosemary said, and suddenly understood the expression better than she ever had.

"Come on," Sissix said. The thrusters on her boots fired. They flew farther out.

Rosemary looked back to the *Wayfarer*. Through the windows, she could see the familiar rooms and corridors, but it was all so different from out here, like watching a vid, or looking into a dollhouse. The ship looked so small, so fragile.

"Rosemary."

She turned her head.

Sissix raised their clasped hands and smiled. "Let go."

She let Sissix's curved fingers slip from her grasp. They drifted apart, still holding the other in their eyes. Rosemary turned away from her ship, away from her companion, turned out to face the void. There was a nebula there, an explosion of dust and light, the fiery corpse of an ancient giant. Within the gaseous folds slept clusters of unborn stars, shining softly. She took inventory of her body. She felt her breath, her blood, the ties binding it all together. Every piece, down to the last atom, had been made out here, flung through the open in a moment of violence, until they had swirled around and around, churning and coalescing, becoming heavy, weighing each other down. But not anymore. The pieces were floating free now. They had returned home.

She was exactly where she was supposed to be.

JULY 2, 2015

||||||||||||||||||||||||||||

ACKNOWLEDGMENTS

In early 2012, I had a problem. Two-thirds of the way through the first draft of this book, the freelance work I relied on to support myself dried up. I was faced with a two-month lull between paying gigs, and it was starting to look like finishing my book and keeping a roof over my head were mutually exclusive. I had two options: set the book aside and use the time to search for work, or find a way to keep the book (and myself) going. I went with option B, and turned to Kickstarter. I told myself that if the campaign wasn't successful, it was time for me to focus my efforts elsewhere. Fifty-three people (mostly strangers) convinced me to stick with it. *The Long Way* exists thanks to their generosity and their encouragement. I am more grateful for that than I can put into words.

Since then, this book has continued to be something of a community effort. I owe much to my posse of beta readers, who donated their brainpower toward helping me unravel the messy bits. Without their insights, their honesty, and most of all, their time, I would never have gotten this far.

My friend Mike Grinti deserves special thanks not only for his invaluable critique of my second draft and for being my anxiety sponge, but for connecting me with Joe Monti, who believed in my book, and from whom I have learned so much.

Though she probably doesn't think that she had a hand in this, I extend a sincere bundle of thanks to Susana Polo, my editor at The Mary Sue. She not only gave me the time I needed to finish the final edit of my manuscript, but her giving me a place at TMS back in 2011 started the domino chain that led to this book. Plus, she's the only other person in the world who likes *Myst IV*.

A salute to Anne Perry, my editor at Hodder & Stoughton, who is a joy to work with. I never imagined that my book would get a second start, but she went out of her way to make me feel right at home. My thanks to her for holding my hand through this, and for giving me the confidence to move on to the next. Huge thanks, too, to Kelly O'Connor at Harper Voyager, for all her hard work in getting my crew back stateside. First round of Little Sumpin' is on me.

On the personal side of things, I am indebted to my friends and family for . . . well, everything. Somehow, even though I fell off the face of the planet while working on this, they stuck by me. Extra hugs to Chimp and Greg, for being my steadfast sanity check; to Cian, for being a good listener; and to Matt, for being my first buddy.

Bear with the seeming nonsequitur: in 2010, I found myself in Sedona with my friend Jessica McKay, who bought me a fancy dinner and more than a few drinks. It may have been the margaritas talking, but she waved aside my concern about her picking up the bill by saying that I had to thank her in print whenever I got a book out. Jess, please take note: thank you for the tacos, the tequila and the fine company. We are now square.

I can't sign off on a science fiction book without giving credit to my mom and dad, who filled my head with spaceships, and who have always, always been there for me. My mom gets additional thanks for being my science consultant, and for giving me courage when I needed it most.

Finally, all my love and gratitude to my partner, Berglaug, who held my hand, sketched my ship, brought me meals, proofread my manuscript (twice!) and put up with all the late nights and Post-it notes. She believed in this book more than I did some days, and her ferocious support kept me grounded and hopeful. If you enjoyed the read, she's the one you should thank.

ABOUT THE AUTHOR

BECKY CHAMBERS was raised in California as the progeny of an astrobiology educator, an aerospace engineer and an *Apollo*-era rocket scientist. An inevitable space enthusiast, she made the obvious choice of studying performing arts. After a few years in theater administration, she shifted her focus toward writing. Her creative work has appeared at The Mary Sue, Tor.com, Five Out of Ten, the Toast and Pornokitsch. Her writing time for *The Long Way to a Small, Angry Planet* was funded in 2012 thanks to a successful Kickstarter campaign. She is now employed as a technical writer, which grants her the ability to devote more time to science fiction.

After living in Scotland and Iceland, Becky is now back in her home state, where she lives with her partner. She is an ardent proponent of video and tabletop games, and enjoys spending time in nature. She hopes to see Earth from orbit one day.

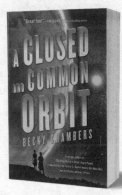